DEVIL IN THE GRAVITY LOUNGE

All Things Found

Book 2

ANTHONY W. EICHENLAUB

Copyright © 2024 by Anthony W. Eichenlaub

All rights reserved.

Print ISBN: 978-1-950542-35-2

No part of this book may be reproduced in any form or by any electronic or mechanical means, including information storage and retrieval systems, without written permission from the author, except for the use of brief quotations in a book review.

This is a work of fiction. All characters, organizations, and events are either fictional or reproduced as fiction.

All text produced within these pages was written by a human being.

For my wonderful wife, might she continue to grant me her faith and support.

PART I

the case of the scientist's daughter

Chapter 1

THERE ARE three stages of the hopeless.

The first is denial. When hope is threatened, everyone—every single last person—bends past the plausible into that place in their hearts where hope still somehow survives.

For me that last hope lurked in the Gravity Garden, near the top of the city-station Nicodemia. Thick trumpetvines snaked over fiberstone arches, blooming in shocks of red and orange, grown huge from the absence of adversity in the Hallow bead of the station. Up here in the bead closest to the core, the simulated gravity was barely a stern suggestion let alone the law. Somewhere, a lilac bloomed, its heady aroma meandering through the smooth, narrow pathways like the specter of a lost spirit.

Above me, the luminous violet glow of simulated night filtered through the fingers of the sprawling honeylocust trees.

"Are you sure you haven't seen her?" I was asking a pair of stereotypical Travelers. The descendants of Nicodemia's original passengers tended to be heavyset and tall, with soft features and upturned noses. I pressed a printout image closer so they could see it in the dim light. "She might not have been smiling."

The man, to his credit, took the time to peer at the image of the grinning girl. The printed photograph was the only recent image her desperate father could find. In the picture, Destiny Alverez wore a yellow dress. Bright makeup covered half her face.

"She isn't from here, is she?" the woman asked in the haughty accent of someone who had never left the luxurious prison of her Hallow home.

Nicodemia was composed of three beads. Heavy Nicodemia dangled at the end of the long chain, where the spin gravity crushed its working populace in both body and spirit. Haven was named for the refuge from Earth it became when Nicodemia was a generation ship hundreds of years ago. Hallow Nicodemia, where the garden lay, was the bead with the lowest simulated gravity and the highest concentration of generational wealth.

"Maybe the gardener would recognize her," said the man.

"Yes," said the woman. "Maybe check back in the morning, and Mr. Mance can help you."

The man nodded. "I'm sure he would know her." It wasn't the first time someone had mentioned the gardener. According to these people, being from the lower beads meant that the woman I was looking for was of the servant class, and all servants knew each other, right?

I did my best to bury my frustration. "She's someone's daughter, asshole." I towered almost as tall as the man, due to my long childhood in lighter gravity, but a decade living in the Heavies had hardened me. The guy didn't flinch, even though he probably should have.

"She looks old enough to make her own decisions," the woman said. "Maybe she left on her own accord."

"Nicodemia's a closed system," I said. "Destiny Alverez hasn't left the city."

The woman brushed me aside with a wave of her manicured fingers. "Alverez? Honey, don't we know an Alverez?"

The man's brow furrowed. "Any relation to the colony scientist?"

"Maybe she followed her mother," said the woman.

"Planetary colonies are restricted to scientists," I said.

"They can't all be scientists out there," said the man. "Who would do the cleaning?"

"Maybe it's an egalitarian utopia," I said.

They stared at me like I'd spoken in tongues.

Destiny's mother was indeed a scientist on the Magdalene Moon colony. By all accounts, Petunia Alverez *ran* the vast terraforming project. Even with that connection, there was no way Destiny would be accepted into the project. Not even to scrub toilets or clean dishes.

The photograph disappeared back into my coat as I left the couple. Like the dozen others I'd questioned that night, they offered nothing useful.

The second stage of the hopeless is desperation. Even when it's too late to deny that hope is lost, we cling to the myth that the world bends to a strong will. Sometimes a stubborn soul can open the gates of heaven.

Reginald Alverez, Destiny's father, was also a scientist, but even he had never been permitted to visit the colonies. Maybe that was because he wasn't the geologist they needed for the project. Or maybe it was because Destiny's mother didn't want him around. Either way, Destiny wasn't exactly the type of girl to follow in her parents' footsteps. She would never have left the Hallows, let alone Nicodemia.

In my search for the young woman, every clue I found led me to this garden. The Gravity Lounge, the Hallow's most opulent, exclusive club, loomed above as I wound my way through the twisting paths. It glowed in the violet night like a big lump of bioluminescent fungi. As I watched from the lush greenery of the garden, flying cabs landed on its summit.

Shadows swallowed the form of a man on the other side of the nearby hedge. He was medium height. Broad shoulders. I caught the hint of a white square decorating his collar.

A priest out in the middle of the night wasn't strange in a station city built by Catholics. They were just as likely to visit a garden in the middle of the night as anyone else. He was a big man, likely a native of the Hallows, but in the shadowed night, through the glossy leaves, I couldn't make out the features of his face.

I thought of speaking out right then but thought better of it. There was no sign that he saw me, and if he was someone I wanted to talk to, then chances were good that he didn't want to talk to me.

The air went still, and it took me a moment to realize the absence of the man's breath. I held my own, hoping he wouldn't hear me in the shadowy dark.

He turned on his heel and stalked away.

I liked to think of myself as a complex person. The greatest tragedy of my life—the death of my parents—shaped me long ago. It got me excommunicated from Trinity, the station's governing AI, so that I was ignored by every computerized system from lights to food vending to automatic doors. It formed me into the kind of person who investigated every shady lie and fixed every broken system. I liked to think of myself as the kind of person who considered every action carefully before acting.

But like a poorly trained Doberman, when someone fled, I chased.

My footsteps thudded on the smooth fiberstone floor. The light gravity made traction tricky, but I grasped a trellis with one hand and pulled myself forward fast enough to see the priest's heel through a narrow gap in the hedge. Three long steps and I rounded a corner to crash into a wall of ivy. I could almost sense the gardener's disapproval as fragile leaves broke under my weight.

A crunch to my right. The priest was escaping on a parallel path. I shoved off the wall, skipped against the cobblestone, and pushed forward. My feet quickly grew accustomed to the low gravity. I'd been raised in this nonsense, and chasing my sister through our garden estate was a memory I would cherish forever. That was before she lost the use of her legs and half her sense of humor in the crash that killed our parents.

Back then, I was fast and skinny. Years in the Heavies had left me fast and huge.

Fast didn't mean much in a maze, though.

A trellis cracked under the force of my grip as I launched myself forward. I heard the priest up ahead. He yelped as he crashed past some innocent sap out for a stroll. His footsteps thudded hard and fast.

I broke into the garden's central court. A fountain shot water in a smooth arc, low gravity allowing the liquid to form into spheres that gently drifted down to settle into the quiet pool. From this central location radiated a dozen paths.

The priest was a shadow in the soft violet of the path straight ahead. He had already rounded the fountain. I jumped straight over.

The lights followed him, illuminating gently as he passed. It helped me spot him as he rounded the next corner. Lights didn't illuminate for me, so when my feet hit the floor, they hit in the complete blackness of the void of space. I misjudged the landing, my ankle twisting under me. A spike of pain lanced up my leg. I swore and limped forward.

By the time I reached the corner, the priest's light was gone. Disappeared in one of three directions. I had no choice but to guess. I took the center path.

Walking now, wincing in pain, I drew a slender lighter from my pocket, lit a cigarette, and kept the lighter out to illuminate the darkness at my feet. The canopy was thick in this part of the garden, and the violet sky was almost hidden.

The floor was smooth. Perfect. Unscuffed. I wouldn't expect to see evidence of the priest's passage, but I wouldn't expect a priest to flee from a man like me. It didn't make much sense, but then again, why wouldn't I expect a priest to act guilty? God-fearing Catholics felt more guilt than anyone else I know.

Except for myself, maybe.

Hairs on the back of my neck prickled. Dread settled into the pit of my stomach. I'd lost the priest, but something was off in this dark section of the garden. Under the warm lilac scent, there lingered the deep sweetness of rot. The candlelight glow of my lighter suffocated in the thick black of the ivy arches.

Paths branched from the central tunnel. I peered into each as I passed by, but my light barely touched the darkness within. The scuff of the priest's footsteps no longer reached my sensitive ears. My chest deflated, and the tension eased from my muscles.

It was probably nothing. The priest – if it even was a priest – might have been there for anything. Secret sex. Clandestine bribery. Priests weren't immune to temptation.

Still, I strolled through the dark, peering into each side

passage. Ahead, the violet glow increased, flickering like a giant purple bonfire. The Gravity Lounge lay up ahead. This path led straight to the gated revelry of the famous club.

At the end of a path, a glint caught my eye. I waved my lighter as I drew a deep pull from my smoldering cigarette.

There. Nestled under the overgrown mass of a clematis, beneath the double-petaled purple inflorescence, sat something covered in mirrored squares. I reached down, brushed the plants away, and peered at the thing.

A purse. Could be anyone's, but the quickening of my heart told me it was Destiny's. I picked it up to check, but my hand came back wet. I flashed my lighter around again and saw the splatter on the smooth stone. Across the leafy green.

Blood. A lot of it.

When hope is undeniably lost, and desperation is a glint of starlight in the great void of space, those who walk the path of the hopeless will find themselves in the final stage.

That final stage is me. I'm Jude Demarco. The last hope for the hopeless.

Chapter 2

THREE PLASTIC TRIANGLES slightly larger than my thumbnail with rounded corners and varying thickness, each with the upward-arrow logo of the Gravity Lounge. A slender silver key with the number seven etched into its handle. A leather journal, half filled with a language nothing like any I've seen on the station. A playing card. Joker, with an image of a leering clown holding the red-and-green planet Mars in his left hand.

A slender bundle of Destiny Alverez's calling cards and a roll of dimes.

In theory, nobody needed money in Nicodemia. Trinity managed Karma for any who wished to pay for the station's non-necessary features. Food and shelter were guaranteed. Clothing, also, to an extent. Anything else depended on Trinity's judgment of a person's actions based on how well those actions supported the AI's interpretation of body, soul, and community. Good deeds boosted Karma.

Being excommunicated meant I wasn't part of the Karma system. Trinity didn't care if I lived or died. For me and others who had failed to maintain a decent Karma rating, there were dimes. Dimes fed appetites and fueled black markets.

I flipped a dime to a driver as he dropped off a couple of Travelers at one of the garden's several entrances. "Fetch the police. Quickly."

He sneered at the coin but pocketed it. "Whatever you say, boss."

It had taken too long to find someone to help, and I was itching for answers. To the newly delivered Travelers, I said, "Get some lights on the upspiral wing."

They stared at me.

"A girl's been hurt."

One of them spoke into a small device. After a delay, the lights for that end of the garden flared to life. It would be hours before the simulated sun rose, but the harsh white maintenance lights washed out the color of the blooming flowers and annihilated the shadows. It turned the serene maze into an affront to the senses.

When I returned to the scene of the crime, the story was much easier to read. It was a story written in blood, and it didn't start with the bloody purse in the back of a dead end. It started on the main path, just outside the central fountain.

"Mark this," I said before I realized nobody was listening. A crowd had gathered to stare, but they weren't about to help.

Two drops of blood glistened on the smooth stone at the base of a currant hedge. Fresh dark blood, same as the blood under the purse. It couldn't have been more than an hour old. Maybe two. I continued down the path toward the Gravity Lounge, noting the spots of red at odd intervals.

Destiny had been attacked first near the central fountain. She had run. A smear of blood on the glossy leaves of a hibiscus shone as bright as the plant's red flowers. She had stumbled. Bad footwear, maybe. The blood here wasn't enough to prove that she had bled out, but if she was attacked again here, maybe—maybe she staggered from another blow.

Another stab.

Bullet wounds don't bleed like this. They spatter. A deep slash would have resulted in more blood than a few drops every dozen feet. A shallow stab might have done this. A cut in the meat of her hand would explain the blood on the plant as she reached out to catch herself.

I drew a long breath. Moving slowly along the path, I did my best to throttle the urgency roaring in my brain. She was hurt. That much was certain. Destiny Alverez might not be dead, but she was definitely badly injured. Everything I saw urged me to work faster. But faster wouldn't get me to her. I needed to know everything I could know.

For instance, why did she have calling cards? The minimalistic cards showed only her first name and a contact number. Anybody with access to a screen could have looked up the same number. These were meant as reminders to her clientele, which was interesting because I didn't know she *had* clients.

Identity was the core of the Trinity AI. It knew who everyone was at all times. Often, people attempted to conceal their identities. They would find a dead spot where Trinity wasn't watching, change their appearance, and emerge supposedly de-identified.

It rarely worked. Sometimes Trinity would see through their ruse, and their crimes would mar their Karma. Sometimes Trinity would respect their attempt at anonymity. But the machine always knew. In the liminal spaces between the station and the deep void, I could access Trinity's subsystems, so I could see a clearer view of what it actually knew. It understood the subterfuge that happened throughout its city.

Mostly, it just didn't care.

Somehow, Trinity sometimes calculated that identity subterfuge was part of a thriving community. It supported "community," one of the core tenets of the governing AI, so the ruse was allowed to continue. Even if that meant criminals walked among us. Sometimes that meant people literally got away with murder.

I hoped this wasn't murder. The blood continued along the long garden path, smeared under a shoe at one point. I peered at the print a long time before realizing it was from my own worn pair of loafers. I had stepped in this spot of blood previously on my way through. A few steps past that, the blood flow increased. Around the corner leading to the dead end, drops came in fives and tens, not just ones and twos. She'd been stabbed again, maybe. Or she had moved slowly.

Stepping carefully past the drops of blood, I made my way to the end of the path, where the purse still sat open on the ground. After discovering the blood, I carefully poked through it, but I hadn't noticed how much blood was around it. It sprayed across the lower leaves of the hedge, spattering the thick leaves. This was enough. My heart pounded in my chest—enough to kill someone if they didn't get medical attention.

But I still didn't know if she was dead. My mouth went dry. A kid like this—only twenty, according to her records—didn't deserve to die. She'd left her father and ventured out on her own, for reasons he hadn't understood—or at least hadn't explained.

It came back to the calling cards. Why had she needed

them? Trinity could drop messages to anyone anywhere on the station.

I nudged the purse with a knuckle and peered inside. The police would want the crime scene to be undisturbed, but I needed to know. If she was alive nearby, I'd need to find her.

What if she was still in the maze?

The path ended in a thick hedge with fat, thorny branches. It wouldn't have been possible to force her way through. Even if she were healthy, that wouldn't work. Not without breaking some branches and leaving some skin. Where had she gone? Could she have bandaged herself and then moved back through the maze? It might have been possible, but then what happened to her attacker?

Something else had happened, and the dread in my belly told me I wasn't going to like it. Every scenario I could think of involved her body being carried away by the killer. Where to, I couldn't guess. How, I wasn't sure. But there was a lot of blood on that ground.

If there was one thing I wasn't any good at finding in the city of Nicodemia, it was hope, but this mystery dug at my gut. I nudged the purse open again. Those calling cards still bothered me, so I took one. The plastic triangles intrigued me too. Some sort of message chip? I picked the small leather book from the purse and flipped through it. Same as the first time I'd handled it, the symbols inside didn't make any sense. It was encoded somehow, and if Destiny was smart, she wasn't going to leave the key anywhere easy to find.

In the eyes of my sister, I was a no-good layabout. My days were spent on trivial things, and nothing I ever did amounted to any worth. In the eyes of the wealthy residents of the Hallows, I was a handyman. I fixed things that needed to be fixed. To the poor of the Heavies, I was a medic. When it was people who needed fixing, I could draw on my tenuous connection to Trinity's complex system and use the medic training I had received long ago.

In my heart, I was an investigator, and when something piqued my curiosity, I grabbed hold of it and never let go, not even if the station around me crumbled and the thin threads of society began to fray.

That journal caught my curiosity, shook it, and held it tight.

I pocketed the little book and stood up. The garden entrance to the Gravity Lounge was only a short walk away. As I approached, I took in the grand, sweeping architecture and the modern clean-cut lines. The building was like a great pink monument to ambition with the bowed pillars of its arched entry.

A man stepped from the shadowed alcove as I mounted the wide steps. In the twilight, he looked like a gargoyle protecting its ancient castle.

"I just need to look around inside," I said.

As it turned out, a person needed to be *someone* to gain entry to the Gravity Lounge, and I was the same old nobody I'd always been.

"I promise you won't get in trouble," I said. I read the stitched name on the breast of his sky-blue polo. "Wesley?"

"This is a private club," Wesley said.

"I'm looking for a girl," I told the bouncer. "She might be in trouble."

He didn't need to flex his bulging muscles to intimidate me. The rigid square of his jaw and the glint of his polished sunglasses did the job well enough. He didn't *need* to flex, but he did anyway. I can appreciate a man going above and beyond to excel at his chosen profession.

"Plenty of trouble to go around." His voice resonated

against the fiberstone of the ornate entryway. "Lot of people are in trouble."

"This one involves a certain kind of life-threatening trouble," I said. "She's around twenty. Medium height. Hair might have been just about any color."

The big guy didn't exactly frown. Something tensed in the rigid musculature of his jaw.

I continued, "Evidence says she'd have been in trouble recently. Maybe around midnight. Lot of blood."

He didn't make the mistake of crossing his arms. That might have slowed him down if I'd decided, like the fool I am, to take a swing at him. Instead, his arms hung like girders of forged steel at his sides, his dark skin glistening in the early morning light.

I met his gaze for several long seconds, trying to show him that I wasn't intimidated by his obvious show of force. I was, though. I *definitely* was, but sometimes it's important not to flinch. "I'll just have a look around outside, then."

"She didn't come this way," he said. For some reason, I believed him.

He watched me all the way back down the stairs to the garden entrance. When he saw me pause, he touched one finger to his ear and spoke. That wasn't going to be good. Then, he crossed his hulking arms and stood up, dwarfed by the enormous building.

People liked buildings. Even on an enormous station in the middle of an unoccupied solar system, homes and businesses and places of worship were crafted to look like the buildings that made up the old Earth cities. There were churches with spires that would have touched the heavens and squat restaurants with quaint decor and unique odors. The propensity for buildings wasn't about having an efficient use of space. It certainly wasn't that. It turned out, after years of experimentation, that there was something hardcoded into the human psyche that made us love the sky. Maybe it was aspirational star-gazing or a quality in the air, but people didn't thrive in tunnels.

There were still tunnels in Nicodemia Station, but the Gravity Lounge sprouted from the edge of the garden like a great glowing cathedral. Rumor was that it had its own recycler and its own access through the airlock. It was a completely independent structure latched onto a system that thrived on its interdependence. Its sheer walls stretched up into the haze of the simulated sky, touching the very topmost layer of Hallow Nicodemia's great spiral. In this position, it was easy to be intimidated by the building's presence and difficult to remember that it was nothing more than one small, knobby lump on the inside of the great chain we call Nicodemia.

Every building had a front door, a back door, and any number of entrances that nobody wanted others to know about. If I was lucky, I might be able to find one of these entrances. All I wanted was to look around. Destiny Alverez wasn't in the garden. If she was, the police would find her. The blue would also find her if she was wandering bloody in the streets downspiral. They might even figure out how to locate her if she was a body being dumped somewhere. There weren't many ways to get rid of a body in Nicodemia.

But the blue wouldn't enter the Gravity Lounge. The Hallows was the wealthiest district, and great wealth bought secrecy and subterfuge. If she was in there, the police might never find her, and that wasn't acceptable.

I tapped my shoe on the grassy path along the upspiral end of the Gravity Garden. If I could find a hollow, I might be able to find a way into the tunnels beneath the building. It was a long shot, but I've taken long shots before.

Thing about long shots is that, by definition, they almost never worked out.

A rumble in an adjacent branch of the maze sounded like the growl of an angry dog.

No. That *was* the growl of an angry dog. I crossed to the dense hedge and tried to hear the movement on the other side. There was a snarl and a snap, followed by a string of curses. Through the foliage, I saw a pair of workers, a massive Doberman, and a man toting a guitar case. They'd run into each other on the path, and the dog looked like he was about ready to tear the guitarist apart.

"Just-Just tranq him," said the guitarist.

"This guy's supposed to meet Cain tonight," replied the man with the leash. He had a thick Heavies accent. He yanked the leash and the dog yelped. "That's right, you little shit," he spat.

There was a struggle and the group moved on. Curious, I followed along my parallel path, wondering if mine would eventually intersect with theirs. It didn't. It veered in the opposite direction.

Wesley was right. There was plenty of trouble to go around.

"Well, well, well," said a voice up ahead as I stepped into the clearing. "If it isn't Big Man Truth himself."

The policeman wore his official blues. He gripped a baton in one hand and a scanner in the other.

In the eyes of the law, I was a no-good, unaccountable, good-for-nothing criminal. I slowly raised my hands in surrender.

Chapter 3

"I'M TELLING YOU," I said for the hundredth time, "you gotta have your guys search the area." I sat in a chair so uncomfortable that it should have been declared a war crime.

The cops shot me a couple of blank stares across a fibersteel table. The two fellas looked about as dim as the single bulb that glowed above us and about half as useful.

The guy on the left, whose badge named him Echo, had a thick mustache, more than the usual allotment of chins, and an expression that was both accusing and bored. "I think you misunderstand who's in charge here."

Halders, the other officer, had a pronounced Adam's apple, searching eyes, and a poorly centered tuft of beard valiantly surviving on his otherwise clean-shaven jaw that might have been an ill-advised attempt at a soul patch. "We have people searching the maze," he said in a rich baritone. "But what we need to understand is *your* involvement."

"Are you supposed to be the likable cop?" I asked. "Because it's not working."

Halders flashed a crooked smile. "We do our best with what charm God gives us."

Dammit, it was working. He was still an asshole, but he was a likable one.

Echo slammed his palm on the table. "Listen, Demarco, we're not screwing around here. If you don't want to spend the next week in lockup, you'll start talking right now."

"Send your people into the Gravity Lounge," I said. "Or let me go so I can find the girl."

Echo's jaw flexed.

"It's a matter of jurisdiction," Halders apologized. "There's only so much we can do up there."

These men weren't native to Hallows. Many of the cops in the bead weren't Travelers, but it felt odd to have an investigation this important run by two yokels from south of the border. Wouldn't the richest district want their policing run in-house?

Then again, most of the natives of the Hallows considered themselves above such a lowly position. They'd rather live off rolling investments and complicated pyramid-style Karma schemes than walk a beat.

I said, "There's a girl out there who needs our help."

Halders peered at me. "You looking for her?"

"We all have jobs to do."

Halders said, "You just looking for this one person or are you going to find all our missing persons?"

"We're on a closed station," I said. "There are no missing people."

Echo said, "That's not what the board in the break room says."

"Maybe those people just don't want to be found by you," I said. "Destiny's actually in danger. If someone took her, you gotta find the creep."

"We found a creep," said Echo.

"I'm the one who called you in," I roared.

"The head gardener called us in," said Echo. "Said there was a suspicious guy lurking around disturbing the guests."

"You've got to get cops into the Gravity Lounge."

"Nobody gets into the Gravity Lounge," said Halders.

"What's your angle?" asked Echo. "Get our boys into the most elite nightclub in all the Hallows to knock around looking for criminal behavior? What's your agenda, Mr. Demarco? Who do you work for?"

That was confidential. "I work for the girl."

Echo's chins got blotchy. "How'd she hire you if she was missing."

"I don't like to get into the business particulars."

Halders glanced at a screen in the palm of his hand. "Her father's in town. You know anything about that?"

I hadn't realized he'd followed me up into the Hallows.

Halders said, "He'll vouch for you?"

"That sounds like a question for him." He had hired me, but I wasn't going to tell them that.

"I don't give a damn," said Echo. "So what if some Haven goon vouches for him?"

This guy was really starting to irritate me. "Call Anders from the Heavies. He's a cop." The only good one I'd found.

"From the Heavies," said Echo, as if that meant the man couldn't be trusted.

"He's got a good record, and he knows my business." Anders didn't know half what I did. He'd been a big help on a few tough cases down in the Heavies, but his trust only went so far. I was willing to push that to its limit if it would get me back on the street.

Halders fired a message off on his tablet screen. "Run us

through this again. How did your bloody footprints end up all over a crime scene?"

I was starting to change my mind about liking this guy. "So you *did* send your people?"

"Answer the question," growled Echo.

"You're wasting your time talking to me," I said.

"You tampered with a crime scene," Echo growled. "So it's *you* wasting *our* time."

The journal burned a hole in my pocket, but I did my best not to draw attention to it. They hadn't technically arrested me yet, so they hadn't confiscated my possessions. After a quick pat-down for weapons, they had locked me in the interrogation room and subjected me to the torture of an uncomfortable chair and slightly warmer-than-ideal temperatures. The technique was about as transparent as it gets, but they'd failed to extract anything resembling a confession from me.

"There was a priest," I said to Halders.

"Isn't there always?"

"He ran from me."

Echo raised an eyebrow. "You chased a priest?"

"He ran."

"Would he have gotten away if he hadn't?" Echo asked in a way that told me he already knew the answer.

I did my best to stay relaxed, but my knuckles cracked. "There's a reason people like me don't like people like you."

"Look," Halders said, "we're doing our best here, but you were acting suspicious around a shiny new crime scene. What do you expect us to do?"

I stood so fast that mankind's worst chair clattered to the floor behind me. "I expect you to find the girl." With that, I pushed past the two men, yanked open the interrogation room door, and stalked out.

To my surprise, neither of them followed. Nobody tried to stop me.

Morning broke as I stepped back into the Hallow Nicodemia streets. A dozen steps away lay the central spiral of the Hallows, with flying craft drifting across the vast open space inside a bead shaped like a child's top—wide in the middle and narrow at top and bottom. The narrowing spiral above was lit with a bright white luminescence that seared through my eyes straight into the back of my caffeine-starved brain.

"They say God's brilliance shines brightest on those who deserve His light," purred a woman's voice beside me.

I squinted against the penetrating sun. "Nobody deserves this."

"It's refreshing, don't you think? All this light after such a long night?"

She leaned against a fibersteel lamppost, one patent leather shoe resting against the lamp's vertical surface. Her suit was a sheer black that struck the morning light like wrought iron. When she saw she had my attention, her ruby lips quirked up in an amused smile, and the amber tips of her short, immaculately styled hair fluttered in the morning's cool breeze.

"Refreshing. Yeah, that was the word I was going to use." I walked past. It would be a long hike upspiral back to the garden, and if I was ever going to get that long night's sleep, I needed to move.

The woman fell in alongside me, matching my pace with ease. Her tall stature didn't leave any doubt that she wasn't a native of the Heavies, but she could have been from either Haven or the Hallows. She was too thin to be a Traveler, but anyone would grow tall if they were raised in the reduced gravity of Hallow Nicodemia.

"You're not an easy man to find, Mr. Demarco," she said.

"People seem to manage."

"I want to help you."

I stopped and turned to her. In the harsh morning light, the traces of amber in her hair shone like veins of copper. "Ma'am, right now I'm on my way to the Gravity Lounge. I'm going to find a girl who needs to be found, whether she's dead or alive, and then I'm going to get some sleep. When that's all done, then maybe you can think about helping me, whatever that means to people like you."

Her voice went flat. "People like me?"

"You know," I said, tasting the long pause on the backs of my teeth. "Jesuits."

Her brow furrowed.

I started walking, and she matched my pace. The pedestrian traffic started to choke the wide streets, and vendors assembled their stalls in well-lit alleys.

"You need to be *someone* to get into the Gravity Lounge," she said.

"I find being no one gets me plenty of places."

She said, "I'm Lorentz, by the way. Ginnie Lorentz."

"And you're someone?"

"Not exactly." She plucked two breakfast burritos from a vendor and paid him with a charming smile. The Karma exchange was handled by Trinity, as indicated by a flash of green on the man's cart. She handed one paper-wrapped burrito to me. "But I'm not exactly no one either."

The burrito was full of eggs and salsa, with a smattering of spicy sausage and green peppers. I would have eaten a dozen, given the opportunity, but one was enough to fight back the crashing pressure of my headache and lightened my mood. "Demarco," I said. "Jude Demarco."

"I know."

"What do you want?"

"I think we have a lot in common," she said.

"It doesn't take many differences to cancel out a whole lot of similarities." A trio of kids ran past us, shouting. "I don't always get along with priests."

Her ruby lips twitched a smile. "Good thing I'm really more of a monk."

"You don't look like much of a monk."

"But you knew I was a Jesuit."

"Why are you here, Sister?"

"You and I both seek the truth."

"In my experience, a priest's truth doesn't look much like the one on the street."

"I'm still not a priest."

"A nun?"

"There are no Jesuit nuns. I'm a monk."

I shrugged.

"Do you know anything about the Jesuit order?"

"Soldiers of God," I said. "Scientists. Evangelicals."

"My studies tend toward the science end of dogma," Lorentz said. "We seek truth, even if it's not convenient to the Church. We always have."

We rounded a lush strawberry patch where a stocky woman plucked her boss's plump breakfast fruit. She had callouses on her knuckles and her blue eyes shone in the morning light. Around the long arc of the upper bead, the entrance to the Gravity Garden was marked by a wide silver arch covered in morning glory.

"The blue should be crawling all over this place," I said to Lorentz. "But they avoid it like the plague."

"Can you blame them for being a little intimidated by their betters?"

"Yes."

"Fair enough."

Our eyes met and I saw a sparkle of mirth in her expression. There was a light openness to her that I'd rarely encountered with anyone from the faith. Still, her mannerisms made me nervous. The more I liked her, the more I was wary of my own gut instinct. I needed to know her agenda.

"Do you know anything about Destiny Alverez that you'd like to share?" I asked.

"Not particularly."

"Then you're wrong. We don't have anything in common."

"This is bigger than Destiny, Demarco. It's bigger than both of us."

"It all is to people like you, isn't it?" I said, not expecting an answer. "God's plan and all that."

"God's plan," she agreed.

I squared off with her and drew a deep, slow breath. It wouldn't do to anger this woman, but I needed her to leave. I pointed at the arch over the garden's entrance.

"Whether it's the best-connected politician in the Hallows or the poorest fisherman down in the Heavies, nobody in Nicodemia is more important to me than Destiny Alverez. She's out there somewhere. Maybe she's dead, maybe she's fine. Maybe she's gasping her last breath bleeding out into a gutter, but right now it's her right to be found. Sure, maybe she doesn't want to be found. Maybe she's desperate for it. I don't care. Finding Destiny Alverez is the right thing to do and for once I want to do something I don't need to feel guilty about. If you don't have something that'll help me do that, then I'm going to have to politely ask you to scram. I have better things to do, and thank you for the burrito."

She stared at me for the span of a long breath. "How did you know I was Jesuit?"

"There's a curiosity about the universe that you only see in scientists and a certainty about the universe's inner workings that you only find in the faith." I drew back and took a good look at her: The slender curves of the black suit that perfectly contoured her body. The quirk of a smile on her full lips. The clever, knowing amusement in her eyes. "You have both, and to be honest, it's a little scary." I tipped my hat. "It was a pleasure meeting you, Lorentz."

Her lips parted in a smile that showed her gleaming teeth. "You'll see me again soon enough."

That's what I was afraid of.

Chapter 4

I HOOFED it up to Saint Lucy of the Light, the Hallow's central cathedral. Inside, the place was that echoing kind of empty that churches got when not in use. A pair of priests lingered in the narthex, mumbling in respectful tones near a pair of sprawling ficus plants. They eyed me as I passed, but neither of them was the tall build of the man I'd seen in the Gravity Garden. Inside the main chapel, I found an old woman lighting a candle at the votive station. She shot me a cold look when I walked past, but she wasn't the guy, so her business wasn't mine.

In the middle pews, a couple of lanky men spoke in hushed voices. I sat directly in front of them, and they shut up fast.

Without turning around, I said, "I hear the middle pews are the best place for bad deeds."

One of them took the bait. "What are you, the blue? We've got sanctuary here."

Sanctuary. Trinity tallied Karma based on their good or bad deeds—measuring against the goods of body, soul, and community. That was suspended inside the church. Nobody but God judged people there. To a point.

"I'm looking for a priest," I said. "Medium build. Tall. Broad shoulders. Enjoys late-night walks in the Gravity Garden."

"I think I know a whore down in the Sinless who fits that description."

"Very funny."

"He doesn't think so."

"Does he wear a collar?" I said.

"Only when he's not wearing a shirt."

"Or pants, for that matter," said the other guy.

"I'm looking for a guy wearing a priest's collar and a shirt and pants, all at the same time."

The other guy whispered, "There are only twelve priests running around Saint Lucy's. Was your priest a Traveler?"

"Likely not."

"A lady?"

"Definitely not."

"Real skinny? Kinda fierce?"

I pictured the man I had seen only in the shadows. He fit none of those descriptions. "No."

"Then nobody knocking around here fits the description. Could be from one of the smaller churches around the district. Might be a traveling priest. The bishop here likes to send clergy all over all three beads."

"How evangelical."

"Yeah, a genuine go-getter."

I stopped and lit a votive on my way out of the church. A single flame signified everyone I had ever lost and every guilt I still carried. It must have been the heaviest candle in the whole church. Once that was lit, I left the cathedral the way

I'd come and started the long walk upspiral. Back toward the Gravity Garden.

"WELL, WELL, WELL," said a familiar voice as I finally reached the arch above the garden's entrance. "What a coincidence to run into Mr. Jude Demarco on a pleasant morning like this."

I turned to see the leering mug of one Leo Shaw, and the morning got a whole lot less pleasant. Leo's shark grin didn't reach his sunken eyes. He cracked his knuckles, touching each of six rings one by one.

"Shaw," I said, blinking through a pair of cheap sunglasses. He was the last guy I'd expect to see here, and my exhausted brain was trying to grasp how he had found me. One of the benefits of being excommunicated was I was tricky to locate when my debts were due. Woe be to the fool debtor who took on my case. But Leo, it seemed, was up for the task. It wouldn't do me any good to ask how he found me. He'd never divulge the secrets of the business. Best odds were that either the bouncer at the Gravity Lounge or someone in the police force had tipped him off. Odds were against it being the Jesuit, but you never knew with religious types.

Odds. Gambling was how I got into financial trouble in the first place.

Leo Shaw collected debts from the lowest of the low and the highest of the high. He knew how to chase a man down, and he knew how to make a man hurt. My best bet was to play it cool. "It's good to see you, Shaw."

"Is it?"

"Which one of them called you? Echo or Halders?"

"I can't even imagine what you're talking about." He stepped closer.

It took all my will not to retreat. "The job I'm on? It pays well. I didn't want to take it, but I hear what you're saying about wanting my debt paid off."

"Smart man like you," said Shaw. "I'd think you'd stay out of debt in the first place."

"Smart's not what it used to be." The casinos down in Haven didn't only offer the sweet release of oblivion. They contained information. A gambling hall was a place to form social connections, gather rumors, and maybe—just maybe—figure out the truth behind the crash that killed my parents.

It was also a place to lose a whole pile of dimes. Maybe I wasn't so smart.

"You're good at your job," I said to Shaw.

"You're not so hard to find."

"This job's almost finished." I gestured up at the Gravity Lounge at the top of the long spiral. "All I need to do is get in there." I don't know why I felt helpless in front of Shaw. All the bluster and bravado I had cultivated in my professional career dissipated like so much sand in the wind.

He said, "Maybe if you were better at smelling bullshit, you wouldn't end up in a pile of manure."

"Blackjack's my game," I said. "Not poker." Maybe I would be better at poker. I filed the idea aside for later investigation.

"Tell me about the job."

"It pays cash."

"Get an advance."

"I got an advance."

He looked at me expectantly.

"Spent it."

Shaw cocked his head as if he were listening to something, but all I heard was the gentle breeze rustling the leaves of a nearby hedge. A hovering cart flew over the nearby garden, hauling vegetative waste to the nearest recycler. I needed to get in there before someone ruined what was left of the crime scene.

"Who are you working for?" Shaw said.

"You know that's confidential, Shaw." The muscles in my shoulders tensed. I didn't like where he was going with this. There was no reason to think that Destiny's father wanted privacy, but secrecy was a matter of policy. It was about integrity. "Can't go telling just anyone about my clients."

Shaw spread his palms. "Am I just anyone?"

"I'm good for the dimes."

"See, it's like this," Shaw explained. "As long as you owe my employers, it's like we're in business together. We share secrets because we're part of the same team."

"My ability to pay you depends on how well I keep secrets."

"That so?"

"It is."

He was a head shorter than me, but when he twitched, I flinched. His fists were like hammers and the line of his jaw set some primal instinct in me on edge. His beady black eyes spotted my reaction and honed in on the helpless prey I'd become. Damn, I hated this guy. I vowed never to gamble with his employers again unless I was absolutely sure I was going to get a winning hand.

"Look at it from my perspective," he said. "How do I even know you're on a job?"

"Faith."

"Faith is for the dumb and the wicked. I'll take proof."

I didn't have proof, but I *did* have a photo of Destiny Alverez. I took it out of the journal where I'd stashed it.

When Shaw saw the photo, his nostrils flared. "She's a looker."

"She's a kid."

"What's in the book?"

"Evidence."

He gestured for me to hand it over, which I did reluctantly. He had me down a dark alley. "Coded, but it's proof I'm close. Just give me another day I'll get to the bottom of all this. My payday is your payday."

"No sidetracks?"

"I would never."

He flipped through the journal. "It's just junk."

"I need to decode it."

He stared at me long enough that it got uncomfortable. He tore a single page out of the journal and pressed it into my open hand.

"What the hell is this?" I asked.

"I'm holding onto the collateral until you can decode that." He took a step back and looked me up and down. "And, Demarco?"

"Yeah?"

"People like you don't get into places like the Gravity Lounge."

"Maybe I'll just have a chat with the guy in charge about that."

Shaw's cruel grin widened. "Guy in charge. Now there's a mystery might earn you a dime or two."

"You don't know who the boss is?"

"Rumor has it the devil runs that place. Just take my advice and check out all your other options first." He nodded at the photograph. "Dames like her don't get into the Gravity Lounge either." With that, he melted back into the bustling crowd of the Hallows morning. A raw pit opened in my stomach, and my hand, the one gripping the single journal page, shook from adrenaline. Leo Shaw put me on edge. He was one of the few men around who intimidated me, and I didn't like it.

But he was right. There wasn't a way into the Gravity Lounge. As my adrenaline crashed, I deflated. All my leads were dead. He had taken my only useful evidence, and if I was being honest with myself, it probably wasn't the lead I had hoped it would be. The journal might hold information about her life, but it probably wouldn't have the address of her kidnapper. And that was *if* I could decode the journal. Which I couldn't.

Not without help.

Chapter 5

BUILDINGS in the middle reaches of the Hallows were nestled into the lush greenery of paradise. Foot traffic bustled by, and people picked their way through the crowded streets on their way to cushy jobs that paid for their extravagant homes and luxurious lifestyles. Twisting vines surrounded the little outdoor cafe, and the aroma of freshly baked scones wafted from the tiny kitchen.

Across from me, a teenager named Retch eyed me over a steaming cup of tea. I'd hired him a while ago to help me interface with the various systems of the station. *Hired* was a relative term. I asked him to help and he did, but certainly not out of kindness. He and the Screaming Jesus gang in the Heavies had been a valuable source of information, but they always came out on the better end of any deal. Retch's necklace, a screaming Jesus suspended on a brutal cross, glittered in the Hallows light. Faded red-dyed hair framed the teen's narrow face.

"I'm just saying," he said, "people care a lot more about

their dogs than they do about their daughters. This would be a quick dime."

Retch wasn't excommunicated, but he wasn't exactly on good terms with the Catholic Church. Something about him being a borderline criminal and teenage transgender boy made the church treat him like a ticking time bomb. Retch was a clever kid, though, and had a streak of decency that was as strong as it was wildly inconsistent.

"Dogs, huh?" I said.

"People lose their dogs all the time."

"You have anything to do with that?"

His eyes narrowed. "I like where you're going with this."

"Somebody was bringing a dog to the Gravity Lounge," I said.

"A Yorkie?"

"Bigger," I said. "A lot bigger."

"Someone's missing a Yorkie. They'll pay a whole stack of dimes for the return."

I took a sip of my black coffee. The brew was somehow both bitter and weak. "I'll keep an eye out."

"His name is King."

"I bet."

"There have been people missing, too," said Retch. "But not the kind anyone pays to find."

"I have to finish this job, Retch," I said. "Then I'll think about looking for people and their dogs."

Retch hmphed. "Destiny Alverez is a dead job. It's time to move on."

"What do you mean?"

He leaned forward. "You've never been good at cutting bait."

"What's it to you?"

"Maybe I like dogs."

"You've always hated my sister's dog."

"*You've* always hated Runt. He's not such a bad monster."

The conversation was starting to irritate me. "I'm going to find Destiny."

"She's not in the Gravity Lounge."

I wanted to know how he knew, but also I really didn't want to know how he knew. It likely involved the kind of illegal, amoral transaction I wasn't comfortable with.

"I bribed a guy," he explained. "And I promised him you'd find his dog."

"What did I tell you about making promises?"

"It's fine, Demarco. I was lying. King's probably dead in a ventilation duct somewhere."

I tried my very best not to roll my eyes. "There was a lot of blood at the scene in the garden, and it was right outside the lounge's back entrance."

"It wasn't enough to kill a person, though."

"You're sure?"

"That's what my sources say. She's probably hiding from the mook who hired you to find her."

"The client is her father."

"A lot of people don't get along with their parents." His tone was deadly serious.

Retch lived on the streets of Heavy Nicodemia, and he'd never told me who his parents were. He also didn't have any formal education, on account of being on poor terms with both Church and State. His Karma rating bottomed out every week, and nobody around was foolish enough to give him a boost. Nobody but me, anyway. I buried my face in my hands. The lack of sleep was smothering my brain like a wet sock.

Retch bounced in place. "You know, I could get used to

this gravity. You should bring me along to more of these things."

"Show me that you know how to stay out of trouble, and I'll think about it."

"Out of trouble? A roll of dimes says it's *me* who's going to have to rescue *you*."

"I'm not taking that action."

He waggled his thin eyebrows. "I heard that Jude Demarco always takes a sure bet."

"Retch."

"Fine, fine. You're not good for that kind of cash, anyway."

"Have you been talking to Shaw?"

Retch stared at me. "That piece of shit?"

"Yeah, that piece of shit."

"I didn't tell him where you were."

"Destiny was attacked in the garden and then relocated somewhere. Maybe on her own, or maybe she was grabbed by her attacker. Where could she have gone other than the Gravity Lounge without drawing too much attention?"

Retch took a sip of his tea. "She could have been flown anywhere. Look, it's a waste of time."

That would explain the lack of footprints leaving the scene. "There's minimal surveillance at the lounge. Trinity might not have sent an ambulance."

"It didn't have to be the medics. Could have been a friend. Could have been the blue."

"Blue didn't know anything about her," I said.

"You questioned them already?"

"Something like that."

We sat in silence for a while. I appreciated Retch helping me with the investigation, but he was inexperienced in many of the ways of the world, especially when it came to the upper crust of society. My plan was to remedy some of that. But that took time.

"So, we think a friend picked her up," said Retch.

"Acquaintance."

"Why not a friend?"

"A friend would have grabbed her purse."

"Could she have signaled for help?"

"Maybe," I said, secretly pleased with the kid's progress. "But where would she have gone?"

Retch leaned forward. "Did you know this bead is haunted?"

"It's not haunted."

"You ever hear of the fuel sludge disaster of transit year twenty?"

"Retch, I grew up in Hallow Nicodemia. The fuel sludge disaster is practically core curriculum."

"So, it really happened." He sipped his tea contemplatively.

"Ancient history," I said. "You need to focus."

"And you need to listen to what people are saying," said Retch. He thought he was the one teaching me how to investigate.

"I *do* listen to people," I said. "But *you* need to learn that they're usually lying."

Retch pushed his tea away. "People always speak their truth."

"What's the truth of the fuel sludge disaster, then?" I asked, trying to keep the condescending amusement from my tone. The disaster *had* been many generations ago, and it had formed a local legend. Rumor was there was a conduit that ran the whole length of the Hallow Nicodemia spiral. It had broken years into Nicodemia's long journey to the stars. The sludge was thick and corrosive. Caustic on everything it touched, toxic to anyone who breathed it. A hundred Travelers had died, and that was back when there weren't many to spare.

"They say you can still smell the sludge on really hot days," Retch said, narrowing his hazel eyes. "And you can hear the spirits of the dead in the tunnels below the streets. They wander at night and watch as the pipes slowly corrode, readying for another disaster much worse than the first."

"They fixed the fuel sludge system," I said. "It's no longer under all that pressure, especially now that the station isn't a ship. There's not as much use for fuel now that we're not moving."

"Oh, we move," said Retch, a hint of a smile on his face. "We move, all right. All the Trinity cities have the same flaw, and every time we do a maneuvering change, we're risking total annihilation."

"Total annihilation? Is that what you heard?"

"Total." He fixed me with a serious stare. "Annihilation."

A wave of exhaustion rolled over me, threatening my tenuous grasp on sanity. It didn't matter that Retch believed in the ghost stories of the out-of-touch people of Hallow Nicodemia. Every fiber of my being told me to argue with the kid until he knew I was right, but it wouldn't matter. As stubborn as I was, he had me beat. He'd wrenched me off topic and left me spinning on ancient history instead of solving Destiny's disappearance.

My knees creaked when I stood. The canopy of honeysuckle draped over us, brushing against my battered fedora. Retch had no such problem when he stood, but he was a native of the Heavies. He was tall for his people, but that didn't mean much this high up the gravity well.

The sun of Hallow Nicodemia had intensified throughout the morning. At almost noon, it was a scouring flame that raked across the district. Downspiral, the shining glass cathedral stood like an ancient monolith, magnifying the too-intense fury of the day's light. Upspiral was an entrance to the dense housing of a university neighborhood.

I started upspiral, and Retch followed.

Something about what he said still bothered me. "Tell me again why you think she's not in the Gravity Lounge?" I asked as we passed a group of studying youths.

"She's not the type," replied Retch.

"What type?"

"Girls who work at places like the Gravity Lounge fit into a certain type. That's all I'm saying."

"The pretty type?"

"That's a little sexist, Demarco."

I navigated the shining alleyways of student housing, making my way through narrow paths deep into the towering structures of the district. The fiberstone buildings were a light gray, almost white, that caught the light and shone almost as bright as the center of the bead, which didn't help my pleasant disposition.

"Fine," Retch said eventually. "She isn't the pretty type. Word is she's a little short, a little plump, and her hair doesn't do that thing they like around here."

"What thing?"

He waved a hand over his head indicating some shape I couldn't quite figure. "That… thing."

"Sure."

"So, she couldn't have worked there. Even if she had good connections, they wouldn't have hired her."

"Someone could have taken her there. When she was bleeding, I mean."

"I thought of that," said Retch. "And no."

"No? That's it? Just no?"

"Demarco, just let it go. Really."

"I'm not dropping this."

He sighed. "Nobody at a reputable place like the Gravity Lounge is going to let some bleeding stranger die in their lobby."

I blinked. How had he misread the place so badly? "Reputable?"

"Reputable," he confirmed. "The more crime happens in a place, the more they have to worry about reputation. It's just common sense, Demarco. How are you so bad at this?"

"So, you don't think the Gravity Lounge is involved at all?"

"Nope."

"I'd still like to take a look around inside that place."

"I bet."

Retch kicked a walnut that had recently fallen from the tree arching high above us. It flew in a long slow arc across the road and landed in a gutter. It was then that I noticed his nice new shoes. They were the right size for his big feet, and they practically shone against the dull gray of the rest of his outfit.

"Nice shoes," I said.

His brow furrowed. "They're all right."

I grabbed his shoulder and turned him to face me. "Where did you get those, kid."

He refused to meet my gaze. "It's nothing."

"You didn't bribe your contact at the lounge. They bribed you."

"I fleeced him," he said.

"How much of what you told me was a lie?" My blood steamed in my veins. Had he betrayed me?

Retch's fists clenched at his sides. He'd been caught, and he didn't like it. "The girl's not in the lounge."

All the exhaustion bubbled up into a fizzy cacophony of emotion directed right at the only kid in the city that I thought I could trust. I knew it would be better to be understanding of his situation. He'd gone through a lot, and this was probably the only new pair of shoes he had ever owned. But—

But.

"I give you a cut, Retch. I help you whenever you need. My sister lets you eat at her cafe, and now you're taking bribes to run me around? You *lie* to me?"

He shoved me away with both hands. "I'm not your charity case."

"You *lied* to me."

"I didn't lie!" His voice went high and tight. "It's none of your fucking business where I got these shoes."

"It is when you sell me out," I said.

"Fuck you, Demarco! Fuck! You!" He stalked away, disappearing into the dense crowds.

It was a full minute before my breathing slowed down. I was surrounded by white university apartments, and the students bustled past as if I hadn't just lost the only help I had in this sour world. As if I hadn't just been betrayed by a kid who was supposed to be the one person on my side.

I stood at the base of one of the tallest buildings in the area. Sharply dressed students steadily filed in and out, rushing to their classes, into the greater city, or even to meetings with others. They lived their lives in ignorance, seeing their world as a stable pursuit of a balance between productivity and happiness. Did any of them know Destiny Alverez? One of them might hold the hint that would lead me to wherever she was now, but I would never know. Of the thousands of students flowing in and out of the building, I could never hope to find anything.

I had nothing. All the work I'd done to find Destiny Alverez left me stranded with only a vague feeling that she might be dead or dying. My only options were to give up or start from the beginning, and I wasn't going to give up.

"Can I help you?" asked a chipper student with smooth chestnut hair and round glasses. She sat at the building's reception desk. She held a smile frozen on her face while I considered my response. Behind her, a boy in a blue sweater buried himself in the cold glow of a tablet screen.

"Yes," I said. "I need you to let me into a room, and I don't care if it's not allowed."

She opened her mouth, then closed it again.

I leaned forward with my two fists pressed against the reception desk. "Listen, kid. I'm looking for Destiny Alverez. Or her corpse. Or some hint as to her intended destination. I got a strong preference for which of those I'd like to find, but I'd give all three even odds. Maybe you help. Maybe you don't. Maybe she's still alive up there, but tomorrow you gotta deal with a corpse. Maybe someone else comes by and covers it all up and you never hear about it again, but you know." I tapped my temple with one finger. "You *know* you could have done something to help someone, and you chose to do nothing."

She chewed her lower lip. "I don't work tomorrow."

"I never stop."

"Fine," she sighed. "Follow me."

Chapter 6

THIS WASN'T the first time I had visited Destiny Alverez's apartment. It was the first place I went when her father hired me. The workers hadn't let me in the first time, so I'd had no choice but to break in and investigate by the light of a lit cigarette.

In an ideal world, the studious daughter of two scientists would have spent the majority of her time in this cramped space. She would have studied here, entertained guests here, and slept the long nights away. This place, out of every other location in the entire city, would surely be the most imprinted with the essence of Destiny—who she was at the very core of her being.

It wasn't.

Destiny lived in a single-room studio with an attached bathroom large enough for me to stand, but not enough to lie down. The mirror shone in the warm light, and the bottles of beauty products were precariously perched atop a tiny sink. Her bed was a jumble of blankets and pillows, expertly tossed to give the appearance of use.

But it *hadn't* been used. I saw that now in the full illumination of the overhead lights. I also smelled it. The blankets had a fresh aroma, but the air hinted at dust and stale air, the way places smell when they've been left in the dark, cut off from the station's general ventilation, which circulates every time someone enters a room.

Had someone staged this room?

If Retch *wasn't* lying to me, then Destiny never got a job at the Gravity Lounge. But right there, dangling on the back of the single chair, was a fitted gravity harness. The piece was stylish, like a rave nightclub number worn to attract the attention of all the wrong sorts of people. In the superconductor framework of a place like the Gravity Lounge, this would give the girl something very close to the ability to fly. She'd float, anyway. It was the gimmick. Combine low-spin gravity with repulsing magnets and watch as everyone defies gravity.

Quaint, really.

There were also receipts and cash scattered on the desk. The receipts all pointed to small purchases near the Gravity Garden. She wasn't spending Karma. She was spending dimes and recording every transaction. Strange behavior for a student, but not entirely out of the norm.

"Can I go?" asked the girl in the round glasses.

"Not yet," I said.

She sighed and leaned against the door frame. If she left, Trinity would close the room. I'd be left in the dark, and it would be that much harder to find anything of use.

I pulled the coded page from my pocket and peered at it in the warm light. The symbols on it—harsh geometric things—appeared more complex in the soft light, as if it were meant for this location. What I really wanted was a way to decode the messages on it.

The more I poked around in the abandoned apartment,

the more things didn't fit. The dust was too thick. The clothes were slightly worn—like castoffs from a previous round of fashion changes. Several of the blouses looked like they wouldn't fit the girl in the picture Reginald Alverez had given me. They were too small. Too conservative. I should have caught it the first time I was here, but back then the job didn't have the same kind of urgency. It wasn't yet an effort to save someone who might be dying somewhere.

"She didn't live here," I muttered.

The girl stared at me.

"She must have crashed somewhere else," I muttered. "Any ideas where? Did she have a boyfriend?"

"It's a big building," the girl said. "I don't actually know everyone."

Of course not. Not everyone made it their business to integrate themselves into the community. Especially not a community like this—ten thousand birds in a flock, all banking the same direction without ever truly understanding why. Science was like that sometimes. Scientists existed in a community of isolation.

"There was a guy with a guitar," she said after a few minutes of poking around on a tablet screen. "He came to visit once at the beginning of the semester. There aren't any records about who he was, though."

"Trinity's telling you this?"

"Well, yeah." Her voice tight with offense.

"Thanks." If Trinity didn't bother to record the identity of the visitor, it probably wasn't significant.

Unless Trinity was hiding that information for the betterment of the community. The AI could be unpredictable that way. In my experience, if I wanted to know something, I needed to ask another person. Preferably someone with a decent memory.

"You live in a room like this?" I asked the girl.

She nodded. "A few stories up."

"Where are the hidden places?"

"Excuse me?"

"You have porn or drugs or a weapon, right?"

"What the hell?"

"You have a secret you want to keep from your significant other or a picture of a loved one you don't want to share. Where do you put it in your room?"

She held out for a long time, locking her gaze with me in a show of impressive determination. The girl had some willpower in her. She almost convinced me that I'd offended her in some way, but I knew there had to be something here. A whole university full of students couldn't exist without a few secrets.

"Behind the sink," she said. When I started looking, she added, "Under it."

The maintenance panel behind the sink took the pressure from my fingertips and a slight twist to open. I might have eventually found it without the girl's help, but knowing exactly where it was saved me the afternoon and a massive headache. The panel clicked and slid open.

Nestled among the pipes, dry inside a plastic pouch, was a crumpled bundle of papers and a few stubs of hand-rolled cigarettes. I opened the pouch and took a sniff. Marijuana, most likely. Typical thing for a kid to have hidden away. It wasn't illegal, necessarily, but it could hurt a person's Karma in certain situations. The rules were unclear, and unclear rules made a good case for secrecy.

The papers were something else. It looked like the transcript of some exceptionally boring scientific communications. Nothing about the odd code in the journal. If there was anything useful in these papers, it was going to take hours of sifting. I filed it away in a coat pocket.

When I looked up, the girl in the round glasses wasn't alone. The boy in the blue sweater from the desk downstairs stood next to her carrying a whole mountain of tension on his shoulders.

"Why are you looking for Destiny?" the boy asked.

I faced him. He was almost as tall as me but soft as a giant teddy bear. "I'm hoping to save her life," I said.

He stared at me, likely trying to judge what he saw in the amber glow of Destiny Alverez's tiny apartment. "All right," he said. "Follow me."

A room down the hall stood open already, and the boy gestured to it. "There was a complaint," he said. "Every floor has an extra room set up just for visitors or emergencies."

"Destiny lived here?"

"No," he said. "But she was here last night."

This was a caricature of the room I'd just left, down to the rumpled blankets and lined-up toiletries. It smelled of stale smoke, sweat, and blood.

And there was plenty of blood, too. Fresh red smeared the sink and mirror. The space under the sink had been torn open by bloody fingers. It was empty.

"Is this Destiny's blood?" I asked.

"I don't know," said the boy. "But the logs say she was here. Someone wanted to use the room this afternoon, but when maintenance came to check, they found it like this."

"She's been here a long time," I said.

"This room hasn't been checked out in ages."

"Sure."

My heart raced. This was it. I'd lucked onto the place Destiny had come after her encounter in the garden. Even more important, this was where she had been living off the books. But why, when she had a room right down the hall?

I checked the drawers and the hotplate. The clothes stashed here were more modern. They looked like Destiny's clothing, and they were on the wild end of fashion, with sleek shapes and bold colors. This wasn't the fashion of the upscale Gravity Lounge. In fact, nothing here pointed to the upper class at all. It was all trash. Servant stuff, but Destiny was supposed to be mingling with the upper class. Her father had expected her to stay at the university so she could develop social connections in the Hallows.

Not this. I held up a shred of cloth that might have passed as a dancer's uniform in one of the sleazier neighborhoods of the Heavies.

The pieces started to fit together. Destiny wanted to maintain her illusion of a nicer life, but she was down on her luck. She got a side gig dancing somewhere. Maybe it started with waitressing or some other servant position, but pretty soon she became the thing her betters kept assuming of her. She got into dancing. She needed to earn dimes fast because by then her Karma was in the gutter.

By the look of the room, dancing had led to something more. Those calling cards were starting to make sense. Whether this was prostitution or a proclivity for profitable relationships was probably a matter of semantics. Whatever the case, she entertained guests in the floor's extra room. Eventually, she started living there more than she lived in her normal room, which meant that if I was looking for clues about where Destiny Alverez ended up, they would be here.

This left me with a lot of questions, but I had a feeling the answers were right here in the room.

The girl in the round glasses had left, but the boy stood in the doorway. His mousy brown hair stood on end, and his hazel eyes watched me from a narrow face.

"Who did she bring here last?" I asked the guy, pretending to still search the room.

"I—I don't know." He punched some controls on his handheld screen. "It's all anonymous."

Anonymous. That kind of thing was only possible with a pretty hefty load of Karma. Trinity would obfuscate logs, but only for people it really trusted. People who were pillars of the community or who helped a lot of people. Philanthropic businessmen, musicians, politicians. But why was Destiny involved with people like that? Even if she was looking to make a quick dime, she wouldn't have been running with that kind of crowd.

"You knew she lived here," I said.

"It's my job to know who lives where."

"But she kept it off the books. Isn't it your job to report things like this?"

The boy chewed his lip. He'd been covering up for her.

I met the guy's gaze for a long breath and waited until he cracked.

The words tumbled out of him like a bad lunch. "We dated. A little. I mean, back when she went to university, we saw each other a lot. She was amazing. Way above my league." He was right, from what I could tell, which made this even more interesting. "When she dropped out, I helped her keep her housing for the rest of the semester, but it was going to run out soon. I didn't know how much she was coming here, but I know she had it unlocked as a backup plan in case she got kicked out."

"How did she get in here without drawing notice?" I nudged a bloody towel with my toe. "She was in a bad way last night."

"Rooftop, maybe?" he said. "She has the code."

"Why wouldn't she have been kicked out of this room?"

"It's not hers. It's not really anyone's. It's on the books as an available rental space for visitors, but it hardly ever gets used."

"You said she dropped out. When did that happen, and why?"

"Early," he said. "Only a month in, I think. I don't know why."

I took off my hat and ran my fingers through my greasy hair. It had been too long since I'd had a proper shower, and I was starting to suffer for it. I had thought Destiny Alverez's case was going to be an easy one, and I had thought I could find her before the sun set the previous night. I was wrong. Reginald Alverez was right to worry about his daughter. She was in much deeper than we thought.

"One last thing," I said, fixing the kid in the steeliest gaze I could manage.

"Yeah?"

I held up the skimpy dancer's outfit. "Where did she dance?"

Chapter 7

NICODEMIA WAS a Catholic city founded by a Catholic need to spread a broken faith to the whole galaxy. The idea that there might be people somewhere who somehow didn't hear the Word of God offended the all-powerful Church, and they weren't about to leave getting the good message out to Protestants or other offshoots of Christianity. It certainly couldn't be left to the Jewish or Muslim members of the coalition. The Church was a major contributor to the space program hundreds of years ago, back when the generation ships were built. They contributed enough that they had the leverage to make one of the generation ship's many cities a truly Catholic-run society.

That didn't mean that *only* Catholics lived in Nicodemia. The Travelers, original descendants of the generation ship's occupants, were predominantly descended from Catholic stock, but faith doesn't run true in the genome. Faith is lost and found more than toys in a playground.

Later, when the ship became a station orbiting a star and Nicodemia became the hub of science and colonization in the cluster, new arrivals started to occupy Nicodemia. Muslims and Buddhists and Jews and Humanists arrived first as a portable workforce, then as colonists hoping to live with their families far from Earth. They gathered in clusters wherever they could, first in the Heavies, where homes were cheap, then in Haven, where the middle class could duke it out for status and wealth.

Finally, clusters of non-Catholic residents established themselves in the lower reaches of the treasured Hallow Nicodemia. Once they had a foothold in a bead, not even the most affluent Travelers could dislodge them.

So they sectioned them off and called it the Sinless District. It was anything but. The Sinless was an outlet for all the things the upper-class Catholic Travelers didn't want to know about. This was where the thinly veiled brothels sat next to synagogues sat next to rave nightclubs. The Sinless hid all the unpleasantness from the heaven above where everything was supposed to be pure and wonderful.

As far as I was concerned, the Sinless was one of the few places in the Hallows that dealt in truth. This was where I had brought Retch so that we could devise a therapy plan for his transition—a medical treatment not referenced in Trinity's Catholic-inspired database. The communities here knew which hormones and blockers were available and which ones were appropriate for a sixteen-year-old kid like Retch.

Even in the brightest afternoon, the Sinless lingered in the filtered shade under tall, arching trees. The scent of decomposition lingered in the foul air wafting out of cramped alleys. This district was nestled behind the hydroponic farms of the lower Hallows, its people as attached to the industry of farming as to the industry of sin.

The Sinless was exclusively a dime economy, its residents, for the most part, having given up long ago on Trinity's

Karma. Nicodemia's few Hindu residents scoffed at the city's perversion of Karma in favor of metal coins. Everyone else spent coins because their Karma wasn't worth the dirt under their fingernails.

The district was quiet during the day. I passed a trio of drag queens on their way to some appointment. They were beautiful, strong, and flamboyant natives of the lower Heavies. The look they shot me as I passed was suspicious—more so than I thought warranted—and the scowls on their painted faces followed me as I disappeared into the darkened alleys.

Once I found the Crushed Velvet, I knew exactly how far Destiny Alverez had fallen. In a district of shady brothels and sleazy dance halls, the Crushed Velvet was about the middle of the pack. Its bouncer looked attentive, and the servers inside appeared well-fed despite the hunger in their eyes. The air hung heavy with the scent of spice cigars cut by the piercing notes of a jazz saxophone.

Behind the bar stood a man with dark skin and a handlebar mustache. He wore a clean white shirt, and his hands looked much younger than his creased face. "Help you?" By his look, I would have identified him as a native of Haven or the Hallows, but his accent pegged him as an immigrant from Earth.

I glanced around at the others in the smoky club. A slender woman danced topless on stage above three men leering in sharp gray suits. A server wearing more feathers than cloth swished between tables occupied by surly customers. "The mood's a little sour in here," I said.

The bartender shrugged. "These are sour times."

"I'm looking for a girl." I slid two dimes across the bar. "And a beer."

"Drinks I can help you with." His mustache twitched as he spoke. "Girls, not so much."

"It's a particular girl," I said. "Word is she works around here."

The man turned his back on me to work the taps. When he finished pouring off the head, he placed it in front of me on a coaster printed with the Crushed Velvet's provocative logo—a scantily clad woman spreading her legs on a cushion of violet and red. "A lot of people work around here."

"She's in trouble." The beer was bitter and strong. The perfect pairing with an empty stomach and a bad mood. "Maybe dead already. I don't know."

The bartender glanced around at nothing in particular, the whites of his eyes hinting at an edge of fear under his sour mood. "I don't know anything about that."

He definitely did. "A man like you doesn't need to get involved," I said. "Stand back, stand aside. Don't utter a word as disquiet turns into a grumbling anger. There's a lot to be said for silence." I took a long pull of beer. "Sells a lot of beers. Silence is survival in a place like this. If there's a killer out there, then words are courage. Courage is dangerous."

"You're not making a strong case, mister."

"I'm not making any case." I flipped another dime onto the table. "I'm looking at this sad sack club in this shitty neighborhood, and I'm wondering if maybe somebody wants something more. Something different. You didn't come all this way for this garbage. You heard you'd be in the best of the three beads of Nicodemia. That's what they promised you, right? You'll live in the Hallows. You'll be light on your feet and raking in cash. The world's yours for the taking."

He met that with a slight twitch of his mustache.

"That's what I thought." I paused as his neck tensed with contained anger. "Ambitious and competent. You're working below your skills because the world you've stepped into doesn't appreciate all the good you can do. It pushes you down."

"There are worse jobs."

"There are better."

"I'm telling you, I don't know anything about any girl."

"Destiny Alverez," I said.

He blinked rapidly. It wasn't what he was expecting.

I leaned close to him and hissed, "Where would she go if she was in trouble?"

"I told you," he said, reeling now. "I don't know anything."

"You know this isn't right." We were drawing attention from the few customers, but I ignored them. "She might be bleeding out as we speak, and this is her one chance at survival."

A slender hand touched my shoulder. The server in the feathers leaned past me and placed a tray on the bar. "Trouble, Moses?"

"No, Ma'am," said the bartender. "Just chatting about Destiny."

"Destiny?" She said with a thoughtful squint. "Can't say I believe in it, but it does what it does anyway, doesn't it?"

"Always," said Moses.

With a swish of feathers, the server glided away.

"Is that what Destiny does here?" I asked. "Serve drinks?"

Moses plucked the tray off the bar and stowed it below. "You sure have a lot of questions for a man only halfway through his first beer."

Despite the beer already going to my head, I said, "Then how about a shot of your best whiskey." I placed my last three dimes on the table. "And some peanuts if you happen to have any back there."

After pouring me a shot of the smokiest, strongest

whiskey I'd ever smelled and retrieving a bowl of popcorn from a machine, he leaned forward and said, "Destiny isn't a server here, mister. She's a dancer. Decent one too."

I cast a glance at the dancer on stage. Her act was morphing from sultry to sexy at a pace that would frustrate a priest. "Does she have a place she would go if she was in trouble?"

"Nobody sticks around here if they're in trouble. Not after—"

The hand rested on my shoulder again. I was starting to think this server was going to be a problem. "I need a trio of Hallow Delights for the gentlemen near the stage, Moses."

"Be right up," he said and turned to work on pouring a noxiously colorful beverage. The sharp bite of gin tickled my nose.

The beer made my head swim, and a rock churned in the pit of my stomach. These people knew more than they were letting on, and if I was reading the situation right, the server was actually the one in charge. She drummed the long daggers of her nails on the polished bar.

I swallowed the rest of my beer and turned to her. "Tell me what you know about Destiny Alverez."

"You're not her type."

"She has a type?"

"Everybody has a type." She took the tray of drinks from Moses. As she glided away, she added, "and it's not you, Traveler."

"Hardly ever is," I muttered.

"Cherry Saint," said Moses, sliding a slip of paper across the bar to me.

"Excuse me?"

"Cherry Saint." He twisted a rag in his calloused hands. "She was the girl I thought you were talking about at first.

Good kid. Danced. She and Destiny weren't exactly friends, but they got along. Maybe they shared something in their past. I don't know. We tend to not ask a lot of questions around here, but those two were close."

"I'm hearing a lot of past tense," I said.

"Cherry disappeared a few weeks ago," said Moses. "Nobody came looking." He leaned close to me and whispered, "She sometimes shared an apartment with Destiny."

"They were close, huh?"

"Maybe closer than a Catholic would like."

"The Church has eased up on that kind of thing over the last few hundred years."

"Way I hear it, the Church says it's always been fine with same-gendered relationships," said Moses, "but that doesn't mean it's ever been true."

I knew what he was saying. The Church didn't like to show that it had ever changed. Instead, it tended to say it had always been exactly as it is now. Cognitive dissonance was a sign of the reverberations of faith echoing through the ages. Women had always been priests, they'd say. Gays were always accepted. Trans people? No, of course not. They were abominations working against God's will.

"Cherry's transgender?" I asked.

"None of my business," Moses said. "But she and Destiny were here. Cherry started talking about leaving as if there was someplace she could go. Now she's gone. Nobody ever bothered to find her."

"The blue's not on it?"

He scoffed, "You see many of them around here?"

I wondered if the disappearance was connected, but my primary concern was Destiny. If she was here, she'd be in the apartment she shared with Cherry Saint. The paper Moses had passed me was a nearly illegible scrawl of an address in the Sinless district. It was one more step in my marathon walk. My day had already stretched on longer than my weary bones could handle. The only thing keeping me up was the barest thread of hope that maybe Destiny Alverez was still alive.

If I was right, this could still end well. If I was wrong—

Well, I was usually wrong.

I stepped out of the Crushed Velvet into the raucous clamor of the Sinless streets. The day was dragging on, and I needed to follow my one lead—but something felt wrong. The hair on the back of my neck was prickling and as a crowd of loud teenagers passed, I felt someone's eyes on me. I lit a cigarette and leaned against the wall, watching as the crowd ebbed and flowed.

Then, I saw him lingering half a block away, half concealed by the worn fiberstone of an adjacent cigar shop.

Reginald Alverez. Destiny's father was following me.

Chapter 8

"I NEVER SHOULD HAVE HIRED a degenerate like you," said Alverez when I caught up to him. His pasty white fists were tight knots at his sides, and he carried all the tension in the world in his rounded shoulders. The man's watery eyes were twisted in anger behind the magnifying distortion of his glasses. I'd never seen him bent up like this, and the sight of him threw me, especially with the alcohol still rumbling around in my otherwise empty belly.

It took a moment, but the implication of his presence clicked. "You've been following me this whole time."

"Since you got arrested," he said. "Now you're drinking your stipend instead of looking for my girl." He jabbed a finger at my chest. "Well, let me tell you, you're not seeing one more dime for this."

"That so?"

"You're fired, Demarco."

I could tell him that I'd been working relentlessly on this job. I could tell him that I'd followed Destiny's trail all the way into the Sinless. That I was on the cusp of maybe rescuing her from whatever danger threatened her. But it wouldn't do any good unleashing all the weak excuses that were dancing on the tip of my tongue. He wouldn't listen. Alverez was a worried father, and if he had gotten in his head that I was down here to blow off some steam, then I'd never convince him otherwise.

There also wasn't any chance of convincing him that his daughter might be something less than pure. "Buy me a kabob, Alverez," I said as I brushed past him.

"A kabob! Why should I buy you anything, you good-for-nothing—"

I spun on him. My nerves ran raw and the back of my neck burned. "You want to know a few things about your daughter? Buy me a damn kabob."

IT WAS MORE vegetables than meat, with green pepper and tomato stuck on a stick with a couple of chunks of brown meat. Lamb, I thought, but it was the stringiest lamb I'd ever had the displeasure of digesting. After a few bites, I handed the paper with the address to Alverez. "That's where we're going."

"What do you mean?"

"Your daughter's been there, and we need to check it out."

He crumpled the paper in his damp hand. "This is just another lie."

"It's been a long day," I said. "This is the next step. We'll find out what happened if we're lucky."

"And you're lucky?"

"Never have been before," I said. "Figure I'm due."

Down the main drag of the Sinless, the residents filtered

out onto the grimy street in anticipation of the approaching night. Flamboyantly dressed men and women crossed women in hijabs and men in robes. A trio of boys in ragged pinstripe suits chatted with a tall lady in sequins. It was an eccentric bunch, and getting more eccentric by the minute. Alverez didn't belong in a district like this. Just admitting that the place existed might be enough to break him.

The alleys of the Sinless were all twisting, narrow passages that doubled back on themselves and served as the best defense anyone had ever designed aboard a Trinity bead. The whole district had been built into the husk of what must have once been a huge building. The structure had long since lost coherency, though, and smaller structures had been constructed inside in a winding, random pattern. The address I had handed Alverez was as much map as it was text, with loops and twists describing directions through the deepest recesses of the district. The farther we traveled, the more dangerous it got.

"I never understood why people didn't just convert when they moved here," Alverez spat.

"Some people can be stubborn in their beliefs."

"Stubborn," he said, eyeing a man in an extravagant feather overcoat. "I bet."

"Think of it this way," I said between my last few bites of tough meat. "Christianity, no matter what flavor, has always thrived on adversity. When it's not under threat, it turns on itself."

"You really believe that?"

"Persecution is fuel for faith," I said. "It can drive it forward or burn it down."

The map took us from the relatively safe gloom of the main drag into an alley covered in arched fiberstone. The lights that followed us—brightening for Alverez, but ignoring me—were a pale warm glow that flickered on the light-starved vines. We were close. I started to doubt my policy of walking around unarmed.

"Stay alert," I told Alverez. "If anything happens, run."

He nodded, finally cowed by the circumstances. "My girl would never come here," he whispered.

"You'd be surprised what some women do to disappoint their fathers."

Above, a shape moved across the lit window of an apartment. A whiff of ammonia kissed the breeze.

"We're here," I said. "So, let's get up there and see who's there."

A shadow ahead of us in the alley moved at my words.

A knife flashed. With a grunt—it sounded like a man—he lurched toward Alverez. My stupid instincts put me in the way of the attack. The knife slashed at my midsection, slicing through the tough cloth of my tan overcoat. Alverez stumbled, catching the tip of the attacker's blade on the backs of his fingers.

"Back!" I shouted, shoving Alverez.

The attacker lunged again at Alverez and struck him with a punishing blow to the shoulder, slamming him against the wall. The blow would have cracked the bones of a native of the Hallows. Lower gravity might give them health and luxury, but it came at a cost. Alverez toppled, and I finally got myself between him and the attacker.

The attacker held off my advance with the glint of his blade. His cloak was blacker than any shadow, and the cloth over his face hid even his eyes from view.

"A silhouette," I said. "Don't see many of those around these days." The cloak was made of an ultra-black material that was highly illegal due to the way it messed up Trinity's sensors.

The attacker's hesitation was enough to let me glance at Alverez. The man was bleeding, but not bad. He wouldn't lose any fingers. Probably.

"What do you want?" I asked the attacker. My gut told me this wasn't a random mugging. A good mugger starts with a request for money, not a swing of the blade. "Why are you here?"

Alverez blubbered something about his fingers. The attacker said nothing.

"The way I figure," I said, "you're in over your head. You're here for a guy like him." I stuck a thumb out at Alverez. "But you got a guy like me. Cross me, and you'll never see a shadow without knowing I'm there. You'll never walk in the open without someone watching you. I'm the guy who lurks just beyond and takes the time to figure out every one of your sins before making you pay for them."

I stepped forward. His face was invisible, but the tense set of his shoulders told me he was affected by my little speech. All I needed to do was take a little more time.

He didn't give it to me.

His free hand took something from an invisible pocket. As soon as he twitched, I was on the move, but I wasn't fast enough. With a downward flick, something shattered on the pavement.

The ammonia blasted across us in a wave. The chemical burn of industrial cleaner spread like a cloud of death. I held my breath and advanced. My vision faltered.

He met me with a slash of his knife. Ammonia burned my eyes and the tears blinded me. I barely avoided his blade, but he danced to the side. A hiss through the air told me he'd swung again. Then again. The cloth of his dark cloak whispered through the air when he moved.

I swung a hard backhand and clipped him in the side of the head. He staggered away. Where did he go?

"Get back," I said to Alverez. The attacker might get me, but he didn't need to get the scientist. "Run!"

"Look out!" shouted Alverez. His voice was a bucket of gravel.

The knife bit into my calf. The pain was like the sting of an insect followed by the static burn of an electrical shock. It tore a shout of pain from the base of my throat.

But I've felt my share of pain. The shadow moved to my right, and I didn't hesitate. Not even the roaring agony running up my leg would stop me from taking this guy down.

My fist connected with meat. My vision cleared enough to see the blade coming in from my left, but I swatted it away. It clattered to the ground.

The attacker wasn't done yet. He struck me in the side of the head with a fist, then kneed me in the gut.

"Run," I gasped.

Finally, Alverez ran.

The attacker snatched his blade from where it had fallen and followed.

I'd be an idiot to go after an armed guy. It had been stupid enough to square off against him in the first place. As big and as tough as I was, a shadow with a knife could end my life in one good slash.

But if that shadow caught up to Alverez, the scientist wouldn't stand a chance.

Alverez didn't know the winding streets of the Sinless. The man barreled away, crashing through the makeshift storefronts and pushing through shocked pedestrians. I glimpsed him as he balked at an enormous man with bronze tattoos on mottled flesh. Alverez pushed into the smoky interior of a club, eliciting shouts of protest from an inattentive bouncer.

The shadow followed, but the bouncer brought me up short. He was a thin man, short like a man from the Heavies but wiry. He held a three-foot-long baton that crackled at the end. A stunstick.

"Out of my way," I said. "I'll get those guys out of your hair."

He eyed me with skepticism. I had no dimes left to bribe the asshole, but after sizing me up, he stepped aside. "Make it quick."

I descended a flight of stairs and stepped into the warm embrace of pulsing music. It wasn't the jazz popular in the rest of the Hallows or even the deep rough blues of the Heavies. This was the pulse of humanity distilled into a single, syncopated noise. Blue and violet lights crashed in waves across the sparsely populated dance floor. It was still early in the night, and only the Sinless's most desperate made their way this early to the drug-fueled orgy of sound and movement.

The shadow was nowhere to be seen, but Alverez stood out like a bad haircut. His pudgy, pale form moved straight across the dance floor, heading for the emergency exit on the far side.

"You see a guy in all black?" I asked a woman with a red mohawk and more piercings than teeth.

She looked at me like I was speaking in tongues. Maybe I was.

I stepped onto the dance floor. He had to be here somewhere, but in the dark, he was invisible. When the lights throbbed blue, I thought I saw a dark shape shifting through the crowd, but it was gone when the lights went violet. He could be anywhere. The incessant pulse of light played with my bone-deep exhaustion, making everything into a haunting phantom ready to strike at any second. The music crushed all other sound. I had to think, but thinking was so hard.

He would be somewhere that he could strike Alverez. That much was clear. He could have circled the floor or made his way straight through, but he wouldn't have waited for me in ambush. Not at the risk of losing Alverez.

Why he wanted Alverez over me didn't matter. Not yet.

There!

Skirting behind a group of leather-clad teens, the shadows shifted unnaturally. I ran, bowling past an angry guy in an ill-fitting halter top. The shadow moved.

Then the lights shifted and the shadow disappeared. I swore, but kept moving.

Lights shifted to blue again. The shadow wasn't where I expected. Gone. I stopped a dozen steps from where Alverez struggled to get past a cluster of women swaying to the low thump of the music. They were the only thing blocking him from the exit. He pushed forward.

"Alverez!" I shouted. If I could get him to stop—but he couldn't hear me over the noise. It was no use. Where was the attacker, though?

I spun just in time to catch the arm swinging a blade at my neck. I shoved the shadow away, and the crowd parted before me into a loose circle. Alverez pushed closer to the exit.

"Who are you?" I shouted.

Again my words were swallowed by waves of noise. I moved so that I was between the attacker and Alverez.

The shadow slashed his blade low. I was ready for him and grabbed his wrist. He had thin arms, but he was strong. I didn't need to buy Alverez time anymore. I'd captured his attacker.

The attacker's fist slammed into the side of my head. Once. Twice. Three times. I went dizzy and red flashed before me. I rolled back, still holding the man's wrist, trying desperately to take away his best angle of attack.

He hooked my knee so I dropped in front of him. He pounded the side of my neck with an elbow and I gasped from the pain. My grip loosened. Nobody helped.

People are garbage sometimes.

I slammed a fist into the man's solar plexus and smiled at the resulting gasp. I punched his face and gut. Anything I could get a fist to. But my angle was bad. I couldn't bring the full force of my strength to bear. Not without losing my grip on his knife hand.

With a twist, he finally yanked free. A kick sent me reeling.

The music stopped. A blare of an emergency alarm sounded, and the lights flared to the brightest white I'd ever seen.

The shadow stood over me, knife in hand. For an eternity, the world was only me and him, with my life wholly in his hands. He could have finished me, but it would have been in front of dozens of witnesses. His silhouette might protect him from being identified, but nobody wants that kind of attention.

He bolted to the front entrance. Then, he was gone.

And so was Alverez.

Chapter 9

SOMETIMES THINGS JUST WORKED OUT. The Fates decreed that the world would move on and everything could be fine.

The stab wound in my leg sealed up easily enough with a med patch. My knee ached, but it wasn't broken. The tendons would be sore for a few days, but they weren't torn. Unlike my ego, the knee would be fine.

I made my way down the spiral toward the alley where we'd been attacked. My odds of catching up to Alverez or the attacker were just shy of null, and I didn't see any reason not to finish what I'd come for. Another stop on the unending slog. Another clue in the long mystery. Destiny needed to be found. With a little luck, I was going to find her.

The only luck I had was bad, but I found her anyway.

Sometimes things just work out.

It was dark except for the neon glow oozing from the slick holograms of thumping nightclubs. Above, the purple haze of the Hallow sky was heavily filtered by a drooping canopy of dark ivy. The people in this part of the city brought their own light to the party. Incandescent makeup covered pasty faces, and lines of illumination accented the extravagant clothing of the most eccentrically dressed people. Kings and queens wandered the streets. Their material wealth was the flow of glitter trailing them wherever they walked.

For once, I wasn't alone in the dark. Every shadow reminded me that the attacker could still be stalking me, but these people valued their privacy. They lurked not out of malice, but out of a desire for quiet solitude even in the presence of many. The people of the Sinless originated mostly from a crowded Earth. Their ancestors were not the Travelers who developed a tradition of ubiquitous surveillance. Instead, their culture demanded a level of independence not wholly at ease in the confined space of a generation ship. Even though many of those here were second- or third-generation residents of the Hallows, that aspect of the culture never quite dissipated. I wasn't sure it ever would.

Or ever should.

A trio of revelers toasted me as I passed. Two tall men flanked a woman with scarlet hair, and at first I thought they recognized me. They didn't. These were friendly people, happy in their revelry.

It was easy to think of the residents of the Sinless as an oppressed people, but it wasn't apparent in the rumbling music as the night's festivities commenced.

The alley transformed from shadowed gloom to stifling black. I used the candlelight glow of my lighter to show me the way through the place where the attacker had gone after Alverez.

Why had he attacked us? It had been apparent from how he fought that he wasn't as interested in me. Even now, I hoped Alverez had been smart enough to get free before the man caught up with him.

Everything about this case led me to believe there was more going on, and I didn't like it.

But sometimes things just worked out. The pieces clicked and everything was fine.

There was an elevator in the old apartment complex, but it wouldn't work for me. Even here in the Sinless, automated systems like elevators were entirely run by Trinity. Instead, I took the unlit stairs using a tongue of flame as guidance. My shoes scuffed against the fiberstone steps, echoing quietly above as I worked my way up to the apartment.

The stairway door opened into a dimly lit hallway, so I extinguished my flame. The click of the lighter sent the dull throb of desire through my chest. I'd have to have a cigarette sooner rather than later. Smoking was one more manageable vice digging its claws into my heart. My nose again detected the trace of ammonia, which reminded me of the attacker. For a long time, I stood perfectly still in the corner, not sure what I was waiting for.

Nothing, apparently.

Halfway down the hall, Cherry Saint's apartment door was painted a pink so wild it almost glowed. It stood slightly ajar, and the flickering glow of a screen lit the space beyond.

Sometimes things just—

I pushed the door open before I could suffer the indignity of hope. The raw dark core of my heart knew I wouldn't like what I saw beyond that door, and there was no reason to utter a prayer, knock on wood, or grasp at one last shred of denial.

The hitching static of a broken wall screen was the room's only illumination. It played across walls glistening with dark splatters that could only be blood. Blood pooled like oil on the floor, slick and sharp in the juddering light.

The thick smell of shit and death choked me, and I had to step out of the room to swallow back the urge to vomit.

I drew as many cool breaths from the hallway as I could before venturing into the room again. I had once claimed I could find and fix anything. People called me when things were about to go badly wrong. Maybe this was still true, but there were some things God himself couldn't fix.

I pushed the door open again and stared at the scene inside. An investigator's work is never easy.

Sometimes things just worked out.

And sometimes they didn't.

Destiny Alverez was dead.

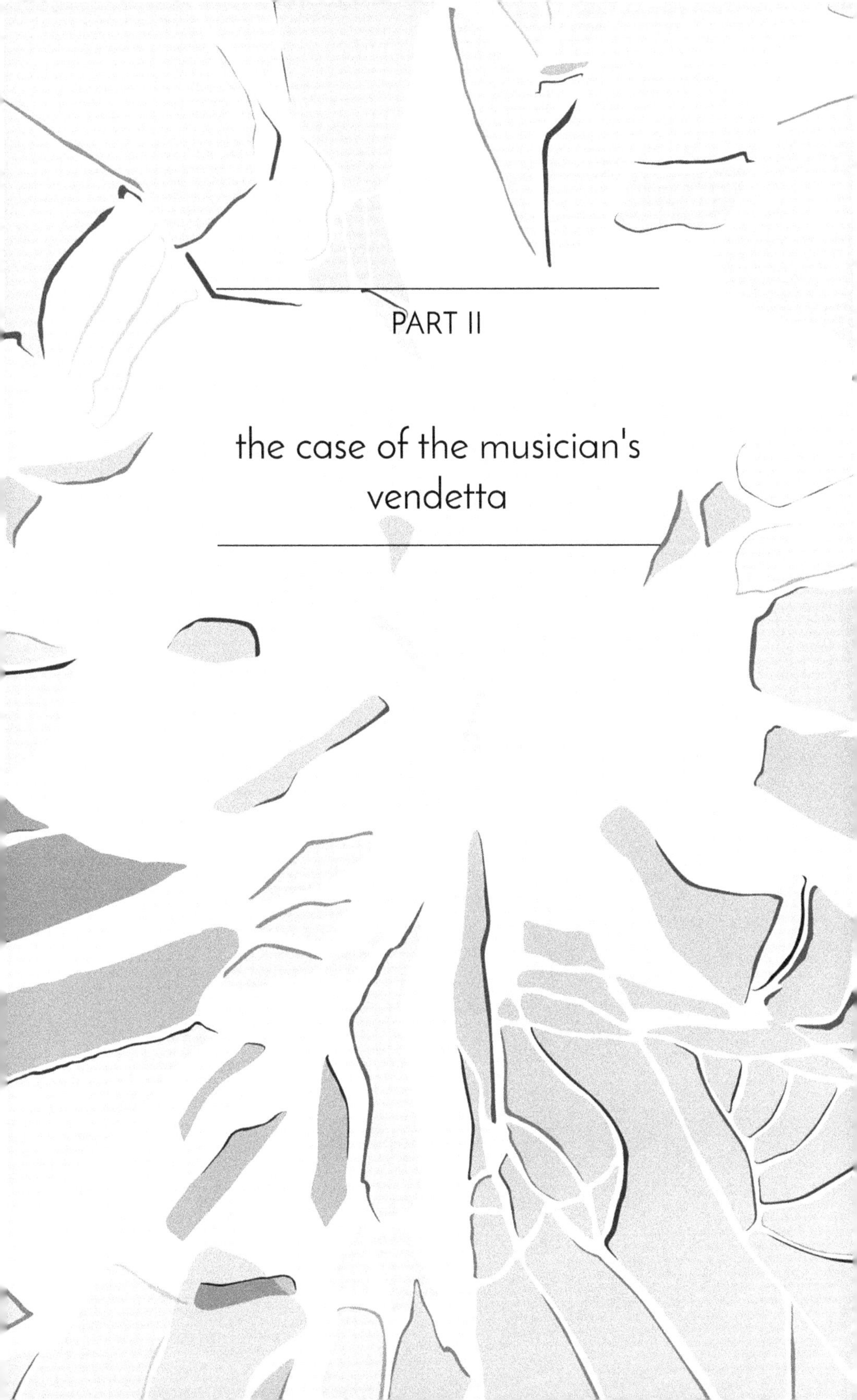

PART II

the case of the musician's vendetta

Chapter 10

MY SHOES STUCK to the thick carpet, pressing imprints everywhere I went, ruining evidence even as I prepared to search for it. My heart pounded in my throat as I breathed the scent of the grisly death. The metallic mix of blood and oil mingled with an undertone of some earthy, sweet scent. It made my stomach turn.

Illumination was the first problem. I could see well enough to know that Destiny was dead, but I needed better light. I didn't want to call one of the neighbors over to convince Trinity to activate the lights, so instead I jimmied open a wall panel using a kitchen knife that I hoped wasn't the murder weapon. Behind the panel was a maintenance interface. After several minutes of struggle and a non-zero number of mild electrocutions, the lights flickered on and I saw everything.

Her throat had been slashed. Blood soaked her flimsy top and pooled on the floor. There were shallow, pale cuts on her arms and face. What bothered me most were her dead open eyes, which seemed to be following me wherever I stood. Judging me.

Something deep inside me had to either harden or break. It didn't break.

Destiny hadn't been missing for long, but she had suffered every second that I had failed to find her. Those thousand shallow cuts told a horrible story on her pale, bloodless flesh. Her nose had been nearly cut from her face, ruining the beauty she'd been known for. The glittering dancer's outfit dangled from her, her left breast hanging scandalously exposed from the shredded bra. A single clean line along her neck was the most likely killing wound. It decorated the wall in an uneven pattern near the kitchenette.

The soft flesh between her breasts was covered in dark tattoos—something Reginald Alverez failed to note in his description. The geometric symbols resembled those in her journal, but when I compared the writings on my last remaining sheet of paper with her tattoos, I found they were different. Denser. Less space to deal with, I figured. Using a pen that I hoped also wasn't a murder weapon, I copied her tattoos onto the back of a page of sheet music.

The lights flickered. In the exposed wall panel, a tiny crab-like robot worked to fix the damage I had done to the lighting system. I needed to work fast.

I took Destiny's hands in my own and turned them palm up. They were doll's hands in my giant hamhocks. Pale and soft, except for the thick callouses on the fingers of her left hand.

When I moved, my shoes sucked against the congealing blood, and that hardened thing inside me allowed a single shudder to run the length of my spine.

Blue and red danced against the closed curtains. The police were coming. How had they known? The Sinless wasn't on their usual beat. Maybe Alverez had tipped them off. Maybe the Sinless's hobbled version of Trinity had triggered an alarm.

I didn't want to be around when they arrived. I gave the room one more once-over, hoping to find the clue that would lead me to Destiny's killer. That hard thing inside me wasn't just the calcification of my own humanity. It wasn't *just* the hardening of my own emotions. It was tied to a desire—a bone-deep need—for revenge. Call it justice if that makes it easier, but I *needed* to find Destiny's killer. Every fiber of my being demanded it.

There was a mark on the windowsill. A thin smudge of blood accompanied by a hard scrape in the fiberoak frame. The lock on the window was disengaged. I peered close at the mark on the window. It was only a few inches long, but it had been made with considerable pressure.

From my position by the window, I could see behind the dresser where the fluttering corner of a photograph peeked from the shadows. Quickly, I plucked it out and peered at it. It wasn't Destiny, but it was someone I recognized.

It was the musician I had run into in the Gravity Garden. Why did everything always turn back to the Gravity Lounge?

Boots tromped in the long hallway. I threw open the unlocked window and realized immediately what the scuff mark was. A footprint. Carefully, trying my best not to ruin the mark on the window, I stepped out onto the narrow ledge and closed the window behind me. My footprints added to another set on the sill. After the murder, someone had left through this window.

In the room, the door flew open and the bright lights fell on the Echo and Halders. The policemen stood, frozen and framed by the scene of horror. When the light they brought spread across the bloody wall near the kitchenette, I thought I saw the shape of a tall man in the gaps between drops of blood.

Echo met my gaze through the window. “Demarco.”

I launched myself from the ledge, letting the reduced gravity guide my arc downward, and landed on the street. My feet hit the fiberstone in a run.

A fire burned deep in my belly as I made my way upspiral through the Sinless. The man who had attacked Alverez was my best suspect. Faceless, formless, and invisible to Trinity, he’d be the toughest person I’d ever track, but I was determined to find him. If my best lead was the guitarist, then I’d find that damn guitarist. If he wasn’t the killer, then he might know something.

But it didn’t take long for that flame to die to embers. Exhaustion rolled over me like a wave as I stepped out from under the Sinless canopy and into the violet aurora of the Hallows night. It had been days since I’d had any real sleep. I needed rest, and I needed it badly.

Retch had secured a place to crash, but I debated skipping it for the nice cozy comfort of hard pavement. I didn’t like where things stood with Retch. He’d have words for me about everything I’d done and I’d have to fill him in on what I’d discovered. It would take time and energy, and Retch wasn’t the kind of kid to wait around and let a man sleep.

In the end, the decision wasn’t hard. My feet carried me to the Coffins, an apartment complex designed for servant-class long-term residents of the Hallows. The Coffins were as small as apartments could get, and there was about as much room for customization as the inside of a casket. Retch’s coffin was on the tenth floor, an almost insurmountable summit in my exhausted state, but one foot went in front of the other, and I managed.

The door was closed. Locked. Retch was supposed to

leave it unlocked for me, but he'd sealed it up tight. I leaned my back to the door and slid down until my sore ass hit the thinly carpeted floor. I must have dozed off. The next thing I knew, Retch was jabbing me in the chest with an inert stunstick.

My mouth tasted like old socks. "Don't make me regret giving that stunstick to you." I remembered our argument from earlier that day, but all the anger had drained from me.

Retch stuck the stunstick in his belt. "I don't think you're capable of regret, old man."

"I'm not sure I've ever known anything else."

He gestured at the door and it slid open, forcing me to catch myself or fall backward into the room. I put on a brave face and pushed myself up.

The room wasn't much, but in the days we had taken to track Destiny Alverez, Retch had turned it into his own space. He'd covered every wall in his art—mostly crafts projects like cross-stitchings of swear words, obscene embroidery, and the occasional nearly surreal nude painting. The images were quaint and offensive all at once, just like the kid who had created them. I'd found Retch on the street, making his own way through the world. Since working for me, he'd proven his ability to carve a place to belong wherever I took him.

It was a little annoying.

"This place is supposed to be temporary," I said as I cleared a spot on the bed—the room's only furniture.

He swatted me away. "You get the floor tonight."

"You were supposed to sleep during the day so I can have the place at night."

He flopped onto the bed. "I'm a busy person."

I settled on the floor. "What do I pay you for again?"

"My relentless charm," he deadpanned. Shit, he was

starting to sound like me. He gestured, and the lights dimmed to almost nothing.

Sleep fought me, despite my exhaustion. Images of Destiny Alverez's corpse played on the backs of my eyelids. Her horror-stricken face and ruined body sent my heart racing every time I neared sleep. I pulled my music rig from my coat, put the earpieces in, and listened to the soothing tones of T-Bone Walker. His blues guitar resonated against the taught tension in my muscles and eventually sleep took me.

When I woke up, Retch was making scrambled eggs on a tiny fold-out stove. He slopped half of the mess onto a plate and handed it to me. I ate like I hadn't seen a decent meal in a week, which was pretty restrained of me, I thought, since it had been over a month.

"You gotta stop doing this," Retch said, sitting in the far corner of his bed. "You keep burning yourself out like this and you'll end up like those wasted druggies in the bottom of the Heavies."

"What's the alternative? Go on the take?"

"You push and push and push like there's some reason not to get a decent night's sleep or eat a good meal. What's the rush, anyway? Like you always say, we're in a closed system. It's not like the woman's going to get any more lost."

"She's dead," I said.

"Oh."

The eggs churned in my stomach as Destiny's image flashed before me again. "It's bad, Retch. Really bad."

"You should have gotten me," he said.

"For what?"

"How am I supposed to help if you won't let me investigate?"

I pressed my palms to my eyes, wishing I could unsee Destiny's ruined body. "Go save the Yorkie," I said.

"The King job is good money."

"All yours."

He spun on me. "I just want to help, Demarco. Quit forcing me out."

"That scene isn't something you want in your brain, kid," I said.

"See, that's the problem," he said. "You think I'm a kid."

"You *are* a kid," I growled.

"My life's way worse than anything your lousy investigation can throw at me."

"You might be surprised."

He didn't say anything for a long time. Quietly, he injected his meds. Those hormone shots were the best anyone could do for a trans man in a Catholic society, even with the doctors practicing in the Sinless. The Catholic Church's stranglehold on medical practice meant that there wasn't a legitimate surgical transition available. For now, the injections would do.

"Destiny's connected to a musician from the Gravity Lounge," I said after brushing my teeth and splashing water on my head in lieu of a shower. "We need to find him."

"Casor Vin," said Retch. "He left in a hurry, but he couldn't be Destiny's killer, could he?"

I remembered the callouses on her fingers and the photograph of the musician. I'd seen those same callouses on blues musicians in Heavy Nicodemia. They practiced for hours every day bending metal strings, and their callouses were the pride of the very best of them. They were the one possession that could never be taken away. Destiny had spent significant time with the guitarist. Whatever else they were doing, he was also teaching her how to play. That also explained the plastic triangles in her purse. They were guitar picks.

"I'd like to talk to him," I said.

"Then we're heading south," Retch said. "He left for Haven almost immediately after you found Destiny's blood in that garden." Retch had his own sources. In only a couple of weeks in the district—his first time visiting the Hallows—he had made allies in the dark underbelly of this shining jewel of a station city. I don't know how he did it, but his network of rats collected rumors like a white shirt collected pasta sauce.

"Are you coming with?" I asked.

"Maybe I'm busy."

"Looking for a Yorkie?"

"It's good money."

I bit back a retort. "I could use your help."

"What would you even do without me?"

I stretched until my back popped. "I'd probably find someone that would let me sleep in a bed."

He slapped me on the back and let out a sharp laugh. "You're not that good-looking, Demarco."

As we made our way out of the apartment building—via the elevator this time because it worked for Retch—I said, under my breath, "I like to think my relentless charm makes up for that."

Retch had the tact not to disagree.

Chapter 11

REGINALD ALVEREZ WAS A MESS. Alive, but a mess. His sunken eyes were twitchy, and his hair was a frayed nest. When Retch messaged him, he met us right away.

"You gotta help me," he said, sliding into the pew across the aisle from us at the tiny Church of Saint Joseph near the bottom of the Hallow Nicodemia spiral.

I gazed up at the altar. It was a gaudy mix of fiberoak and gold, but the artistry was well done. The cross above the draped slab had one of the more gruesomely injured Jesus figures I'd ever seen. "I seem to recall that I was fired."

"After that nightclub, I made myself scarce, just like you said. Didn't see that guy again at all. I set up alerts, so if he comes close to me, Trinity will drop me a ping, but…"

I said, "He wore a silhouette."

Retch, watching from the church's entrance, said, "What the fuck is a silhouette?"

"Go home," I said to Alverez. "Lock your doors. Try to stay in brightly lit public places when you're out. You'll get a funeral for your girl. Life will move on."

"I—I can't do that," said Alverez, deflated. "I'll need to talk to Petunia." A stricken expression flashed across his face.

"Call her."

He grasped my arm. "You don't understand. We were married for a decade. Destiny was nine when she left. Things were… they got pretty rocky between us toward the end. Petunia was going through some changes."

"And you didn't want change."

He flashed a weak smile. "I'm a theoretical geologist. Change is fine, so long as it takes eons."

"Maybe you should work for the Church."

"She'll come in from the colony for the funeral. I can apologize."

"There's a guy with a silhouette after you, Alverez. He ignored me and went straight for you."

"I know, I know." To his credit, Alverez made something that looked like a brave expression.

Retch hissed, "What the hell is a silhouette?"

"It's something you don't want," I said, a little shocked at how my voice boomed in the church. "It won't help the guy in brightly lit areas."

"But it'll help in the dark?" Retch said.

"It obscures Trinity's identity-linking abilities by concealing a person in low-light conditions. You wouldn't like it."

"The hell I wouldn't!"

"Have your daughter's body shipped down the chain," I said to Reginald.

"No." The response came fast enough that I knew without a doubt that he'd already considered it. "She deserves a Hallows funeral. Best of the best. Petunia would never forgive me if I swept this under the rug."

"You need protection," I said.

Alverez leaned forward and whispered, "I know where I can get a gun."

"Hire a hand to hold it." I trusted this guy with a gun about as much as I trusted a dog with a rasher of bacon.

"Who do I trust?" Alverez cast a sideways glance at me. "You?" He said it like he was spitting bad tobacco.

Retch called from the door, "Hey, hurry up, guys. There's people coming."

The gold of the tortured Jesus's halo caught the light from a stained-glass window and shone in the tiny building. The altar was flanked with statues of Joseph and Mary.

As the elderly priest started the Mass with a song, I whispered across the aisle to Alverez, "What aren't you telling me?"

He clasped his hands tightly in his lap, the perfect imitation of the reverent parishioner. Around us, a dozen other patrons stood in their pews. After the song finished, the priest started his short introduction. It was Ordinary Time. After another song, someone stood to do the first reading.

Alverez started, "I—"

"Don't lie in church, Alverez."

He cursed under his breath. I couldn't tell if he was upset because he was really a devout Catholic or if he didn't like the fact that I'd spotted his lie before he even made it. Either way, it was the middle of the Homily before he spoke again.

"I'll get some protection," he whispered. "I'm sorry I blamed you for not finding my girl before—" He choked on his next words, but I didn't need to hear them. "I'm just sorry," he said again. He genuflected and left the church.

In his place, he'd left several rolls of dimes. My payment for finding Destiny. He thought our contract was over, and by any reasonable reading, it was.

But I wasn't done.

I left before the Eucharist, dropping a few dimes in the collection plate on my way out.

Sister Lorentz stood opposite Retch in the narthex. Her radiant skin shone under the rose light of the stained glass, and the scarlet of her loose-fitting suit danced around the curves of her body.

Retch had the expression he got right before slugging someone. I recognized it well.

Cursing under my breath, I stepped up to the two. "Can I help you, Sister?"

She turned her kind gaze to me, and I regretted getting involved. She had a way of peering straight into a person's soul with her dark eyes, and I didn't like it. Speaking to her was like saying confession with a basset hound.

Lorentz whispered, "I heard about Destiny. I'm sorry."

"A lot of people are sorry," I said. "Maybe people should be apologizing to Destiny."

"She's in a better place."

"What does a soldier of God say about hunting down and killing the murderer?"

"I think you know the answer to that, Jude."

Retch stepped back, watching the monk warily.

"You can meet me outside, kid," I said, and like a rabbit released from a trap, he darted away. To Lorentz, I said, "Leave him alone."

Lorentz flashed a quirk of a smile. "He has an interesting history, doesn't he?"

"Most of us do."

"His is the kind of story that puts him at odds with the Church." She said it as if it were a mild amusement and not a vicious accusation.

"I like to think it's the Church's story that puts it at odds with him."

She gestured for me to follow her out of the church, and for some reason I obeyed. "My help wouldn't have saved Destiny."

"Who said I was asking?"

"You carry so much guilt in your shoulders it looks painful."

Her help might have gotten me to Destiny sooner. Maybe she would have lived. I tried not to show the pang of guilt I felt for not asking her to help me. "You could have gotten me into the Gravity Lounge."

"A place she wasn't at."

True. "It might have helped."

"*I* don't have the kind of pull it takes to get into a place like that."

"What about your boss?"

"The bishop? I'm having trouble imagining him at a club like the Gravity Lounge."

"Think of the good someone could do if the Catholic Church threw around its weight to help people from time to time."

"Also, he's not really my boss."

"Head of the local diocese. He's got to have some sway."

"Quit fooling yourself, Jude," she said. Did she sound amused? "There's nothing we could have done."

"Why rub it in, then? Why give my assistant a hard time?"

"He said he was your partner."

"It's a working relationship," I said.

Her slender fingers wrapped around my big, calloused hand. "You have a good heart, Jude. I've seen what you do for this city."

I pulled away. My flesh shivered where her warm hands

had touched me. "Good hearts are for martyrs and marathon runners."

"You don't run?" she said.

"Do you?"

"Not if I can help it." She peered at me and amber limbal rings around her brown irises glowed in the full light of the Hallows. "There's something happening in the scientific community. I need your help finding out what."

"Someone threatening to disprove a fundamental particle? Slight variation in the speed of light? Did they redefine the kilogram again?"

"People are scared."

"Reassure them that they'll be in a better place," I said. "I've got a killer to find."

"Let the cops handle it."

"The blue would only get in the way."

"Alverez hired you to find Destiny's killer?"

I peered up at the too-bright sky. "Sometimes I work pro bono."

"I think your killer is involved in whatever has the scientists worked up."

"Maybe I'll ask some questions as I crush his trachea."

"Then we're working together."

"Is that what you got out of that?"

She sighed. "I can't let you murder someone. You know that."

"You don't get along with my assistant."

"Partner."

"Accomplice."

Lorentz cast her gaze upward. Whether she was looking to the burning sky or to God himself, I couldn't tell. "You can take me places I wouldn't dare go alone. You know people—people like your partner—who don't feel comfortable talking to me. If I'm going to get to the bottom of this, I'm going to need your help. Not only that, but I can offer you access to information you would never reach."

"And you can lend me your church's influence," I said. "That sounds too good to be true."

"Try it," she purred. "If you think I'm not worth it, you can tell me to leave."

"I'm still stuck on the fact that Retch doesn't like you."

"From what I've seen, he doesn't like you either."

I closed my eyes, but the brightness of the Hallows cut right through my eyelids. There was no end to the brightness in this damn place, and I was looking forward to moving down the chain as soon as possible. "I don't have a lead," I said. "Only the name of one of Destiny's known associates." I couldn't believe that I'd given in to Lorentz's demands, but the dimes Alverez had given me wouldn't last forever.

"Maybe that'll turn into a lead," said Lorentz. "Maybe we'll end up back here sifting for answers."

"Is that all you're looking for? Information?"

"It's all we ever need."

"A roll of dimes," I said. "Every day." It was ten times my usual rate, but if her church wanted me this badly, she'd pay. "In advance."

"Cash isn't really my thing."

"Karma isn't really mine." I opened my eyes and let out a long breath. "You have a deal as soon as the dimes are in my hand, but give me a chance to smooth things over with Retch first."

The kid hadn't gone far. He sat atop a fibersteel bull statue in an adjacent courtyard. The shining figure blazed in the light, and I couldn't figure out how he endured the heat that must be radiating from the metal.

He didn't open his eyes before speaking. "She's your next client?"

"Same job, different funding."

"Sounds suspect."

"I need to know something."

He glanced at me. "You want me to promise that I won't pound the shit out of her."

"I want to know what she said to you that made you so mad."

His fists clenched so hard his knuckles went white. "She said I was welcome there."

"And that made you upset?"

"You're not supposed to lie in a church." He rolled to the side and dropped down from the bull. His boots struck the dry ground with a resounding thump. Without another word, he turned toward the Customs office, which led to the chain downward.

I waved for Lorentz to join me, and together, we followed.

Chapter 12

SOME SAY the Trinity station was built to resemble a giant spinning rosary. The inner beads were all connected in a single chain that orbited an artificial sun. The false sun was a miniature fusion reactor that folks said would burn for ten thousand years. Every few beads, instead of a single city, there were three. This was the case for Nicodemia. Hallow Nicodemia, named because it was the most hollow and also, pretentiously, the most hallowed of the three cities, was accompanied by two nearly identical beads farther down its chain.

Haven Nicodemia had a similar layout to the Hallows above, but its tighter spiral meant more city in which its people were crammed together in tighter quarters. Instead of the arching displays of plant growth, Haven featured animal pens nestled among zones of manufacturing and commerce.

Traveling down from Hallows to Haven was always easier than the other direction. Neither Lorentz nor Retch encountered any trouble, and as a person excommunicated from the entire automated system, all I needed to do was tip my hat at the customs officer and be on my way.

"Does it ever strike you as strange?" asked Lorentz as we strolled past the heaviest security.

"The existence of social hierarchies?" I said. "Every single day."

Retch rolled his eyes and pushed ahead, leaving me alone with Lorentz.

"He doesn't like you," I said.

"I mean your excommunication," Lorentz said.

"Oh." I scratched the stubble on my chin. The crowd bustled past, and we became a pebble in a torrent. "Does being a monk strike you as strange?"

"Every single day."

"We are what we are," I said. "It would be strange to be anything else."

Life wasn't so easy for the crowds attempting to go the opposite direction. A dense line of travelers wove a block down through the Customs building and almost stretched out into the street. The poor sods in the front of the line stood like swaying zombies after their long slog through the government bureaucracy. At the end of the line, people tended to be brighter and more alert. They were ready for their wait, or so they thought.

It was in the middle where a grumbling discontent ate away at morale. As we passed, anger flared when a woman pushed her way through the crowd.

"You bring him back!" she shouted. She wore a loose-fitting dress, natty black hair, and fingernails that could legitimately be called weapons.

"Not a chance," growled a man in the middle of the line. He was built like a brick wall and twice as thick. In one hand he held the leash of an equally muscular mutt.

I was about to move on when Lorentz touched the woman's arm. Only a waist-high barrier divided us from them. "Excuse me," she said in the most infuriatingly calm tone I'd ever heard. "Can we be of some service?"

The woman pulled away from her and elbowed her way forward through the crowd, earning some seething looks from those around her.

"Excuse me," said Lorentz, more insistent.

The woman looked at Lorentz, her eyes brimming with angry tears. She pointed at the man. "He took my baby."

Lorentz turned to the man. The crowd parted so that the two could finally confront each other directly.

The man was a bundle of muscle and aggression. "The dog's mine."

"Buster was always my dog!" shouted the woman. She stepped up, but Lorentz cut her off.

Buster sat quietly watching as the two people fought over him. He was a tough-looking breed, like a handful of pit bull mixed with a Great Dane or a Bernese mountain dog. Despite his tough image, he didn't seem bothered by all the excitement.

"I'm sure this can be resolved," Lorentz said.

But the man was a wall.

Some situations are too fraught to get involved with lightly. Custody battles were the worst of them. When it was only children, that was bad enough, but these two were fighting over a dog. If I stepped in, there would be a mess. Someone would get hurt. Maybe the woman would end up with the pit bull. Maybe it would be the man. Either way, I had no way of knowing who the rightful owner was. I had no way of doing the right thing.

If Lorentz hadn't opened her Jesuit mouth, I probably

could have stayed out of it, but things had escalated fast, so I felt an obligation.

I stepped forward, palms out to make the peace. "Now hold on."

The woman saw her opportunity. "He stole Buster."

"I paid for him with my own money," said the man. His grip on Buster's leash was like iron. He didn't even bother to look at me. "If you weren't so stuck in your own world, you'd remember that."

"He didn't pay for that dog!" shouted the woman, gesturing at the man. "Look at him. He never paid one dime for nothin'."

The man wore a threadbare white muscle shirt and heavy cargo pants. His knuckles were calloused and his nose had been broken more than once. I couldn't judge whether he was the kind of guy who would buy a puppy for his girlfriend, but he sure as hell didn't look like a man with business up in the Hallows. Not legitimate business, anyway. I shot a glance at Lorentz, but she shooed me forward like it was my job to clean up the mess she had made. Retch was nowhere to be seen.

Then the man muttered, "Bitch," and the woman's claws came out.

She launched herself past me, raking at his face with a wide left. His feet moved like a prize fighter's, dancing and tapping as she kept coming. Buster barked, but not at anyone in particular.

"See this?" the man laughed. "See what I gotta put up with?"

I took the woman by her arms. My big hands felt clumsy against her thin, thrashing elbows, but I held her tight. "Stop," I roared. A customs officer watched along with the whole crowd. This was turning into a spectacle, and I didn't like it. "Stop!"

Finally, her struggle eased. I hoped I hadn't left bruises on her arms.

She glared at the man with the dog. "You bought him for me."

The man's jaw jutted out and his lips pressed together hard. "He was always an investment. Even when I first got him."

"An investment?" the woman mocked. "You? Oh yeah, that's real smart of you. You're some fancy investor."

Tension returned to the man's shoulders. He could strike at any moment, but I was no longer sure who would win that fight. The man was clearly a professional fighter, but the woman was vicious. I didn't like my odds if they turned on me, and it was going to get ugly if they went after each other again.

"Look," I said. "Maybe we can work something out."

"Work something out?" snapped the woman. "He's leaving with Buster. You think he'd ever dare show his face back here after he got caught stealing my dog? My brothers will kill him."

"I'd like to see them try," said the man, but there was a hint of fear in the corners of his eyes. "I beat them all once. I'll beat them again."

"Not all at once, asshole," she said. "And I'm not talking about coming after you in the ring. You better train a dozen more dogs to guard your ass while you sleep because it's going to get ugly."

The man yanked on Buster's collar. "C'mon, stupid mutt. We're leaving."

"You fucking aren't!" The woman tried to push past me again, but I held her back.

I said to the man, "Why do you want the dog."

He glanced at the woman. "Like I said, he was an investment. Some rich assholes up the chain are paying a fortune for dogs. I had a line on puppies. I didn't know my stupid girlfriend was going to get attached."

The woman thrashed again, and it was all I could do to stop her. "You didn't know nothin' about that when you bought him. You probably didn't even buy him. You stole that damn puppy, didn't you? Investment my ass. You never invested in anything that wasn't a pair of aces."

"Give her the dog." I pulled the stacks of dimes from my pocket and tossed them on the ground at the man's feet. "Take your investment and get out of here."

For a long held breath the man stared at me. Finally, he glared at the money at his feet, then looked up at the woman. His expression softened.

"Fine," he said. He dropped the leash and Buster padded over to the woman. The man picked up the money and hefted it. "This is short, but I'm feeling nice today."

"Sure you are," spat the woman. She hugged her big-headed pit bull. "Who's my good Buster?"

She left with the dog and didn't even bother to utter a word of thanks. The man melted back into the crowd, and everyone around pretended like they hadn't been gawking. I said to Lorentz, "You owe me a meal."

She sidled up next to me. "She loves that dog."

"Love doesn't make the world move forward, though."

She pinched her narrow chin between thumb and forefinger. "Love does a lot more work than you think."

"Maybe," I said again. "But you still owe me lunch for getting us involved in that mess."

Lorentz smiled. Her slender form straightened in her

loose-fitting clothes. She gave a slight bow. "I would love to take you for a meal, my friend."

Friend sounded a bit presumptuous to me, but I wasn't going to turn down a meal. We made our way down the spiral, heading toward the halfway point where the massive Cathedral of Saint Benedict's brutal architecture jutted from the surrounding warehouse districts like a broken thumb.

"*You* owe me a meal, too," I whispered to Retch when he caught up to us. Lorentz was walking ahead, cheerfully greeting perfect strangers for no good reason.

"What for?" asked Retch, feigning his best innocent look.

"Because otherwise I might let slip that you used the distraction around that dog to pick about a dozen pockets."

He narrowed his eyes. "That's blackmail, and you know I don't even care what she thinks."

"It wouldn't be blackmail if you didn't care."

"I told you, people care more about their dogs than they do about other people."

"You're welcome to start your own pet detective agency."

The muscles in his neck twitched. "Sometimes I wonder why we're even partners."

I mugged my best big grin. "You're my assistant because you can't stand to see a guy in need."

"You don't need shit."

"I need your help finding that musician," I said. "We know he's in Haven, but we don't know where."

He ran his fingers through his hair, and for a fraction of a heartbeat his hardened features softened. "I hate this, you know."

I didn't know if I should lay a comforting hand on his shoulder or tell him to tough it up, so I opted for an awkward nothing.

"This place—this goddamn city, the Church, that fucking

monk of yours—do you ever just want to leave?" Retch stepped back and looked up at me. "No, you wouldn't, would you? You *belong* here."

"*You* belong, too, kid."

"Not in this fucking city." He sighed. "I'm a trans guy, an orphan, and a criminal. If they put it to a vote, this city would kick me out."

"Good thing there's nowhere to send you."

"By a landslide," Retch said.

On a gut instinct, I decided I better start trusting the kid again. At least a little. I handed him the journal page and the copy I'd made of Destiny's tattoo. "This is important," I said.

He peered at the papers, turned them upside down, and looked at them again. "Some kind of puzzle?"

"Let me know if you can solve it."

He stuffed the papers in a pocket. "No promises."

"Lorentz doesn't have a problem with you."

"Hate takes a lot of forms," Retch said. "But it's worst when it looks like kindness."

"She's not that bad."

"She's your type."

"I don't have a type."

"Skinny and smart," said Retch. "What's the point in having her around, Demarco."

"You didn't see Destiny's body."

"Yeah," he snapped. "I *didn't*."

"Destiny…" I couldn't form the words I needed to describe it. My gut churned and the back of my spine bristled. "The killer's still out there, Retch. I don't know if this guitarist is going to help, but it's our only lead. That means we pull every string we can to find him, and we take all the help we can get."

Retch stopped in the middle of the street, gripping my

elbow so I had to stop too. For several seconds, he watched Lorentz walking away. He was right. Lorentz was thin and graceful. Beautiful in her own way. The fact that she was a monk likely sworn to celibacy didn't do much to dull her attractiveness to me, but the thought of it drove an ugly spike of guilt right through my chest.

"I'll tell you what your type is," said Retch. "Your type is any lady who's no good for you."

"And that's her?"

"Guaranteed."

Chapter 13

FOR A PERFORMER WITH A PUBLIC PRESENCE, Castor Vin turned out to be a needle in a stack of needles. The musician had melted into the cobblestones the second he entered Haven Nicodemia, slipping between the cracks of society to become a ghost in the halls of the enormous station. Retch didn't have very many connections in Haven, so he searched the networks, looking for traces of the man as he moved around town, but found nothing but the occasional fuzzy image of him in the darkest alleys.

Lorentz asked around in the more reputable parts of town. When every lead turned up dry, she flashed a smile and uttered something about trusting God in all things.

I didn't trust God for much of anything these days, but I wasn't brave enough to say it.

"Can't you talk to Trinity about this?" Retch whispered over a ham and provolone sandwich.

"It's not that easy," I said. In a way it *was* that easy. I could find a liminal space—a border between worlds—and interact directly with Trinity's systems. All I needed to do was find my way through the complicated airlocks or pause at the bottom of a bead. Unfortunately, communing directly with the machine was always a last resort. It tended to cause more problems than it fixed.

"Maybe if I had seen all the evidence, I'd be able to help more," Retch said.

"Not now, kid." Every time I blinked, I still saw Destiny's ruined body.

"Fine."

Retch secured a place for me to sleep that was slightly larger than the coffin in the Hallows but lacked his personalized touches. I don't know where he slept, but it was nice to have the privacy. I wasn't sure how much I could stand his surly mood. I don't know how much he could stand mine. Days passed.

"Vin's got to be here somewhere," Lorentz said as she sipped her morning tea.

My preferred beverage was coffee—the exquisite brew that could only be achieved in Haven Nicodemia. "He might have passed straight through to the Heavies."

"We checked Customs."

"Customs is more holey than the Catholic Church on Easter."

"He's here," Lorentz said. "He's got to be." Something about how she said it set my teeth on edge.

"Is it really just information you're looking for, *boss*?" I asked, extra emphasis on the *boss*, since she hadn't paid me yet.

She took a sip of tea and pursed her beautiful lips. "I didn't get the impression you cared what my motivations are."

"Information gets people in trouble," I said. "Revenge gets people killed." Nobody ever said I wasn't a hypocrite.

"You think I want revenge for Destiny's murder?"

"It makes more sense is all."

"You'll get your dimes," she said. "With back pay."

"Swear on the Bible?"

Vin was nowhere to be found in the official channels, but a man's nature always betrays him. Starting the first night, I visited the seediest subdued nightclubs. Lorentz sought out band shells, auditoriums, and every stage she could find. Eventually, Castor Vin would be there practicing, performing, or simply listening. I knew what kind of addiction music formed in the brain. My own need for the blues was proof enough of that.

"This isn't really your kind of haunt, is it, sister?" I sat with Lorentz at a tiny two-person table in the smoky basement digs of an underground jazz club. The place was a warm hug of leather and velvet, with a trophy wall of metal records and ancient guitars and saxophones. One wall held a list of names written in cursive black handwriting, spiraling out from a central list. Dim blue lighting cast shadows in Lorentz's dark eyes.

She gave her straight whiskey a sniff and swirled it in the glass. She tapped the table where an ashtray held my smoldering cigarette and peered through the smoke at the stage where two women were setting up a band's equipment. "Incense, altar, devout worship. I'd say I'm familiar with a similar setup."

"You make anything from the names on that display?"

"Nobody I recognize, and I've been listening to jazz all my life."

I chuckled despite myself. "I bet you thought this investigation was going to be a whole lot more exciting."

She sipped her whiskey. "On the contrary, Demarco. This is the most excitement I've had since seminary."

Having finished setting up, the band descended into a swirling mess of jazz. A saxophone solo tore a hole in the smoky atmosphere, and for a while, I lost myself in the sheer creative energy of it. I closed my eyes and let the notes wash over me.

Lorentz broke the reverie. "I think that's him." Her whiskey glass was empty, and she had a warm expression on her rosy cheeks. "Don't look."

I didn't look. "Who's he with?"

"Alone," Lorentz whispered. "He's wearing a terrible disguise. It's that makeup that's supposed to fool Trinity's facial recognition."

"That stuff doesn't work."

"He's been hard to track down." The monk leaned forward, her eyes narrowing into slits. "Too hard."

I cocked my head. "Are you drunk, Sister Lorentz?"

Her slow blink said *yes*, but her mouth said, "No."

"What's he doing here?" I asked, still avoiding looking at the man directly.

She glanced over my shoulder. "Nodding his head. Having a drink."

"Are his eyes up or down?"

"That's an odd question."

I drank down the rest of my fiery whiskey and stubbed out my cigarette in the empty glass. "If his eyes are up, scanning the crowd, then he's either looking for someone or he's nervous about someone following him. If his eyes are down, he's either reading a screen or actually enjoying the music."

After a long pause, Lorentz said, "Down."

"Good."

I left the tiny table and made my way in a long arc around the club, keeping the lone figure in the corner of my eye at all times without ever really looking directly at him.

When I'd acquired a new drink—whiskey, on rocks—I stepped up next to the musician and tapped my toe to the lilting sax.

After a particularly complex solo, I said, "Yeah, that's what I'm talking about." To Vin next to me, I said, "She always this good?"

"Best in the bead," he replied without a second's hesitation. His dark skin shone under the rolling chartreuse lights of the nightclub. Bright streaks of makeup ran down his cheeks. He was also dressed differently from when I'd seen him in front of the Gravity Lounge. He wore a baggy shirt that concealed the loose musculature of his body. He pulled his goatee reflexively. "It's a shock she hasn't moved up the chain."

"That how it works?"

He glanced over at the wall of names. "I thought I was going to be on that wall."

"You have the skills?"

His brow furrowed. "Skills? No, that's a wall of missing people." He closed his eyes as the music washed over us. "Nobody's going to miss me, though."

I watched the way his fingers moved to the music. "Guitar?"

"Guitar." He flashed a wide grin. The man was all smooth charm. Maybe that's what Destiny saw in him. He looked up at me—I stood a full head taller. "It's a calling, you know? A guy's gotta play what he's gotta play."

"Blues?"

"Whenever I can."

"I have a lot of respect for a true bluesman." I needed to know as much as I could from this guy, but there was a line of tension just under his skin. If I spooked him, he'd shut up like a clam. Luckily, he liked talking about himself and his music.

"I used to know a guy who taught blues guitar down in the Heavies. A true hero if I ever heard one."

"They say those who can't do, teach."

I chuckled. "But those who can't teach, disappear."

It took the better part of a long jazz routine for that to sink in before he responded. "I used to teach. Had a good student too."

"Sometimes they outgrow you." I took a sip of my whiskey and closed my eyes to listen as the drummer pounded out a swirling rhythm.

"Sometimes they die," said Castor Vin so quietly that I barely heard him over the soft sax. The tight tension of guilt strangled his voice, but I couldn't tell if it was because he thought he should have saved her or if he was somehow involved in her killing.

I needed more answers, so I took a risk. "It wasn't your fault, Vin."

He shot a scowl in my direction.

"I know about Destiny."

"So do your friends over there," he said, tilting his head toward the bar where a couple of slabs of muscle acted so nonchalant they might have forgotten they were in a club. They wore sky-blue suits and sunglasses that hid their eyes. One of them was Wesley, the gargoyle I'd locked horns with in front of the Gravity Lounge. Vin pounded back his drink. "Buy me another, won't you? If you're going to finish me off when the concert's done, I might as well tie one last drink on, right?"

Even if I wasn't all out of dimes, I wouldn't have turned my back on the musician. He was ripe to flee, and I still wanted a word. "You think I'm with them."

"Aren't you?"

"What happened the night she was killed?"

He eyed me for a long time before waving down a server in a black shirt and tie. He must have given up on the hope for a free drink because he ordered a round for the both of us. "You almost had me, you know," he said.

The server returned with our drinks—a pair of awful blue cocktails that glowed in the low light. I finished my whiskey and took a sip of the new beverage. It was sweet and sour with a lingering burn of alcohol. Terrible. I shot a glance at Lorentz, still sitting at our table. The chartreuse lights played across the contours of her elegant face as she watched the band play. Her eyes sparkled in the swell of emotion rolling off the stage.

I turned to Vin. "People listen to jazz because they like the energy. They like the joy in every lick. Do you know why people listen to the blues?"

"I've had enough of this."

"The blues is permission, Vin," I said. "When everything's gone to crap, the blues don't try to fix it. They don't try to gloss it over and make things look all pretty. It's the kind of music that tells you that there are two goons ready to kick you around, a dead girl with your fingerprints all over the crime scene, and an excommunicated man asking hard questions you don't want to answer."

Vin pounded back his awful cocktail. "You think I'm going to believe you're not with those guys? Then you're the blue. Either way, I've got nothing to say about Destiny." A flash of white in his eyes betrayed his fear, but I got the impression he wasn't afraid of me, and he wasn't afraid of the goons. The blue, then? No, the police didn't have the kind of reach or coordination it would take to harass a guy like Castor Vin once he crossed to a new bead.

The saxophonist started the last solo of their set. I set my drink down on a nearby table and put a hand on Castor Vin's shoulder. "You know about the door below the stage?"

He twitched. "They'll be on me like a rabid dog soon as I step up there. Doesn't matter which way I leave."

"I'll make a distraction."

"They'll kill you."

"It'll be nice and peaceful." I hoped. "I promise."

It took a moment for his lack of choices to work their way through his alcohol haze.

"Meet me at the Ever Upward," I said. "We need to talk." With that, I picked up my drink from the table, pushed past him, and waved down the two goons from the Gravity Lounge. "Hey," I said, exaggerating a drunken slur. "Wesley. Great to see you here."

I feigned a trip, sloshed my sickly blue drink all over Wesley's suit, and crashed into the other guy. From there, the whole evening went downhill.

Chapter 14

ALL HOPE OF MAKING A NICE, peaceful distraction flew out the window when I flew out the door.

The alley was a dark pit in the poorly lit Haven Nicodemia night. The walls were slick with condensation or piss, and the whole space smelled like the ripe leftovers from a particularly bad night of drinking.

It wasn't going to be nice and peaceful, but it could still be a distraction.

"What are you hiding about Destiny Alverez?" I slurred, raising my hands in surrender as I backed away. Let them think I was still drunk. That way I could at least surprise them and dodge the first punch.

The goon, Wesley—the gargoyle who had guarded the Gravity Lounge—popped me in the jaw with a rabbit punch so fast I didn't have time to blink. Fireworks flashed before my eyes.

"Hold on. Hold on." My words were tangled up in a jumble of misfired neurons. "I was supposed to dodge that."

Wesley responded with his fists, and his fists were

eloquent. A slug to my gut stole my breath. A pounding of my chest made my heart flutter. The ground was wet and cold on my face when I fell. I spat blood and watched it mix with the oily surface of a puddle.

When the two goons started to walk away, I said, “Wait.” It hurt saying it.

Wesley heaved me up and slammed me against the wall. His breath smelled like lemons.

“It’s just…” My brain wasn’t functioning very well anymore. Maybe it never had been. “It’s like we’re old friends.”

He slammed my head against the brick so hard it snuffed out the fireworks. A woman’s voice chimed like a bell somewhere far away. I slumped, unsupported, to the ground.

Lorentz leaned close with her brow knit with worry. “Demarco? Come on, you idiot.”

“Bleargh.” I don’t know what I was trying to say, but that wasn’t it.

“What were you thinking? Those guys are professional muscle, Demarco.”

When I sat up, a wave of dizziness threatened to topple me back over, but Lorentz provided the extra support I needed.

“I was interrogating them,” I said.

Her lips pressed into a line. “Did you learn anything?”

“Yeah,” I rubbed my jaw. “I learned that Wesley has a mean left hook.”

She threw up her hands. “Great. While you were fighting, the musician ducked out.”

“I’m a professional, too, you know,” I said as we passed from the alley into the main drag. “Basically a goon.”

“You are decidedly amateur.”

That rankled more than it should have. "Why did you come to me instead of following Vin?"

"Those guys could have killed you."

"I'm excommunicated. Anyone could kill me."

"They might have actually done it."

I pressed my fingers to my lip, and they came back slick with blood. When I breathed, my ribs ached. Not broken, probably, but they'd be sore.

We found a bench outside a shuttered café, and I lay across it, letting out a long slow breath. The world still spun around me, and everything ached all the way down to my bones, but I was alive. More alive than I'd felt in a while. Somewhere in the back of my head, I heard my sister—my actual sister, not Sister Lorentz—reprimanding me for my self-loathing.

"You must really hate yourself, Jude," said Lorentz sitting at my feet. Crap.

"I get the job done."

"There are better ways."

"I need that money, Lorentz," I said after finally catching my breath.

She took one of my hands and inspected the scrapes on my tough knuckles. Her hands felt cool against my over-heated skin. "The Church won't pay until they see results."

"I'd think a church would have a little more faith."

"It hasn't been easy getting a hold of Bishop Barton, and let's just say the rest of the liturgical crowd is a tad risk-averse."

"Nothing moves without proper funding. A dime or two a day isn't even a retainer. I can't extract information from anyone without spending a few dimes." I thought of the journal Leo Shaw had taken from me and the single page I'd left in Retch's care. My lack of funds was actively working against us.

"Do you want to know why I became a Jesuit?"

Not particularly. "I'm just saying that I'm not running a charity."

She drew a long breath and stared into the distance. "My parents were good Catholics. Farmers. They provided not only a good example for me to learn what it meant to be Catholic, but they were very strict about the rules. Church on Sunday. Fast during Lent. That kind of thing."

"Maybe I should talk to this Barton fellow face to face," I said.

She shot me the look I deserved. "Don't ruin a good thing."

"I'd take payment in indulgences if he's short on dimes."

"Both of my fathers were strict. Like any kid growing up in a rules-heavy environment, I rebelled, but I didn't rebel by disobeying rules. I rebelled by asking why. Why do we genuflect before sitting in a pew? Why do we believe that God exists throughout the entire universe? Why is there mystery in the transformation of bread into flesh during the Mass? Wine into blood? Why did my fathers have a blessing in union but not a true marriage? It wasn't enough for me to learn the rituals and perform them. I needed to know not only the history behind every act we made but also the scientific reasoning behind it."

When she didn't speak for a while, I prompted her, "Sounds like you were a real pain in the ass."

That drew a chuckle from her. "My parents didn't know what to do with me. The priests over at Saint Benedict didn't know either. Turns out they weren't sure if women were allowed to be Jesuits, the same way they aren't entirely sure women are allowed to be priests." She flashed a wry smile.

"You should have seen the looks on their faces when I asked what part of Mass involved the penis and whether it was just the cock or were balls involved too."

"Damn." Laughing hurt like hell.

"But you know how the Church works. They don't say, 'It's allowed now.' They say, 'It's always been this way,' even though we know it hasn't. Part of the Church's authority comes from being the same Church it's always been. Its roots grow in the clay of tradition. It makes it hard to topple but stunts its growth."

"Seems big enough to me."

"It's all about psychology. A science. The Church has faded almost to nothing on Earth. Did you know that? It still has its hold on the Vatican and some parts of South America, but most of the rest of the world has smothered it or splintered apart into strange offshoots." She laughed to herself and leaned back on the bench. The more she spoke, the more relaxed she became, and it made me like her despite my distrust of the church she served. "Nicodemia was built with Catholic funds during the height of the Church's power. It was meant to be a way to expand influence to the stars. If there was going to be a colony somewhere in the universe, that better be a Catholic colony or it might be rooted in evil and would surely fail. The logic is a little hard to follow."

I refrained from making a snide comment, and she nodded her approval.

"My fathers were both home when our apartment was robbed. I was ten and ridiculously faithful by that time. I prayed every night. Went to church. Played absolutely everything by the book, and you *know* what book I'm talking about."

"The Bible."

"The Catechism of the Catholic Church."

"Right." I took her hands in mine. "What happened to your fathers?"

"Did you know that the Church hasn't always blessed homosexual relationships?"

"That's not what the priests say."

"If you ask enough, you'll get the long version. How they always deep down knew that certain relationships were fine, but interpreting the scripture was an ongoing struggle. They'll tell you that the confinement of the generation ship revealed wisdom that they hadn't previously noticed in the text, but of course, the souls of those historically turned away from the Church were able to reach heaven."

"Does it matter that the Church sent them there early?"

She waved my comment away. "What I'm saying is, when my fathers were attacked, I had a crisis of faith. My perfect childish beliefs had formed a rigid system that could never bend. When a crisis came, my faith shattered."

"But you still went to seminary. You still became a Jesuit."

She flashed a crooked grin. "I'm putting the pieces back together one by one, and I do that by seeking the truth. No matter how long it takes, I'll find the truth behind the Gravity Lounge. I'll learn who killed Destiny Alverez. I'll find the scientific secrets tying everything together. It'll take patience, and it'll take the use of every resource at my disposal."

I looked at my hands, still bloody from my beating. In that blood I saw the vacant expression on Destiny's corpse. "Some things are too broken to fix," I said. "And some things aren't meant to be known."

"That's the first blasphemy I've heard from you that really bothers me, Demarco."

I closed my eyes and waited as the quiet of the Haven night surrounded us. Haven wasn't the lively bright of the Hallows, and it wasn't the raucous revelry of the Heavies. It was a strict curfew covering the simmering boil of a dissident middle class. There were nightclubs and gambling halls hidden in the corners of basements, but the noise and the fun didn't spill out into the street. There under the flickering lamp, I lay in silence next to Lorentz, chewing on her words.

"So this Barton fellow isn't so risk averse?" I finally said.

"He plays by his own rules."

"If you get a hold of him," I said, "tell him I took a beating so that I could meet with the musician. Tell him I can get any answer from anyone, in all of Nicodemia, and tell him I never stop." I looked her in the eyes. "But I don't work for free."

Chapter 15

"YOU'RE NOT COMING WITH," I told Lorentz.

"You need my help," she said.

"You need to meet with Retch."

"He's patient."

"We both know that's not true."

"He can take care of himself."

"That's a very Christian sentiment."

Lorentz wasn't going to nibble on that bait. "Those goons will be looking for Vin."

"All the better if I can stay in the dark."

She searched my face for something, but I don't know if she found it. "We'll stay close."

"Try not to cause too much trouble," I told her.

"I could ask the same of you," she said over her shoulder, "but I think I've heard enough lies for one night."

Once she'd left, the first thing I did was locate an ice pack to press against my swelling eye. It felt like the orbital bone was jutting out the side of my face. It wasn't. When I looked in the mirror, I didn't even find much swelling. Hopefully, the ice would keep it down.

I'd given Vin the name of a bar, the Ever Upward, but he wouldn't go there right away, if at all. I made my way down-spiral. The lower half of the bead was riddled with farm stacks. Plants choked the empty streets. Pigs and cattle lived in cramped quarters, genetically engineered to give the most efficient payload possible.

Most of the people in this district couldn't afford meat on a daily basis, but there was a lifecycle to maintain. The plants fed the animals, and the animals fed the plants. Byproducts of both were used in all manner of manufacture, including oxygen and organic plastics.

My feet took me down among the dark alleys of towering apartments. Here, the light of busy gambling halls and speakeasies spilled onto the street. The siren call of dealers taking bids whispered of opportunities for the entrepreneurial spirit.

Then, I stood in the indigo glow of a swanky place called the Blue Mongoose.

This was where I'd lost it all, but it wasn't the first *all* that I'd lost. If I'd had a single dime in my pocket I might have stepped inside for a game. Damn Leo Shaw and his debt collecting. I could win it all back. I could take the house for all it's worth and buy that journal back.

I *needed* the journal translated. Even after several days, Retch hadn't made any progress on the single page.

Temptation is a funny thing. It's most dangerous when it comes in like a ghost in the night, not when it faces a person head-on. When I'd lost it all—the most recent loss—it wasn't that I faced off against temptation and failed. It was that I didn't realize I was gambling until the cards hit the table. I was only out for a drink and a chat, and the stubborn side of my brain wasn't even active.

My history was catching up with me. Someday soon my life would collapse. Maybe that's what I glimpsed that night.

But not this night. This time I was paying attention when temptation rolled my way, and I faced it down. My fists clenched. I tossed the ice pack in the recycler and pushed my way into the Blue Mongoose.

"I'm here to talk to the boss," I told the woman at the door.

Jasmine wore a black button-down shirt with a black bow tie. It was the uniform around these parts, and she wore it well. She looked me up and down like she was pricing a side of beef. "Jade's busy, Demarco."

"I'll wait." I parked my ugly, bruised self near the door and folded my arms.

Jasmine had worked the door of the Blue Mongoose for years. Rumor had it she was part owner of the establishment, but rumors had a way of running on their own steam. I didn't put too many dimes in that one way or the other. She touched her ear and whispered. After a brief conversation, she met my gaze and said, "Follow me."

"I know the way."

"It's safer for everyone if you have an escort."

She left her post at the door and led me past quiet tables of people playing blackjack and poker. We weaved through the basement club, brushing against the craps table and a row of slot machines. If I didn't know any better, I'd have guessed that Jasmine was walking me past every gambling opportunity in the whole place.

"Can I get you a drink?" she asked as we passed the bar.

"No dimes."

"On the house."

I must really be in trouble. “I’m fine, thanks.”

Finally, we arrived at a plain fibersteel door with a stenciled *EMPLOYEES ONLY* sign. Jasmine led me through, up some stairs, and into a wide office with deep amber lamps and a fiberoak desk, behind which sat Jasmine’s well-dressed twin sister. A window overlooked the gambling hall below.

“Jade,” I said.

Jade lingered on the papers in front of her, taking a long time before looking up to acknowledge me. She had the same frown lines in her young face and the same startling brown eyes, but other than that she couldn’t be more different from her twin. Her hair was a shocking pink, and the glasses perched on the end of her nose made her look like a rebel librarian. She drummed her long fingernails on the desk next to a red panic button and tsked several times before speaking.

“You know, a lot of people won’t lend to excommunicated individuals.”

“I can’t imagine why.”

“Leo tells me he was able to track you down in the Hallows and remind you about your fiscal responsibilities”

“Shaw’s the reason I’m here.”

“Delivering your payment?”

“Not exactly.”

“If you have something to say about him that isn’t regarding the efficiency with which he does his job, then I think you might be in the wrong place.” Jade blinked once. It was a shark’s blink. Slow and bloodless.

“Shaw took something I need.”

“It’s called collateral.”

“It’s called theft. I need what he took so I can earn your dimes.”

“Maybe you need a better job.”

“I’m uniquely qualified for this one.”

"Poverty's a qualification?"

"I need that journal."

Jade spread her hands. "And I need that money. I think we have an understanding, don't we?"

"This is bigger than our little debt." I knew the argument wouldn't work as soon as I said it. Jade was a numbers woman, and I was negative. "There was a murder in the Hallows. Something bad."

Jade raised one dark eyebrow. "Seems fortunate that it wasn't down here."

My fists clenched. This was going about as well as I'd expected, which wasn't very well. "Let me meet with Shaw. He can be there the whole time I decipher the book."

"And this is going to get me my money?"

"I have a client," I said. "She'll pay well for this information."

She must have heard the hesitation in my voice. "Who is this client and what do they pay?"

A Jesuit and not much. "That's confidential."

Jade glanced at Jasmine again. "Jasmine told me yesterday that Shaw's having trouble fulfilling a few of his contracts."

"No." I saw exactly where she was going with this.

"I give you a list of names and how much they owe. You find them and get them to pay. Everyone's happy."

"That's not what I do."

"Isn't it? Rumor is you're very good at finding people."

"I'm busy."

Jade slammed her fists on the desk hard enough that her paperweight jumped. "You *owe* me, Demarco. As long as you owe me, you *work* for me."

I glanced at Jasmine. She raised an eyebrow.

"The day you lost all those dimes, you came in here

looking for something," Jade said, her voice saccharine and soft. "Rumor is it was information. You ever get what you needed?"

"I'm still looking."

"There aren't a whole lot of people around who know about the Benevolent, are there?"

My parents had been on the Benevolent. I'd been the one who had aborted the catastrophic docking sequence. That action had gotten me excommunicated. It had been the traumatic experience my teenage self had never recovered from, and it was the event that put my sister in her wheelchair.

It was also why I'd set foot in the Blue Mongoose in the first place, but recording devices didn't work on me. Trinity edited my words out of every recording. If Jade had overheard my questioning, it meant she had someone listening in on me.

This smelled like a setup.

"I think we're done here." I turned to leave, but Jasmine stepped in front of the doorway. She fixed me with her piercing dark gaze and held out a tiny slip of paper. The list.

Pride told me not to take the job. I had plenty to do finding Destiny's killer, and there were better ways I could use my ability to locate people.

But I needed that journal. Working off the debt would be my penance.

I took the paper from Jasmine, dropped it into a pocket, and left.

Chapter 16

THE EVER UPWARD SAT IN an auspicious junction between the muck of the Haven farms and the bustling activity of the lower city. It was the nexus between the maintenance workers who toiled relentlessly in the buildings above and the farmers who worked to feed all three beads of Nicodemia. It was officially closed in the dark of the Haven curfew, as were all reputable pubs.

It was also unofficially open.

I made my way into the back entrance, where a single subtle light above the door indicated that it was open for business. Inside, the lights were dimmed, the air was smoky, and the drinks were flowing. A waitress wearing a halter top and golden angel wings brushed past me with a tray of florescent shots.

The Ever Upward favored privacy over community. High sound-proof walls separated the booths and draped beads divided sections of the floor. During the day it was quaint and comfortable. A nice place to enjoy a quiet conversation with a friend. In its nighttime configuration, it was a den of vipers hissing quietly under the shelter of a cold rock.

"I'm meeting someone," I said to the winged waitress.

Her eyes narrowed slightly, but she shrugged and gestured me toward a booth. On my way there, the club's owner, Aiken, gave me a nod. He was a heavyset man with an unkempt beard, but his bright soccer jersey clashed with the decor. I made myself comfortable and listened to the long tail of a jazz guitarist playing somewhere unseen in the secluded sections of the pub.

"Give me something with too much rum," I said to the waitress as she disappeared into the smoky haze. I gave it even odds that she was gone for good, but I couldn't pay for it anyway, so it all worked out.

I also figured it was fifty-fifty whether Vin showed. He'd been paranoid, and for good reason. Those thugs weren't there to mess around. The smart move for him was to disappear again, but nobody ever really disappeared in Nicodemia. Not for long, anyway. The bent guitar notes and the dim lights and the thrum of my own headache lulled me into something resembling calm. I may have fallen asleep, but I jolted awake at a voice.

"That partner of yours is insane."

It was Lorentz. She slid into the booth next to me. A glass of amber liquid sat in front of me, its ice cubes having melted almost to nothing. "He tried to hit me with that stunstick."

I licked my dry lips. "Retch is my assistant."

"Well, he's headed back to the Heavies. Said if he was going to make no progress on the journal, he might as well do it at home."

"Makes sense."

"No luck with the musician?"

"Not yet. If he's coming, it'll be late."

"It *is* late."

"Then maybe he's not coming." I pushed my drink over to Lorentz.

After a brief hesitation, she took a sip and made a face. "Rum?"

"Sometimes I feel like a pirate."

"Yar," she said with little enthusiasm. We sat in silence until the guitarist ended his set. Lorentz finally said, "I've always appreciated the guitar. There are some amazing jazz guitarists up in the Hallows."

"Guitar will always mean the blues to me," I said. "Anything else sounds disingenuous."

"You're kidding me." She gave me a punch on the shoulder that actually hurt. "Django Reinhardt? The soul jazz of Grant Green?"

"Green's basically playing blues." I set my music rig on the table and handed Lorentz one of the earpieces. "Listen to this."

She hesitantly placed one earpiece in and I took the other. I set my rig to play B. B. King's "Got'em Bad." We listened as the old blues guitarist bent strings and wailed into some of the best blues ever played.

When it was done, she set down the earpiece and said, "Not bad. Do you have any Charlie Byrd on that thing?"

"Every song recorded before Nicodemia left Earth," I said.

"Nothing new?"

"New music isn't my speed." I found Charlie Byrd and we listened to "Speak Low," a quick little guitar piece that popped from the speakers and had me tapping my toe.

"Your speed?" the Sister asked when it was finished.

I said, "Good guitar should take its time."

"Sometimes guitarists like to take their time too." Castor

Vin slid into the booth across from us. He wore a gray tracksuit with white stripes running the length of his arms and legs. His dark skin shone with a sheen of sweat that made his weird makeup smear.

"As long as you make it," I said. I stowed my music rig. "Now spill."

"Not so fast," he said. "It's hard to trust anyone these days."

Lorentz said, "You can trust the bruises on Demarco's face."

Vin pressed his lips together. "Could have been for show."

"You wouldn't be here if you weren't going to talk," I said. "Now, what do you know about Destiny Alverez?"

Vin said, "Talented musician. Pretty. She had the talent to play the best gigs in the Hallows and she spent all her free time practicing."

"Were you a thing?" Lorentz asked.

Vin said, "With a flame like that, it's hard not to be a moth."

"She was going to carry on your legacy," I said.

"No need to sound so fatalistic about it." He scratched his thin goatee. "But yeah."

"What else?" I asked. "You were pretty unhinged when I saw you in the Gravity Garden that night."

"I thought I recognized you from somewhere," he said.

"I've got one of those faces."

He shot a wary glance at Lorentz, who innocently sipped my rum. "How do you know I didn't kill her?"

"I don't."

His gaze darted across the pub. The problem with the secluded layout was poor sight lines to the door.

"Did you know who was coming for her?" I said.

Vin touched the breast pocket of his tracksuit. "It don't feel right."

"What?" I leaned forward. "What was it, Vin?"

"You hear that?"

I didn't hear anything.

"The band," Vin said. "It's not time to end their set, and I know these guys. They soak every second out of a gig."

Vin's paranoia must have been rubbing off on me because I motioned for him to follow. Lorentz swallowed the last of the rum and the three of us made our way toward the back.

We were halfway there when the lights flared to life above us, washing the whole place in white that penetrated even the darkest corners of the pub.

"Shit," I muttered.

On the overhead speakers, a gruff voice said, "This establishment is in violation of Haven curfew. Everyone in this establishment has been found in violation of curfew ordinance 11.49.b with respect to the lawful and organized community standards agreed upon in the council four hundred sixty-seven. Please proceed with calm deliberation to the nearest exit and submit."

Calm deliberation was *not* what the patrons of the Ever Upward had in mind. Calm deliberation would have scored them expensive citations. It would have ended with them spending the night in jail and the rest of the day explaining to loved ones why they'd been out when there was clearly a community-supported curfew.

Getting caught by a curfew crew hurt their Karma with Trinity. They'd feel that impact for years. Running was their only chance.

Which is why everyone ran.

"Stay close," I said, seeing Vin's panicked expression.

"This is how it happens," he whispered.

The crowd pressed toward the emergency exits—the front, rear, and side doors were wide open. Those who went through first were immediately taken down by the blue. I led Lorentz and Vin through a hidden door behind the bar and up a tight spiral staircase. It spat us out on the roof.

The area below was awash in red and blue. The flashing strobe was a blaze of madness surrounding the dark building at its center. Aiken and the Ever Upward would suffer due to the loss of Karma and reputation. It would be worse if he were caught. That's why he stood atop the roof with a long fiberoak plank in his hands.

"Aiken," I said as we stepped over toward him.

He shot me a murderous look. His scraggly beard twitched in a strong wind. "You brought this trouble, didn't you, Demarco?"

"I'm the only one here without a curfew."

Aiken dropped the board across the alley, creating a dangerous bridge between buildings. "Then go back down if you're so cozy with the blue." He made to step out onto the board, but a strong breeze ruffled his bright jersey. He glanced back at me, terrified.

"Wait," I said. The breeze roared across the alley. If he fell from that height, his odds of walking away weren't great. Not in this gravity. I started forward to hold the bridge as he crossed.

He didn't wait for me. Taking a deep breath, he ran the few steps across the board. It wobbled under his feet, but he made it. He turned and grabbed the board, but I reached it at the same time.

"Let go!" he hollered across the gap.

Below, the crowd pressed the blue. People broke through

and spilled out into the city's dark streets. At any moment, the distracted authorities would glance up and see us.

Lorentz stepped up beside me. "We're here doing God's work," she called across the gap.

Something about the way she said it—the way she settled her piercing gaze on the bar owner—convinced him to drop the plank. He retreated into the adjacent building. No doubt he would descend the stairs and disappear into the night.

I waved Vin forward. "Go."

The musician stepped up to the plank. The blue and red played across the sheen of sweat on his brow and the whites showed in his glassy eyes. "I don't—"

"Go!" I commanded. We didn't have time to mess around.

He stepped out onto the bridge. Despite my best efforts, the warped plank wobbled under his feet.

"You have to move," I told him. "It's three steps. One, two, three. Quick, like Aiken did. Then you're over."

Vin's jaw worked, but he didn't have any words. The guy was a mess—a bundle of nerves wrapped around a panicked jelly core.

But he did it. He took the three steps above certain death and collapsed in a heap on the other side.

"You go next," said Lorentz.

A wave of vertigo washed over me as I stood on the ledge. Heights had never been my thing. Never would be. Plus, I was heavy—significantly heavier than the rest of them. Not only that, but I wasn't in any danger leaving through the front door. The blue might rough me up a little and detain me, but part of being excommunicated meant I was outside the Karma economy. Unless the Haven blue had a particularly bad bug up its butt, I would get away.

But I saw the fear in Vin's eyes. He needed me by his side.

Lorentz held the board steady. "Move it, big guy."

"Will God catch me if I fall?" I asked, meaning it as a joke but tasting the bitter tilt of the words.

"Not a chance." At least she was honest.

I stepped onto the board. It had been three steps to Vin, but I managed in two. With solid stone under me again, I stretched a hand out and hefted the guitarist to his feet.

Just then, from down below, Wesley shouted, "There he is!" I looked down in time to see the Gravity Lounge gargoyle running toward our building.

With no desire to retreat back through the Ever Upward and no chance of sneaking through our current building, I made the least bad choice I could think of. I pointed across the building roofs, gave the guitarist a shove, and said, "Run!"

We ran.

Chapter 17

I WAS BORN in the Hallows, where the gravity is below Earth's normal. I lived well into my tragic teens in that lesser gravity, then moved to Haven, where the single G of simulated gravity roughly matched Earth.

Then, I lived in the Heavies. The Heavies made me strong. It made my bones dense, my muscles powerful, and my heart hard. None of that made me very good at running, and all of it made me genuinely bad at jumping.

I had the strength to jump from roof to roof, but not the instinct to know how hard to jump. Leaping over the first gap, I overshot and bowled the musician over onto the rough fiberstone. Together, we skidded across and slammed into a utility box.

"They're coming," said Vin.

The two thugs from the Gravity Lounge emerged onto the roof. Lorentz was nowhere to be seen. Wesley spotted me. The other guy drew a small plastic pistol.

"This just got serious," I said.

"It hasn't been?" Vin exclaimed.

The guitarist took three steps and jumped to the next roof. We moved downspiral and outward, each roof was slightly lower than the last. I followed, almost undershooting this time. My feet landed hard on the rocky roof.

We didn't slow, and the next roof was easier. I could see the end of the string of buildings coming up. I tested a door and found it locked.

"Keep going!" I shouted.

The bouncers made their first leap. Damn, these guys were good. I expected them to struggle with the gravity, but they launched themselves with expert precision, hardly slowing as they vaulted to the next roof.

"It's too far!" shouted Vin.

I grabbed his shirt in my fists and looked him straight in the eye. "You can do this, Vin. Run and jump. Don't slow down and just keep going."

The bouncer's first shot whistled past my ear. Vin jumped for the next roof.

He didn't make it. His chest slammed into the far wall, but he managed to grasp the railing. I swore and followed, leaping as hard as I could. My knee—the one that already hurt—twisted under me and I collapsed. Not missing a beat, I scrambled over to Vin and yanked him up onto the roof.

The bouncers landed on the adjacent roof. One jump away and they'd be on top of us.

Police drones decorated the skies. The blue had finally copped to the escape route and they were sending eyes. Lot of good they would do.

I stood my ground. "Vin, check the door." To Wesley, I held my hands up high.

The bouncer with the gun stopped before leaping across the gap. If he had continued, I could have easily knocked him off the ledge, and he probably didn't want to take that chance.

Not that he needed to.

He pointed the gun at my face. "You're not the top dog in this fight, mister."

Wesley shot the guy a worried look. "Demarco," he boomed. "You can walk away."

"It's like you hardly know me," I said.

Wesley walked along the length of the roof. Behind me, I heard the scrabble of Vin moving toward the door.

I stared down the barrel of the gun.

In that moment, I didn't care whether or not he pulled the trigger. Maybe people got what they deserved. Maybe if that trigger was pulled and the bullet slammed into my brain, it would be my destiny.

Penance.

Seconds stretched into an agonizing eternity. Behind me, the door slammed open. In front of me, the thug with the gun blinked. Re-aimed. "Don't move, Vin." I was still between him and the musician. Did the bouncer have a shot? I didn't dare look back to check.

Wesley found a gap he could jump. He was too far down the roof to get to Vin fast enough, but he was also far enough away that if I moved to stop him the other guy would be able to jump.

Everything happened at once. Wesley jumped. I lunged across the roof to stop him. Vin dove for the door. The gun fired once. Twice.

I slammed into the big guy, stopping him at the ledge.

Vin slammed against the open door, leaving a smear of blood. He tumbled into the building and out of sight.

Wesley toppled, and I grabbed his shirt to keep him from falling. He stared at his partner in horror, but he didn't have the angle to help him. If he shot me, Wesley would drop.

I shouted in Wesley's face, "Why are you after Vin?"

As an answer, he swung a sloppy left hook, forcing me to flinch backward. Cloth tore under my huge fingers, and panic flashed across his face.

Seeing a big guy like that in a state of pure terror does something to a man's soul. This giant of a man, all muscle and mean, couldn't possibly be afraid of anything.

But he was. He was terrified.

The other bouncer bolted. He jumped to another roof then disappeared behind a building. Some partner.

The cloth of Wesley's shirt tore again.

Our eyes met. He swallowed back his fear, but he knew I had him. He gripped my wrists. His hands were like shackles tying me to a weight that would sink me to the bottom of the deepest fisheries.

"Who do you work for?" I repeated. "Who runs the Gravity Lounge?" Because I was coming for them. Soon as I figured out who Destiny's killer was, I was going to go straight for whoever sent these thugs after Castor Vin.

But I didn't get an answer. The big guy cast his gaze upward, staring for a moment at the bright lights on the spiral ceiling almost as if he were casting his eyes to God. Then, with a shove, he launched himself out of my grip. The shirt tore the rest of the way, and he fell.

I didn't wait to watch the slab of meat hit the ground. Maybe it was a death sentence, and maybe not. It wasn't going to matter one way or another. What mattered was Castor Vin.

The musician was still alive when I reached him. Blood pulsed from a hole in the side of his neck. If I had a medical kiosk and a full surgery suite, maybe I could help him die slower. As it was, the pressure I placed on his spurting wound only served to strangle his air supply.

"Girls," he bubbled.

I didn't say anything. If there was anyone with something to say, it was going to be him, and I didn't want to fill that space with empty promises.

"Girls," he whispered again. He was fading fast. He touched his breast pocket. There was an envelope there, and he handed it to me, marking it with his bloody fingerprints. "Destiny…" The light in his eyes faded, and he drew a ragged, bloody breath. "Not the only one."

With that, the musician gurgled his last breath. His pulse stopped, and his whole body melted from lack of a motivating force.

Lorentz ran up the stairwell and stopped in front of the bloody scene. She stared for a long time, taking it in as if there were something she desperately needed to memorize.

I looked at the envelope in my hand. Wiping everything as clean as I could get it, I carefully opened the flap and looked at what was inside. What had Castor Vin been so desperate to tell me yet so afraid to speak of?

The only content of the envelope was a single glossy photograph—the kind that used a chemical paper to bypass any digital manipulation.

The photograph showed a woman in a dancing outfit similar to the ones at the jazz club we'd visited earlier in the evening.

Fresh blood marked the girl's beautiful face from a clean slash across her slender throat.

She had been murdered, same as Destiny Alverez.

"What?" Lorentz asked from the stairwell. She could have approached, but the expanding pool of blood got in her way. "What is it?"

"I don't care how evil you think God lets people get," I said, "you're wrong." I put the picture in my pocket and stepped over the musician's corpse. "There's always someone worse."

We returned to the city, where false stars failed to lend light to the stifling black.

PART III

the case of the scientist's daughter

Chapter 18

HEAVY NICODEMIA WAS the lowest of the three beads—farther from the center of the spinning chain and the bead that suffered the highest simulated gravity. Lights were dim in the late afternoon when we arrived, a sharp contrast to the almost invasive brilliance of the Hallows. My eyes adjusted quickly to shadows so dim they washed out everything in grays and blues. This was home. Despite all that had happened in my life, this was the one place I felt almost comfortable.

"I can drop you off at the cathedral," I told Lorentz.

The corners of her lips turned down for a sliver of a second, but she said nothing.

I said, "I'm sorry it went down like that with Vin."

We walked for a long time before she said anything, and when she did, her voice was swallowed by the grumble of the Heavy Nicodemia crowds. It sounded something like, "I should have been faster."

"You're feeling guilt for the first time in your life."

"I'm Catholic."

"You were innocent," I said. "In a bubble. Now you're not."

Her fists clenched at her sides. "I'm not responsible for what happened back there."

"Guilt isn't about responsibility. Guilt is about guilt. It clutches at your chest and weighs on your shoulders, but it's not about what you did or didn't do. It has its own weight."

"That doesn't make any sense."

"It doesn't need to," I said. "It never has."

Again, she was silent for a long time.

"You get used to it," I finally said. "But it takes time."

A crowd was gathered in front of the Cathedral of Saint Francis of Assisi in front of its enormous fiberoak doors. The Catholic Church ruled everything in Heavy Nicodemia, even more so than in the upper beads. Even the non-Catholic—even the non-Christian—residents of the bead respected the authority of the Church. Crime bosses and business leaders alike paid tribute to the station's most powerful entity, and the priesthood never let anyone forget about it.

Now, in the warm glow of the evening sunset, Priest Cecilia Cano spoke to the masses. She was a bulldozer of a woman, built sturdy in both mind and body by God to bowl through mountains of bureaucracy and crush the doubts of a skeptical population. Her gray hair was uncharacteristically skewed, as if she'd had as rough a week as me.

Her voice boomed over the crowd, amplified through a mic clipped to her priestly blacks. "All we can do is look to our own," she said. "Care for those around us and tend to our own needs."

A grumble rolled through the crowd. The Heavies were a tense place, but this felt like something more.

"We don't own the ideas of the other beads," Cano continued. "We can only consider our own—"

"It's blasphemy!" shouted a man in the crowd. Assent rippled through the crowd.

"The structure of the Church is designed to root out such blasphemy," said Cano. Her eyes fell on me in the back of the crowd, and for a fraction of a second, I thought I saw a hint of annoyance. I couldn't figure out why. We'd always gotten along fairly well. "The Church has always researched its own history. It has always delved into new ideas and it has thrived on the acceptance of new understanding."

"Let's go," said Lorentz. I had almost forgotten she was there.

"I thought this was your jam," I said.

"It's complicated."

"You sound like you know what this is about."

She stared at me. "It's about Trinity."

"Machine worship?"

"It's not like that."

I pushed through the crowd, and Lorentz followed. There was a trend in the church of the Hallows that confused the will of God with the programming of the AI Trinity. As someone raised on a hearty mix of Catholic tradition and disdain for our mechanized authority, the new policies didn't settle well.

Lorentz grasped my elbow and pulled me back. "I need to learn more about the colonies."

"Will that help us find Destiny's killer?"

"This is the best way to find him." Her voice was raw, and her brow knit together with the embers of frustration.

"I should take more plumbing jobs."

"Because they're cleaner?"

"Nobody tries to plumb for the plumber."

She put her fists on her hips. "I'm not telling you how to do your job. I'm telling you what your job is."

I patted my pockets. "I don't recall being paid."

"Fine." It wasn't fine. "What do you think is the next step?"

"Police."

"Someone was just recently telling me that the blue would just get in the way."

"Whoever told you that is a troublemaker."

"So, let's go," she said.

"The guy walks a beat. He might not be much help with something like this," I warned her.

"Not much help is better than none at all," she said.

"Sometimes."

Leaving the crowd behind, we continued downspiral. Rows of tenement housing passed and as we drew lower, the sharp odor of the fish farms wafted up on the cool breeze. A chill ran over my arms, and I pressed my hat down on my head. This was home to me, but home wasn't always pleasant. In the last row of a rundown business center sat my sister Angel's small diner.

Angel was a force to be reckoned with. The same crash that had killed my parents and left me excommunicated had left her wheelchair-bound. Sometimes I thought she got the better end of that deal. At first we'd struggled through life in Haven, but she'd earned her way back into the good graces of Trinity's Karma system while I'd spiraled into a life of gambling and regret. When I finally burned all my bridges in that bead, we'd moved together down to the Heavies—a lousy place for a woman in a wheelchair.

But my sister greeted opposition like a heavyweight boxer. She bought a diner, married the woman of her dreams, and spent her free time generally succeeding in every way that her big brother had failed.

"Sis," I said as the bell over Angel's Diner's door rang.

Angel looked up from behind the counter. "Corner booth." What better greeting could a big brother expect?

A white lump near the kitchen door unfolded itself and pointed black eyes my direction. The compact bundle of muscle and muzzle was Runt, my sister's tough little pit bull. His nose twitched at the rush of air from outside, but we must have passed inspection because he curled back up into a ball.

In the corner booth sat Officer Anders in his full formal blues. The crisp lines of his uniform made the young cop look like a teenager playing dress-up. In front of him sat two untouched slices of boysenberry pie—one of my sister's favorites—and a half-empty cup of black coffee. When he saw me approaching with Lorentz, a pleasant smile crossed his lips and he slid both slices of pie across the table.

"Demarco," said Anders. "Good to see you. And this is…"

"Ginnie Lorentz," said Lorentz, sitting across from him. I squeezed into the booth next to her, but I didn't touch the pie. "You must be Anders."

"Guilty." His smile was as sweet as the pie in front of him.

Lorentz elbowed me. "You never said he was a charmer."

"Only a matter of time before he's jaded and bitter."

Pride told me not to eat my sister's pie. It told me to show some restraint and get down to business with Anders. There was a killer out there, after all. Someone needed to find him, and fast.

But it was my sister's boysenberry pie, and it wasn't like I was going to get more anytime soon. I ate while Lorentz and Anders chatted it up. Their conversation about sports teams (the soccer season was coming to a close) and crime waves (we were in one, due to a recent power vacuum in organized crime) and favorite pies (boysenberry was edging its way up) washed over me as I worked my way through the fantastic slice. Angel brought Anders a third piece, scowling at me as I used my fork to scrape the last remnants from the plate.

"What do you think, Demarco?" Anders asked, eventually. The young cop's serious expression was thwarted by his curly hair and the smudge of boysenberry on his cheek.

"I need to know if you recognize a victim," I said.

Lorentz pressed her lips into a hard line.

Anders said, "Lot of victims out there these days."

"Sure." I took the photo from my pocket and tossed it onto the table. "But this perp is forming a pattern."

Anders gawked at the photo. His already pale face went another two steps toward white. "I don't work homicide."

"I'm looking for rumors. Recognition. Anything. There's been a similar victim by the name of Destiny Alverez, but I haven't ID'd this one."

"Which bead?"

"Destiny was in Hallow," I said, tapping on the pictures. "Hard to say where this one was. Maybe Haven."

"Sounds like you need Trinity's help."

"We ran a basic search," said Lorentz. Her voice was surprisingly strong, but her eyes avoided the three photos. "There were no hits."

Anders blinked at that. "Is she from Earth or a colony system?"

"Not a chance." I slid the photo toward Anders. I pointed to the tattoo on her neck, which depicted a turtle carrying the world on its back.

Anders peered at the image. The angle of the girl's head wasn't good, so only part of the tattoo was visible.

"What is it?" Lorentz asked, finally looking at the picture. There was a tension in her voice.

Before I could answer, Anders surprised me by saying, "Turtles are a common theme down here in the Heavies. It's a reference to stories about the world being carried on the back of a turtle. Like, we're getting crushed down here."

"But the turtle doesn't get crushed," said Lorentz.

"Exactly," I said. "The turtle just keeps going while all the world is oblivious. It's not rebellion, exactly, and that keeps them straight with regard to Karma. Open rebellion costs points because it hurts the community."

"Unless it doesn't," said Lorentz.

I said, "Pointing out the inequality is sometimes a net gain."

Lorentz pursed her lips. "For someone outside of the Karma system, you sure seem to know a lot about it."

"Sometimes it takes an outsider's view," I said. "But this tattoo is fairly common down here, which is why I'm coming to Anders here."

Anders studied the photo for a long time. "What are the odds these are the only two victims?" He picked up his fork, looked at his pie, and set the fork back down. "Where did you get this, anyway?"

"A musician," I said.

"Is he the killer?"

"Probably not. He was offed by a couple of goons from the Gravity Lounge."

"That place at the top of the Hallows?"

"You know it?"

"Never been," said Anders.

"It's pretty exclusive," said Lorentz.

"Seems like a big coincidence if your informant was digging into these murders and the Gravity Lounge sent someone to kill him." Anders leaned forward. "Are the blue up there in contact with whoever's running that place?"

"The blue up north won't touch the Gravity Lounge," I said. "Not without proof. Any chance your boys can look into it?"

A flush bloomed in Anders' cheeks. "Cross-bead operations get complicated," he said.

"You're right," Lorentz said to me. "He's not much help."

"Look, I'll try," Anders said, "but you have to understand, there's not a lot I can do without a special task force."

I leaned forward. "And for that, you need proof that there's been a cross-bead crime."

"Exactly."

I slid Anders's pie over to my side of the table and took a bite. "There *is* the other victim," I said. "Destiny Alverez."

"Right," Anders said, "but what I mean is, can we show that her murder is connected to this one? If Trinity's hiding these vics, then there might be more, right?"

"Has anyone been going missing in the Heavies?" I asked.

Anders' brow furrowed. "Not more than the usual."

"What's usual?" I said.

"More than zero. Less than a lot."

"Seems funny for a closed system, don't you think?"

Anders put his palms forward in surrender. "Lot of people disappear for legitimate reasons. It's complicated."

"Sounds like a lot of things are complicated," I said.

Lorentz said, "Trinity's focus is on body, soul, and community. There has to be something about these killings that causes a conflict between two of those priorities—otherwise it'd be an obvious threat to the bodies of these women."

"What's more important than people's lives?" I wondered.

Anders tapped the photos. “It doesn’t look like the killer is interested in saving anyone’s soul.”

Lorentz frowned and turned away. After a moment, she stood and crossed the diner to pet Runt. I got the distinct impression that the conversation was taking a toll on her, and after recent events, I didn’t blame her.

Anders thumbed in her direction. “What’s with the lady?”

“Jesuit,” I said.

“She’s in the wrong crowd if she doesn’t like the look of blood.”

I pushed the photos over to Anders. “Scan this into the police systems. We need to identify her, and then maybe we can figure out how they’re connected. If more girls are in danger…”

“I’m on it,” Anders said, pocketing the pic. “But if Trinity didn’t ping these on a civilian scan, there’s not much our database is going to do.” He dropped a few dimes on the table and stood to leave.

“The best database is the one you carry around in your skull,” I said. “Make sure you check a few of those.”

“Will do, Demarco.” When he passed Lorentz, he said, “Pleasure meeting you, ma’am.”

She flashed a weak smile. “Likewise, officer.”

Once he was gone, Lorentz slid into the booth across from me. Her skin was pale, and her eyes shone with unshed tears. “How do you do it, Demarco?” she asked. “How do you talk about these killings and not let it get to you?”

Something deep in my chest ached, but I drew a deep breath and held it back. There’s no telling what floodgates that would open. “When a person walks in the dark long enough, their soul gets tough or withers away. I chose tough.”

Angel wheeled up to the table. “If you’re so tough, Jude, why don’t you finish that pie?”

I looked down at the uneaten pie. Boysenberry was the best pie Angel made, and this was just going to go to waste.

But try as I might, I couldn't eat another bite.

"Some tough guy," she said, and she wheeled away with the plate. When she reached the corner, she dumped the pie into Runt's dish, and he ate it in one bite.

Sometimes I hated my sister for being so damn right.

Chapter 19

AFTER A FITFUL REST in my tiny apartment above Angel's Diner, I ventured back upspiral toward the cathedral. The Heavy Nicodemia morning hung in the air like damp wool. Residents shuffled on their way and rode the trolley to their places of business. By all measures, it was a typical day in the downtrodden districts.

Lorentz still hadn't paid me. She was out visiting churches and libraries in the area, shoring up the gaps in her local knowledge. A message had been sent to the bishop. After giving the photo to Anders, we'd decided our best option was to familiarize ourselves with the details of the case. She'd go learn about the turtle tattoo. I'd shake down some contacts to see if I could rustle up more leads.

Someone had to know this murdered girl. If anyone could help, it would be Retch.

I didn't like how I'd last parted with Retch. He was a volatile kid, but his animosity toward Lorentz didn't sit well with me, and I got the distinct feeling that there was something else there that I needed to be aware of.

First, I tried all the usual places his gang typically lurked. There was a nook in the cathedral's shadow where Trinity's cameras formed a dead spot. Several kids lingered there in the shadows, entertaining onlookers with feats of juggling, magic, and some mild pickpocketing. When they saw me approach, they ran. Apparently I had a reputation.

Retch wasn't there, so I wandered to the warehouse district behind the cathedral where the half-used box-like buildings collected the unwanted remnants of society. The ancient structures stood testament to the bureaucratic nightmare of zoning a closed space station. Everywhere else in the Heavies was crowded to the point of collapse, but this warehouse district was underused and sparsely populated. The only people living there were unhoused children who had run from their parents, disabled adults whom society had failed, and those evil enough to prey upon the other two. Many fit more than one category. A few fit all three.

Retch once lived back there, securing an abandoned warehouse as his own solitary home. He'd since moved into another of the tiny rooms above Angel's Diner, but I always suspected that he'd kept a place back here somewhere. A kid doesn't grow up on the streets without learning to always have a backup plan.

Turned out I was right.

"I'd say it's fresh meat in the slums, but this cut's looking a little dried up." Retch lounged atop the dumpster and waved his stunstick lazily in front of him like a magic wand.

"Hey, kid," I said, trying not to sound resigned and failing miserably. "Any trouble getting through Customs?"

"Down's always easier than up," he said.

True enough. "Lorentz—"

He slapped the dumpster with an open palm. "I'd rather

be on top of shit mountain than anywhere near the church, Demarco."

"She's not the Church."

Retch shrugged. "I don't care what your girlfriend gets up to."

"If the Church bothers you, then stay away from it."

"Three of my best disappeared while I was gone," Retch said.

"You think the Catholic Church took them?"

"They were the three queerest motherfuckers in Screaming Jesus, Demarco. Who do *you* think would target them?"

Retch's crew was a group of transient kids bent on nothing but trouble. There were a dozen reasons three of them might disappear. "The Catholic Church is guilty of a lot of things, but kidnapping isn't their gig." I furrowed my brow. "Recently."

"Very convincing." Retch jumped down from the dumpster and poked me in the chest with his inert stunstick. "You know what bothers me? Lady shows up and you shut me out. We had a chance at blowing that case wide open, and you decided to go it without me."

"You're not ready yet, kid."

He took a step back and his stunstick crackled with energy. "Call me kid again."

"It got too heavy. Too dark."

"Are you kidding me?" Retch stalked down the alley, then spun back to me. "Do you even know who you're talking to? Too dark for *me?* Do you know what kind of life I live?"

I bristled. "I lived through the wreck of the Benevolent."

"So fucking what?"

"Death lingers." My fists clenched, but I couldn't relax

them. "In your dreams. In the scent in the air. In the way you see everyone you meet. It lingers."

He sheathed his stunstick. His expression was carefully flat. "It does."

"I need you to work with Lorentz," I said. "Without hitting her with that stick."

"I'm not making that promise."

The irritation was starting to get to me. "It's not like you can't just go back on the promise, right?"

"Oh, is that what you think of me? I'm just a lying kid with no moral fiber? I'll just promise to get along with the evil lady and then smack her on the bottom with a stunstick?"

"It's a distinct possibility."

"Do you want to know what she asked me?"

"She told you that you'd be welcome back in the Church."

He jabbed a finger at me. "She knows her Church, Demarco. She knows just exactly how the Church has always treated people like me, all the way back to the days on Earth. It's part of the moral fiber of the station that trans men and women don't exist."

"That's not true."

"Tell *her* that."

I could see by the set of his jaw that he wasn't going to listen, but I kept right on anyway. "Girls are getting murdered, Retch. This is bigger than just Destiny Alverez. You're my best bet to track down the identity of the other victim." I pointed to a spot on my neck. "She had the world turtle tattoo. Blonde. Now she's dead."

He spread his arms. "Once they're dead, they're out of my jurisdiction. Remember? I'm not allowed to see dead people. Might wound my fragile psyche."

"That's not what I meant," I said.

"People mean a lot of things," he said, turning to leave. "Maybe if you work at it hard enough, you can figure out why you really need me around."

Retch disappeared into the nearest warehouse, passing through a jagged wound in the building's fibersteel walls. I might have been stupid enough to follow if the hole had been any wider, but he'd planned this well. There was no way I would fit, and by the time I circled the building, he'd be gone.

All my irons were in the fire, so I headed back to the center of the bead. Downspiral from the cathedral, I crossed the tracks where a rickety trolley shuttled people up and down the long spiral. There, I found a bench not too close to the edge of the vast inner space and set to work at diligently smoking a cigarette. Somewhere, someone played a trombone, chaining the introductions of various blues tunes into each other as if the signature riffs of each were the only important part of the whole song.

Beginnings and ends matter, of course, but they weren't the whole story. It made me wonder what Destiny Alverez's story was. Did she really, in a fit of desperation, get involved with the wrong people? She'd wanted to play the Gravity Lounge. That much was clear, but where had she gone from there? Who had she met along the way?

And how was this killer killing in more than one bead? That was the strange part. Most folks stuck to their home, moving up a bead in times of good fortune or down whenever the world worked the way it worked. What if we were looking in the wrong place?

I didn't know how old Vin's photograph was. It could have been years old or days. I should have mentioned that to Anders when I asked him to show it around. A lungful of death cleared my thoughts as I stared up into the hazy sky.

It was an illusion, of course. The sky was just a vast

empty space and then more city. More buildings spiraled inward to the narrow point where Customs managed the elevator to the bead above. They told us that the station was designed the way it was because humans needed the illusion of a sky. We need to be able to gaze upward and see distance. Without that, the human condition degrades into depression and anxiety.

The butt of my cigarette smoldered. I dropped it to the ground and stepped on it. Then, I picked it up and tossed it into a recycler.

It was with that extra movement that I spotted Leo Shaw watching me from across the tracks. He met my gaze and flashed an innocent smile as if he just happened to be in the area. The muscled toad folded his arms and watched as another trolley rumbled between us.

When it was gone, I said, "I need that book back, Shaw."

"How's the money situation?"

"I've cracked the code." I lied, strolling upspiral along the track. Stepping onto the track was dangerous for me. The trolleys would stop for anyone else in the district, but machines didn't see an excommunicated person like myself. They wouldn't even slow down after grinding my bones to dust. "You said you'd give it back."

"I said I wanted proof."

Damn. Retch still had the page and my drawing of Destiny's tattoos. I had forgotten to ask if he'd gotten anywhere with it, but it didn't matter if I couldn't show Shaw any proof. The list of names still burned in my pocket. Shaw hadn't been able to collect on any of them. "I'm looking for a girl," I said. "Blonde. Twenties. Tattoo of a world turtle on her neck."

His expression was so carefully controlled I knew I'd hit

something. “People disappear, Demarco.” Another trolley rumbled past, spiraling downward and away.

Our eyes met. There was something he wasn’t telling me. A secret he didn’t want to share. “I need that journal,” I finally said.

“And I need that money.” A cruel grin flashed his straight teeth. “Preferably before you disappear.”

The next trolley rumbled upspiral, and as it passed I hooked it with one arm. It was going too fast for a graceful boarding, but I held on hard and it yanked me up and away from Shaw.

He’d get his dimes, but not today. Not until Lorentz started paying. Not until I found Destiny’s killer.

Not until I had some answers.

As I approached the Cathedral of Saint Francis of Assisi, I saw Anders waiting on a nearby bench where we sometimes meet. He spotted me right away and stood to greet me.

“Dig something up already?” I said.

“Paydirt.” He tipped his hat to a passerby. “One of the other patrolmen recognized your vic.”

“Recent?”

“Recent, but not local. The body came down from Haven yesterday.”

“Vin must have taken the picture after tracking her down a little too late.”

“You sure he’s not the killer?” Anders asked.

I thought about it. “I’m not sure of much of anything.”

“Well, here’s one thing you can be sure of.” He handed me the photograph. “There’s a funeral tonight for Lacie van Esters that you might want to attend.”

Chapter 20

FUNERALS ON A STATION were nothing like funerals on Earth. Bodies weren't interred in the ground or built into structures. Every resident of Nicodemia was part of the grand cycle. Every fingernail, every drop of blood, every resilient bone. The worst of us and the best of us all ended up part of the system at some point. A funeral in Nicodemia was the last chance to say goodbye to a person's mortal form. To their lingering soul.

Even I had enough tact to avoid hard interrogations during the funeral ceremony in the main chapel of Saint Francis of Assisi. The place was three-quarters full of mourners. Family and friends packed toward the front of the church. Spectators like myself—and there were several of us—lingered toward the back. Priest Cano delivered the service in her best droning monotone. A few of the girl's family spoke.

Then, contrary to my expectations, the ceremony did not end by sending the deceased into the cathedral's sanctified recycler. The bearers closed the girl's casket, picked it up, and started a procession down the long aisle out of the church.

"Suicide," explained the man next to me. "Damn shame."

I was still considering the implications when the family processed past me. Lacie van Esters's mother wore a dark veil and walked next to her husband.

The dead woman trailed her mother. Alive. I recognized her from the picture. She had the same blonde hair and the same tattoo. Her eyes shone with the same blue. It was *her*.

It wasn't her.

"Twin sister," explained the man next to me.

The woman at the funeral was Cherie van Esters, twin sister to the girl in my photograph. That made a little more sense than seeing a ghost, but it wasn't any more settling on the soul. Cherie was distraught. As the procession continued out of the church and downspiral, she oscillated between screaming mess and crying fury. Approaching her wasn't going to do anybody any good. Not in this state.

I still wasn't going to press my investigation, but I could listen as I followed.

Lacie had been a waitress in Haven, according to a couple of gossiping uncles near the back of the procession. That wasn't much of a connection to the dancer Destiny. A pair of elderly gentlemen discussed the girl's rumored promiscuousness. She had dated a number of sketchy individuals in the Heavies and even in Haven, where she'd died, but she'd lately settled in with a regular guy somewhere in the lower districts.

"Do you know who?" I asked.

They shot me sour looks and shuffled away.

Third, the whispers among the younger crowd told me

that Lacie was well-liked, but unstable. This wasn't anything like Destiny, who had been something of a loner. It was these social connections that made people murmur when they spoke of Lacie's cause of death.

Suicide, the rumors said. It was a real shame that nobody saw it coming. One self-indulgent asshole even hypothesized that it was her mother's fault. Bad parenting. Everyone's always so eager to point to the parents.

What didn't make sense was the funeral itself. Lacie van Esters was a waitress. A nobody. Even worse, she was a suicide.

So, what was she doing getting a full Catholic service from the biggest cathedral in the Heavies? They weren't using Saint Francis's sanctified recycler because of her suicide, but Priest Cano still walked ahead of the family. Even if Lacie were a social creature, she wouldn't justify the biggest service in town. The crowd walking the slow procession downspiral was ten times what I'd expect for a young waitress without an ounce of celebrity influence.

Which meant somebody in her family must be important. I watched the crowd carefully to try to figure out who.

What I really wanted was a connection between Lacie and Destiny—something other than their brutal deaths. I wondered when Destiny's funeral would be. How would Reginald Alverez react when I showed up at the funeral of the daughter I had failed to save?

Did it matter?

I caught a familiar whiff of bad perfume as the slow-moving procession approached the recycler. Someone wore an awful astringent aroma that wafted over the crowd and fought back even the odor of the fisheries farther downspiral. I looked around for the source, but the black-clad masses shuffled forward, and most of the women's faces were obscured behind dark veils.

Pushing on, I found a place in the procession where I could watch Lacie's mother. The plump woman's blonde hair and sharply upturned nose made her unmistakable as a relative, but the crowd around her was the real indication of her status. She was surrounded by a dense group of well-wishers, and they moved quietly as a single unit.

Beyond them was the casket, carried by six bearded men. Each face was a grim mask, and the familial resemblance to Lacie and Cherie was undeniable. A big family, then. These were likely brothers and uncles, carrying one of their own to the great recycler. It was a proud tradition in the more respected families of the district.

We arrived at a non-denominational ceremonial recycler housed just upspiral from the docks. It led straight into the best, most efficient materials recycling unit in the bead and would deliver the body straight to the processors where she'd be returned to the station's closed cycle.

"What are you doing here?" hissed a voice at my side. I looked down to see Priest Cano walking in her white ceremonial robes. The stocky woman carried a Bible and an expression of stern disapproval.

"Blending in," I whispered back.

"You're two heads taller than anyone here."

"I slouched." When she didn't back away, I tried a different tack. "You know why I'm here."

That gave her pause. "There's a lot you don't know."

"Fill me in."

"You're not the only suspicious character at this funeral, you know."

"I don't like to think of myself as suspicious."

"I'd love to see you in reconciliation sometime, Jude," she said, moving away. "I bet you have some good stories to tell."

"I'm saving them up."

I lingered until the procession moved past me, keeping an eye out for the suspicious character Cano had mentioned. As the group passed into the richly decorated hallways of the ceremonial recycler, I spotted him.

He wore black, but everyone wore black. This wasn't the black of mourning, though. This was the black that sucked light from the skies and swallowed it whole. The black that ached to look at.

The black that the attacker in the Sinless had worn to avoid detection by Trinity. The black of a killer. His veil was a similar material, but I felt his eyes as he turned my way. It was probably too much to have hoped he hadn't seen me.

The silhouette wouldn't work in the light of day. The figure might be marginally harder for Trinity to identify, but the suit wouldn't give him any real advantage. So, what was the play?

I watched the dark figure as the group moved through a long hall to the secular recycling chamber. Images on the walls showed the history of the city's voyage to the stars like Stations of the Cross. How it first built the spinning cathedral in space, then expanded into a city, and finally became dozens of cities surrounding a single fusion core. The imagery made not-very-subtle comparisons between the heaven of Christian mythology and the literal place we were living. Ironic, considering the Heavies were considered by many to be Nicodemia's hell.

The lighting dimmed as we moved farther down the hall. It became harder and harder to see the man in black. He kept shifting his position so that I had to frantically search the shadows for him. Finally, we reached the end, where a large altar served as the entry point to the recycler. Fiberoak and stone surrounded a shrouded hole like the cave where Jesus had his three-day nap. There'd be no walking out of this tomb, though. The altar was part of a conveyance system, ready to accept our mortal forms into the great cycle.

The bearers placed the casket on the dais and Priest Cano took position on an adjacent podium.

"It is with great sadness that we gather together today," the priest began.

The figure was gone—melted into the crowd. This was his element, where the shadows merged the mourners with the somber darkness of the ashen walls. This is why he'd worn that suit here. In the shadows of this ceremonial space, he could disappear, not only from the cameras, but also from anyone genuinely trying to find him. He could strike me dead in a second if I wasn't careful.

I stood far enough away from the crowds that I would be able to see him coming. I felt horribly conspicuous in my tan coat and hat.

"Her father once came to me," said Cano, "on the eve before her mother left for the colony, and he asked me if Lacie and Cherie could possibly succeed without her. This tragedy today might look like failure. It might look like God is punishing us in our misery."

My heart pounded. If the man in black was going to attack, he would do it soon. There wasn't any advantage in waiting. All he needed was a sharp blade or a small firearm and he could kill. He'd disappear easily in the chaos.

What if it wasn't dark?

I cast around frantically, an icy sweat forming on my brow. These older sections of the ship were often built with maintenance lighting. Even the ceremonial spaces needed a good cleaning from time to time, and the lighting was designed to help.

Unfortunately, I couldn't activate the lights. I was excommunicated. The controls would simply ignore me, and it would take too long to find a manual override.

There! A flash of black in the center of the crowd—blacker even than the darkest mourning cloth. He was working his way to the front. I pushed forward, elbowing aside the funeral crowd to grumbles of discontent.

I slammed into Cherie. Her face was a pale ghost behind a thin veil, and when she looked up at me, I felt a rush of fear that I knew was irrational. This was the dead girl, looking at me. Scowling. Judging.

The harsh judgment was deserved, wasn't it? I pushed past the girl. At my height, I could see how the deepest black flowed through the crowd like an eel through the depths of the oceans. He was too far away. I'd never catch him. If only Retch were there. Even Lorentz would be able to help me. They could make Trinity turn on the lights. They could flank and trap the killer. They could be my eyes and my ears in places I could never travel.

Doubt clouded my every move. The shadow and I converged on the front of the crowd, making our way to the family of the victim—the mother and father who Cano was still talking about.

"When she was little, her parents would bring her to church," Cano said. "And in Sunday school, little Lacie would ask the hardest questions. She asked, 'What happens when fish die?' and 'How do we know that Trinity isn't the same as the Holy Trinity?'" Cano paused as if considering her next words. "She was a smart girl. Brilliant and beautiful. We know she didn't deserve the death she got, but nor can we believe that God will judge her poorly."

There was something fatalistic about Cano's tone. Her eyes locked with mine, and an intense sense of wrongness tightened in my gut.

The dark figure was gone. Disappeared somewhere in the crowd ahead. My heart pounded in my ears, drowning out Priest Cano's droning words. Why wouldn't she wrap things up? Why did she have to keep talking while there was an obvious threat lurking in the crowd—a threat that *she* had warned me about.

Black shifted, and I lunged, shoving aside the crowd. Cries of anger and frustration swelled. Cano ignored my offense and droned on as I crashed through the innocent onlookers and caught—

Nobody.

I burst out of the funeral procession into the open space between the mourners and the altar. There was nobody there. No dark shadow attacked the innocent bystanders. No black-clad assassin waited to strike. I faced the crowd and peered at their shining faces in the flickering ceremonial lights.

He wasn't there. He had escaped in the chaos, melted into the darkest shadows. My eyes met those of the dead girl's mother, and I felt the full weight of her judging disapproval. She was a hard woman, short and solid like so many other denizens of Heavy Nicodemia. She stared at me with cold eyes.

Then, the wall behind the casket opened and Lacie van Esters started her journey into the great beyond. Cano watched quietly as the casket rolled into an expansive corridor lined with bright, shining steel.

The ceremony was over, and Lacie van Esters would soon be lost, at long last—sent into the great recycler to give herself fully to the community that had failed to support her in her time of need.

Her last good deed.

"Jude!" Cano shouted.

A force slammed into me, and I staggered over the recycler threshold. A flash of almost invisible black darted away as I slipped on the smooth surface and landed hard next to the coffin.

The wall slammed shut, dooming me to be recycled by the machine.

Chapter 21

MY FISTS SLAMMED USELESSLY against the shining metal wall. The door was gone, having disappeared into the smooth cylinder's circular end.

Because of the ancient programming by long-dead Catholic scholars, Trinity ignored excommunicated agents outside of liminal spaces. It wouldn't open the door for me because it didn't acknowledge that I existed. The recycling sequence was going to kill me.

The casket reached its destination in the center of the recycling chamber with a resounding boom. Sound echoed strangely in the enclosed space. The material was like nothing I'd seen in the city. It was hard and heavy. Nothing I did would penetrate that barrier. It wouldn't move until the cycle finished.

That cycle would consume everything inside the chamber.

A sharp chemical odor oozed out of hidden vents below the casket. The mechanism that moved the casket suspended it over a rectangular opening. Even as I watched, acidic mist rose from the pit and etched the fiberoak box. Soon, that mist would reach me, and I'd die as horrible a death as I could imagine. Heart racing, I pounded on the wall.

Blue lights flickered somewhere behind the reflective surface of the walls. I stared, breathing hard. My lungs ached. My throat was raw. I fought hard to focus. This light reminded me of something. I recalled the liminal spaces where Nicodemia touched the outside world.

"Trinity?"

The voice that answered was smooth and low. "Reconcile?" it asked, because that was what it always asked.

"Not today, Trinity." Maybe someday. Probably never. "Pause the recycling, Trinity," I ordered. The hiss of mist stopped, but the casket now sat suspended over a rectangular hole in the floor. I stayed as far as I could from the open processing pit center. The mist still in the air stung where it touched my skin.

This was a liminal space. It was the space between life and death, where the long arc of the recycler bent back upon itself to form its full circle. Because it was a liminal space, Trinity listened to me. It responded to my voice.

"I have some questions," I said. My chest still ached from the adrenaline rush. I had been so close to death. I still was. The mist cleared, but significant portions of the casket were missing or compromised where the corrosive solution of the pit sloshed onto its polished exterior.

Cautiously, I opened the casket to reveal the shrouded corpse.

"Tell me about Lacie van Esters," I said, pacing around the platform. If this was my chance to talk directly to Trinity, then I needed to make use of it.

Trinity processed the question for several seconds before

answering. “There is no record of a Lacie van Esters in Nicodemia.”

“Bullshit.” I pulled the shroud off the body with a flourish. “Then who is this?”

The girl had been cleaned up since the photo was taken, but all the injuries were still there. Her light blonde hair was styled in a tight curl on her forehead. The low cut of the collar revealed the angry red of the wound on her throat, even through the cover-up makeup. Burns on her chest and arms were covered by a pristine black jumper, but when I touched her shoulder, I could feel where the bones had been shattered and shunted back in place. Someone had worked very hard to make this corpse presentable, but this was definitely a murder, not a suicide.

Finally, after far more processing than I expected from the governing AI, Trinity said, “Unknown suicide.”

“That’s not a name.”

“Name is unknown.”

I threw the shroud back over Lacie’s corpse. “You know damn well who she is, Trinity. You’re lying to me.”

But Trinity *couldn’t* lie to me. Part of our arrangement was that I always got the truth, no matter how painful or inconvenient or dangerous. This wasn’t the machine lying to me. This was worse. Trinity truly didn’t know.

I paced around the casket. “Continue recycling, Trinity. Without the mist.”

“Skipping pretreatment.”

Trinity didn’t know Lacie van Esters. But how could that be? Did it erase its own memory just to keep information hidden? Why would it do that? No, it made more sense if someone else was erasing data. The question, then, was *how*?

“Tell me about Cherie van Esters,” I said.

Without hesitation, the machine responded, “Cherie van

Esters is the twenty-two-year-old daughter of Saria van Esters and—"

"Hold on," I said. "Does Cherie have a sister?"

Again, the long pause. "Cherie does not have a sister." The casket descended, and the slurry ate its fiberoak panels.

"How many daughters does Saria van Esters have?"

A pause. "One."

"You know there's someone else," I said. "Tell me more about Cherie van Esters," I finally said, desperately grasping for some clues.

Trinity's voice was low when it continued, "Cherie van Esters is an accountant in the upper government district of Heavy Nicodemia. She is the daughter of Saria and Benjamin van Esters—"

"I don't need her family history." Asking the computer for help made me sick, but I needed to find the connection between Lacie and Destiny. Without that, there was nothing I could do for either. "Tell me about Cherie's social sphere."

A long list of names appeared in blue text on the wall.

"Cross reference with Destiny Alverez."

After a brief pause, a network diagram appeared. Social connections linked to social connections in a vast network for each girl. Where the connections overlapped, the nodes glowed bright blue.

There were only a few, but one stood out.

"How does Saria van Esters know Petunia Alverez?" Their mothers were acquainted. The dim node noted that they weren't a close contact, but their spheres had overlapped long ago.

"Reconcile?" asked Trinity.

What the hell? "I said, how does Saria know Petunia?"

The social network diagram disappeared, as did the

image of Cherie. "Reconcile?" Trinity repeated. The word appeared in giant blue type along the wall.

This. This was why I hated dealing directly with the machine. It was the same reason I hated dealing with the priests of the Catholic Church. They always wanted to hear my sins, and there were simply too many to list. I wouldn't reconcile until I'd paid my penance, and the penance was only going to get worse.

"You know damn well what my sins are, Trinity," I said. "I caused the wreck of the *Benevolent*." My wealthy family had often used the ship to avoid customs between the Hallows and Haven. When its docking attachment had failed, I was the one who chose to eject the ship rather than risk the city. Maybe that earned me respect from the machine, but killing my parents would always be a dark stain on my soul.

At least, it would until I found whoever had sabotaged the ship's life support systems. Detachment had meant death for almost everyone aboard the ship, but it *shouldn't* have.

"I've stopped looking," I finally said to Trinity. "There are no more leads." I stared at the body of Lacie van Esters for a long time—a body Trinity still swore was an unidentified suicide. As the bottom of the casket fell away, the slurry started to eat the girl's clothes and flesh. I closed the lid so that I didn't need to watch. "I'm not going to reconcile, Trinity."

But it would always ask. That was the funny thing about the AI and the Church. They were both relentless.

Trinity said, "Saria van Esters and Petunia Alverez were coworkers on a scientific endeavor."

The wording struck me as strange. "What endeavor?"

"Unknown."

"What do you mean, 'unknown?'" We were back to Trinity's missing information and the deeper we delved, the more worried I got. Trinity was a complex and highly efficient AI. It was designed for comprehensive management of Nicodemia's social structures. If it was missing this much information, what were the downstream effects?

"The project has been archived."

Archived. That meant it existed in paper format somewhere, but the digital records had been purged. Again, this was not the standard procedure. The paper versions were nothing more than a temporary backup in case of digital file failure. Trinity wouldn't willingly purge that information.

"Who ordered the archive of that information?" I asked.

"Unknown."

Dammit.

The casket was halfway submerged and dissolving quickly. The chemical smell washed over me in a wave of ammonia. I stepped back from the edge.

"Who has access to change your memory files?" I asked.

"You do, Jude Demarco."

There were other excommunicated people. If I had access, then so did they. I didn't know who any of them were. All I knew was that they'd experienced similar trauma, making a hard selfless decision to save the city. They were also the hardest people in the city to find, since they left no digital trail and people tended to let them sink into the shadows.

"Who else?" I asked, hoping there would be some other lead. "There has to be someone high enough up in government. The Church? Jesus himself? Come on, Trinity, there has to be someone with the power to make this happen who would actually dare to make these changes. Someone's covering up for Lacie van Esters' murderer."

After a brief pause, Trinity said, "There is no record of Lacie van Esters."

Slurry finally swallowed Lacie's casket. The air filled with a vile mixture of chemical and flesh, forcing me back toward the closed door.

"Open the door, Trinity," I said.

The wall opened, and I stumbled out into Priest Cano's arms. I coughed and heaved as the door closed behind me. I'd breathed more of that vile substance than I'd thought. My knees were weak.

The ceremonial space was dark and cold, empty of the mourners who had recently occupied it. I stepped outside, letting the door close behind me.

"Did he get away?" I rasped.

"They all fled," said Cano. "Jude, I'm sorry—"

"It's fine," I said.

Trinity would process the corpse of Lacie van Esters, recording her as an unknown suicide. Even as her soul went to the great beyond, the molecules of her body would be processed into feed for the fish. The fish would feed the plants. The plants would feed the people. It was all part of the grand cycle.

But there would never be a record of Lacie van Esters, save for the memories of her family.

Chapter 22

"I WENT to a funeral and spoke with a god," I said to the Jesuit in a small side chapel of the Cathedral of Saint Francis of Assisi. "How was your morning?"

Lorentz didn't even twitch. She knelt before the subdued altar wearing a black suit and priest's collar, breathing in the heavy incense.

I sat on the pew behind her without genuflecting and let out a slow breath. "I think Saria van Esters is in danger."

Eventually, Lorentz finished her prayer, stood up, and exited the chapel. I followed like a well-trained dog. We reached a wide hall decorated with statues of Saint Francis himself. An army of forest creatures trailed behind him like obedient little servants.

Frustrated, I growled, "A woman is in danger." My raised voice echoed. A trio of young men in white collars glanced up from their hushed discussion.

"Where have I heard that name?" whispered Lorentz, almost to herself.

"Did you see a woman in fancy blacks around here after the funeral?"

"I was in prayer."

"Did God see her?"

"I didn't ask." She peered up at me. "You don't know where she is?"

"Was hoping she came back here."

"I suppose you'll tell me you need money to find her."

"Money makes the clock tick, Sister." I turned to leave, but she grabbed my arm.

She said, "I feel like there are pieces missing from your story."

"There's nothing *but* missing pieces." I extracted my arm, but I didn't leave. "Did you learn anything?"

"In prayer?"

"Sometimes prayers are answered." Rarely.

"Yeah," she said. "Sometimes they are." She took my hand in both of hers and pressed a roll of dimes into my palm. Her fingers lingered there for a moment too long. "Seems you have a friend here who vouched for you."

"Priest Cano and I go way back," I said.

"She said the same thing, as a matter of fact." Lorentz glanced at the three young priests. "I guess you're officially an employee now?"

"I like to think of myself as an independent contractor."

"Fair enough."

"Do I work for you directly? Or is this from the bishop?"

"Bishop Barton is still too busy for this kind of action."

"Doing what?"

"Bishop stuff." She frowned. "I don't know. He's not an easy guy to track down, but I finally got a wire to him through Cano and he authorized your payments."

"Can he get us into the Gravity Lounge?"

"Maybe."

"In time for Destiny's funeral?"

"We'll see."

"The morass of bureaucracy is the one reason I don't fear the Church." I cracked the roll open and dropped a few coins into the collection plate. I led Lorentz beyond the drab offices toward the cathedral's back exit.

We were dumped out near the edge of the warehouse district. I wanted to wander back into the seedier parts of the city to find Retch, but I also didn't want to do that at all.

"Tell me more about Van Esters," said Lorentz as we strolled upspiral. "What's her connection to this?"

"The dead girl was the one in the photo. Her mother might have worked with Destiny's mother a long time ago."

"Pretty big coincidence."

"You know what they say, right?"

"There are no coincidences?"

"No good ones." I dropped my voice, even though there was nobody close. "We were attacked by someone with a silhouette."

"Same guy as before?"

"It was dark," I said.

"You think he followed you down here?"

I wasn't sure. I had disrupted the funeral before I could be sure who he was targeting. I settled for, "Takes a sick man to attend the funeral of his victim."

"You're really earning your dimes, Demarco," Lorentz deadpanned. She led us up through a narrow alley full of food vendors. The aroma of fried spices made my mouth water. "Do you think the connection between Van Esters and Alverez means anything?"

"We might never know." I peeled a dime from my freshly acquired roll and bought a couple of bowls of noodles, handing one to Lorentz. “Trinity’s records were doctored.”

“That’s not possible.”

“Tell that to your machine god.”

“I’ll pass.”

“Lacie van Esters was treated as a suicide.” I watched as the implications sunk in. Lorentz’s eyes brightened with understanding. “The church knows more than the official records.”

“I can ask around,” said Lorentz.

We stopped at the corner and slurped noodles. After inhaling the delicious carbohydrates, I looked up and saw a trio of priests. “Those the guys we saw in their cathedral?”

Lorentz stole a glance. “Maybe.” Lot of help she was.

“What do you know about the science colonies?” I asked.

Lorentz’s eyes really lit up at that. “Everything,” she said. “And not enough.”

“What kind of work are they doing there?”

“Mining and research,” Lorentz said. “They found new kinds of minerals in the rock there. The mining operations help supply the city, but the science colonies will eventually make the Cabrini habitable for permanent colonization.”

“I thought the air was poisonous.”

Lorentz pursed her lips. “Not exactly. Well, a little. It’s a slow poison. It’s not like the atmosphere is fifty percent arsenic. Cabrini’s the closest we have to a habitable planet. It’s right around as poisonous as those cigarettes you’re always smoking.”

That reminded me—

“Not right now, Jude,” Lorentz said.

I abandoned a cigarette halfway to my lips and placed it back in the pack. “What happens to Nicodemia if people start moving to the colonies in large numbers?”

She blinked. The three priests walked casually past, pretending to not even notice us on the corner. They sat at a cafe a short distance away and ordered drinks.

"They're not local," I whispered. The shortest was taller than most residents of the Heavies. There was a tension in the set of his shoulders and he kept glancing at us.

"Maybe Priest Cano friend wants to keep an eye on you."

I stared up at the hazy sky. "Humanity will fill any space given it."

"Cabrini's not the first candidate for colonization. Magdalene Moon has a solid profile, but even that's years away. Same toxic atmosphere." Her eyes narrowed. "That's where I recognize the name. Saria van Esters is a Cabrini colony scientist. You think someone's got it in for the colony scientists?"

"I would very much like to speak with Van Esters about that." I tossed my bowl into a recycler. "She just left her daughter's funeral an hour ago. Where would a woman like that go to mourn? Home? Church? Is there a bar where scientists let loose?"

Lorentz cast her gaze upward toward through the hazy light above. Here, farther out from the inner spiral, the simulation of sky wasn't as convincing. A person could focus on the underside of the city above, and the gray structure of the roof stood out against the reddish fiberbrick of the local buildings.

"If she's a scientist, she'll be at work."

"She just buried her kid."

"Work."

"How can she work? If she's living on the colony, wouldn't she need to secure transit back?"

"People bury themselves in work to avoid grief," said Lorentz quietly. "It's human nature."

"Has it ever worked?"

"Maybe."

"Lacie was killed two days after Destiny. How was her mother able to get here already?"

"I thought I hired you to find answers, not more questions."

I said, "Investigating is more about asking the right questions."

"Same thing for being a Jesuit."

"Where would she work this afternoon, assuming she wasn't already booked to leave the city?"

Lorentz pinched the bridge of her nose and leaned back against the fiberbrick wall. After several deep breaths, she said, "Do you know why Heavy Nicodemia exists?"

"Because sinners need a place to live that isn't overly pleasant."

"There's a spot about three-quarters of the way down. Just above the first of the fisheries. Near the Yards where the simulated gravity matches the gravity Cabrini." She opened her eyes. "That's where she'll be."

"You're sure?"

"As sure as I can be."

"I need you to back off Retch," I said.

She blinked, taken by surprise by my request. "I've shown him nothing but kindness."

"Some people don't know what kindness looks like."

"He's pretty smart."

"He's also dealt a lot with people who look a whole lot like you."

An icy edge laced her quiet voice. "All the more reason to show him kindness."

"All the more reason to back off," I said through my teeth. She was finally paying me, so I didn't bother telling her to drop her Catholicism into the slurry pits. "If you want me getting to the bottom of all this, you'll stay away from him."

"I'm not an evangelist."

"Sure."

"I can help him," she said.

"Help isn't all it's cracked up to be." I knew it was too much, but I couldn't take my words back. Lorentz didn't need the kind of bitterness I felt for the Catholic Church and its version of the truth. She didn't deserve that. "He's my best resource."

"Isn't that what he is to you?"

"Absolutely." I glanced at the trio of priests drinking their frothy beverages. "Where is this lab?"

"I'll show you," said Lorentz.

When we finally left, one of the three priests signaled to his fellows. As one, they stood and followed. We wove our way downspiral through the twisted and tiny bends of the outer districts. Rows of warehouses gave way to seedy residential areas choked with stunted vegetables and defunct maintenance equipment. Every turn we made, the priests followed. Every time we doubled back, they acted innocent and lost.

Amateurs.

But two could play the game.

"Change of plans," I said to Lorentz as we circled the research district where the planetary lab was located. "I think I need to have a little chat with these gentlemen."

When I'd finished telling her my plan, she flashed me a smile so wicked I wasn't sure it belonged on the face of a holy woman.

Chapter 23

NOBODY EVER LOOKS for a man in the dark.

In a city of light—even in the dimly lit gloom of Heavy Nicodemia—the shadows were an empty void. Light lingered on people through the alleys of the public districts, and the gutters of the city below. It clung to the priests as they skulked through blind intersections and narrow streets. It illuminated Lorentz as she crept quietly into a neighborhood known as the Maze.

No light touched me.

"We can't keep this up," gasped the short priest. He had a scraggly black beard and hair like a tangle of wires. He was so close I could have reached out and touched him, but the shadows made me invisible.

"Quiet, brother," snapped the tallest of the three priests. His black shirt was loose-fitting over the slight paunch of his belly. He peered at the light ahead, where Lorentz still moved through the alley.

"We should split up," said the third priest. "We could

follow without being so obvious." Apparently, he was the clever one. He had a narrow, shaved skull and art deco cheekbones.

I wondered if any of these three were the priest I'd seen in the Gravity Garden. I hadn't gotten a look at that man's face, but something didn't settle right about their bearing. The tallest was close, but even he wasn't filled out enough. It wasn't them. Could they have been sent by Cano? She was usually more straightforward in her meddling attempts.

With a nod, two priests split. The shortest headed straight into the Maze after Lorentz. The one with the shaved skull took a side passage that I was almost positive wouldn't take him where he wanted to go. The Maze was a collection of old tenements, each only a few stories tall and encroaching on each other's courtyards in a seemingly haphazard fashion. There were no proper streets through the Maze, but the postage stamp yards opened at odd angles, which allowed passage to those who knew their way.

Once his companions were out of sight, the tallest priest leaned forward with his palms on his knees and gulped oxygen.

I placed a cigarette on my lips and flicked my lighter, letting the flame illuminate my grim face. "Some folks aren't built for the Heavies."

He hyperventilated, stumbled backward, and struck his temple on the corner of a fiberstone wall.

When the cigarette was properly lit, I blew out a stream of smoke. "What good deeds have I done to attract the attention of three upstanding priests?"

He looked up at me, the light of the abandoned storefront casting a pearly sheen across the trickle of blood cutting a path down his pale flesh. His thin lips quavered.

"Thou shalt not lie, Father. Who are you working for?"

His back pressed against the wall. His eyes darted to the paths his fellows had taken.

I said, "Is this official Church business? Or are you three running some kind of criminal side gig?"

"It's not criminal," he spat.

"Official, then. What's the Church following me for? Or is it my friend you're after?"

This time, the priest kept his lips pressed in a straight line.

"The Jesuit's too smart for her own good, isn't she?" I said. "She's a threat to folks like you."

"I—I don't know what you mean."

"Maybe I'm misreading the situation." Another long stream of smoke.

He straightened, making an obvious effort to feign confidence. His black button-down shirt was rumpled and untucked. His priest's collar sat askew. "We know who you are," he said.

"That so?" I drew a long pull on the cigarette and let the smoke curl around my face.

"You're trouble, Demarco."

I folded my arms and leaned against the wall. He had a clear shot at an exit, but he'd have to turn his back on me to take it. "I've been trouble since long before I stepped into the dark."

He bolted down the alley, running smack into the shortest priest, who had already doubled back after a quickly failed foray into the Maze.

I stubbed my cigarette out and retreated back into the shadows. "I'll see you gentlemen later."

They stared at me, as if unsure whether or not they should follow. After a minute, their bald friend joined them and together they left the way they'd come.

This was when the fun part began.

Lorentz knew to follow them first. She'd already climbed to the rooftops and perched somewhere with a view. Now, her job was to stay with them for as many blocks as she could. I strolled along a parallel street, staying in the deepest shadows. Sunset hadn't officially happened yet, but the darkness lapped like a rising tide. There were always plenty of places to hide.

When Lorentz signaled with a low whistle, I darted along a cross street and found the three men. They were making their way upspiral.

At first, they proceeded inward toward the nearest trolley system. Trolleys would make life harder for me. It wasn't easy to keep up with one on foot, and hopping on would be too obvious, even for my oblivious quarry.

Luckily, they didn't take the trolley. They entered a business district, where the day workers swarmed like ants on a dead fish. The shadows abandoned me, but the crowds swallowed me whole. I caught sight of Lorentz on another rooftop and signaled with a wave of my hat. She took over the trail, and I dropped back, angling to the outer end of the district where I'd be able to follow from a greater distance.

Lorentz followed them into a residential district—a densely packed cluster of towering apartments that made the Maze look like the dingy backwater it was. She couldn't follow on the roofs, so she signaled for me to pick up the tail.

And I lost them. The straight streets and inadequate shadows forced me to leave a long lead. They rounded a corner and were gone.

"You really think they're up to something?" Lorentz asked when she caught up to me.

"I've never met a priest who wasn't up to something."

"Well," Lorentz sighed. "I guess we'd better try to find them."

We split up again. The pattern of their movement, while

slightly erratic, hinted at a nearby destination. Lorentz asked the meandering workers in the crowd while I checked the nearby shops.

I was just about to give in when a woman running a small tamale stand said, "The tall priests went back that way." She indicated a narrow alley with her pepper-stained thumb. "They always go there."

I thanked her and dropped a few dimes as a tip. I'd run out pretty fast if I kept spending, but a good tip was worth the coins. I thought of the debt owed and of Leo Shaw tracking me down in the Hallows. It'd be a shame if I spent my payday too fast for him to collect. A damn shame.

Instead of barreling down the alley at full speed, I crept as light on my toes as I could manage. The alley was an access to a maintenance port. It didn't go anywhere in particular, but it separated two towering apartment complexes and opened up into a series of air processing units. The units hummed, their fans sucking in city air and spitting out something close to clean.

The back of the alley was all shadow. They couldn't have picked a better place for me to sneak up on them. Dim lights illuminated their movements through the narrow maze, but lights never touched me.

A silhouette moved at the edge of the tallest priests' column of light.

I had found him, but what could I do about it? The priests weren't much of a threat, but four against one wasn't a set of odds I was prepared to take. I found a place down in the shadows between air processing units and I listened.

"He's with her now," said the tallest priest between gasps for air. "I'm certain he was headed to the Cabrini Colony Lab."

"You were supposed to stop him," the shadow said.

The priest with the shaved head said, "You should have followed her from the funeral."

The shadow took a single step forward into the light, and the trio of priests stepped back. A shining blade appeared in the shadow's left hand.

"All we can tell you is that Demarco thinks she is in her lab," said the tallest priest. "You can do what you want with that information."

"People think she's scheduled to leave tomorrow morning," said the bald priest.

"Leave for where?" asked the shadow. "There hasn't been a shuttle to or from Cabrini in ages."

The tall one said, "That's absurd."

"My sources are solid," said the shadow. "I'll pay her a visit in the lab if you think she's there. If she's not—"

"She needs to be stopped," said the tall priest.

"Of course," said the shadow.

"No," said the clever priest. "You don't understand. This is critical."

"I get it," hissed the shadow.

"I don't think you do," said the tall priest. His voice was low. Dangerous. "We're not going to get this opportunity again."

"She has another daughter," said the shadow.

The three priests stared in uncomfortable silence for a long time. Finally, the bald one said, "We don't approve of your methods."

"I'd be disappointed if you did," said the shadow.

That confirmed it. He had lured Saria van Esters into the open by killing the daughter. They needed to be stopped. Three priests and one shadow-clad asshole? My fists cracked in anticipation of a fight. I could end this right now.

A flash of yellow plastic danced in the shadow's hand. A gun. "I'll have Demarco's number if he shows up again."

I froze. A gun didn't exactly change my odds of going up against four guys, but it made the split a whole lot more obvious.

The short priest sputtered, "You know we don't like guns."

"You can keep not liking them," said the shadow. "But I don't like getting my ass handed to me by an overzealous detective. He ruined my chances at the funeral. Put the whole place on high alert."

The tallest priest said, "I don't like any of this."

The shadow stowed the gun. "Just think of it as the greater good."

"Be sure that gun of yours isn't the thing that tips the balance of your Karma."

Plasti-ceramic bullets killed well enough but turned to powder when they hit anything really hard. Trinity suffered their existence because removing them was expensive and the risk posed to the station as a whole was minimal. Unfortunately, the risk posed to me was still significant.

I was lost in this thought when I realized that the four men in the alley had gone very quiet. They peered into the darkness where I still stood. My breath came out slow and stiff, aching in my chest as I struggled to stay completely quiet.

"I don't know," the shadow finally said. "Demarco could be anywhere."

"He went straight to the lab," said the tall priest. "He knows where Van Esters is, and I think he knows we're looking for her."

With their meeting finished, the three priests shuffled down the alley, bringing their cone of light with them. Trinity illuminated the way of the righteous traveler, they said. These three men had plenty of light to go around.

Which left me alone with the man in black. Once he left, I could work my way back to Lorentz and to the lab—or I could try to take him out now. I strained my ears to locate the man and heard nothing but the low hum of the air handlers. The only light left was the ambient glow from the low sunset striking the buildings high above.

"I know you're there," the shadow finally said. "Step out here, and we can come to an agreement."

Yellow plastic flashed in the shadows, and I knew what kind of agreement he'd have for me.

But he couldn't possibly know I was there. If he did, he wouldn't be speaking to the darkness. He'd been seeking me out. Hunting me.

Maybe he was.

Slowly, carefully, I crept back through the alley. If I found enough light, he wouldn't be able to follow—or at least he wouldn't be able to strike without consequences. His shadow suit only hid him when he was in sufficient darkness.

My foot scuffed against a raised cobblestone, and I silently swore.

The hunter shifted behind me in the alley. "I hear you, Demarco. You're on the wrong side in this, you know. Everything we're doing is to save this city. An upstanding excommunicated detective like yourself ought to respect that."

I rounded the last of the air processing units and saw the light of the street up ahead. It wasn't as bright as when I'd entered. Night had fallen and the only lights were the personal auras around the few pedestrians. Still, witnesses and light might be enough to avoid the shadow's attack.

Feeling the light on my face, I straightened and walked into the middle of the street. The shadow would see me as soon as he stepped out, but he would be revealed. I didn't think he would dare bring his silhouette into broad daylight.

He had another idea.

Harold Mance, the gardener, stepped from the shadows with a silhouette wadded up in one hand and a gun in the other.

Chapter 24

THERE ISN'T REALLY a commandment that says to avoid violence. Sure, there's *thou shalt not kill*, but that's a narrow subset of the overall preponderance of violence. Killing is the end result of an excess of violence, and if I'm honest, I'm not convinced killing is always something that should be avoided.

Mance was looking like a pretty good candidate.

I raised my hands, showing him my palms. "You're going to let me go."

He raised an eyebrow. "That so?"

"You could have killed me this morning at the funeral."

"I thought I had."

"No, you thought you got me out of the way. It would have been Trinity doing the killing." I stepped back. A few more steps and I'd have a straight shot for the cover of an old merchant's cart. "I don't think you'll kill me in full view."

"One more step and you'll find out."

I stopped, still too far to escape without a pair of shiny bullets in my back. "What's your business with Van Esters?"

"That only concerns her, me, and the man upstairs."

"Really? Because I'm feeling pretty concerned about it too."

"She's dangerous."

My eyes darted to the man's gun. "It's all relative."

"I don't want to kill you," he said.

"No, what you want is a good look at me."

"I've seen you plenty." He fingered the trigger.

I stepped forward. He was more than an arm's length away, but close enough that I could smell the aura of ammonia surrounding him. "Tell me why you're after Saria van Esters."

"Dead men don't need to know things like that."

"I'm curious."

"Curious enough to get yourself killed?"

"Seems to me I'm getting killed anyway." I eased forward half a step more and breathed through flared nostrils. "It'd be mighty Christian of you to give a man his last wish."

"Who says I'm Christian?"

"You keep some mighty interesting company if you aren't." Our eyes locked, and I saw deep into his cold soul. This man was a calculating monster. He wasn't here for idealistic reasons. The realization closed a steel clamp on my spine. "What would your priest friends think?"

His eyes flicked to something beyond my left shoulder. It was a shattered moment of distraction. A brief crack in an otherwise perfect façade. An opportunity.

I struck the gun with the heel of my right hand. It fired as it snapped free of Mance's grip. My ears rang. The gun clattered to the pavement. Mance drew his knife.

When I turned to run, I saw the three priests. The tall one had a look of horror on his face. The brick near his head had shattered from the shot. I bowled through the three. One of them grasped my sleeve as I passed, but I spun and slammed a fist into his jaw. Something cracked when I struck, and a ragged stab of pain ran the length of my forearm.

The priest collapsed, and I ran.

They were after me. A glance back showed only the flickering shadows of the Heavy night, but I could hear the scuff of footsteps. The panting of breath. The dark had always been my safety, but I sprinted for light as fast as I could.

The footsteps stopped.

It wasn't light enough, but there were people around. Witnesses. Clusters of residents moved between the busy restaurants and hurried through the packed streets. The smoky aroma of seared meat wafted over the crowd. I fixed my hat on my head and pushed forward, skirting the crowds.

A glance back gave me nothing again, and I could no longer hear my pursuer under the din of the crowded street. He would strike as soon as he had the chance, and his chance would come as soon as he had a clear shot. The shadows might keep him safe, even if there were witnesses.

I wondered where Lorentz was. She was nearby, but where? I pushed across the wide street, weaving between vendor stalls and a group of shabbily dressed dock workers. Distance. That's what I needed. Distance and obstacles. I glanced back again and thought I saw Mance in the crowd. It could have been my imagination. It could have been my death coming for me.

Lungs heaving, muscles burning, I crashed through the lingering crowds toward the trolley tracks.

In my imagination, it struck me down a thousand times. It sprayed my blood across a group of teens. It shattered my bones as I reached the trolley. It made me stumble onto the tracks.

But it never came.

The trolley rumbled into place and stopped in front of

me. If I took it, I'd be leaving Lorentz behind, but something told me I needed to reach Van Esters as quickly as possible. Slowly, carefully, I moved into place next to the trolley. I hooked an arm on the bar, placed a foot on the step, and waited.

The trolley accelerated downward around the spiral. Cool wind pulled at my coat and the night's mist kissed my face. The city's cool presence wrapped itself around me.

I didn't know where Mance was, but I knew where he was going. I hopped off near Angel's Diner and took a moment to straighten my coat. I felt like a burning recycler full of trash, and my wrist still ached. I poked my head in the door. Runt stood at attention, the corded muscles at the base of his neck working overtime.

"What?" said Angel, as irritated as her dog.

The harsh reception took me off guard. "Anders around?"

She gestured to the corner table where Anders sat with a cup of coffee and a half-eaten slice of pie.

"It's time," I said to Anders.

He fumbled with his police hat, touched his stunstick to make sure it was in the right place, and hurried for the door. "You look awful," he said as he fell in step next to me.

"Lacie van Esters's mother is a scientist at the Cabrini Colony Lab," I said as we hurried through the dark streets. The streetlights illuminated as Anders approached, then died as he left. It lit our way but didn't show us if anyone was lurking further ahead in the darkness.

Anders said, "I just came here to tell you that the connection to the world turtle isn't suspected to have anything to do with her murder. They're just a protest group that likes to harass the Church."

"That sounds to me like the kind of thing that might get someone killed."

"It's the Church."

"Exactly." I rounded a bend and found a long street that would take us over to the lab. I debated telling Anders about data getting rewritten in Trinity's memory but decided against it. I didn't know what kind of disruption that information would cause if it got out. "The killer's name is Harold Mance."

"Doesn't ring a bell."

"He works for the Gravity Lounge."

"That's a long walk north of here."

"Makes me wonder why he's so far from home."

We rounded the corner and the entrance to the lab glowed before us in the murky night.

"This Mance guy is dangerous," I said to Anders.

Anders cast me a nervous glance. "Should I call in support?"

"I don't want him spooked."

"I'm spooked."

"We don't have eyes on Mance," I said. "If you called them in right now, would they come?"

"They're busy."

"We're all busy, aren't we?"

I pushed the door open. The sparse lobby was fully lit, and a man at the desk looked up at us in surprise. Wire-frame glasses sat atop his weasel nose, and the nametag pinned to his crisp white shirt claimed his name was Evan.

"Can I help you?" asked Evan in a tone that clearly implied that he could not.

"You can help in one of two ways," I said. "Would you rather show us around now or help clean up after a murder later?"

Chapter 25

THE CABRINI COLONY LAB was a sprawling cancer of a structure, taking up significant space in a district choked for real estate. It had seven gangly arms that stretched into the nearby residential zones and a large central hub housing office space and chemical laboratories. Rumor had it that the same design was mimicked in both the planetary and lunar colonies. While those arms were designed to keep the most dangerous experiments far from the central hub, here in Heavy Nicodemia the design only served to place those same dangerous experiments adjacent to the encroaching housing.

Anders and I entered the dark wing that Saria van Esters would most likely inhabit. She was a botanist, and the third wing was a greenhouse under a sharply angled roof. This was her home away from home when she wasn't visiting the planetary colony. Or rather, the lunar colony.

Evan said, "Everyone works on Madeline Moon these days."

"But this is a planetary lab," I said. "Shouldn't people here work planetside?"

He shook his head. “Maybe they’d like to, but the big focus is on getting the moon habitable. Scientists chase funding the way dachshunds chase rats.”

“I bet they love that comparison,” I said.

“They don’t care what they get compared to, as long as they get to keep the rat.”

Anders scrawled something in his notebook. “How long has Van Esters been here today?”

“Oh, I have no idea,” said the receptionist. “She comes and goes as she pleases. She’s on the list.”

“The list?” Anders asked.

“Some scientists are working on things so important that they no longer need to deal with petty inconveniences like nodding a friendly hello to a receptionist. They get separate entrances and a free pass to the lunar shuttles.”

“But not the shuttles to the planet,” I said.

“Depends on which rat they catch.”

“Do many shuttles leave from around here?” I said.

“None. It’s safer to dock as far up the chain as possible due to angular velocities.” Evan cast his eyes upward. “Even then, it’s extremely rare.”

We passed several dark greenhouses. The air smelled of ammonia and the green of damp earth. It settled something in my chest that had been uneasy for a long time. A deep-down instinct binding me to a planet I’d never visited. Something about the growing things of Earth did that to us. That’s why people considered the verdant Hallows to be paradise, more so even than the lower gravity and extravagant fashions.

I said, “Do these—”

“I’m not supposed to talk about the science,” interrupted the receptionist.

Ahead, a door opened and the dazzling light of its greenhouse spilled into the hall. Saria van Esters stepped out, carrying a tray of seedlings. A blue apron covered her black funeral dress. She didn't notice us—didn't seem to notice anything—before turning around and entering the blazing light of the next greenhouse. A knot in my chest unclenched. At least for now, the woman was safe.

"Where are these lights controlled?" I asked.

The receptionist looked at me with a curious expression on his face. "I'll show you," he finally said. He led me away while Anders took up a post near where Van Esters worked.

Later, after a quick tour of the wing, I stepped into the blazing bright of Saria van Esters' greenhouse. The air smelled of lemon and ash, and the bright light had a slight orange tint. Saria van Esters worked at a bench on the far side, sticking clippings into wet sand in tidy rows. When she looked up at me, I saw that she wore the same makeup from the morning's funeral, now smeared from the day's grief.

"Haven't you done enough damage today?" she said without looking up.

"Never."

She stuck another twig into the damp sand. "Mind what you touch. We don't need to contend with contamination."

My hand froze a hair's breadth from the sand.

"Terraforming is tricky business, you know." Van Esters spoke as if to herself. "First you establish the microbiome, then plants and fungi, then animals. Every stage requires genetic modification on every level. Intricate stuff. All that happens before regular humans can visit without full protection. It takes hundreds of years."

"It's *been* hundreds of years," I said.

"Some say we could use a couple hundred more."

"I'm sorry about your daughter," I said.

She shot a look at me that was part glare, part grief.

"I don't think she was a suicide," I said.

"Tell that to the Church."

"Priest Cano told me she didn't think it was suicide either."

"Then why the non-sanctified recycler? You think our pallbearers wanted to stretch their legs?" She threw her cutting down, and it landed like a wet rag on the sand. Tears shone in her red eyes. "Lacie was my baby girl, and now she's gone, and I wasted—I wasted all these years."

"We all get caught up in what we think is important."

She fixed me with a stare so cold my fingers got frostbite.

I moved through the narrow aisles between greenhouse plots in various stages of growth. They were making vines of some sort, and many of them were thriving. "If this Cabrini colony work is so important, why is all the funding going to Madeline Moon?"

"I know who you are, Mr. Demarco, and I know who you work for. You won't get anything from me."

"You're in danger."

Saria quietly peeled the protective gloves from her hands and deposited them in a waste bin. "There was a time when I would spend every waking hour in this greenhouse. Have you ever worked on something that wouldn't be finished until your daughter's granddaughter was alive to finish it?"

"Did Lacie disappoint you by refusing to follow the family business?"

Her chin quivered. "A career in the service industry. Can you believe that? She even worked in the Hallows for a while."

"Some consider that respectable."

"I suppose they would." Her shoulders slumped, and she looked up at me with pleading eyes. "What are you waiting for? You might as well ask me the question."

"What question?"

The lights flickered. Saria looked up at them curiously. "It's not time for these lights to go into their night cycle."

"Anders," I said.

"I saw it," he replied from the hall.

The lights died, casting the greenhouse into a bluish night. My eyes adjusted quickly, and I crouched low to make the most of what little cover the greenhouse benches offered.

"What is happening?" Saria said.

Motioning for her to follow, I moved toward the door where the hallway light still glowed a pleasant white near Anders. As he moved away down the hall, the lights followed.

We didn't even make it halfway before the man in the black suit pushed through the side door connecting this greenhouse to the next. My eyes registered the black figure moving into the room and the shape of it as an arm raised to point at us.

The lights flared to life. Even though I was expecting it, the light seared the back of my skull. I lunged from memory, toppling benches and scattering sand and plants. My hands closed on the attacker's arm, and I twisted as hard as I could until I felt the shuddering snap of tendon and bone. The attacker screamed. His gun clattered to the floor.

I wrenched his arm until he was flat on his chest and pulled the hood from his face.

Harold Mance looked up at me with dark hatred.

I finally had him, alone and unarmed. This was the man who had killed Destiny Alverez. He had murdered Lacie Van Esters and was about to kill her mother.

My meaty fist closed around his windpipe.

"Demarco!" snapped Anders from the door.

I slammed Mance to the floor again. "I'm fine," I gasped. I wasn't fine.

Anders crossed to Van Esters who was weeping and trying

her best to salvage the ruined benches. She might as well have tried to push back the void of space. He pulled her up and hugged her. It must have been the right thing to do, because she gathered herself and followed him. He shot me a look as he passed, which I took as a warning.

Without a word, I hefted Mance and dragged him along to follow. Once he was cuffed to a chair in the breakroom, Anders settled Van Esters onto the sofa. Anders pulled me to the side.

"You were right," said Anders. "He knew exactly how the greenhouse light controls worked. All I had to do was come in after him and flip the lights back on."

"He's the gardener for the Gravity Lounge up in the Hallows. I figured it would be similar controls to his own greenhouse."

"Why's he doing this, though?"

I kicked Mance in the shin. "Now's a decent time to talk, Mance."

He stared hatred at me with hooded eyes.

"Why did you kill Destiny?" I grabbed hold of his broken arm.

All he did was laugh. The ragged, raw sound of it made me sick to my stomach.

"Demarco," Anders said, placing a hand on my shoulder.

"Fine." I let go of Mance and noticed Saria staring at me with a mix of disgust and horror.

Saria rose from the sofa, brushed herself off, and left the room.

"You should go after her," I said to Anders.

He shook his head. "I'm not leaving you alone with Mance."

Smart. I could barely contain the hate I felt for Mance at that moment. "He's a danger as long as he's alive."

"You're not a killer, Demarco," said Anders.

He was wrong. The vision of my parents' deaths flashed before my eyes. I'd killed every single person on that ship. How could I hesitate to kill a man like Harold Mance? "I could be."

Again, that ragged laugh, more mocking this time. Mance turned his blade of a nose up at me. "If you want answers, you're going to have to let me walk."

"Who were those priests you were with today?" I asked.

He barked a laugh. "That's the wrong question, Demarco. You think I killed those girls? I didn't kill anyone. I just *find* them."

The hairs on my arm bristled. "What are you talking about?"

"Let me go and I'll tell you."

Anders said, "The blue's on the way, Mance. No need to try to get away. We have you on attempted murder."

"Really?"

We didn't. At best, he could be held on trespassing charges. His gun might be legit, but having it wasn't going to do us much good. If Mance knew someone high up in the hierarchy, he'd be out within the year.

I slammed a fist down on the table. "Tell me who those priests were!" I shouted. "Who do you work for?"

Mance's laugh was maniacal and high.

"Tell us," I roared, stepping toward him.

Anders cut me off. "Back down, Demarco." He put two hands on my chest.

The policeman was taller than most Heavies, but I loomed over him by a head and a half. I could push past him and wreck Destiny's killer without hardly breaking a sweat. I fixed my gaze on the killer, boring a hole through his skull with all the hate I could muster.

But it didn't help. I couldn't raise a hand against a decent guy like Officer Anders, no matter how much I wanted to.

"You're a good man," Anders said. "You'll regret it if you hurt this man while he's in custody."

"I'll regret it if I don't," I growled. Electric adrenaline coursed through my veins. The image of Destiny's corpse flashed before me every time I blinked.

"Go check on Van Esters," Anders said.

Seething, I obeyed. The hallway lights were still a pleasant warm tone. The greenhouse door was wide open.

And Saria wasn't there. On the floor, I saw the scattered sand hadn't been touched since we left. In the center of it all sat a yellow chunk of plastic in the shape of a gun. I picked it up, hoping it would be the evidence we needed to convict Mance of something serious.

It wasn't. The plastic wasn't the gun Mance had carried in the alley. It wasn't a gun at all, only a clumsy facsimile that wouldn't have fooled anyone in the full light of day.

This wasn't a murder weapon.

And Saria wasn't here.

The sharp snap of gunshots broke the quiet night.

Chapter 26

ANDERS SAT against the far wall under the flickering light. Blood painted a grim figure on the stark white wall above him.

"Anders." I took hold of his arm.

His unfocused eyes searched the ceiling. "Go," he rasped.

"Not a chance." The lights stuttered. My eyes burned.

His wound was in the meaty part of his left armpit. I turned to look for a med kit but froze when I saw Mance's body.

Harold Mance was dead. A ceramic bullet had shattered against his skull and removed the better part of the upper half of his brain box. If there had been any coherent answers in there, we sure as hell weren't going to get them.

The nearby med station was easily available and well stocked, as it should be in any lab. I used a pair of shears to cut away Anders' uniform to expose the wound. It looked painful. The bullet had chipped bone and shredded muscle. Without anything in the way of warning, I slapped a med patch on the wound. He choked back a scream.

"Who shot you?" I asked.

He tried to stand up, but it didn't take. His skin was pale and cold. "Tall. Brown hair."

I thought of the priests. "Alone?"

"The lights," Anders said, waving me out the door. He shook his head as if to clear it. The painkillers from the patch would knock him out soon. "Find her."

Mance was dead, but the manner of his death asked more questions than it answered. My mouth tasted of bitter bile as I rushed back out into the hall. Saria van Esters was still in danger. That's all that mattered. We'd sort everything else out later.

Where would she have gone? Had she heard the gunshots and fled? I looked both ways down the long, dimly lit hallway. All of the doors to the greenhouses were closed, so I started toward the far end and checked them one by one. My heart pounded. If the killer was still here, he could hide in the dark greenhouses, but the safety lights in the hallway were Trinity-controlled. They would reveal his presence. I had to put that out of my mind. The only important thing was to find Van Esters, and then… what?

It didn't matter. I checked the next greenhouse. Dark. Empty. It smelled of the thick rot of humidity with a sour undertone. The next was empty, dry, and warm. It was ready for some botanist's new experiment. They were all dark, all the way down the row.

Where would Van Esters have gone?

A door at the end of the hall sat ajar. I cast a glance back behind me to verify that the hall was still dark. If the killer moved closer, the lights would betray his presence.

A soft light glowed from the cracked door, and the sound of a pen on paper scratched like a rat in the ducts.

"Saria," I whispered.

The pen stopped. "Yes?"

I pushed open the door. The room looked like a janitor's closet except for a single desk shoved into one corner and a cot along one wall. Among the mop buckets and chemical cleaners, Saria van Esters sat with a notebook and a pen. She glanced at me, cleared her throat, and resumed writing.

"We need to leave," I whispered. "Mance is dead, but you're still in danger."

"*I'm* in danger? You're in danger."

I grabbed her shoulders and didn't let go until she looked me in the eyes. There was a touch of madness in the way her eyes danced. Tears streaked her cheeks. "Saria," I said, "you'll be safe if we get you out of here."

"What about my daughter?"

She's dead, I wanted to say, but she wasn't talking about Lacie. "We can keep Cherie safe too."

"You can't." She sobbed. "*I* can't."

I released her. She wasn't going to budge, and it wasn't my job to make powerful women give an inch. I listened at the door while she scratched strange symbols into her notepad. "What is that, anyway?" I asked.

She didn't stop working.

"Destiny Alverez had a notebook full of scratch like that," I said.

"Did she?" Van Esters stared at me for several seconds before returning to her work. "Did she?"

"Can you help me interpret it?"

"It's trivial." Van Esters was annoyed at me for interrupting.

"You have a back exit," I said. "If we can get out, we can disappear. Buy you time to write everything you need and get back to the colony."

"The colony!" She chuckled to herself.

"Didn't you come from Magdalene Moon?"

She gestured at the cot and desk. "Welcome to the colony."

"We can buy you more time."

"People always think they'll have enough time," the woman said. "Day after day after day. They think they'll always be able to tell their loved ones how they feel. They think they'll be able to finish that one final project. People don't understand that they're mortal. Not really. They never have. *Humanity* has never understood that it'll one day vanish into that great beyond."

I didn't have a clue what she was getting at. "I understand."

"There's going to be an end, you know. It might be a tragic explosion or a slow diminishment of the species, but humanity will eventually vanish. We can't last forever. Maybe there will be something else in our place."

Somewhere down the hall, a door slammed. I hazarded a peek around the end of the filing cabinet but saw no movement in the hallway lights.

"The blue is on the way," I said.

She wrote, flipping pages with a fervor that one normally associated with starving dogs and raw meat.

"Saria—"

"Let me concentrate," she hissed.

I swore under my breath. She wasn't going to move, and if the killer stumbled onto us in the closet, we'd be fish in a barrel. Another door boomed, echoing down the hall. I held my breath until I heard the creak of another hinge. Whoever was down there was working their way closer. The hallway lights were all dimmed, giving no hint as to where the intruder lurked.

"Can you lock this door?" I asked, knowing the answer as

soon as I asked it. The door only locked from the outside, and then, only with a key. I thought of Evan, the administrative assistant who had greeted us at the door. The odds of getting to him and back were about as good as winning a hand of poker with a pair of sixes.

I only had one advantage against the killer. The dark. I stepped out of the closet, closed the door, and crept down the hall. The lights didn't respond to my movement. I might be able to get the jump on him.

My breath ached in my chest before I realized I was holding it. Silence was my only friend. I pressed my hands against the third greenhouse door and shoved. It glided open without a sound.

The greenhouse was dark except for a row of emergency guidelights along the floor. They cast the room in tones of gray and blue, and the room smelled of sharp ammonia and damp earth. I felt along the wall and found a storage cabinet. Each greenhouse had its own tools, to better avoid cross-contamination. The cabinet creaked when I opened it, and the sound was like the scream of a banshee in the otherwise quiet space.

Greenhouse tools weren't the best weapons. The only shovels were handheld trowels. The only blades were pruning shears. I took one of each, hoping I wouldn't need to bear the humiliation of my sister needing to identify my corpse next to those as my only weapons.

"Yeah," she would say, "that's my idiot brother. Brings a trowel to a gunfight."

I pressed my ear to the door. If I got the timing right, I might be able to follow the killer into a greenhouse. He'd be as blind as me in the dark greenhouses. All I needed to do was prevent him from making it to the end of the hall where Van Esters still scratched away at her notebook.

Through the crack between the door and frame, I heard a swish of movement in the hall. Still no light. He was on the move, but Trinity's lights weren't responding to him. Did he have a silhouette like Mance's? Breath held, I waited, straining to hear movement. Soft footsteps moved across the hard floor. An errant breath sounded like a sign in the echoing halls of a museum.

Then the door to the adjacent greenhouse opened and closed again. The hallway lights still didn't change.

I moved, taking my steps as slowly as I dared. As quietly as I could. At the greenhouse door, I paused. Would he see my door move?

"Saria," a man's deep, sonorous voice called on the other side of the door. "I know you're in here."

My grips on the trowel and clippers tightened.

"Saria," he said. He sounded serious.

I stood by the side of the door, ready to pounce as soon as he stepped out.

Instead, he moved farther into the dark greenhouse. I drew a deep breath and waited. He must be moving through the space methodically, checking all the corners and under all the benches. If he did that, it would take time. Maybe he'd be here long enough for the blue to arrive. Backup from Anders's allies sounded like a great idea at this point, even if they were a bunch of incompetent assholes.

Seconds dragged like hours, and the killer didn't return. I couldn't hear him anymore, and I started to worry. What if there was another way out? What if he had left through the side door where it connected to the next greenhouse? He'd have the jump on me for sure. What if there was a back exit and I'd lost him already? He could be out in the city blending with the Heavy Nicodemia nights.

Then again, maybe waiting wasn't the best option.

I pushed the door open and ducked into the darkness, shuffling as quickly as I could to one side. When I heard nothing, I knew I'd done something wrong. The killer had escaped.

That thought continued right up until the first gunshot. A muzzle flash lit the room like lightning and something cracked into the wall next to me. I dropped low and scrambled behind the greenhouse bench.

I crouch-ran as quickly as I could along the end of the greenhouse. The roar of my heart in my ears drowned out any hope of hearing the killer.

"Saria's gone," I said. "Fled out the back door."

Another flash and the fiberoak bench three rows down shattered. Not even close, asshole.

"You're not great at this," I taunted, still on the move. Maybe he would run out of bullets.

Nobody knew the dark like me. I moved through the space like a shadow in the night—an oil slick in the center of the blue-black sea. Breath held, I crouched and moved until my legs burned and my lungs cried out in agony. I heard his labored breath only a few paces ahead on the other side of the bench. His clothing rustled as he crept forward. I could almost hear the sweat dripping from his brow. I had him.

Lights above flashed once, then blazed with the full brilliance of a Hallow noon. The door slammed open and Saria van Esters filled the doorway, bathed in the light from the hallway, notebook in hand. Her eyes were wide with panic. The woman was a terror of smeared makeup and wild hair.

I made my advance, still nearly blind. I launched myself over the bench, scooped sand with my trowel, and flung it at the killer. It struck him square in the face and he cried out in frustration and pain. The gun fired. Fired again.

Then I was on him. I wrenched the gun free and threw it

to the ground. With a stomp, I shattered the plastic casing. The killer was big. Strong. He used my distraction with the gun to twist free.

He smashed against a greenhouse bench and staggered away. All I saw was the flash of his black clothes against the dark hallway as he shoved past Van Esters. He wore a strip of ultra-black cloth over the upper half of his face.

Saria van Esters clutched a spurting hole in her chest.

"Why?" I asked, helping her to the ground. The notebook tumbled from her hand.

I tried pressure, but the bullet had shattered, perforating her chest with fragments of bone and bullet. She stared at me with something like serenity. A calm resignation washed over her, and her hand grasped for the notebook, leaving a bloody handprint.

"I can fix this," I said. "Be calm." Into the hall, I shouted down the hall, "Anders! Bring that medpack!"

Anders either didn't hear or he had his own problems because he didn't come. Saria's pale lips moved with words not granted sound. I tried again to stop her from moving, but she wouldn't listen. Her face was so white. Breaths came in shallow gasps.

"Why, Saria?" This was too much. The failure. The death. I couldn't stomach it. I could fix anything. I *needed* to fix this. "Why didn't you just stay hidden?"

She pressed the bloody notebook into my hands. Her mouth worked as if to talk, but it only caused more blood to spurt from her wound.

Saria van Esters faded into pale dark death, slipping through my fingers like sand. With the final shreds of life left in her, she pointed a finger at the bloody notebook.

The lights in the hallway dimmed, no longer detecting a human presence. I stared after the fleeing attacker. The lights hadn't changed for him either, but the black of his clothes hadn't been the black of a silhouette.

He was like me. Excommunicated.

I opened the notebook and flipped through its yellowed pages. At the end, where Saria had just scrawled out the most important message she'd ever written—her last words—I found more of the squarish code.

She was dead and all I had left was another notebook that I couldn't read.

PART IV

the case of the three debtors

Chapter 27

"FORGIVE ME, Priest, for I have sinned." My knees ached from kneeling in the confessional, and through the flimsy screen I could see Priest Cano's downcast gaze. The heady scent of incense lingered in the air, but it didn't calm my unsettled spirit. "It has been a lifetime since my last confession."

For a long time, the priest said nothing, and I thought she was going to reject me for my false attempt at reconciliation. She must know that I couldn't truly confess. Any attempt was nothing more than grasping at drops in the mist.

Finally, she said, "In the name of the Father, and of the Son, and the Holy Spirit."

"Amen," I muttered.

"Tell me, Jude," said Cano. "What made you decide to come in today?"

Desperation. There wasn't anywhere else to go. Nowhere else to seek the answers I needed or the sanctity I craved. There was no way to get the weight off my chest or the devil off my shoulder. Everywhere I went was sin and squalor.

Suffering. I came in for the holy rite of reconciliation because if I didn't do that, I was afraid I might do something far worse.

"Pride," I said.

Cano sat in silence, but despite the mounting pressure, I didn't elaborate. She said, finally, "Pride can lead us to sin, but pride itself is not a sin."

"I thought I could fix everything, Cano." I drew a deep breath, trying my best not to swear in the confessional. "Shit." Dammit. "I thought I could fix *one* thing. If I just made one thing better, then I believed that maybe I could convince myself I was walking the right path."

I closed my eyes and pictured Mance's bound form. I could have squeezed the answers out of him, but Anders was right. I didn't regret letting him live. Not that he'd lasted long. I just wasn't sure if my soul could take another battering.

Through the screen, I saw Cano's bright eyes searching my face. These screens were a joke meant to make confession easier. Instead, they made it feel like Cano was spying on something private—something between God and myself. At least one of them was listening.

"I've only made things worse," I said. "In my pride, I thought I could save someone, but I failed. In my pride, I thought I could catch a killer without help, but it just led to someone else's death, and one of my only allies is injured."

Cano said, "It's your pride that tells you everything is your fault."

"I know!" It took a full minute before my breathing was under control and I could speak again. "I know. There's a decision I need to make, and I was hoping I could have your advice before I take it."

"That's… not really what the Rite of Reconciliation is about, Jude."

"No, but it's the best way to get a private conversation."

"All our conversations are private if you want them to be."

"Sure." I drew another deep breath. My mouth tasted like cotton, and my bruises ached like a bad memory. "There's something wrong in the Catholic Church, Priest. Something rotten right up to the top. I saw three priests making a deal with a contract killer. I've heard talk about machine worship as if it was something to be considered seriously. There are priests in the church telling their parishioners that science is full of lies. That the colonies are a threat to our faith. There's something wrong here, Cano, and I'm not sure, but I think we might need to hurt the Church to make it better."

Again, Priest Cano didn't speak for a long time. She and I had a history. I knew that she was faithful to God and her Church—in that order. She was a good person, and while I didn't exactly share her faith, we at least had similar values when it came to human life and the pursuit of good in the world. The difference was that I saw how there would never be enough good to make up for all the bad.

"Nobody is perfect but God," Cano whispered. "The Holy Trinity is our source of perfection, but even those in the highest ranks of the Catholic Church are not perfect conveyors of their truth."

"Not even the Pope?" I asked.

"The Pope is only infallible when he speaks the doctrine of Jesus Christ. Even he makes mistakes. Every priest is constantly made aware of their own fallibility, but some take it to heart while others become lost."

"What about you?"

"I do my best, Jude. You know that."

"I don't think there are enough rosaries to say my penance."

The fiberoak door creaked as I opened it and stepped outside into the back of the cathedral's central sanctuary. A dozen parishioners lined up outside the confessionals, ready for their weekly reconciliation.

Cano caught me as I entered the narthex. "Jude," she said. Her voice echoed.

I turned to face her, a little surprised that she'd followed. "What is it, Priest? You expect me to pray the Act of Contrition with you? My God, I am sorry with all my heart—"

"Jude, stop."

I stopped.

"You need to be careful who you talk to." Her large eyes bore right into my soul. "But I think you can trust the Jesuit."

Without another word, she returned to the confessionals, taking a moment to murmur a greeting to those waiting in line.

"Thanks," I muttered. Trust the Jesuit. As if I could trust anyone.

The morning was a bright one for the Heavies—almost as obnoxiously bright as the higher beads. Light shone down from the top of the spiral city, glinting off the gold spires of the Cathedral of Saint Francis of Assisi. It was Sunday morning, and the well-dressed crowds were shuffling toward the church with all the urgency of a log floating downriver. The day promised to be pleasantly cool, with a hint of a spiral wind to dissipate some of the stink from the fisheries below.

Mance had access to Destiny in the garden. He flew her across town in one of the Gravity Garden's waste haulers in the middle of the night. Nobody stopped him. Together, they had visited her flat at the university. Why? From there they went to a place she'd used in the Sinless—a place where another girl had gone missing. There, he had tortured and killed her. Why all the stops? What did he expect to learn from the torture? How was Mance's killer involved in all of this?

Destiny's killer might be dead, but his death left more questions, and every one of them irritated me like a bad sweater.

I avoided my sister's diner. Everybody I knew who wanted to find me would find me there, and I wasn't ready for it. Cano thought I could trust Lorentz, but I wasn't ready to face the Jesuit. Not yet. Not after what happened. My failure to save Saria van Esters gnawed at me. I wanted to find her killer, but this was a precipice. A long spiral started here if I stepped off this cliff, and I couldn't see the bottom of it.

Reginald Alverez had hired me to find Destiny, and, by extension, her killer. Nobody hired me to help Saria van Esters. Nobody wanted me to find her killer. I needed the kind of work that paid. As much as I love running off and solving the hardest problems in the city, I needed food. Shelter.

There *were* paying jobs. Lorentz still had me on retainer, but with Van Esters dead, that couldn't last. Retch probably wouldn't talk to me, let alone bring me work.

That left the list of names Jade had given me. I could track down each of them, shake them down for what they owed, and get back on the good sides of Jade and Jasmine. It would pay, and it would get me closer to having my grubby hands on the journal Leo Shaw had taken from me—the journal with code that matched the scrawlings of Saria van Esters.

Jade's list was my next big job, but I itched to know what was written in those journals and why they used such a strange code. If I was going to figure that out, then I needed to do something first.

My feet took me upspiral to a neighborhood filled with

jagged apartments built in the angry architectural style of a district designed for utility above beauty. In my eye, it had a certain elegance, but that elegance was born from the efficiency with which it packed bodies into buildings. Families crammed into one- or two-bedroom apartments, and those apartments were stacked almost up to the bottom of the spiral above. This was the Stacks, where the poor and unfortunate could disappear among their kind, living their lives with little hope of escape.

It was a hope that many would never realize.

Trinity's priorities of body, soul, and community leaned hard toward community here. Nothing helped the body thrive in a close-packed district like this. The souls of its inhabitants atrophied in rundown churches and dingy meeting halls. But community? Community flourished. Boys kicked soccer balls on fields crammed into cramped parks. Girls played stickball in pickup games played on the cleared-out streets. The smell of seared meats wafted over the district in preparation for lunchtime crowds coming down to eat in shared kitchens and community barbecues. This was a place closely knit with its people, and the one thing that drove that community was a shared desire to leave.

Destiny's mother needed my help. I had no doubt that there was a plan to assassinate her the same Saria van Esters. The two scientists shared something in common: their work on the Magdalene Moon colony. What I didn't know was why that would put them in danger. What did those three priests have against the work on the colonies?

There was another thing the Stacks were good for. Despite the tightly knit community, the Stacks were the place people went to hide. A tiny apartment in the upper reaches of a building could disappear a person as good as burying them in a deep hole.

According to Anders, the blue had discovered that Harold Mance had a place somewhere in the Stacks. They didn't know exactly where, and they didn't know how to find out, but they had enough records of him in the area to hint that he probably had a place.

From my pocket, I removed two photos: one of Mance's corpse, the other of him alive. I chose the less disturbing picture and showed it to a trio of teens. The blue might not know where to find Mance's place among the rank-and-file nobodies of the Stacks, but I could walk that beat. I could dive into the masses and come up gasping for air with a cold hard truth gripped in my claws.

"You ever seen this guy around here?" I asked the kids.

I'd find the truth behind it all, whether I starved doing it or not. I was the man who walked in the dark, and nothing—not one damn thing—could make me drop a case once a hard question was asked.

Chapter 28

I STEPPED into the dingy apartment at the top of Tower Three of the Stacks, and the pungent aroma of ammonia and sweat brought me back to the body of Destiny Alverez. I could almost picture the blood spatters—the image of the figure on the wall written in the absence of red, the pool on the floor, and the scuff mark on the windowsill.

The floor manager, a portly man with a bushy mustache and a cauliflower ear, rigged the lights to stay on while I worked. "He's a good tenant," he said.

"Quiet?"

"Morbidly."

"Did he ever have visitors?"

"None that made themselves known."

I thanked him with a dime before he left, wishing I had more to grease the wheels. It would have saved me half a dozen hours and a whole lot of sour looks. The tiny apartment was cluttered with a lifetime of detritus, and a haze of dust hung in the rancid air.

I put my earpieces in, and Howlin' Wolf wailed as I delved into the drudgery of detective work.

"Smokestack Lightnin'" played while I skimmed the surface of Mance's possessions. The bed was covered in ragged gray sheets, rumpled from a recent stay. A box under the bed held a few possessions—knives, clothes, and a copy of a gardening magazine. A single hard-backed chair in the room sat next to a bundle of papers. I decided to look through those later. Paperwork exhausted me.

Bottles of pills lined the sink in the bathroom. I noted each as Howlin' Wolf strummed his blues guitar for "The Red Rooster." Painkillers. More painkillers. Most of his meds were designed to help with joint stiffness and other tissue maladies. He had arthritis or something related. It would have been exacerbated by the heavy gravity. Interesting, but not particularly useful.

I remembered Destiny's apartment with its hidden cache. While "Poor Boy" played, I tapped and prodded every surface of every wall in a desperate attempt to scour Mance's lousy life. It wasn't until "Gettin' Old and Gray" that I found the photos. They were in a slender fiberoak box under a stack of chemical photo blanks and a camera.

They were all women. Most were blondes. All in their early twenties. Each woman in all twelve photographs was clearly dead. Blood stained their soft skin. Ragged injuries ranged from stabs in the chest to crushing wounds to the temple. They all showed signs of bruising, and several showed signs of healed bruises alongside the fresh ones.

Mance had been torturing Destiny not because he wanted to learn something from her. He had been torturing her because he enjoyed it. I splashed water on my face in the bathroom to keep from vomiting. My face was a hollow mask in the mirror.

The stack of papers was the only remaining potential clue. They were receipts, mostly. Payment details, contracts, and records of ownership.

It was the middle of "Mr. Highway Man" when I realized I wasn't alone. Lorentz leaned against the doorframe, arms folded over a black button-down shirt. Her white priest's collar shone in the hazy light. At the end of the song, I stowed my music rig, carefully folding the pieces together so they would stow nicely in my pocket. I flipped through the papers. The chair wasn't comfortable, and my back ached.

"You're not an easy man to find," Lorentz finally said.

"Mance had a lot of debts." My voice sounded calm despite my ragged nerves. I flipped through the papers. "He owed a lot of bad people."

"Your sister had some sharp words for you."

"It tells a story," I said, "but I'm still not following the plot."

"I heard you went to the church after what happened yesterday. There's no shame in seeking guidance, you know."

A receipt fluttered to the floor, and I snatched it up so that I could place it back in the stack.

"You might be invisible on the surveillance systems," she said, "but kids always notice when you go by. Funny thing, really. It's like the adults in the area willfully forget about you the second you're gone, but the kids see you. They think you're someone they should respect."

I paused in my search, letting her words trickle into my skull. "Kids are wrong most of the time."

Lorentz strolled into the room and nudged the yellowed mattress with a toe. "I still need to know about the science, Demarco. Saria's death is evidence that there's something more going on with the colony projects. Mance was involved, but he's not the real story. He was lowlife scum."

"He's not worthy enough to get your holy attention?"

"I'm a Jesuit, not a pastor. My concern is with the truth, not the people."

"What's one life in the face of the truth?"

"I've given my life for the truth."

"Not yet you haven't." I tossed another unpaid bill on my growing stack of discards. "Plenty of truth down here in the gutters, boss."

"Why is it nobody knows what the colony scientists were working on?"

I glanced at Lorentz. Her penetrating gaze bore a hole right through me. I pretended to be very interested in the receipt on the top of my stack. "You think people have a problem with the science?"

"I think there's a problem with the scientists, and people are starting to notice."

"People murder each other for the worst reasons." I stood and stretched. My nervous energy wouldn't let me sit any longer. "What you're looking for is a good, clean, logical reason for Saria van Esters to be dead. You're looking for a reasonable connection that'll tie everything together." I stepped up to her. She smelled of lavender and the scented oils they used during holiday Mass. It reminded me of Destiny's murder scene. "I'm looking for that too, but I need to warn you: it might not exist. Most killings are messy, ugly things, filled with anger and fear. This guy—Mance—I think he got his jollies off killing girls. This kind of murder wasn't the sort of thing a person does for a reason."

"This wasn't random either."

"Far from it." I handed her the stack of photographs. "Far from it."

"What?" she said, reading the expression on my face. She flipped through the photos and her breath caught. "This…"

"He was a killer."

"He was a monster," she said. "But *whose* monster was he?"

The top paper in my pile of receipts showed gambling debts cleared in one massive lump. It didn't say whether Mance had a particularly lucky night at the tables or if he paid it off from savings. All it said was that it was paid.

And that the collector was Leo Shaw, the same asshole who was collecting on me. The same asshole who took Destiny Alverez's journal almost as soon as I got my hands on it.

"What is it, Demarco?" Her voice sounded as hollow as I felt. She set the photos down on the mattress.

I showed her the receipt. "Mance owed a significant amount, and it was collected by Shaw."

"So?"

"So, why is Mance paying off huge debts?"

"A lot of people pay off their debts," Lorentz said. "You might want to try it sometime."

I waved the paper. "Not like this. Listen, I know this kind of guy. In some very uncomfortable ways, I *am* this kind of guy. If I get a bunch of money, I'm not paying off my debts. I'm gambling. I only pay what *needs* to be paid."

She blinked slowly.

"If he paid it all off at once, it was because the payment was a job. Just like Jade's asking me to do a job." I flipped quickly through the rest of the papers. None of them held any obvious clues about the state of Mance's finances, except to indicate that he owed a lot of people a lot of money. It was only the debt being collected by Shaw that got paid down, even though he had older and larger debts to worry about.

Lorentz dropped the photos on the mattress. "I want to keep you on, Demarco."

"Are you going to front me enough dimes to get out of debt with Shaw?"

"Would you actually pay off that debt?"

"Maybe I can win enough to pay off all my debts."

She shook her head in disgust and passed the paper back to me. I stowed it, donned my hat, and ushered her out. We wouldn't find anything else in Mance's crash pad, and if my theory was correct, we had some work to do before the sun set.

"When is the Alverez funeral?" I asked as we descended the apartment's elevator.

"Two days," said Lorentz. "Petunia Alverez had it delayed so that she could hitch a ride in from the lunar colony with the cargo vessel."

"Her daughter's funeral didn't warrant a special trip?"

"Space travel's expensive."

"Petunia Alverez is rich."

"Petunia Alverez is busy."

"Doing what?"

She gave me a soft slug in the arm. "That's what I'm hiring you for, big guy."

All the research I'd done on the family before I started looking for Destiny had shown that Petunia's work on Madeline Moon paid well. Quite well. She was richer than most Travelers and had enough pull in the government to move mountains of red tape. And this wasn't the Trinity kind of payment where a person gains Karma and therefore influence. Petunia Alverez was living on a mountain of dimes. Her family traded in the kind of currency that could be carried to other cities. It could be taken out into the vast worlds beyond Nicodemia.

And even there, she was rich.

The fact that she wouldn't leave immediately for

Nicodemia upon hearing of her daughter's death meant one of two things. Either she didn't care much for her daughter, or there was something very interesting happening on the lunar colony.

The elevator door opened, and we stepped into the bustling lobby. Amber lights cast warmth on shabby brown walls and the apartment's tall glass doors.

"Tell me about Madeline Moon," I said.

"I don't know anything." She pushed through the glass doors. The sky was still bright, but a haze of smoke and mist hung in the air.

"If you weren't a religious type, I'd probably call that a lie."

"I don't make a habit of lying."

"It's a colony. The scientists have been working on it for a hundred years. That's the kind of thing you could say."

She spun on me. "Don't waste my time, Demarco. You and I both know you're not looking for a grade school education. You want recent information? Find out why none of the scientists' notes have made it back to Nicodemia in twenty years. Figure out the clues left behind in shipping manifests and personnel requests. I don't know—dig into it a little."

"Is that what you're doing?"

"It's what I'm *trying* to do. It's what I'm hiring you to do, but you keep getting distracted."

"Murders are pretty distracting," I said.

Her nostrils flared. When she spoke, she was so close her breath brushed against my cheek. "Please, Jude."

I touched the pocket of my coat which still held Van Esters's notebook with the scrawled code that was her last message to the living. I don't know why I hadn't told Lorentz about the notebook. It wouldn't do any good until we had the other journal and some way to decode them both. That pocket also held the list Jade had given me for collections. "I think I can get you the information you need, but it's going to take time."

"We have two days," Lorentz said.

"Two days," I said. "Three people. Then we'll get Destiny's journal back."

"What good will that do if we can't decode it?"

I held out a hand, palm up. "Let me worry about that."

She placed three rolls of dimes in my open palm and didn't look one bit pleased about it.

Chapter 29

THE FIRST NAME on Jade's list was Francesca Frank, a trolley mechanic from the Yards District. She'd gotten in too deep at the Blue Mongoose one night on a Haven vacation. After an evening of drinking and debauchery, she'd fled back down to the Heavies, thinking she could escape her debts by moving south.

She'd been correct until now, but it had cost her. Even the legendary Leo Shaw hadn't been able to collect on her debt, but hiding from him had cost her a job, a family, and a reasonably comfortable life fixing broken trolleys down by the docks.

At least, that was the story.

"Three debts," I said to Lorentz, "and then Shaw will give up the journal."

She raised a doubtful eyebrow at me. "And you think the journal has something to do with the Madeline Moon project, even though Destiny couldn't have been directly involved in it?"

"Her mother worked on Madeline Moon."

"Why would Destiny have her mother's journal?"

"Look," I said. We stood at the edge of the Stacks looking out on the central trolley tracks for the Heavy Nicodemia spiral. "I can handle this. Finding people is what I do. Why don't you go up to the Hallows so you can warn Alverez about the danger she might be in?"

She gazed at me through half-lidded eyes. "Why are you always trying to get rid of me, Demarco?"

"I'm an independent spirit."

"Is that why you ditched me after the priests?"

"Priests make me skittish."

"I'm not a priest."

"This job going to be easy," I said as we hopped the next trolley downspiral. "There's only one place a person like Frank would hide in a pinch."

"I'm coming with," she said in a voice that left no room for argument. "You're on my dime, Jude."

"I remember."

After a short ride, the trolley rolled into the last stop, where the air smelled green and damp from the fisheries. Trolley tracks branched here because there were tracks that went even farther downspiral than even the last public stop. They bent and twisted outward toward the sprawling lower reaches of the bead, bending their way toward the warehouse where mechanics and engineers worked on the big electric machines.

It was the middle of the workday, and the shift was still in full swing. Metal pounded on metal in the syncopated rhythm of workers bending their will against molded fibersteel.

When we stepped into the warehouse, one of the workers stopped greasing the wheels on an older model trolley. Its shining side panels were dented and worn, but the motor inside looked as clean and fresh as the day it was manufactured.

"Can I help you?" asked the scruffy man, wiping his greasy hands on a greasier cloth. He wore a badge on his jumper designating him as a head engineer named Rollins.

"Looking for a friend," I said. "She used to work here. Lady by the name of Frank."

If I hadn't been watching closely, I might have missed his eyes darting to one side. "Haven't seen Frankie around here in a while," he said with an apologetic shrug.

"Mind if I look around?"

"We do, actually," Rollins stepped in front of me. He was a solid guy, but I towered over him. "It's not safe."

Lorentz said, "We'll be careful."

The man blinked, like he hadn't noticed her there. "Of course," he said finally. "Have a look around. Nobody's seen her."

The line was the same from everyone we asked. "Nobody's seen her," was a funny kind of mantra repeated both for its apparent truth and the fact that it was clearly meant to misdirect. Nobody had seen her, but that didn't mean she wasn't there. I made my way around the outer walls of the building, taking time to touch the cold metal tools arranged neatly on workbenches.

"Where's her bench?" I asked Rollins when I was halfway around the building.

"Cleared out," he said.

"Did anyone see her do it?"

He gave an exaggerated shrug.

"Got it," I said. "Nobody's seen her." I stepped over a set of tracks and continued around. The right side of the warehouse was dedicated to the printing and storage of machine parts. Huge gears sat in stacks on a shelf, print-in-place motors occupied a bank of fiberstone storage bins, and freshly polished railings leaned against the corner. A fiber printer in the center of the space slowly extruded a replacement front grill for an older model of trolley. Beyond that, an old grill sat in a bin marked for recycling. The benefit of fiber-based materials was the many times that they could be recycled and rebuilt into something new. Even the hardest fibersteels could be worked down into their component materials, re-configured, and turned into parts that were as strong as the originals.

When we reached the open entrance of the maintenance warehouse, where a completed trolley was being moved back out into the world, I said to Lorentz, "Did you see it?"

"I saw a lot of hard-working people," Lorentz said. "But I didn't see her."

The lead engineer still watched us from several paces back.

"Yeah," I said loud enough for Rollins to hear. "Nobody's seen her."

I crossed back into the warehouse, cutting straight across the center.

"Wait," waved the guy with the greasy rag. "You can't go through there."

I sidestepped to avoid two women carrying a heavy gear between them.

"I'm going to need this open," I said, gesturing at the place where the tracks met the seemingly solid barrier.

Rollins ran up beside me. "We can't—"

"I'm here to talk," I said in my best placating voice. Out of the corner of my eye, I saw Lorentz relax. I wondered briefly how much having her along was muting my interactions with these people. I could have easily gotten the man to open the door with the judicious application of muscle. It was still an option if this didn't work. "You're not doing Frank any favors by keeping me away."

The man peered at me for several uncomfortable breaths. Then, he tossed his rag on the nearest bench and waved a couple of workers over. At first, I thought we might have some trouble, and I wondered how far I was willing to take this if things got ugly. Then, the two workers gripped the wall and pulled.

The whole segment split around the tracks, and workshop lights flooded into the dark space beyond. I stepped forward, but Rollins stopped me with a greasy hand.

"You're here to talk," he said. "Nothing more."

All around us, the workers of the trolley repair station stopped what they were doing and watched with furrowed brows. They gripped wrenches and clenched fists.

I said, "I don't want any trouble."

"Liar," Lorentz whispered as we stepped into the hidden workshop.

"Well," I said, "I don't want any trouble with them."

The first thing that hit in the space was the smell. It was a mix of old noodles, urine, and grease. The air was dense and humid and warm, like the underbelly of a great beast. Ahead, a single light cast an enormous trolley car into silhouette. It loomed in the dark room, and the ceilings might have been the void of the stars above for all I could tell. The darkness stretched high above into nothing.

Stepping to one side, I spotted the workbench on the other side of the trolley car. The flicker of a lightning welder flashed under the cold glow of a naked bulb. A single worker hunched over the operation, using the welder to affix pieces of torn fibersteel onto…

Something.

The welder wore a full facemask, but it wasn't hard to guess who it was.

"Frankie," I said.

She froze, then continued her work.

"I think you know why I'm here," I said.

Lorentz put a hand on my elbow and gestured to the corner of the room. In the flashing light of the welder, I could see the bundle of blankets in the corner that must have made up Francesca Frank's bed.

"You have a debt with the Blue Mongoose." I almost told her that I wanted to help—that I could maybe find a solution to her problems and figure out a way to get the gang off her back. If I had known a solution for that, though, wouldn't I have used it myself?

She finished a weld of a long joint, shut down her equipment, and turned to face us. Pulling her mask up so that it was a dark visor that kept her face in shadow, she said, "You can't squeeze grease from a brick."

"I'm not looking for grease," I said.

"I don't have any dimes." She pulled off her mask and threw it to the bench. Her eyes were dark and fierce, peering at me from sunken sockets. "Mechanics earn Karma, not dimes."

"You had enough to gamble."

Lorentz wandered to the corner with the woman's bundle of blankets. She kicked one with a toe and nodded her satisfaction. Frankie's story checked out, then. She didn't have a dime to her name.

I didn't realize I was clenching my fists until my knuckles cracked. The sound was a thunderclap in the big empty space. "All they gave me was a number, Frankie."

But Frankie didn't back down. Her whole body tensed. "I'm nothing." She gestured at the corner where she lived.

"This is all there is to me. You want my blankets? You want a share of my rock-bottom Karma? You can have it."

"Where'd the dimes you gambled come from?" I asked. "Maybe there's more."

"There's not more!" she roared.

I glanced back the entrance, where Rollins still watched, arms folded. He glowered at me, and I felt the full weight of his judgment. This wasn't going well.

"My brother died," said Frankie. "A year ago. He left me a roll of dimes and some tickets up to Haven. I thought, 'Hey, might as well enjoy a vacation.' I deserved it, right?" She rested a hand on her workbench. "Work every day for a decade, and what does it get you? Nothing, I'm telling you. A decent Karma rating and a kink in the back of your neck that'll never go away. Well, fuck it. It's not worth it."

"Tell me how you lost the money," I said. I didn't like how she was spiraling, but I couldn't think of any way to fix what was going wrong in her life.

"I told you, it was a free roll of dimes." Her jaw hardened. "I won at first. The Mongoose was one of Parvel's favorite places, so that's where I went. Won a whole stack."

"And you got hooked." I glanced at Lorentz, and she nodded. We both knew how this story went from here.

"It wasn't bad at first. I'd stop for a day and go see the sights. By the end of my week, though, I was spending every night gambling my fortune until it wasn't a fortune anymore. I took out a loan. Then a bigger loan. I had to lie about my profession to get them to give it to me."

"What did you tell them?"

She glared at me. "I don't have any more brothers who can die and leave me money. It's just not going to happen. I stay down here where Trinity can't keep an eye on me, and I figure as long as mooks like you don't show up, I'm fine."

But she wasn't fine. Even I could see that. "Your friends bring you food. They help you keep your space clean, and they bring you supplies."

She scoffed. "Supplies and work is what they bring. Work that I'm not getting any Karma for because Trinity can't monitor this space."

A good deed unseen was a good deed wasted in Nicodemia. Frankie knew it, and I didn't have the heart to argue.

She spread her hands wide in supplication. "So, what's it going to be? You going to take me away from all this? Rough me up a little and press me into service?"

"You *could* work for them," I said, hating the words as they came out of my mouth. It was exactly the deal I had taken, and I knew it wasn't a good one.

"And every job they sent me on would wreck my Karma even more." She glanced at Lorentz. "I think you'll understand why I don't want that job."

The scene behind Frankie finally came into focus. In the dim white light of her workbench lamp, I saw the shapes she had been working on.

They were birds. Birds standing in rippling pools. Birds in flight above lush forests. Birds of prey striking animals running across the ground. They were all formed from folded sheets of fibersteel, with the textured weave of the substance carefully softened with heat, reshaped, and welded. These were gorgeous pieces, and Frankie was hiding them away in the recesses of her workshop dungeon.

"I can't sell them," Frankie said.

"You mean you won't sell them." I picked up the piece she had been working on when we arrived. It was still warm.

"Can't," she insisted. She thumbed back at the trolley behind her. "The materials are stolen."

Then, it all made sense. Frankie had always wanted to be an artist, but art wasn't something everyone could easily manage, especially in the Heavies. She needed funding to get the materials. If she took apart the trolley and didn't recycle the parts, the theft would hurt her Karma, which would impact her ability to acquire more materials or gain access to the parts of the station where art was better appreciated.

She had seen her brother's dimes as an opportunity, but it hadn't been enough. She gambled them, winning at first, but losing in the end, same as any gambler. When that didn't work, she fled back to her old job, and her friends in the trolley shop helped her hide in the unused workshop. Since then, she had passed her time making beautiful things that she knew would never earn her a way to freedom. It was a self-imposed prison sentence, and she'd be here her whole life if nobody did anything.

Except, it couldn't last forever. A glance at Rollins in the doorway told me there was already some stress in their relationship. He was worried more than angry, but that wouldn't last.

Frankie said, "What are you going to do?"

I could hand her over to Leo Shaw. I could force her into indentured servitude in the criminal underground. I could do nothing and leave her to rot in her cave.

No, I couldn't do nothing. That wasn't an option anymore.

"What's it going to be?" Lorentz asked. Her gaze was as judging as any priest's.

I set the half-formed bird on the bench and left Frankie's hideout. Once Lorentz was out, I pulled the heavy double doors closed and made sure they were hidden from casual observers.

To Rollins, I said, "I need three things from you."

He crossed his arms and a scowl deepened the lines at the corners of his mouth.

"First, I need you to fix Trinity's surveillance in that room."

"That won't be easy."

"Good deeds often aren't, and this will be one of the best."

"She won't like it."

"She doesn't have to."

"What else do you need?"

"Get her some better equipment. Make sure she has the best welding tools, the best burners, the best forge."

"How can that—"

"I need money." I looked around at the rest of the mechanics. "Every dime you can scrounge up." A rumble of discontent rolled through the crowd, but I put my hands up. "Call it a loan if you need to, but if I don't go back with a stack of dimes to show progress against this loan, then it's coming down bad on all of you."

"What's your plan?" Lorentz asked as we walked away with more dimes than I'd carried in years. It was only a fraction of what Frankie owed, but it was a solid show of intent. This would have to be enough. For now. "You're going to make her an artist?"

"She *is* an artist, Jesuit. I'm just going to make sure people realize it." I checked Francesca Frank off my list. "One down, two to go."

Chapter 30

AS THE HEAVY Nicodemia sky grew orange with one of its better-simulated sunsets, I sat across the counter from my sister. She sat in her wheelchair and assembled sandwiches while her wife Helen worked the grill in back. Next to me sat Lorentz, her slender form perched atop a black stool like a particularly elegant bird posing for a photograph.

"Apologize to him," said Angel.

"Retch doesn't listen to apologies," I protested. "He says they're for the weak."

"Apologize anyway," Angel said, more insistent. She slammed a slice of tomato on top of the sandwich.

Responding to her raised voice, the white lump near the far wall unfolded, walked up to her, and curled up at her feet. The muscular little pit bull emitted a single low whine.

"I don't think you understand our delicate relationship," I said.

Lorentz coughed gently into her hand.

"Something to say?" I asked.

Angel answered for her. "If there's anyone around here who doesn't understand relationships, Jude—"

"Yeah, it's me. I get it." I didn't. "Can I get that sandwich to go?"

"Not going to stay and chat with your sister?"

"Let me know if Retch comes back." I *was* worried about him. As rough as our friendship always was, he'd never stayed out of contact for very long. I placed a slip of paper on the counter. "And ask him to see if his people can find this guy." The third name on my list, Orville Ward, was proving difficult.

Outside, the fiery sky cast a warm glow over the moving city. Streets bustled with activity, showing no sign of slowing in the day's waning hours. This was Heavy Nicodemia, different from Haven or the Hallows. Life continually pulsed through spiral veins, no matter the time of day. I crossed the trolley tracks and stood at the edge of the open center of the district.

Above, blue and red flashed as the police moved downspiral. Their lights met those of a rave as they approached the districts near the bottom quarter. People moved. They went their merry ways ignoring the stifling chaos around them, as they always have and always will. I stood for a moment of quiet in the press of it all, wondering how anyone ever found peace in this press of madness.

"You're lucky you have her, you know," said Lorentz by my side. I didn't know how long she had been standing there. "She's a good sister." She handed me a sandwich wrapped in paper.

"Tomato and mayonnaise," I said.

"Maybe one day you'll earn bacon or lettuce."

"Not both?"

She flashed a crooked smile. “Let’s not get too ambitious.”

“I never am.”

“You handled Frankie’s situation well.”

“That was luck,” I said.

“You saw her potential.”

“Does that mean you’ll leave me to handle the next job on my own?”

“Not a chance.”

I finished my sandwich as we walked down the spiral. “This would have been simpler with Retch’s help, but I have a pretty good guess where the next guy will be.”

“The worst part of town?”

“How did you know?”

She threw an arm around my waist and laughed a deep laugh.

The bead grew dark as we moved downspiral. The crowds thinned, moving from the kind of shady revelers who moved happily through the dim district to the kind of shadowed individuals who watched me and Lorentz as if every step were a trespass. The air reeked of fish and industry. Mist wafted across the path.

The Docks were the heaviest place in the Heavies, where the fisheries produced the bulk of Heavy Nicodemia’s protein. The fiberstone ground was slick and gray, the buildings were rudimentary and simple, and the air was filled with the raw stink of dead fish. At night, most of the fishermen left the area, preferring to spend their time above the stench of their daily grind. Only the worst of the worst chose to stay down here at night, living, breathing, and drinking as true fishermen.

“His name’s Lonnie Grant,” I said. “My background check said he was a fisherman who used to do courier duty up to Haven and sometimes to the Hallows. Customs caught him smuggling a while back, and they decided his punishment was that he couldn't travel anymore."

"Stuck back home in the Heavies, then? Not so bad."

"Not bad, but not great either. He disappeared not long after that, but he had some outstanding debts at the Mongoose. When Leo Shaw came looking for him, he knew exactly where the guy spent his days. Problem is, Leo couldn't get anywhere near it."

"Too dangerous?"

"Too dangerous."

"And why is it different for us?" Lorentz asked.

"Hide the collar," I said. "People around here don't like being reminded of their guilt."

She pulled the white out of her collar, folded it, and stuffed it in a pocket. Dressed in her sharp black shirt, she almost looked like she belonged in the seedy underground.

I lit a cigarette and let its warm glow fail to penetrate the dark. The shadows watched as I peered into the mists. Somewhere, something splashed in one of the pools. No doubt the fishermen in the farms were giving their last meal of the night—or becoming one.

It was full dark by the time we found the Guttered Spine. The seedy bar was nestled among a cluster of fishing shacks. Yellow neon set the surrounding mist on fire, and a trio of men out front eyed us like we were a bad rash.

I offered a cigarette to a blond pile of muscle in an olive-green jacket. "I'm looking for Lonnie Grant."

He took the cigarette, lit it with the flick of a match, and shot a glance at Lorentz. She had hidden her priest's collar, but she still glowed like a religious zealot. The man flicked his first ash in her direction. "I think you're in the wrong place, Miss."

She didn't miss a beat. "We're looking for Lonnie Grant," she said. "You can tell us where to find him through the smoke of a free cigarette, or you can tell us through a set of broken teeth."

Damn.

The blond guy glanced at his two partners. She had their attention, which was about the worst thing a person could have in a neighborhood like that.

"Look," I said. "There's no reason for this to get ugly."

The blond drew a long pull at his cigarette. The ash glowed. "It's already ugly, fella. We're just trying to decide if it's going to end with a fresh batch of fish feed."

The thing about the Karma system was that once a person bottomed out, there wasn't much incentive to play nice. What's another murder when the systems were all turned against a person? Some of the fish grown under the docks were carnivorous, preferring the flesh of other fish or animals.

This was the danger that kept Shaw from pursuing Grant. The mists meant that nobody would see us murdered in the night. The fisheries meant our bodies wouldn't be found. The ruined Karma of the lowlife thugs meant that there were no doubts about how intruders ought to be treated.

All we had were my two fists and the fact that I outweighed any two of them combined.

The blond clicked his tongue and the guy on my left swung. I was ready for it, but the blow caught me in the ribs anyway. Story of my life.

But the wild swing opened him up.

I jabbed the guy, turning my back on Lorentz. The blond came in hard, grabbing my elbow and scuffing a kick off my shin. If it had been a solid blow, it would have shattered the bone. As it was, it slammed hard into the muscle. I didn't know what kind of boots he was wearing, but they were reinforced with fibersteel, and I didn't like it.

Reach didn't do me much good up close, so I backpedaled and shot a couple hard punches at the two guys on me. I heard Lorentz behind me, but I couldn't turn my back on the guy with the metal boots. He came at me again with a wild haymaker, and I pounded him in the jaw. A boxing match I could handle, even if they doubled up on me.

My left thumped the other guy in the neck, and he stumbled back, gasping.

The blond closed inside my swing and rabbit punched me in the gut. I doubled over and he grabbed a handful of my hair. My hat was gone. He slammed a fist into my face and it was like running full speed into a brick wall. Again. The world spun and my vision went black around the edges.

He cried out and dropped me. My legs wouldn't hold my weight. The other guy tried to grab my arm, but I blindly reversed the grip and slammed him down hard enough to shake the docks.

Lorentz squared off against two of them. The guy on the right and the blond guy. They had her outmatched, but she was in a ready position that looked like she knew her way around a dojo. The blond clicked his tongue again, and the other guy made his move.

A long leg snapped out and caught him under the chin. His eyes rolled back and he collapsed. By the time the blond closed, Lorentz was ready. It wasn't enough. The guy caught her punch and twisted her elbow, throwing her off balance.

The guy I'd slammed started to move, so I dropped a crunching elbow down on his chest. Heaving myself to my feet, I tackled the blond just as he was about to break Lorentz's wrist.

An elbow pounded into my neck, breaking my grip. A

brick of a fist slammed into my shoulder and we both went down in a heap.

"Break it up," growled a voice from the door. A big man stepped into the cool night air. He wore an olive fisherman's jacket like the others, but it was cut longer, like a trench coat. His hands were covered in fingerless gloves and clenched into huge meaty fists. "I hear someone's here to talk to me."

I extracted myself from the blond, who managed to get one last shove in for good measure. The other two guys groaned and complained, but were otherwise none the worse for wear. They'd have a painful time at work the next day, but that wasn't my problem. I wiped some blood from my lip and plucked my hat from the ground. My head ached, and the ground swayed under my feet.

"Been a long time since anyone got brave enough to find me down here," said Lonnie Grant. He stuck out a meaty hand and shook Lorentz's hand, then mine. His grip was so massive it had its own gravity. "You here to tell me I owe something?"

"I'm here to talk," I said.

Lorentz stepped forward. "We're here to get what you owe the Blue Mongoose."

Grant chuckled at that. The misty air consumed the laugh, swallowing the sound of it like there wasn't anything for a million miles. After laughing too long, he said, "Throw them in the shark tank."

"Wait," Lorentz said. "Don't you want to hear our proposal?"

I gave her a questioning look. There wasn't any proposal as far as I knew.

"You wanna know why I owe that money?" said Grant.

"Let me guess," I said. "The house cheated."

His laugh was razor-sharp. “I used to live like a goddamn king.” He waved at the shack behind him where the sounds of raucous drinking grew in waves. “Not this nice, but pretty good. I brought the best sablefish to some fellas in the Hallows every week. Nothing too fancy, but they liked it fresh. Didn’t want to wait for Customs. On the way home every week, I’d visit—” His voice hitched, and instead of continuing, he gestured for to the bar behind him. “You want a drink?”

“You’re not going to kill us?” I asked.

“I’m still thinking about it.” He disappeared through the door, its corroded hinges creaking in the night.

I raised an eyebrow at Lorentz, but she shrugged. Tipping my hat to the trio guarding the door, I stepped over and entered the seedy bar.

Inside was a cloud of steam and smoke all mingling together in a warm sludge of atmosphere. Filters in the corners of the room churned the sludge but only seemed to move it around. Grant gestured to a table where a deck of cards sat in the center. The room wasn’t packed, but clusters of fishers lined the bars and occupied almost half of the rickety tables. I earned a few sour looks when I moved my massive body through the room.

When Lorentz stepped inside, they all stared. In a place like this, a well-dressed woman was even more anomalous than a visiting giant. This was something to write home about. We crossed under the heavy gazes of the men and women of the Guttered Spine and sat across from Grant at his felt-topped table.

A deck of cards sat enticingly in the center of the table.

“I don’t owe those ladies a thing,” Grant said. He picked up the cards and started to shuffle.

“That’s not what the number on my paper says.” I tapped

the pocket where I kept Jade's note. "Says you owe quite the handful of dimes."

A man in a soiled apron approached and gave us each a mug of golden ale that smelled like fish and tasted like bitter hops. I gulped half mine down before Grant started talking again.

His eyes grew unfocused, and he stared into the great void beyond. "At first you think they're just being nice, you know? There's that kind of smile they give you that you know in your heart is just for you even when you know in your head it's the same smile they give everyone else. That's how it was at first, but it turned into something different." He shuffled the deck a few times, its rhythm settling me into a hypnotic trance. "We got talking, sometimes. Some nights I wouldn't gamble at all, and she'd just sit at the table with me and talk." His eyes met mine.

The weight of what he was saying snapped me from my trance. "You're telling me you didn't go there to gamble."

"I *did* gamble. There was plenty of that. I even lost some, because, hell, nobody ever wins at gambling."

"Only the house," I said.

That put a grin on his face. "Around here, I'm the house." He shuffled his cards.

"I'm not here to gamble," I said, trying not to watch his hands.

"And I'm not here to give you any money." He dealt five cards each to himself, Lorentz, and me. "But I can see in your eyes that you're a man who knows his cards."

My heart hammered in my chest. All the aches of the fight were gone, a fresh wave of adrenaline soaking them up like gravy. Some part of my brain told me that I could win. My pocket was full of Frankie's dimes. If I doubled those—or even tripled them—then I could have everyone's debts paid off in no time. The job would be done and I could get that damn journal off of Shaw.

But I knew I wouldn't stop. Lorentz's gaze burrowed into the side of my bruised face. The Jesuit knew how to judge a man, and nothing in my addled brain could come up with a reason I shouldn't be judged.

"I'm here with a number," I growled, not touching the cards. "And I'm not here to gamble."

Grant smiled a shark's smile. "One hand. Is poker your game?"

"Maybe."

He knew exactly what he was doing. There was no such thing as one hand for people like me. If I won, I'd want to win again. If I lost, it would be a long slog until I'd lost everything. No, I couldn't pick up those cards, and I knew it.

Only, what if it was only one hand? What if I could manage this time, and I could come out as the hero in all of this? My mind raced with all the things that could be done with a single big win.

Lorentz leaned forward over the table and said, "I'll trade you."

She reached into her pocket and withdrew a rosary, tossing it onto the table. "God and Trinity might not watch my friend here, but he listens to me."

Grant's voice went flat. "A woman of God out collecting gambling debts?"

"Honesty benefits us all, Mr. Grant," she purred.

Damn.

Grant chuckled again, this time with a hint of tension making the laugh high and strained. He reached into a case at his side, opened it, and withdrew a tightly packed brick of dimes. He slammed it on the table and took the rosary.

Considering it carefully, he nodded to himself and wrapped Lorentz's beaded rosary around his wrist.

"Maybe I'll take up prayer," he said, sitting back down. A murmur of nervous laughter rippled through the room. He reached across the table and flipped my five cards over. Full house. Kings and nines. "Stop by for a game sometime," he said to me.

I picked up the brick and stowed it in my biggest pocket. My nerves shook. Sweat made my palms clammy. I led Lorentz out of the room. Nobody followed us into the night, and by the time we left the mists of the lower fisheries, all my aches had returned with vengeance.

"At least I know one thing now," I said.

"What's that?"

"Poker's not my game."

Chapter 31

I HURT.

I would have taken painkillers, but my brain was already a bowl of thick soup. I sat on a bench in front of the Cathedral of Saint Francis of Assisi, not remembering how I got there. Lorentz leaned over me, dabbing the blood from my cut lip. Her face was close to mine. I could smell her sweet breath on the cool wind, and the simulated moonlight above turned her into a sleek silhouette in the night.

"You got knocked around pretty good," she said.

I closed my eyes and saw her deliver a perfect kick to a man's chin. "You handled yourself pretty well for a priest."

"Monk."

"Right."

"We all have hidden truths," she whispered.

"Usually it's not anything good."

Lorentz dabbed at my lip again. "It's almost stopped bleeding, but try not to let anyone punch it for the next few days."

I closed my eyes and let the world spin. She might have said something, but her words jumbled away into the thick haze of my muddled brain. When I opened my eyes again, she was gone.

"Impressive work," said a voice next to me. Leo Shaw sat on the bench. "I didn't think you'd make it back up from the docks."

My head had cleared, but the white glow of the moon was still an ice pick in the back of my skull. "Just doing my job."

"At first I thought you were just messing around," Shaw said. He sat with one leg crossed over the other in a relaxed pose. "It felt like you weren't taking Jade's mission seriously, which is quite disrespectful if you ask me."

I thought of the journal he still held and his name appearing in Mance's papers. He was involved somehow, but I decided I better not give away how much I knew. If he suspected me of knowing too much, then I'd be more likely to see the bottom of a fish pond than the journal.

"It's almost making a guy look bad." A rime of ice lined Shaw's words. "Two impossible collections in one day."

"Frankie hasn't paid yet. Just a deferment cost. We'll get the rest when she has her art show."

"Clever," Shaw said. "But that wasn't the deal."

I stretched my sore neck. It was like flexing a fibersteel girder. "All I want is the journal, Shaw. Give that back and maybe I'll stop showing you up."

"I'd hate to go back on a deal."

"Maybe I'll take it from you."

Shaw showed his open palms. "I'd never carry something so valuable on my person, Demarco. If you want the journal, you're going to have to visit the Mongoose."

"You're pretty clever for a thug."

He bristled. "You know why I got into this business, Demarco?" He paused, as if expecting a response, but I had no time for guessing games. "My pops always weaseled out of deals. He was a shirk and a cheapskate. Any time he acquired any Karma—by accident, usually—he squandered it by reneging on a deal. Pretty soon people wouldn't make deals with him, so he had my ma make the deals. They got a decent pile of dimes that way, moving around a lot and gambling money they didn't have."

"Your pops sounds like a real piece of shit."

A wicked smile crossed Shaw's lips. "He does, doesn't he?" He pulled a pack of cigarettes from his pocket and offered me one. When I declined, he stuck one between his lips and lit it with a flick of an old steel lighter. "I was ten when it happened. We went to a show and cut through the Sinless on the way home. Stupid fucking idea if you ask me." The smoke of his breath mingled with the heavy haze of night air. "Stupid fucking idea."

"Who did it?"

"Doesn't matter. Could have been any of a dozen sharks. I'm not looking for revenge. Took me a decade to figure it out, but when I did, I realized they were right. My parents deserved what they got. Maybe they didn't deserve all the suffering. Pops took a week to die from the wound in his gut. Ma went quick." He drew a long pull from his burner. "Yeah, she went quick. It was better that way."

Behind us, the stained glass of the cathedral cast a red light into the haze that resembled spilled blood. The glow from its mighty sanctuary illuminated the streets for blocks, cutting a swath through the gloomy night.

Shaw continued, "My point is that I find people and I

collect debts. It's an important role in the community. If debts aren't collected promptly—" He plucked the cigarette from his lips and peered at its burning embers. "The longer it takes for people to face their consequences, the harder it is."

"You're a damn hero."

"Without people like me, debts don't mean anything. Without that—"

"Was Mance an important part of the community?"

He blinked. "What?"

"Harold Mance," I said. "Saria van Esters's attacker. Probably Destiny Alverez's killer."

The debt collector's tight lips strangled his cigarette. He didn't speak a word, but I knew from the flare of his nostrils that there was something he didn't want to share.

"You're scum, Shaw," I said. "A real piece of shit, just like your pops."

"Sweet talk from a guy who wants something from me."

"Help me with the final job. Solves all our problems."

Shaw stood from the bench and paced in front of me. His smoke formed a sickly halo. "I don't think you've been listening to me, Demarco." He tossed his spent cig to the ground and stepped on it with a leather boot. "It's a man's moral duty to pay his debts. Wouldn't be right for me to pay for you, would it?"

I almost offered to owe him one, but wise restraint stopped me. Leo Shaw wasn't the kind of guy I wanted to owe a favor. Not with his ties to Mance, if there really were any. Instead, I said, "What's the lowdown on Orville Ward?"

He turned away. I almost thought he was going to leave. "Orville Ward's dead. You need to talk to his last living relative, Frida."

"Wife?"

"Granddaughter." He handed me a thin folder, then disappeared into the mist.

Frida Ward. There wasn't much on the printout, but it was enough. Orville had been a craftsman, working on the materials printers all his life. He'd done a fair amount of gambling, landing himself in trouble after a bad weekend at the blackjack tables.

Unfortunately, heart failure due to a rare genetic disorder was his get-out-of-debt card. Any decent debtor would have called that the end of it. Going after a man's family was low. Hurt the Karma. This must have been enough dimes to make it worth the stain on the soul, though. Jade had signed the paper to press the matter. Legally, she was well within her right. The girl had inherited everything from her grandfather, including the debt.

Something still didn't add up.

I forced myself to my feet, knowing that if I stayed inert much longer, I'd grow roots and sprout leaves. My feet took me to all of Retch's haunts with the weary, automatic movement of a man burning his last luck. The kid was nowhere to be found, but his accomplices watched me with dark eyes as I moved through the gloomiest sections of the warehouse district.

"Where is he?" I asked a kid with sallow cheeks and grimy hair.

He stared at me like I was speaking tongues.

"I'm looking for Retch," I said to a girl with chopped blonde hair and sparkling eyes. "I want to apologize."

She watched me from atop a huge recycler. The machine could swallow a whole trolley car if needed, but the girl had somehow climbed atop it and claimed it as her own. "Retch doesn't want to see you."

The shadows down the alley twitched as more of their

gang attempted to move without drawing my attention. It wasn't working. "Tell your friends they might as well not bother."

The girl leaned dangerously out over the edge of the recycler. "Maybe we want payment for our services."

I thought of the bundle of dimes in my pocket. It was stupid for me to wander into the dark corners of the city with this kind of cash. Losing this would undo all of the work I'd already done collecting from Jade's debtors. I forced the thought away. I'd taken down Lonnie Grant's goons. I could manage a bunch of kids.

"Tell him I need his help, and I can give him something he's definitely going to want."

The girl's laugh was like the tinkling of bells. "Retch *takes* whatever he wants."

"Not this," I said. "I'll get him a silhouette."

The kid froze. Her mocking smile turned strained and her eyes grew cold. In the alleys around me, dim lights followed the movements of at least half a dozen children. These were the dejected. The disowned. They were the orphans of the city, gathered together into the Heavies' most dangerous gang.

And I was talking about giving their leader one of the most dangerous tools a criminal could possess. It was a tool that had just been used to murder a string of innocent women.

Behind me, Retch's voice rang out strong and wry. "I thought you were going to say friendship," he said, stepping from the broken doorway of an abandoned warehouse.

I turned to face him. "Can't sell you something you've already got."

His eyes scanned me, taking in my battered body and my ragged clothes. He searched me, and I couldn't help but feel like all my pains were being judged by the highest court. Had I suffered enough to earn Retch's pity? After an aching eternity, he grunted, turned, and disappeared back into the warehouse.

After glancing around and getting a noncommittal shrug from the girl on the recycler, I followed.

Chapter 32

RETCH HAD CLEANED himself up since I'd seen him last. His hair was buzzed in a tight undercut, and the tips were dyed a hazy red. His skin was hard like the brick façade of a government building, and his clothes were the muted grays of an undercover cop. He almost looked legitimate sitting on the oversized fibersteel throne in the center of the warehouse.

His hands gripped the armrests like claws. "I hear you're still with her."

It almost felt like I should kneel in King Retch's court. The corners of the warehouse were dark, with the only light being a single spot blasting down from above to bake the circle in which I stood.

"I'm looking for someone named Frida Ward," I said.

"I know." Retch leaned forward. "I got the message that you were going after her family."

"You know where she is?"

"I do," said Retch.

"Just because Lorentz pays my bills doesn't mean I'm siding with the Church."

Retch spit on the ground, sharply contrasting his current stylish image. "We all take money."

I paced, unable to stand still for this farce of a meeting. The spotlight followed me. "This is bigger than your dislike of the Catholic Church, Retch."

"Nothing's bigger than the Church, Demarco," Retch snapped.

"Have you cracked the code?"

He stared at me for a long time, his eyes a flat, emotionless drudge in the dark shadows. "I have," he said finally.

"What did you find out?"

"You gave me one page from a longer work. I got about one page worth of data from a larger experiment."

"What kind of experiment?"

"Get me the rest of that journal."

"Tell me where to find Frida Ward."

"You're a piece of shit, Demarco."

"I was just telling someone else that," I said. "Did you listen in on that conversation, too?"

"Didn't you wonder why Shaw refused to go after Ward?"

"I wonder what it means to you." My mind was still clouded from the beating, but it was starting to click that Retch had something else to tell me.

"Leave this one alone."

"You know I can't do that."

Retch said, "You're such an optimist."

"Not a very good one."

"People are a lot worse than you think. *That woman* is a lot worse than you think." It took me a hard blink to realize he was talking about Lorentz. "Take her money if you want, but don't let her in on people's secrets."

He called me an optimist, but every instinct in my big

Traveler's chest told me I couldn't trust anyone in this damn city, least of all a Jesuit.

"I'll trust who I want," I told Retch. Fighting my own pessimistic integrity, I pulled Saria van Esters's notebook from my pocket and tossed it to Retch. "Don't let me down."

"Such a fucking optimist, Demarco," Retch said, but something had softened in his voice. "Such a fucking optimist."

I didn't see a single soul on my way out of the warehouse district. Not the girl on the recycler. Not the urchin with the grimy hair. It was an abandoned wasteland that stretched on into the darkness of the Heavy Nicodemia night.

When I reached the bench where Lorentz had left me, I found she'd returned. She looked up at me as I approached, and a knowing smile touched her lips. "Any luck?"

I walked past and she fell in step beside me. "There's more to this that I'm not seeing."

"Do you want to know what I learned?"

"I'm waiting."

"Frida Ward is a mystery. Disappeared several years ago after an incident with her uncle." Lorentz's gaze burrowed into the side of my head. "The uncle's dead now. No leads there."

"How old is she?"

"No records. Could be a kid. Could be an old lady."

We passed the flashing police lights surrounding the storefront of a kabob eatery. The frosted glass danced with blue and red, making it impossible to witness the drama inside, but shouting voices and furious explosions of anger escalated into a crescendo and then stifling silence.

"The records are all purged?" I asked.

"Paper's probably still available." Lorentz gave me a sideways glance. She knew that I could dig directly through the paper records.

"Government buildings will be closed this time of night," I said.

"Doors can be opened."

Retch's warnings ran through my head. If Lorentz couldn't be trusted—if she was manipulating me—then what was her goal? Here she was trying to get me to break into the documents archive—something I could easily do—and for what? To find one lousy debtor?

"Information should be free," said Lorentz.

"She doesn't want to be found."

"It's not up to the individual whether or not they participate in society. They only get to decide *how* they participate."

"And Frida wants to participate by staying hidden."

"She can't stay disconnected if she owes money. That's a connection."

I said, "Sounds like you really want to find her."

"We *need* to find her. We need the notebook."

"That's not true. I could go up to the Hallows and have a talk with the legendary Petunia Alverez when she arrives for the funeral. She might be able to tell me what was in Destiny's notebook." Even as I said it, I understood the hopelessness of it. If it turned out Petunia didn't know anything about the journal, it would be too late to follow up with Shaw. "Shaw's around here somewhere," I said grimly.

"Does that do us any good?"

"Shaw's notoriously hard to follow, but Retch might be able to find him."

"You rely on that kid too much."

"He's reliable," I said.

"Is he?"

"Shaw's not carrying the journal anyway. It's at the Blue Mongoose."

"We'll go learn something about Frida Ward." When Lorentz saw my hesitation, she took my hand in both of hers and pulled me close. Her warm body pressed up against mine, and I had thoughts that were not appropriate anywhere in the vicinity of a religious vow. "Let's learn more about her and then we can make the decision."

"Why do I feel like you're the devil whispering in my ear?"

"You don't think the Church can tempt a person?"

I thought of Retch on his throne. There was more to this than he was letting on. Some piece of information that he was trying to get me to discover on my own. He had called me an optimist when he damn well knew I was about as pessimistic as they came.

"Frida might have been in Retch's gang," I hypothesized, putting the pieces together. "There's probably history there."

Lorentz stopped and looked at me. Behind us, down the long spiral, the blue and red lights went dark and vehicles scattered into the night. "All those kids have tragic stories."

"It would explain why he doesn't want me to try to collect. If I discover that it's one of his people, there's a chance I'd out that person."

"Would you do that?"

"Accidents happen."

"Our souls can't thrive in shadows."

"Some of us don't do well in the light."

"Always the pessimist," Lorentz chided, elbowing me. She pulled away from me and spun in the brilliant light of a streetlamp. "Step into Trinity's embrace, Jude. It'll do you good."

"You sound like a machinist."

She spread her arms wide. The light from above cast her face in shadow. “Step into the light, Jude Demarco. Let it burn away your sins.” When I didn’t step forward, she sighed, her shoulders slumped. “You know I’m not with them, right?”

“Those guys back there? Or the Catholic Church in general? It seems to me that for a church that’s supposed to be preaching one message, there sure are a lot of factions.” Warm night air blew down from upspiral. The morning’s warmth would spread through the district soon. An idea occurred to me. “Is this the start of a schism?”

“That’s a dangerous word.”

“I’m a dangerous guy.”

Lorentz showed me her palms in surrender. “I was hoping you’d shed some light for me.”

“That’s a lot of pressure.”

“Any Jesuit would give their life for the truth.”

“You folks keep a lot of secrets for someone so bent on free information,” I said.

Her hands slowly closed into fists in frustration. She spoke through gritted teeth. “If we can learn what’s in the journal, then I can give you a theory.”

“If I’m tracking down this Frida Ward when everyone says not to, then I need an assurance that it’s for something worthwhile.”

Lorentz seethed. “From what I hear, you’re the bulldog tearing the throat out of a dead rival. You never stop. You trample over whatever’s necessary to get the truth, just like any decent investigator.”

“Just like any decent Jesuit.”

“Only you do it for dimes.”

“I like to eat.”

She stepped back. “Join the order if you like,” she said. “It comes with free food, and we could use the help.”

"Never," I spat.

The venom in the word hit her like a closed-fist punch. She blinked rapidly, staggered back, and stared at me with her mouth hanging half open.

"Lorentz." My voice was too hard for the apology that I desperately wanted to make. Instead, I said, "Let me do this one alone. Retch doesn't want you near it."

"Can I trust you?"

"Please."

She turned on her heel. "Stick to the dark, then. Gather whatever information you can."

Then, she was gone.

Chapter 33

WHAT HARM COULD there be in knowing?

I asked myself the question as I broke into the records archive at the top of Heavy Nicodemia. The entrances were all locked, and the buildings were dark, but there were ways around even the toughest security in Heavy Nicodemia. An excommunicated person like myself might have trouble opening even the most basic doors, but in darkness I could move through maintenance tunnels, and in silence I could squeeze through access ports that weren't meant for humans. It was through these tunnels that I made my way into the archive building, but the door to the archive itself was sealed.

There were several theories about why Trinity kept paper archives on a space station where every shred of mass needed to justify its existence. Some said the archives were meant to build Trinity's redundancy, making it more resilient against catastrophic harm. Meteor strikes or electromagnetic storms might take out memory banks, but everything important could be rebuilt from the archives.

Others said the archives were there for the convenience

of historians. Back when the colony ship was designed, the ancient Catholics valued history above all else. They loved history more than they loved the future, and bringing that history to the stars was even more important than bringing people.

To the dismay of historians everywhere, paper archives didn't last forever. Trinity cycled them away and eventually destroyed them, using the pulp to make new paper printed with new records.

I chose to believe that the archives existed not because the designers wanted to preserve history, but because they didn't trust Trinity.

If the disappearance of Lacie van Esters was any indication, they were right not to trust the machine's digital record. Consulting the paper record was the only way to know what had been recently deleted, whether that was the location of Frida Ward, the employment records around the docks, or simply the preferred hangouts of the bead's most notorious criminals.

It took me only half an hour to break the door's control panel and expose the important wires. I disengaged the locking mechanism and pried the door open. It wasn't pretty, but it worked. Trinity didn't fire any alerts because Trinity always ignored me. The ruined panel would be someone else's bad day. Thus, the benefits of being excommunicated.

One thing the ancient Catholics had done well was devise a method of organizing their archives. The records showed the work of Saria van Esters in the Cabrini Colony Lab. Before she started working directly for Petunia Alverez, she had specialized in a strain of biologics specific to colony establishment—water-born microbiomes, in particular.

"Genetic manipulation," I muttered to myself, reading

the term for the hundredth time. "Programmable adaptive algae." Was that what drew Alverez's interest?

Could this be what the Church had a problem with? Could this genetic manipulation trigger that same antiquated irrational response? Was this all Lorentz needed?

It seemed unlikely. After all, this lab had existed for a hundred years. Their plans to terraform Cabrini and Magdalene Moon had been kicked around for hundreds of years before that. The ethics of the basic concepts of colonization were considered before the colony ship left Earth.

This was Saria van Esters's specialty, though, and whatever she was working on now must have been derived from that somehow. The answers wouldn't be in this archive. It likely wouldn't even be in the archive in the Hallows. *That* was why the scientists worked on the colony. They wanted to hide their results from Trinity. I blinked away my exhaustion and exhaled a long dry breath. After all this work, I was no closer to knowing what was happening. I still needed that journal, and for that I needed Ward.

Retch's request came back to me. Don't track her down. Leave this *one* thing alone. The request of a friend echoed in my ears, and I almost dropped the case right there. I valued Retch's opinion. His help had been invaluable in the time I'd known him, even if he was always, always difficult. He asked this one thing.

But what harm could there be in knowing?

Once I knew, then I could decide. Did he think that I couldn't make a reasonable decision once I had all the information? Was there any chance I could make the right decision if I *didn't* have all the pertinent info? Lorentz thought information should be free. Maybe she had a point.

Then again, maybe she couldn't be trusted.

I located the latest information on Frida Ward without

much trouble, and by the glow of my tiny lighter, I peered at the documents, locating her last known address. The redacted files came out as a thick bundle of ultra-thin sheets of archival paper.

So, I read. I located the records for the day she left and scoured through her documented connections. Why had she disappeared? Why did Trinity remove her from the public records? I read until my eyes were muddy from lack of sleep and my arms were leaden with exhaustion.

It all came back to her uncle, but the uncle's records would be in a different row. I wasn't sure if I had time to find them.

A noise from somewhere down the long hall snapped me from a numb haze. I didn't know how much time had passed. A door closed far away.

There was something else on the bottom sheet of the last file in Frida Ward's record. A single line denoting her connections to known relatives. It was written in an archaic code, meant to be read by machines and used as a pointer to a whole new archive. Everything I had read up to that point had mentioned the uncle, Gerry Ward, but there was a second row in the familial connections line. It pointed to a child not yet named at the time of this document's creation.

The day's workers would find me soon, and I didn't want to stick around to explain the damage I was doing to their pristine archives. I stuffed the final few pages into my pocket—the records that would give me my best chance to locate Ward—and I filed everything else back in its proper place.

I needed to speak with her. It was the only way.

After all, what harm could there be in knowing?

Chapter 34

FRIDA WARD HUGGED ME. It hit before I even had a chance to say my name. Before I made any kind of attempt at a greeting. It was a warm hug—a friendly one—and at first, I didn't know what to do. My arms stuck out at odd angles. Her head buried in my chest. She smelled of lavender shampoo. Eventually, I pressed my hands to her back and squeezed, and, finally, she released me.

Breakfast was being served at the Saint Teresa Home for the Needy, so I sidled into the line and worked my way through the gathering crowd. The home was a dime-funded residence for those of any Karma level who could not care for themselves. People who could pay lived here in a nicer facility than the Church-funded homes scattered throughout the bead. Saint Teresa served people whether they suffered from an injury that prevented them from working, from mental health problems that kept them from effectively participating in society, or, as in Frida Ward's case, from congenital disability.

Frida was a beautiful woman with flat features and

almond eyes typical for a person with Down syndrome. She had thin red-blonde hair framing her wide-set face and her blue eyes shone in the morning light. Her records put her at thirty-two years old, but her soft features and cheerful demeanor made her appear much younger. She smiled at me as I sat next to her. Something about her felt familiar, but it might have been the familiarity with which she addressed me and everyone around her.

"Hi, Frida," I said.

Her grin widened. "You have to get up extra early to get sausage." She took a bite of a link and grinned. "It's the best part."

I looked down at the sausage and eggs on my plate. "I'll trade you my sausage if you tell me a story."

She looked at me as if I'd just made a very serious proposition. "Stories are free."

"Not this one," I said. "This one is about your family."

"I'm not supposed to."

"I know." I pushed my sausages to the edge of my plate. "And I'm not supposed to ask you to. I'm supposed to come here and take your money." I gestured at the room we were in. The decor was centered around a cheerful yellow, like sunlight blasting through the stainless steel. "But I don't want to take this life away from you."

Frida accepted my sausages, rolling each one carefully from my plate to hers. After she had taken her first few bites, she said, "Uncle Gerry was always nice to me."

A chill ran down my spine. Gerry. The uncle that the records had identified as her only remaining relative. "What's his last name?"

She shrugged. "Gerry was nice but the boys he made me play with weren't always nice." She touched her cheek as if remembering a pain long since passed. Her breaths became shallow and her skin flushed.

Watching her sent a shiver through my chest at the realization that Retch was right. I was going to learn something here that I couldn't possibly ignore. It was already too late.

"They always came at night," Frida said. "Sometimes there were lots of them." A tear rolled down her cheek. "Sometimes they were Heavies. Sometimes they were tall boys like you."

"From the Hallows?"

Frida nodded. She bit another piece of sausage, chewing it slowly. A piece of it stuck to the corner of her mouth, but she didn't seem to notice. "They were always mean."

"How did you get them to stop?"

Another tear fell. "I didn't," she whispered.

She shook in her seat and pressed her eyes closed. I was stressing her out, and I still didn't know what I was going to do about the collection contract. If I kept pressing, I'd hurt her, and she had been hurt enough. I could see it in the quaver of her jaw and the flush of her cheeks. One of the workers—a Heavy woman in blue scrubs—scowled at me from the corner. The workers had taken my bribe, but it would only take the slightest outburst before I was on my ass out the back door.

"What do you do that's fun here?" I asked, looking around. My eggs sat on the plate in front of me, but I had lost my appetite.

Her flush faded. She mumbled an answer too quiet to hear.

"What was that?" I asked.

"Flippers."

"Flippers? I don't know flippers. Would you care to show it to me?"

She glanced at my eggs. The two orange yolks stared up at me from the plate. Getting the hint, I ate them, sopping up the yolk with a slice of buttered toast. Despite my lack of appetite, they were the best eggs I'd ever had. Frida finished the sausages and cleared her plate. We carried our dishes over to a window where a conveyor belt carried them away to the kitchen.

"It's my day to do dishes," Frida said.

The place was run as a coop. Everybody did their part to the best of their ability. Frida and two men showed me where the aprons and gloves were, and they set me up at a station next to Frida. She didn't hesitate a second, diving right into her work without complaint. The spray wand blasted food from plates and silverware, and she had me scrub down the larger cookware. Together with the others drying and putting away dishes, the chore was quickly finished. The work had settled Frida.

"Come on," she said, tossing her gloves and apron into a laundry chute.

Flippers was a game involving oversized coins flipping across a flat surface. It was low-tech, luck-based, and surprisingly addictive. Maybe it was the expression of absolute glee on Frida's face when she landed a coin in the three-point spot on the table, or maybe it was my competitive impulse, but I couldn't bring myself to break the game for more questions. We didn't speak until we finished a full twenty-one-point game in which Frida destroyed what was left of my ego.

"You have a nice life here, Frida," I said.

"Yeah," she said as if it was a comment she got a lot.

I knew the moment I met her that I wasn't going to take her money. I didn't care what kind of debt I had to incur or what kind of bones needed breaking, I wasn't going to steal this life from her. I wasn't that much of a piece of shit.

That didn't mean the lingering questions didn't bother me. I could guess that her uncle got what was coming to him, but it was something I'd have to follow up on. Uncle Gerry was a steaming pile of frothy waste left over after a fish harvest, and I found myself hoping he'd died a particularly painful death. Maybe I could follow up on that to make sure it really happened.

But there was still one thing.

It was instinct, really. Maybe my gut was permanently poisoned by the sickness of my pessimism, but the truth was my gut was right more often than not. I knew darkness when I saw it. Hell, I wallowed in the dark slime of the Nicodemia underworld long enough to probe the edges of the great abyss. There was a sickness in a world that lived in this sort of perverse logic. People hurt other people. Even when there were so many reasons to treat humans with decency, people still hurt people.

Frida had been hurt. The outline of the plot was clear enough, and I didn't need any more details. Sure, it would have been nice to track down every abuser, but that was an impossible task. Even I knew not to take that one on. What bothered me was how she escaped. There were only a few ways I could think of that would get a girl like her away from a man like Uncle Gerry.

And only one of those ways made much sense.

"Frida," I said as I put my hat back on my aching head. "What happened to your baby?"

I caught a glare from the helper in blue scrubs a few paces away. She scowled a hole in my head, but I'd asked the question so quickly—so casually—that she didn't have a chance to stop me.

At first, I thought Frida wasn't going to respond. She looked at me with her bright blue eyes, and her tongue tasted her dry lips as if the answer danced right there ready to be spoken.

Then, the tears came, heralding the most anguished wail I'd ever heard. Frida cried so hard and so loud that only one conclusion was possible.

Turned out, I was a piece of shit after all.

The others closed ranks on her. The boys scowled at me and crossed their arms. The girls wrapped Frida up in the biggest hug imaginable. Together, they absorbed her pain in a big ball of kindness.

As I left—a moment after I passed through the exit from the Saint Teresa Home for the Needy—I heard one name claw its way free from Frida's miserable howls.

"Gretchen," she wailed. "M-My Gretchen."

Then, all the familial similarities clicked. The amber tint in her hair. The light coloring of her skin. There was a bright flicker in her eyes that I should have recognized. Frida had once had a child. She'd wanted desperately to keep her, but the broken system had allowed that child to fall through the cracks.

Frida's Gretchen had become Retch.

Chapter 35

I WOKE with the dirty dishrag of exhaustion settled deep into my bones. My aches tugged at the muscles of my face, making every expression painful. Every movement was the grinding of an ancient, rusted machine. All sleep gave me was a sore back and a few more ticks on the clock.

A shower helped, but I couldn't bring myself to go through the effort of a decent shave. The scruff along my jawline rasped when I ran a hand along it, but it hid the worst bruise that I barely remembered getting.

"You're a living Adonis," drolled my sister when I sat across from her at the diner booth.

"I guarantee you I look better than I feel."

"And I guarantee that can't possibly be true as long as you insist on wearing that hat."

I plucked my fedora from my head and peered at it. The battered hat didn't look so bad, in my opinion. According to ancient traditions, it told people I was an investigator. Maybe I didn't have any right to wear it, since my investigations of late didn't seem to go anywhere.

"Lovely for you to join us this afternoon," said Helen, setting a plate of fried potatoes in front of me. She cast a glare at my sister, but Angel wasn't the sort to go easy on her big brother just because her wife thought it was a good idea. "I'm sorry your night didn't go well."

"Thanks, Helen," I said without breaking the locked gaze with my sister. "You don't know how much I appreciate everything you do here."

Helen wandered back to the counter, where a pair of elderly men in fishing coveralls muttered their gossip over cups of black coffee.

"Is it true you got all the way down to the Guttering Spine last night?" asked Angel as she scooped food into Runt's dish. The muscular slab of a dog waited for her permission before approaching the food like the good dog he was.

The fried potatoes filled an empty hole in my gut, and I washed them down with a glass of too-sweet pineapple juice. "It wasn't the worst thing I did since I saw you last."

She opened her mouth to spit more acid, but something in my expression stopped her. She plucked a potato from my plate, dipped it in ketchup, and popped it into her mouth. "Dad always said you were the hard worker."

"Sometimes I think maybe being a hard worker isn't the ideal he thought it was."

"I'm pretty sure he was insulting you." Angel clicked her tongue and Runt left his food to stand by her side. She scratched him behind the ears before releasing him so that he could finish his meal.

"Don't you feel guilty for being so mean to him?" I asked.

"You're the only one with guilt issues around here, bro." She leaned forward. "Dogs need structure." Angel plucked another piece of potato from my plate and tossed it to her dog, who snatched it out of the air. "Knowing who's boss gives him a sense of purpose."

"He must have one hell of a sense of purpose."

The bell over the door rang, and Retch strode in looking like a brick of dimes on a Saturday night. He wore a sleek button-down shirt, sunglasses, and a pair of thin black gloves.

The dog nearly bowled him over as a greeting. Standing on his back legs, Runt did his best to reach Retch's face with his slobbery tongue. Retch cried out in dismay and did his best to shove the ball of muscle away, but it didn't work.

"Come on, dog!" Retch exclaimed, backpedaling.

Runt dropped to the floor but didn't let up. He licked Retch's hand, sniffed his crotch, and ran about a dozen circles around him in half as many seconds.

"Runt," Angel said in a calm voice.

The dog stopped. He pranced over to his owner and lay his head in her lap. She gave him another little scratch behind the ears. "Likes to know whose boss," she said.

"Always you, sis," I said. "We all know it."

Retch nudged me over and sat in the booth next to me. He straightened his stylish shirt, checked it for dog-related damage, and set his sunglasses on the table. "You always lend me the best books, Demarco."

"It looked a little dense to me."

He opened Saria van Esters' journal to a marked page. "It's a modified Vigenere cipher. Very hard to break. Without the key, I probably would have been stuck."

When he didn't speak for a few breaths, I prompted him. "Well?"

"Did you know the key was backwards?"

I thought about the tattoos on Destiny's chest. She would have needed to read it in a mirror. "Makes sense."

"You know I'm still mad at you, right?"

I thought of Frida Ward and her wailing cries. "I'm a piece of shit. I thought we were just agreeing on that."

He had the decency to look abashed, but Angel saved him. "I think that's unanimous."

"Saria van Esters wrote this before she died," I said, tapping the journal, "and there's one that Destiny Alverez had in her possession before she died."

"Suspicious," said Angel.

"It's about the colony," said Retch. "At least, that's what's in Saria's notes. She talks about the steps needed to make Magdalene Moon habitable as soon as possible. It's pretty technical."

"Why would she write it?" I asked because I was always asking too many questions. It was my job.

"You said the other journal was more complete," said Retch. He was getting into it now. It almost felt like he'd stopped being angry at me. "Maybe there's something in that one."

I said, "Shaw's probably tossed it into the recycler by now."

"He'd be an idiot to get rid of something that valuable," said Retch.

"A lot of people are idiots," said Angel. "Idiocy makes the world spin."

"What exactly does it say?" I asked.

"That's the thing," said Retch. "When she says she's speeding things up, she says it should have always moved this fast—like they've known how to colonize the moon since the day Nicodemia first started orbiting this solar system. These are just some final calculations."

"It's been a hundred years," I said. "More."

Angel leaned forward and whispered, "I'm going to let

you kids work out your conspiracy theories." With that, she rolled away into the kitchen.

With a shrug, Retch crossed to the other side of the table. I paged through the journal. Retch's neat handwriting covered the previously blank pages, first decoding the odd geometric shapes into letters and then substituting the letters through a complex, variable cipher.

"This is incredible," I muttered as I read his translations.

"Scientists get pretty full of themselves," said Retch.

"No, not that. I mean your work here. Retch, this is a tough cipher and you've decoded it. You transcribed the whole document."

"All while you were busy getting your face bashed in."

"Literally and figuratively," I said.

"You had it coming."

"We all have our talents." I peered at Retch. His hair was immaculately styled. The line of his jaw was set against the judging world. "I really missed you, Retch."

"Yeah, you could have used my help," he said.

"Frida Ward—"

"Drop it," he said.

"Retch—"

"We don't need this right now," Retch snapped.

"Later?"

He tapped the journal, bringing my attention back to the task at hand. "It's also her confessional. Almost like Last Rites."

Saria van Esters had written every sin of her long career in the journal, starting from dropping microbial genetic studies in favor of larger organisms, despite ethical dilemmas. She thought it was against God's will for her to modify higher organisms, but she'd seen the utility of it. A simple tweak to survive in the lighter gravity. A change to accept the toxins of the moon's atmosphere. The microbiome around a plant's roots could do wonders, but it only went so far. They were so close, she thought, and how could she possibly not be involved in that last step?

At the very end, in a messy script, was written, *My love, you were right. Everything you do is for a greater good.* After that, the text remained untranslated.

I said, "Why the code?"

Retch shook his head, clearly pitying my stupidity. "Oh, old man. You don't get it, do you? They write this code because they're afraid of it being read. This is something they've done so much that to them it's easier to write like this than in any regular language."

"It looks like a lot of effort, for something that can just be decoded."

Retch pointed up at the ceiling. "There's only one set of eyes they need to hide it from."

Trinity. The journals were coded because Trinity would struggle to scan and read the oddly coded message. That was why it was written not only in a cipher but also in another more obscure geometric code. As long as the two pieces weren't together, Trinity wouldn't be able to judge anyone writing the notes. Their Karma would be safe. Probably.

And here we were putting the pieces together. I closed the journal and sat with my hand on the cover for a long time. "There must be more to this."

"Oh, there is."

"You stopped translating because you knew Trinity would pick it up."

He winked at me.

"All right. When are you going to tell me?"

Retch flashed a charming smile. "Let's get that second journal first."

Something about how he said it made me uneasy, like he was hiding some crucial piece of information. What had he read in that journal that he hadn't bothered to translate for me? What was it that was so critical that Saria van Esters wanted to hide it from Trinity—and Retch had agreed? I took the journal and the key Retch had derived from Destiny's tattoo, and I tucked them away in my pocket.

"I know where Shaw hid Destiny's journal," I said finally. "And we're going to get it back."

His grin widened.

Chapter 36

"YOU'LL BE POLITE?" I asked Retch.

"Absolutely." He jammed a syringe into the muscle of his leg and gave himself his daily dose of hormones. Trinity offered very little in the way of support to a transitioning teen, but between the small support community we'd visited in the Sinless district and my access to restricted medications, Retch was settling into an acceptable hormone regime. For now. "Wouldn't dream of anything else."

His reaction seemed sincere, which worried me. He was hiding something. "You sure seem a lot more cooperative," I said.

"What's wrong with cooperative?"

We sat at a cafe in a lower section of Haven only a few blocks from the Blue Mongoose. The dimes I'd collected sat heavily in my satchel, just waiting to be delivered to Jade and Jasmine. The sun had set, and one by one the Haven streets went dark with curfew. The cafe owner—a heavyset man with a well-trimmed beard—polished mugs behind the counter, waiting politely for us to leave before shutting down.

Lorentz entered, looking every bit the dashing beauty that she was. She wore a slender black suit and thin sunglasses. The white tails of her monk's collar fell down crisp and straight against her perfectly tailored shirt. Her amber-tipped hair was slicked back, accentuating a sharp widow's peak.

Between her and Retch's new extravagant styling, I felt like a homeless thug.

"You look like a homeless thug," Retch said, eyeing me up and down.

"Shut it," I growled.

"Ready?" Lorentz said.

"Always." I led the group through the dimly lit street.

Shaw had said I needed to visit the Mongoose if I wanted the journal. He had put the journal in the safest place he could find. Not a bank. Banks could be robbed. Banks had suspicious items disappear from deposit boxes all the time if you believed the mistrustful miscreants of Retch's Screaming Jesus gang. No, Shaw wouldn't have put the journal in any official lockbox. Nor would he have stashed it in one of his caches around town. Too easy to find. Retch's people had been following Shaw for a long time, and they knew where half his hiding spots were.

If he wanted something safe, it had to be stashed *and* guarded, and for that, he would have taken it to the Blue Mongoose, one of the most protected illegal gambling halls in all of Haven.

Retch hooked elbows with Lorentz, flashing her a saccharine smile. "You know your part?"

"Do you know yours?" she replied.

Retch pulled away from her. "Bitch, it's *my* plan."

"Polite," I said.

"That *was* polite," snapped Retch.

I shot Lorentz an apologetic look.

We separated, and I charged into the Blue Mongoose like a bull. I lowered my head and pushed past Jasmine.

"Jude," she cried as I passed. She waved her bouncer to follow and trailed me past the glittering lights. "We're not expecting you—"

"Shut it, Jas," I said. "I'm here for the boss."

"You know that—"

I shouldered my way through the door into the stairwell. When the bouncer grabbed my arm, I stopped him with a glare cold as the dead of space.

It didn't faze him one bit. Behind him, Lorentz made her way into the club unmolested. Retch was nowhere to be seen, but that was the plan. The silhouette wouldn't be perfect in the dimly lit casino, but with a well-placed distraction, he'd be able to sneak in. A couple more goons patrolled the casino floor—one woman near the blackjack tables and the other back by the cash register by the row of personal vaults.

"All right." I wrenched my arm away from the goon. "I'll go slow, but you know I need to meet with Jade."

"Jade's busy," Jasmine said.

"Aren't we all?"

With a sigh, Jasmine ascended the stairs, leaving me guarded by the bouncer. Minutes passed with the thick-headed thug staring holes in the side of my skull. He was taller than me and built like the kind of guy who might push trolleys around down in the Heavies.

"Name's Demarco," I said once the awkward silence started to get to me. "Jude Demarco. All things found, all things fixed."

He continued to stare.

"Nice to meet you, too," I said.

"She'll see you now," said Jasmine. She nodded to the

bouncer and he followed us up into the suite at the top of the stairs, breathing hot breath down my neck the whole way.

I burst into the room like a man on fire, throwing the satchel down in front of Jade. I leaned forward, two fists down on the smooth top of her heavy desk. "I've had enough of this bullshit."

She met my gaze and held it, answering in her own casual time. "I've been listening to reports about your work," she said. "It's subpar."

"It's better than what Shaw's giving you, and I need what he stole from me."

"Better? We sent you to make three collections." She raised an eyebrow at the satchel in front of her. "Unless I'm mistaken, you've only collected one."

"One and a half," I said. Behind Jasmine, through the window that looked out on the gambling hall below, I saw Lorentz throwing dice on a craps table. Behind her, the goon who had been near the blackjack tables crossed the floor to man the host's station in Jasmine's absence. "The rest of Frankie's payment will come when she has her first art show."

Jade leaned back, lacing her fingers behind her head. "Maybe you don't know how things are done around here, Demarco. We collect money, not art."

I glanced back at Jasmine, who now stood in the corner of the room. I moved to close the gap between us, but the thug stepped in my way. Suddenly I didn't like my chances. I held my hands up in surrender. "You'll get Frankie's money," I said.

"But not Orville Ward?" asked Jade.

"Orville's dead," I said. The goon towered over me.

"Yet his debt lives on," said Jade.

I sighed. There wasn't any other way to play this. Not one that would get the journal anytime soon.

I clenched my fists. “Frida’s off limits.”

“You misunderstand how this works,” said Jade.

“If I need to tear this place to the ground—”

The bouncer tried to grab my arm, so I reversed the grip and shoved him until his hip crunched into the corner of Jade’s desk.

Jade scowled. “If you can’t behave—”

“She’s disabled,” I said.

“And wealthy,” said Jasmine.

The bouncer looked like he was going to fight my grip, but Jade waved him off. Her eyes flicked to the red button on her desk, which would summon more bouncers. I released her bouncer.

Jasmine peered at me with her brow knit in a pleading expression. “A lot of people wonder how Haven’s Trinity allows us to operate. We’re up past curfew. We drive the vice of the entire neighborhood and a fair share of the surrounding communities.” She circled the outside of the room. “But that’s what it’s about, isn’t it? Community. One of Trinity’s three pillars. Body, soul, community. Do you know what the skeleton of the community we’ve built is?”

“Trust?”

“Trust,” spat Jade. “Trust is worthless. This club is built on *money*, Demarco. No exceptions. Not for kindness. Not for corruption. Money that’s owed gets paid. Never trust anyone.”

What she said made sense. Even though they operated outside Haven’s laws, they didn’t operate outside of Trinity. They built a community here, and that community couldn’t exist if people didn’t pay their debts. Things would get real messy real fast. That was why Shaw was able to put physical pressure on people. Owing money made them part of this community.

But me? I was outside of it all. "Anything I collect doesn't count," I said.

"No, but Shaw didn't mind taking credit for your work." She gestured at the corner of the desk, where a bundle of dimes sat. "Turns out Frankie had access to more money after all."

Blood rushed through my skull. Shaw had been following me all along, and he'd collected from Frankie. Would he do the same for Frida? Suddenly it didn't matter that I was outmatched by the bouncer. I was too mad to care.

I slammed a fist into the bouncer's gut. Despite how alert he'd been—despite how much he'd been watching me—I caught him off guard. Like a good bodyguard, he had been waiting for me to attack his boss. His belly crumpled under my fist and he grunted.

Then he recovered.

Jade's hand hovered above the red button. If she hit it, there would be a swarm of bouncers on me in seconds.

The bouncer swung a wild fist at my head, but I'd had enough head injuries to last me a whole week. I ducked and did a double jab to his stomach and neck, connecting hard with the second. I held a boxer's stance with my fists up for defense.

I shot a glance at Jade, who watched without a shred of emotion. She thought the big guy was going to take me down, and wouldn't call for backup unless it was needed. Jasmine fled.

Then the bouncer was back in business again. He came hard, a glint of metal in his hand. Brass knuckles. Damn.

His stance matched my own. Fists up, feet spread. This guy knew how to match my style beat for beat, only his beats were going to be bone-crushing, and mine wouldn't knock the wind out of a balloon. A guy with knuckles like his didn't need to swing hard. A light jab would break ribs, meaning he didn't need to overbalance himself with a haymaker or over-commit with a furious assault.

But everyone did that anyway.

He came at me hard. I ducked, but not too hard or fast. I stayed a breath out of reach, leading him forward to match me.

He bit the bait. Feet fell out of position. I stepped forward, slugged him as hard as I could in the solar plexus, and slammed him against the glass, hoping to land him on the gambling hall floor below.

Below, Lorentz glanced up at us, breaking character with the worried crease between her eyebrows before smoothing herself off again and returning to her game.

"Demarco," said Jade. "Have you had enough?"

The bouncer pulled himself to his feet. He stretched his neck, clenched his fists, and put up his dukes.

"No," I said to Jade, raising my own fists. "I think I can take him."

This time I didn't bother baiting him. I launched myself hard and fast, feinting left, going right. My feet moved like we were on a dance floor. He anticipated the move, but I was fast. I landed a fist in his side, then ducked back as he swung an elbow. My back hit the wall, so I braced myself and kicked hard and low.

Big guys. They're all about the muscle, and it's hard to hit through solid muscle. A padded stomach or the heavy meat of a shoulder—they're like punching bricks. Thighs will eventually bruise enough to cause a problem for even the biggest guy. I'm a big guy myself, I know what I'm talking about.

But knees? Knees are the same on big guys as they are on skinny ones. Hit them hard enough, and they tear. Hit them harder and they crack. Braced against the wall, facing the full force of my Heavy-trained muscles, the bouncer's knee was a twig in a hurricane. With a sickening crunch, it bent backward and I felt the kneecap crumble under my boot.

I darted away as he screamed in pain.

Jade finally pushed the panic button. She wasn't obvious about it, but her hand brushed across the surface of her desk and the two bouncers down on the casino floor moved.

"Things are going to get real interesting real fast, aren't they?" I said.

Her voice was laced with venom. "You don't know what you've done."

"Let Frida's debt drop, Jade," I said. "And since I don't like how this is going, let Frankie's drop too."

"You've made an enemy today," said Jasmine from the doorway. The two thugs crashed past her through the door. "I hope you understand that, Demarco."

I nodded to the bouncer crying on the floor. "I think we had a fair fight. No hard feelings there, right, buddy?"

The two bouncers advanced. I glanced at the window to the floor below. My lungs ached with every breath. The two thugs were about to make short work of me.

"Look," I said, raising my open palms in supplication. "I've always liked you, Jasmine. Lonnie Grant always liked you. You're a good person down under it all. All you want to do is run a good gambling hall in a bad place, and nobody's going to blame you if things get a little rough." I stepped away from the window and let my appeasing smile drop back into my usual resting frown. "But there are lines we don't cross. It doesn't matter how Trinity weighs your deeds. It doesn't matter what your customers think. Some debts don't get paid, and that's the end of it. No matter what."

Jasmine's eyes narrowed. "Or what?"

My smile came back, but this time it was wicked.

"Wherever the shadows fall on the shallow graves of sinners, wherever blood pools under a wounded man, wherever the sky goes dark and the reckoning comes, that's where I'll be. You make an enemy of me, and you'll never be safe. Your customers will never walk near a shadow. If you're doing this, then you'd better kill me now and hope I stay dead, because I'll make your life miserable until the day you crawl to the lowest of the low in the Heavies for hope of reprieve. I'll plague you until your bones turn to dust."

Jade's fingernails drummed on the desk. "What makes you think I won't kill you right now?"

"Corpses are bad business."

Jasmine stared at me, her jaw as tense as I'd ever seen it. Finally, she stepped aside so I could leave. When I tried to walk past, she held out a hand to stop me. "You won't set foot in this establishment ever again."

I said, "So long as you never collect on Frida's debt, we're even."

Jasmine glanced at Jade, who nodded.

That was it.

I descended the stairs and walked past the empty tables of the Blue Mongoose, cleared of all the night's customers by the alarm. I walked past the moaning body of the cashier, who was just starting to recover from the wrenching agony of a stunstick. I walked past the open safe, where Leo Shaw had once stored items most valuable to him.

I had lied to Jasmine. We weren't even. Jade and Jasmine would know soon enough that I was their enemy. This wouldn't make my life any easier, but that would be a problem for another day.

And I walked out the door directly into Leo Shaw. He leaned against a lamppost, lit cigarette dangling from his lip, arms crossed. His calculating eyes watched me as I approached.

"I don't want trouble with you," I said.

He exhaled a cloud of smoke. "A certain way of looking at things says that you just stole something from me."

I showed my palms. "My hands are clean."

"But your knuckles are bloody."

"Professional hazard." My hands closed into fists. He was right, my knuckles ached from the abuse. "Who sent you after the journal?"

"Easy fella." Shaw plucked the cigarette from his lips and grinned a toothy smile. "Nobody's got any fight around here."

"Way I see it," I said, "Jade and Jasmine sent you after my debt, but someone else paid you to take the journal. Otherwise, there was no way for you to know its value."

"Interesting theory."

"I'm just hypothesizing."

"Then hypothesize."

"The journal's important to whatever the colony is doing. Science stuff. Could be that the scientists were after it, but also there's nowhere science goes that the Church doesn't take interest, so I'm guessing someone with a religious affiliation hit you up for the contents." I watched Shaw closely but saw no hint of a reaction. "Instead of handing it over, you used it as leverage against me. The way I figure it, you were hoping I could decode it for you so that its value would skyrocket."

"That's a clever hypothesis," Shaw said.

"I thought so."

Shaw stubbed his cigarette out on the wall and flicked the butt at my feet. "The way I measure it, we're clear. Stay out of debt and I won't have to come chasing you down again."

"Who hired you?"

He folded his arms again. "I'd hate for you to owe me."

I picked up the cigarette butt, folded it neatly, and dropped it in a nearby recycler. If we were even, then I didn't want anything else to do with Leonard Shaw. It wasn't worth owing him again.

As I left, he said, "Barton. Bishop Theodore Barton"

Without turning back to him, I said, "Is that so?"

"It's a good hypothesis, don't you think?"

I met Retch and Lorentz in the gloom of an alley several blocks away. The silhouette draped from the kid's body and its extra length pooled around his ankles like blood, but he had the hood off, so I could see the rapt expression on his face as he paged through the book.

"You got it," I said, stating the obvious.

He flashed a mischievous smile. "I told you those vaults weren't so hard to crack."

"Well?"

"It's worse than you think," Retch said, returning to the journal. "A lot worse."

"I think things are pretty bad," I said.

"Always such a pessimist," said Lorentz.

"I prefer to think of myself as an optimist in a lousy world."

"You can read it?" Lorentz said. "Just like that?"

Retch nodded but didn't say anything.

"Smart kid," said Lorentz.

"Destiny needed a tattoo to allow her to read it," I said.

The muscles in Retch's face relaxed long enough for the smallest sigh to pass through his lips. He flipped another page. His eyes focused into the distance, and for the first time ever I had the impression that I was seeing him unguarded.

"What is it?" I asked when he didn't volunteer anything.

His eyes darted to Lorentz and then to me. "You're going to the Gravity Lounge," he said, "and I'm coming with."

"I've wanted to get into that gig from the start," I said.

Lorentz stepped back, tilting her head. "What does it say?"

"I know a guy who can get us into the Gravity Lounge," Retch said meeting Lorentz's steady gaze.

Lorentz said, "I need to know what's in that journal."

To Lorentz, I said, "You don't want to bring Retch, do you?"

"You shouldn't come either. I need to confront Petunia, and to do that I need the contents of that journal." She met my gaze. "It won't be safe for anyone else."

"To hell with *safe*," said Retch. "Nothing's safe."

Lorentz said, "I—"

"What we just did wasn't safe," snapped Retch. "You're the one we don't need."

Lorentz said, "The Church—"

"Your Church never did anyone any good," Retch said.

They both looked at me as if I had the answer to it all. I wished that I did.

"Barton's scheduled for a service," I said. "I'm going to have a chat with him, then we're all going to the lounge."

"Oh, by the way," Retch said, "our ticket in involves your sister's dog."

I swore under my breath.

So much for optimism.

PART V

the case of the gravity lounge

Chapter 37

THE FUSION STAR in the center of the spinning station shone directly into Nicodemia's topmost bead providing life-giving light for all its lush plant life. In the center of the vast spiral, Saint Lucy of the Light's crystal parapets focused God's scouring luminescence like a giant magnifying glass on a swarm of penitent ants.

I sat in a pew during the main chapel's morning service staring into the brightest of the bright, trying my best to adjust to the blinding light.

The pews were half full with the penitent and the performative, and the bishop at the altar raised his hands, blessing the body and blood of Christ. The gold trim on his purple vestments draped over his broad shoulders. His miter caught the light and cast dancing reflections across the ornate statuary high above.

The moment I saw him, I knew my mistake. I had scoured the ranks of the priesthood in my search for the man I'd met in the garden the night of Destiny's murder, but priests weren't the only ones who wore collars. The bishop made the sign of the cross with immaculately manicured hands, touched the bread to the wine, and spoke sweltering truths from the bottom of his soul. When he was finished, he administered the body and blood to five parishioners, and they distributed it to the rest of the parish. Same as in any church for the past thousand years.

I didn't take the Eucharist. Maybe I wasn't worthy. Maybe I wasn't pure.

Maybe I was just in a bad mood.

I could taste the dry wafers in my memory. The subtle vinegar of cheap wine lingered on my tongue. How many Masses had my parents brought me to before they died? Had they ever really believed the teachings of the Church? My father certainly hadn't let it keep him from his dubious dealings in stolen art.

Here I was—walking in his footsteps, questioning my faith, walking the shaded path. He'd be so proud.

"Go in peace to love and serve the world," chanted the bishop. His words resonated in the enormous space, caught by godly acoustics formed of gold leaf and stained glass. The final song of Mass was a celebratory one, sung by a congregation devoid of all emotion and flat as the cardboard circles offered up for transubstantiation.

"Theodore Barton," I said to the bishop as he exited the sanctuary in procession. "We need to talk."

He ignored me, keeping his chin high and his eyes forward. When he reached the narthex, he turned to face the approaching wave of parishioners and caught an eyeful of me.

"We need to talk," I repeated, not moving to the side.

"Peace be with you," Barton said to the first woman to exit the sanctuary. She smiled weakly and shook his hand. To me, Barton said, "Reconciliation hours are posted, my son."

"A confession would be nice," I said. "But not mine. Not today."

"Peace be with you."

"I thought I saw a priest in the garden the other day," I said.

He spread his hands to indicate the lush plants growing throughout the narthex. "The whole of the Hallows is our garden."

"But I wasn't looking for a priest at all, was I?" I said.

"Peace be with you," said the bishop to a pair of scantily dressed teens. The sharp line of his lips pressed together in disapproval, but he said nothing. "Perhaps we could have this conversation another time?"

"Why were you in the Gravity Garden the night of Destiny's murder?"

"Are you speaking of Destiny Alverez?"

"I am."

"Unfortunately, her funeral will be a private affair," he said, "and it will not take place in the church."

"I can assure you she wasn't a suicide."

His gaze flicked to me for a fraction of a second before returning to the flow of parishioners vomiting into the narthex. "Peace be with you."

"Harold Mance is dead," I said, pitching my voice so that it would carry to the nearest parishioners.

Barton's serene expression slipped for a heartbeat. I was getting under his skin. "He was a disturbed man, but I'm sorry to see him pass."

"Were you sorry to see Destiny pass?"

"All life is precious."

"You didn't know her?"

"There are many parishioners in my diocese. It's impossible to know everyone, as much as I try."

"But you know her mother, don't you?"

Barton raised an eyebrow. "Perhaps you should talk to the priests. They deal more closely with the parishioners."

"I've had words with three of your finest."

He spread his palms. "Peace be with you." A gaggle of old women passed.

The room had almost cleared, and only a few parishioners lingered near the exit. If there was one thing Catholics were good at, it was clearing the room once Mass was finished. The smell of sweat and incense lingered in the air. Barton preened as if proud of all the good work he'd done that day. I'd had enough of his sanctimonious garbage.

"Mr. Demarco," he said as I turned to leave. "Let me offer you some free advice."

"Advice is never free," I said.

"Reconcile."

"You first."

I pushed through the grand cathedral doors, blinking away the blind spots burned into my retinas. Barton's involvement in all of this still eluded me, but I had an appointment to keep. Retch was going to bring our ticket to the Gravity Lounge, and he'd be meeting us in the garden. If I was late—well, I didn't know that he'd wait.

"Jude Demarco," came a familiar voice. Officer Echo emerged from the blinding morning light, a stunstick held loosely in his left hand. "Funny meeting you here."

Halders stepped up to me from the other side, dressed in his on-duty blues. "A coincidence, probably." His Adam's apple bobbed under the scruff of his beard. "Just a chance meeting."

"Still," said Echo. "I'd like to get some questions answered, now that we have the opportunity."

"Like how did the Destiny Alverez crime scene get messed up?" said Halders.

"And why wasn't the killer caught on Trinity's surveillance? Seems like there aren't too many people who can get away with something like that."

"Come on, guys," I said. They flanked me, making it impossible to talk to them both at once. "You know I didn't kill Destiny."

"Do we?" asked Echo. "Seems like a pretty straight gig. Kill someone. Earn a few dimes investigating the murder. A crime never solved keeps paying, right?" When I didn't answer, he barked, "Right?"

That asshole bishop must have tipped them off to my presence, but I couldn't figure out how. He'd been in Mass the whole time. "I'm not looking for trouble right now."

"When *are* you looking for trouble?" asked Echo.

"At night?" Halders said.

"Sure." Anything to get them to leave me alone.

"Sure?" Echo mocked. "Sure? Halders, you hear this guy? He said *sure*."

"Sounds like a confession to me," said Halders. "He's admitting to some pretty shady practices."

"I'm not—"

"Looks like I win," said Halders.

Echo flipped a dime to his partner. "Fair enough." To me, he said, "You're not going to try to run, are you?"

"Do I look like a guy who runs?"

Echo prodded me with the inert stunstick.

"I wouldn't run if I were you," said Halders.

"I promise I won't run," I said. "Happy?"

Halders said to Echo, "Can we trust this guy at his word?"

"You figured I'm a good God-fearing Catholic, right?" I said. "Isn't that how you knew I'd be here?"

"He bet you'd take a swing at me and make a run for it," said Echo. "I bet you'd just run."

"Looks like nobody wins," I said. "Welcome to real life."

Echo shrugged. His chins jiggled and his thick mustache twitched. "You ever take a long bet, Demarco?"

"Fella by the name of Harold Mance killed Destiny," I said. "If you're looking for a clue in your case, that one's free."

"Leave the investigation to us, is what we said," said Halders. "I remember saying it. I remember telling you to get out of town for a while."

"It's been a while."

He placed a hand on my shoulder. "We have a different opinion about the movement of time."

"Sure."

"'*Sure*,' he said," Echo mocked again. "What an agreeable guy."

"Look, fellas," I said, starting to walk down the cathedral's massive steps. The space in front of the church was a magnified focus of uncomfortable heat, and I'd had enough of it. "I'm telling you what I know. Harold Mance helped kill Destiny Alverez. He was involved in the death of Saria van Esters in the Heavies, and now he's dead."

"He's a pretty helpful guy," Echo mused.

"He's been busy," I said.

"Busy enough that he had an alibi for Destiny's killing?" said Halders.

Echo's lips puckered like he had tasted something sour. "Rock solid."

"Star witness," said Halders. "Real respectable too."

"Maybe he had an accomplice," I said.

"And who might that be?" asked Halders.

I thought of how the bishop ran from me in the garden. I didn't have any evidence on the guy. Only a hunch that he was involved. "It's a work in progress."

Echo said, "Maybe we should collaborate."

"I'd only slow you down." They followed me down the steps, still inconveniently flanking me. If I made a move they'd knock me flat.

Echo jabbed me in the kidneys with his stunstick—still not activated, thankfully. It prodded me into walking faster but didn't land me in a heap. "You know what gets me?" he said, glancing at the cathedral spires high above. "The duplicitousness of some Catholics."

"That's a mighty big word, Echo," I said.

He jabbed me again. This time, a low-grade electrical buzz ran up my spine. "Watch your mouth, asshole."

I tried to veer upspiral, but Echo nudged me downward. Toward the jail.

"I saw you, you know," said Halders. "That night Destiny was killed."

"Just because I was too late to save Destiny doesn't mean I'm guilty of her murder." It was a weak argument, and I knew it.

"Doesn't mean you're innocent," said Echo.

"Harold Mance killed her."

"I told you," Echo said, "he had an alibi."

"Video?"

"Witnesses. A whole prayer group full of them," said Echo.

"I sure would like to meet those witnesses." I pushed forward faster, forcing them to keep up. "The man didn't strike me as the prayer group type."

"Told you this guy was going to run," said Echo.

Halders said, “This is a fast walk.”

“I promised I wouldn’t run,” I said.

Echo said, “Sure.”

“Sure?” These guys were making me nervous. “Sure? What an agreeable couple of cops you turned out to be.”

Echo poked me with the stick. Harder this time, and with more juice. It made my knees wobble and my mouth taste like limes. He flipped a switch, and the stunstick’s buzz whirred louder.

“Fair enough,” I rasped. “I won’t accuse you of being agreeable. I didn’t mean to offend.”

“We need to talk,” said Halders. “That’s all.”

“You guys are right,” I said. “It’s the duplicitous nature of some Catholics that’s really the problem around here, isn’t it?”

“Every day,” said Halders.

“I mean, the ones in the Gravity Lounge are the worst, aren’t they?”

Halders frowned. “You know we don’t go there.”

“Not even to follow a fugitive?” I asked.

“Maybe if he’s a real asshole,” said Halders.

“And you never know what you’ll find once you’re in the door,” I said.

Echo said, “Sounds like a guy getting ready to run.”

“I’m not going to run.” I casually stepped up my pace. I wanted the cops winded, and I was in much better shape, even after all the beatings. “I promise.”

“That so?” wheezed Echo.

“I’d hate to give you fellas the satisfaction.”

Halders said, “Disappointing.”

“That’s what my father always said.”

“You run from him, too?” asked Echo.

"Did Lorentz tell you I'd run?" I asked, taking a stab in the dark.

Halders said, "She said you might."

"I bet she says a lot of things," I said.

Echo shot his partner a harsh glare. "The Jesuit's a whole lot more trustworthy than some excommunicated handyman."

"And a whole lot smarter than a couple of cops."

When Echo's predictable jab came, I took his stunstick and jammed it into Halders's chest. The taller cop dropped like a sack of dead fish. With a twist and a flourish, I separated the stunstick from Echo's sweaty grasp and swung it around to land a crippling pulse in the man's gut.

The tough guy folded in on himself and deflated onto the pavement. They both convulsed violently, vomited, and then settled into fitful unconsciousness.

"I won't run," I said, switching the stunstick off and tucking it under Echo's arm. "I prefer to walk."

With that, I disappeared into the too-bright Hallows morning. It was almost time to meet Lorentz, and things were about to get complicated.

Chapter 38

TRUST IS A POISONED WELL, slick and sour with the lies of those who came before us. Trust can't exist in a society based on greed. It can't thrive in a world built on the ashes of the distrusted. All three beads of this great heaven in the sky were constructed from the displaced trust in higher powers that betray the needy if it meant one single step toward glory.

Trust in the Church? Not the church that rejects its most destitute followers. It purports to support the poor, but only if they abandon their own truths. The Church embraces those bent toward sin. After all, we're all sinners. But those like Retch who seek to exist in their truths? They are sinners beyond reconciliation.

And for what?

Trust the machine? Trinity was a collection of rules designed by faithful engineers who had no idea what society they would create in the future of humanity. They saw their generation ship as a way to form the perfect Catholic society in the stars. A replica of Dante's Paradiso, bright and perfect, with the sin scoured from our poor souls by the relentless judgment of pure white light.

The machine had more loopholes and contradictions than the Bible itself. And to make it all work, all they needed to do was abandon a needy Earth.

Trust people? The average chump in the city of Nicodemia could be trusted to keep their head down, help when it wasn't inconvenient, and disappear when the going got tough. They weren't necessarily bad, but they weren't exactly good either.

Then, there were people like Lorentz. Her eyes widened as I approached under the long arched trellis. Roses brushed the top of my hat and the heavy sweet scent of the brilliant flowers filled the air. The scent dominated the atmosphere, reminding me of concealed corruption. Of hidden death. We were in the Gravity Garden, the minimally surveilled space outside of the esteemed Gravity Lounge. This was the meeting place we had arranged.

And now I didn't trust her one bit.

I plucked a rose from the trellis and pressed a thumb against its thorn. "Sorry I'm late, boss. The blue cornered me."

She held out a hand as if to take mine, but when I didn't respond she dropped it again. The set of her shoulders was tense like she was expecting a punch. "The police are not our enemies, Jude. They can help us."

"They've only ever helped people like us into an early grave."

"People like *you*."

"If the grave's big enough, maybe you can join me."

"I gladly will if it gets me the answers I need."

It was too much. All of it was too much. I hated myself

for putting my trust in her, and I hated myself for not. "When I need help, I'll find it myself."

"When you need help, it won't be there."

"No," I said. "It won't. And that's why I work so damn hard making sure I have things under control."

"Under control!" Now it was her turn to rage. "Under control? You think you have *anything* under control? You've thrown yourself at the mercy of thugs and criminals how many times these past few days?"

"At least I know how they'll treat me."

"You have the bruises to prove it."

"I'm not locked in a jail cell."

"What about Retch? You trust him, but you won't trust me?"

"You *just* betrayed my trust, Lorentz."

"You're too good for what's going to happen up there," she said, calm again.

I stared at her, unable to process what she had said.

"I watched you handle yourself. You fight only when you need to fight. You're fair to those who are fair to you." She pointed up at the Gravity Lounge. "Up there things are going to get ugly. It would be better if you missed it."

"What are you afraid of me learning?" I asked.

She said, "Retch knows more than he's letting on."

"Retch knows who he can trust."

Lorentz placed a hand on my arm and looked up into my eyes. "There's something broken in the Church, Jude. This has been a problem throughout its whole history. When the tenets of our faith part from the truth discovered by science, we break, and it's always ugly."

"It's tough learning that the universe doesn't revolve around you."

"It's even tougher to learn that you've caused thousands

of years of suffering when Jesus's only mandate was that we love each other."

I pulled my arm away. "You think Petunia Alverez learned something that challenges the faith?"

Lorentz shook her head. "I think God works through science in ways that the Church doesn't always appreciate."

"Is that why you sent the blue after me?"

"I alerted the blue about the danger to Petunia Alverez," Lorentz said, turning away. "If there's anyone who can help us keep her safe—"

"It's not them," I growled. "It's never them. The blue is the problem here in the Hallows. Hell, they're a problem everywhere. Just another gang of thugs trying to impose order on a world swirling around in the chaos."

"We're living on a space station, Demarco," Lorentz drolled. "Imposed order keeps us alive."

"It *crushes* us." My thumb bled where I'd pressed too hard on the rose's thorn, but I didn't feel the pain. I threw the flower to the ground. "We don't see it because it's all we've ever known, but this place is slowly killing us."

Lorentz stared at the rose. "Maybe the colony on Magdalene Moon has the solution."

"All I want is justice for Destiny."

"Retch knows something," Lorentz said. "He read something in that journal and he's hiding it from us. Why do you think that is?"

Lorentz had always been a mystery to me. Her love of science almost eclipsed her love of the Catholic Church. When I first met her, I was struck by her relentless search for the truth, which I assumed meant she supported the advances of science that would eventually lead us to colonize the system. It would give us the release valve Nicodemia desperately needed—the release it was unable to truly fulfill in places like the Sinless or the Gravity Lounge. An escape from the Church. It was the only reason I could think of that would motivate Retch.

It was also the reason I was still excommunicated after all these years. Living without the machine—without the Church—breathing down my neck for every mistake and every single sin was the only way I could still draw breath. I lived and died by the kindness of strangers, and they lived and died by mine.

Lately, too many of them were dying.

So, yes. I believed that escaping from Trinity was one solution to the problems people were facing. I didn't say it to Lorentz, afraid of what she would think of me.

"All we can give is everything, Jude," she said. "Neither of us can fix the world. We just have to give everything we can to what we believe is right and trust God to carry the rest."

"I'm here to solve a murder, prevent a murder, and maybe bruise my knuckles along the way."

"You have a hell of a job to do, Demarco." The voice came from down the short end of the arched tunnel. Retch approached holding a short leash and a backpack. On the leash was my sister's compact pit bull Runt, his white face contorted into that dumb grin all pit bulls get when they try to breathe.

"You have any trouble with Customs?"

"Dropped a few dimes and mentioned the Gravity Lounge, and they let me right through." He glanced at Lorentz. "You two getting along?"

"Yeah," I said. "Yeah, we're good." We weren't good. "What did my sister say about taking Runt?"

Retch pulled the dog past us.

"Retch." My voice dripped with warning.

"She didn't want to give him up," he said. "Even after I said you only needed him for a few hours."

"You stole him." I leaned down and patted the dog's big dumb head.

"Well, here's the thing," said Retch, taking Runt's face in his hands and jostling his jowls.

Around the corner rolled my sister in her wheelchair, dressed to perfection and sporting something I hadn't seen in a long time—a smile.

"Goddamn it," I said.

"Demarco," said Lorentz.

"I know, I know."

"No, that's not—" Her throat made a dry click when she swallowed. "What I said before…"

"You can't come," I told Angel.

She clicked her tongue, and Runt came to her side.

"I only need Runt to get us in the door," I explained. "The Gravity Lounge has been scooping up dogs, and Retch has someone who will let us all in if we bring the pooch."

"Then you need me, too," said Angel.

I knew that stubborn expression like it was the one I stared at in the mirror every single morning. Angel was going to join us or we were going to lose the use of her solid little brick of a dog.

"You know the plan?" I asked, finally.

"Bust heads, take names," Angel said.

I glanced at Retch, who shrugged. I said, "Petunia Alverez lands in one hour, and her airlock opens directly into the Gravity Lounge. If anyone's coming after her, it'll have to be at the funeral."

"You have Mance's silhouette?" I asked Retch.

He patted his backpack.

"Runt stays with me," said Angel.

"I can't guarantee that'll be easy," I said.

She rolled forward. The dog stayed in step.

"All right, all right." I showed her my palms. "The dog stays with you." It *did* make for one less thing to worry about. "I'll do my best to make sure it's not an issue."

"I've seen you do your best, bro. We're going to need a little better."

Ouch. "You should have stolen the dog, Retch."

Runt looked up at me with joy and forgiveness in his big stupid eyes. I took his leash and led him along the path, letting the others follow at their own pace. When we reached the place where Destiny Alverez was taken, he sniffed the scoured pavers, detecting death or sin or blood—whatever innocent dogs found interesting in places of disrepute. He anointed the shrubs with a splash of urine.

Lorentz did her best to clean my coat, which was a hopeless affair best left to the rain. She brushed invisible specs of dust and straightened the collar. Then, she took a makeup kit and touched up around my eyes and nose to hide the bruising. "Can't have you looking like a meathead," she said.

"I like to think of myself as more of a mook."

"The hat," said Retch, folding his arms from a few paces away. "You gotta ditch the hat."

Angel clicked her tongue. When Runt sat at attention, she tossed him a treat. "I've always told him that."

"It's my signature look," I said, removing the fedora.

Retch blinked. "Oh, God, the hair."

Lorentz plucked the hat from my hands and placed it back on my head. I knew how to win that argument when I needed to. She stepped back next to Retch and Angel and peered at me. I felt fairly judged by the three of them, and I didn't much like it.

"They'll never let you in," said Lorentz.

"What about the kid?" I said, gesturing to Retch.

"Don't worry about me," said Retch, straightening his collar. "I've got class."

He *did* look good. His slow change from street urchin to roguish gentleman had continued with colored tips of his gelled hair, a blazing button-down shirt, and a pair of slacks that absolutely must have been tailored to fit so well. Not only did he look as good as I'd ever seen him, but he looked undeniably male. He *was* undeniably male, and he carried it with a confidence I'd never seen in him. A glittering earring was the only hint of traditional femininity on the boy, and even that was something that changed with the ebb and flow of fashion.

"All right," I said. "What else do we need before we meet this contact of yours?"

"Not a thing," said a voice from around the corner. Wesley rounded the bend from the alcove where Destiny had been taken. "In fact, I think you'll fit in just fine."

Chapter 39

I DID *NOT* FIT IN. Not by a long shot. Wesley led us through the elaborate arches of the front entrance where gilded reliefs depicted angels descending from the glorious clouds of heaven. Bands of real marble were inset into shining metal surfaces, and lights inset into the walls blazed across the floor like rainbow flames. This was the service entrance, and it made me wonder how amazing the fancier upper entrance to the Gravity Lounge must be.

"I thought you died when you fell," I said to Wesley, remembering his expression as he dropped from the building in Haven.

"I didn't."

"It had me pretty broken up. I thought I'd killed a guy. Wrecked my whole day."

Wesley's gargoyle jaw didn't even twitch.

"Do you get that, too?" I touched my chest. "Real tight feeling when you know you've hurt someone?"

He didn't blink.

"Castor Vin was a good man," I said. "He was trying to do the right thing."

"He was a threat." Finally, a response.

"You eat that lie?"

"Maybe you're a threat."

"I like to think so."

Wesley pushed open a door made of genuine cherry and let the way into a dimly lit lobby. Our footsteps were silent on the soft red carpets and the only light came from rows of gilded sconces. The walls themselves were covered in textured tapestries that shone with intricate silver and gold thread among textures of green and blue. Again, the theme was angelic, but here the angels landed to interact with a penitent human population.

"Vin wasn't supposed to die," Wesley said.

"The bullet in your partner's gun had a different opinion."

He fixed me with a stony gaze. "The boss said to let in anyone with a dog, so I'm letting you in."

"All of us get in with just one dog?" I said.

"Your partner made a deal."

I chewed my lip.

"He said you would find King," said Wesley.

"Ah. The Yorkshire terrier."

"He promised."

"No hard feelings, then?"

"Not at the moment, but if the boss tells me to break your legs…"

"Who is your boss, exactly?"

Wesley gestured to the desk on one side of the lobby, which sat in front of a plain, unmarked door. A rack stood next to the desk with a dozen coats hanging from metal hooks.

"If things get ugly," I whispered to my sister as she caught up to me, "I want you out of here. Fast."

She gave a little hop with her wheelchair, testing the gravity. Her wheels floated above the smooth floor for a solid second before landing. "I don't think I'm going anywhere fast. It's hard to get any traction."

Here in the Gravity Lounge, the highest of the high, gravity felt like it might be willing to release us from its oppressive grasp. The heady aroma of lilacs drifted up from the garden below, carried by the low hum of powerful ventilation fans.

"This way, Miss," said Wesley. He gestured for Angel to follow him past the desk into the coat check room.

Angel's brow furrowed with worry but she followed. I followed with Runt.

"This is great," said Retch, hopping next to Lorentz.

Lorentz put a hand on his shoulder. "Something's not right."

Then I was in the coat check room, but it wasn't a coat check. Or rather, it wasn't *only* a coat check. A slender girl with gangly arms and a long nose stood in front of a row of tags. Her name was Jan according to her embroidered name tag, and her hair was fashioned in a kind of curled bob I'd never seen outside of antique novelty photographs. She wore a skimpy outfit that closely resembled the one I'd found in Destiny's apartment.

"Is that the hair thing you were talking about?" I asked Retch, who waited, arms folded, in the doorway.

"That's the hair thing."

"I like it."

"You would."

Jan offered me a harness and gestured at my coat and hat.

I said, "I get cold."

"He has bad hair," said Angel. "And his fashion's about a decade late."

"Or a few hundred years, depending on how you look at it," I said.

"That doesn't make it better, bro," Angel said.

But her attention wasn't on me. It was on Wesley and the work he was doing selecting items of clothing from a rack. These weren't checked coats, but rather sleek, streamlined arm and leg coverings. When he found the pair he was looking for, he offered them to Angel, who tentatively took them.

"All of the customer-accessible hallways in the Gravity Lounge are fitted with superconducting plates," Wesley explained in a voice that told me he'd memorized these lines and delivered them a hundred times. "Thanks to the lower gravity up here and these adjustable rigs, you will be able to free float or even engage in light propulsion."

Angel hefted the weighty fittings. "I'd rather have my chair," she said.

The bouncer scowled. "Most people find it easier to move through the vertical spaces with proper anti-gravity fittings."

"Vertical spaces?" I asked.

"The Gravity Lounge is designed for free space. It's a remnant of the days when the beads were being constructed in a freefall environment." He handed me a pair of fittings.

Every hair on the back of my neck was telling me that this was suspicious, but I clasped the fittings on my arms and legs anyway. The leg units clamped onto my thighs and the arm units fit snugly around my shoulders. They were comfortable enough.

Angel donned her gravity gear, her lips pressed in a hard line.

"Will you manage?" I asked.

"You know I don't like leaving my chair," she said. Her chair was her mobility. It would be like me leaving my legs behind for a chance to fly for an afternoon. Would I get my legs back? Depended on how much I trusted Jan, the coat check girl.

"I'll buy you a new one if they damage it," I said.

She barked a single laugh. Then, she tentatively rose with the assistance of the gravity gear. Floating a hand's breadth above the chair, she made some adjustments to the tools, then pushed up until she was level with my face. "I could get used to this," she said, lifting herself a tidge above me. "Looking down on my big brother."

I tried my own gravity gear, floating at first, and then playing with the adjustment to drop myself down to the floor. The magnetic assist was adjustable using a cuff on the left arm, and after some tinkering, I was able to skip across the floor like a schoolgirl on a moon.

Wesley brought two sets of gravity gear out of the coat check room, only to find Lorentz standing alone in the lobby. A pair of men dressed in flowing blue silk entered from the garden doors.

"Where's the kid?" Wesley asked.

"He decided this wasn't for him," Lorentz explained as she took her gravity gear from the bouncer.

"He might have enjoyed the show." But the bouncer stepped aside and touched a comm unit attached to his ear. After some whispered communications, he returned. "Well, with that in order, you should head to the main stage. There is a show starting soon, and a delegation arriving within the hour that I'm sure you'll want to greet."

Angel floated behind Runt like a balloon, enjoying the full range of freedom promised by the Gravity Lounge. The bouncer left us and greeted the couple at the door, ushering them to the coat check.

"I guess that's all the intro we get," I said.

"Hey, it could have been a punch to the gut and a hard toss off the inner spiral," said Lorentz.

"That would have made me feel like the world was a little more predictable." I bounced forward, still trying to gain my balance with the gravity gear. Two hops across the grand gold-plated lobby took me to the double doors that led to the next room.

The inside of the Gravity Lounge was a marvel of modern architecture. Long cantilevered structures stretched high up into the vast room, with circular portals leading upward and inward to the central chambers. Elegant statuary sprouted from the walls depicting angels and saints in their glory with their swords upraised and Bibles thrust forth. Above, a frescoed ceiling covered a wide dome, coming down across the walls and floor. It was an enormous reimagining of the Sistine Chapel, complete with a full telling of the first five books of the Bible centered around an image of Adam and God touching.

"It's beautiful," whispered Lorentz. "Inspiring."

"Hidden away so nobody can see it but the elite." I pushed myself up, nudged the marble robe of a saint to adjust my direction, and drifted up above the statues.

As I rose, Angel said, "Well isn't my brother just a ray of sunshine."

There were others in the lounge. A cluster of three men floated above the Archangel Michael's flaming sword. They watched as I drifted past, sipping their goblets of wine. I imagined these people were used to seeing newcomers fumbling for the first time using the gravity gear. I tipped my hat to them as I passed on my way upward, mumbling a greeting.

"Not going to help your sister?" Lorentz asked, drifting up beside me. Even with the gravity gear, I was still being pulled downward slightly, and I'd slowed significantly shy of the circular portal to the main stage high above.

"Angel wants help about as much as I want a punch in the face."

"Maybe," said Lorentz. "But I find it's best to help anyone who needs it

"Funny, I feel the same way about punches."

Lorentz was drifting faster than me, so she took my hand so that we would stay together. Below, my sister found another path. A winding walkway up the side of the room wove its way through the elaborate statuary and even cut its way through the fresco itself. She waved at me to keep moving forward to the next room, while Runt pulled her slowly upward.

"Does she know why they want dogs here?" I asked.

"Do you?"

"I assumed it was for a dog show of some sort," I said. "Or a fight."

"Runt doesn't seem like the fighting type," Lorentz said.

"I doubt anybody's going to care." I peered up at the arch high above. "Think we can make it up there?"

A pair of gray-haired women drifted past us on their way up, giggling like schoolgirls.

"I'll race you," said Lorentz. She pushed off of me, caught Michael's extended flaming sword, and launched herself upward toward the exit.

I, on the other hand, tumbled helplessly downward. I tipped my hat to the three chatting men and caught myself on the noble depiction of Joan of Arc's holy shield. With a mighty leap, I launched up after Lorentz, catching up to her just as she passed through the portal. I caught her waist in one hand, pulled her close, and spun until we crashed into the far wall.

At first, I was distracted by her pressed up against me. She was a holy person. A chaste monk wed to her Church. She was never going to be with me. Her path was set long ago when she decided to take the robe and rope of the Jesuit order.

But she was a beautiful woman. Her body pressed up against mine and I felt her melt into me as if we were always meant to be together. There was regret in the way her hand touched my chest. Sadness in the way her forehead pressed against my shoulder.

"Demarco," she whispered.

"I know." I wasn't holding her close, but I didn't push her away either. I desperately wanted to tell her that I was sorry for our argument, but the words were sludge in the back of my throat. "Stay close and stay safe," I said.

Then, I opened my eyes and took in the Gravity Lounge's inner sanctum. Gone were the religious depictions and the noble statuary. Gone were the clusters of quiet patrons whispering secrets in a space where nobody could hear. This place was something else. Something darker. Louder.

The first thing I noticed was the people. The writhing of flesh put the Sinless to shame. A hundred people clung to a cage in the center of the room, dark limbs intertwining around the central stage. Naked men and women writhed within. Others clung to the outside of the expansive room, more conservatively dressed than those in the center, but leering and muttering like rumors of sin gone bad.

A tunnel of iron mesh led from the central cage to the outside of the room. The doorway was closed. Above more circular portals led to dimly lit tunnels. Somewhere in those passages, I'd find the airlock. Seven layers separated Nicodemia from the great void beyond, and this was one of only a few entrances to our great city. Docking was easier here at the top of Hallow Nicodemia. Other open portals led from this central lounge to a dozen other smaller rooms. People passed in and out of these in various stages of undress. Business men and women made deals and exchanged goods.

The light in the vast room was dim and red and foul. The air smelled of sweat and blood, with low undertones of alcohol and drugs. I knew this smell.

It was the smell of gambling.

A bookie had set up near the entrance, and a crowd of shouting men and women surrounded the little booth holding rolls of dimes up for their wagers. Nobody here wagered less than a full stack. The hair on the back of my neck itched to place a bet, even though I didn't even know what they were betting on.

"Dogfighting," said Lorentz, pointing to a digital readout. It was one of dozens of possible bets, but it appeared to be popular.

As if I wasn't worried enough about my sister. "They don't even do that down in the Sinless."

"What is this place?" Lorentz whispered.

Before I could answer, the people attached to the central cage pushed away to drift to the outside of the room, revealing a central figure who addressed the whole crowd with open arms. He wore the long, multicolored sleeves of a showman draped over his broad shoulders, and the flashy long tail of his modified kimono trailed behind him in the low gravity. Every wave of his long arms was a flash of dazzling color.

He wore a black porcelain mask that gleamed with grinning malevolence.

"You know anything about this?" asked Lorentz.

"Maybe that's the boss we've heard so much about," I said. "And I think I know who he is."

"Same." She pushed herself back against the outside wall. Her face was pale, and her breaths came rapid and shallow.

"Welcome!" The man's voice boomed through an amplification system, and I knew exactly who the boss of the Gravity Lounge was. Bishop Theodore Barton's eyes locked with mine. "To the Gravity Lounge."

It was suddenly hard not to notice the number of guards emerging from the shadows around us.

Chapter 40

THE BALCONY WAS one of any overlooking the inner sphere of the Gravity Lounge. As we watched, black-clad workers prepped the cage in the center of the lounge for some kind of show. Lorentz stood next to me. Behind us stood a single guard watching in silence.

When the guard had invited us to wait on the boss's balcony, I hadn't seen any option but to accept. He stood grim-faced and sour, watching us as the activity in the center of the main stage played out.

"I figure we can take him down if we need to," I whispered to Lorentz.

"I figure you'd get killed in the process."

"A win is a win." To the guard, I said, "What's the show, anyway?"

The guard's grin showed too many teeth. "You've never seen the Devil in action, have you?"

"I like to think I have."

A wall panel behind him slid open and Barton floated through, golden goblet in one hand. He had abandoned the grim porcelain mask for a simple strip of ultra-black cloth that covered the upper half of his face. He placed a hand on the guard's shoulder and whispered something in the man's ear. The guard slipped away, and the wall closed behind him.

"Bishop," I said.

He pressed his palms together. "It isn't often I see someone attend both of my services on the same Sunday."

Three vertical lines formed on Lorentz's brow. "What is this about, Father?"

"Consider it outreach for the modern Church," said Barton.

"Dog fighting, flesh shows, and gambling," I said. "Hell of a church you have here."

"It's an outlet for those who deserve it."

Lorentz scoffed.

"The lord provides." Barton touched his wristwatch and the cage in the center of the lounge expanded. Workers drifted away and disappeared into the walls. "I think of this as a reward for our good works."

I didn't want to get into a theological debate with a bishop, but everything he said sounded dubious. "We're here for Destiny Alverez's funeral."

"As I said earlier," said Barton, sipping fortified wine from a golden goblet. "Hers is a private event."

"We think her mother is in danger," said Lorentz.

"I assure you, she is safe."

"As safe as Saria van Esters?" I asked. "Those were your three priests working with Mance, weren't they?"

"Dr. Alverez has used the port attached to the Gravity Lounge a dozen times, and she has always been safe doing so." Barton watched a pair of extravagantly dressed men drift past, arm in arm. "Her ship has arrived already, and she is working her way through the airlocks. When she arrives, the funeral will commence."

"Then take us there," I said.

"I suggest you enjoy the show," Barton said.

Lorentz said, "This is disgusting."

The bishop tipped his glass to her. The liquid inside sloshed in slow motion in the micro gravity. "These people's good works have had enormous influence on the whole city. They have earned their revelry."

"It's not a point system," Lorentz said.

"Ah, but it is," said Barton. "Few know how Trinity weighs deeds, but Church leaders have insight that we do not share."

Trinity. "You're a machinist," I said.

"Such an odd term, don't you think?" He swirled his drink. "Trinity defines the values of our tradition. We certainly don't worship it as an idol."

"Then you must believe that the engineers were inspired by God," said Lorentz, seeming to think that the theological discussion was more important than our other pressing concerns.

"Those who wrote the books of the Bible were inspired by God, as were the people who assembled those documents. Why wouldn't Trinity's engineers be similarly influenced?" The smug smile on Barton's lips told me he'd had this argument before. *That's* why I didn't want to get into a theological debate.

A cheer went up in the crowd. The cage connected to the wall via a long tunnel made of heavy bars. Doors opened with a groan, and a monster emerged.

"God gave man dominion over all His creatures," said Barton.

It was a dog, but it wasn't a dog. Corded muscle roped

around its massive frame and its squat face snarled to reveal rows of wicked teeth. Its cropped ears lay flat against its head and short black hair bristled along its back. Its long claws hooked on the bars of the cage, and it launched itself into the twelve-sided cage in the center of the lounge.

Barton touched the device on his wrist, and his voice boomed throughout the lounge. "Behold, the monster of Magdalene Moon, the creature of the Hallows, the devil of the Gravity Lounge." He paused until the crowd's cheers ebbed. "Genetically modified to build muscle and bone in low gravity. Trained to slaughter its rivals. Vicious in every way that matters. Perfectly obedient to its masters. This is what they make of those they send to the colonies. Welcome, Cain!" The name echoed through the Gravity Lounge, punctuated by the beast itself snarling and launching itself at the inside of the metal cage hard enough to bend the fibersteel bars. It ran a circuit around the cage, using its hooked claws to move as easily on the ceiling as on the floor.

Viewers near the cage flinched, but I wasn't paying attention to the hideous dog. I was watching the door at the other end of the caged tunnel. A chill of dread pierced my spine. You need two dogs for a dogfight.

"Call this off, Barton," I said.

"Bets have been placed, Demarco," said Barton. "You, of all people, can respect the sanctity of a good wager, can't you?"

"Yeah, you're real honorable here."

The doors to the cage tunnel opened a crack, then closed again. A murmur rippled through the crowd.

Barton peered at me. "I thought you might appreciate it if the entertainment you brought for us could jump the queue."

Again, the cage door almost opened but slammed shut

with a boom. A single shout of anger and dismay emerged under the roar of the crowd. Not many would have recognized it, but I did. It was etched into the annals of my youth, inscribed so deeply into my soul that I would recognize it long after I was dead.

It was the sound of my sister's fury.

"I can't let you attend the funeral," said Barton.

"You son of a bitch."

Cain snarled and pounded at the confines of its cage. He launched himself from one side, slamming hard into the walls and rattling the bars. A cheer shook the Gravity Lounge.

Barton pushed away from the viewing platform's mesh, but I grabbed his wrist before he could drift out of reach. "Call this off," I snarled.

The guards had me before I could even think about taking a swing at Barton. They swarmed in through the balcony and slammed me hard against the bars of the viewing platform.

Barton was gone, disappeared into a passage behind the balcony. One of the two bouncers pounded me in the gut with a meaty fist.

"Stop!" shouted Lorentz, real concern bleeding through the tension in her voice. "You'll hurt him!"

They weren't going to stop. They held me down and smashed my face against the mesh so that I could see the show.

Cain had stopped raging at the walls. The big dog faced the door, and his low growl rumbled through the entire Gravity Lounge.

"Shit," I said.

"It's a distraction," Lorentz said.

"A good one."

The guards pressed me harder against the mesh.

The door to the cage opened, and someone shoved Angel and Runt through. Angel clutched the bars of the cage in one hand and Runt in the other. The thin leash was still attached to the dog's collar, and his lips were peeled back in warning. I had never seen him look so fierce.

Cain dwarfed the tough little pit bull. Until I saw them close to each other, I didn't fully comprehend how gigantic Cain was. It was like a rabbit squaring off against a wolf. Poor, tiny Runt wasn't going to stand a chance against the monster.

The crowd went wild. Money changed hands. Wesley floated down in front of me and regarded me carefully. He was sizing me up, probably trying to decide if I'd go quietly or if I'd put up a fight.

"Let him go," Wesley ordered. The two guards released me. My face ached where it had been pressed into the mesh, but I was otherwise uninjured. "He'll behave."

It was hard to imagine anyone being more wrong.

I launched myself out of the balcony and slammed into Wesley's enormous chest. He was ready for me. Ready for wild swings and a furious display of anger.

What he wasn't ready for was my sheer bulk. Living in the Heavies for a decade built me up into a solid brick. He might be a better fighter than me, and he might be bigger than me, but I had something he couldn't match.

I just didn't give a shit.

He swung a stunstick at me, but I swatted it aside. I slammed a boot into his fingers where he gripped the railing, smashing fingers. With a joint lock and a hard kick, I sent both of us toppling toward the cage in the center of the lounge.

We smashed into the bars, and the dogs clashed.

Runt flew hard at the bigger dog. Cain snarled and

snapped, his slavering jaws foaming in fury. The two dogs locked together and the crowd cheered.

Lorentz launched herself high into the air, but she was the furthest thing from my mind. The plan was ruined. My sister was in that cage, and I didn't see any reason Cain would stop once he'd killed Runt.

Then, the music changed. Ram Jam's Black Betty blasted through the great open space to questioning looks from the crowd. Its heavy blues guitar wailed as I swung at the bouncer. He moved like lightning and my face slammed hard into the cage.

Retch had control of the music. That meant he'd found his way into the control center, which meant that he was giving me a ticking clock.

"Jude!" Angel shouted, her voice laced with genuine concern.

"I'm working on it," I said through the taste of blood. "Can you get out the way you came in?"

"Tried," she said. "Look out!"

The bouncer's grip slackened. I rolled away just in time as his stunstick slammed into the cage where my head had been.

I grabbed the guy's arm, yanked him around, and flung him away across the room. Cain launched himself at Runt, but the smaller dog dipped to the side with a snarl.

The patrons of the Gravity Lounge watched the dogfight in cruel fascination. They knew my sister's dog was going to die. They knew she'd be next. That's what they were here to see.

Well, fuck them.

Because I knew something they didn't.

There was a hinge on the cage, not visible from afar. The hinge was attached to a door, and the door spanned nearly a third of the upper surface of the cage. Thin, delicate metal hinges attached to a heavy iron frame?

That's what I call a point of weakness.

I had only seconds before Wesley and the other bouncers were on me. This time they weren't going to foolishly let me off easy. I'd be overwhelmed the moment they decided to move.

So I didn't hesitate. I wrapped my hands around the heavy bars, braced my boots against the cage, and pulled with every ounce of strength all those years in the Heavies had given me.

The structure was strong enough for a resident of the Hallows. Thin bones and unconditioned muscles would never pull apart this cage. Even a resident of Haven would struggle unless they were the showy weightlifters working for one of the big gambling houses, or farmers from down in the meat mills.

But I was something else. I grew tall in the Hallows, but the Heavies had made me strong. Heavy tempered my bones and bound the cords of my muscles. I heaved, and metal bent. Wesley saw what I was doing and launched himself back across the open space toward me. The other bouncers followed suit.

They were too late. With a roar, I tore the entire gate from the cage and flung it at one of the bouncers. It slammed into him and he tumbled downward and away.

Cain swung his jowly face in my direction and growled so deep it made my chest ache.

My sister once told me that only a fool locks gazes with a large, angry dog.

In the yellow depths Cain's huge eyes, I saw something I didn't expect. Cain's gaze wasn't the rage-filled murderfest I was anticipating. It wasn't a pit of mindless fury.

The monster was intelligent. Cain stared at me with a calculating brilliance that I could only think of as sizing me up and weighing my worth. He cocked his head. The short hair on the back of his broad shoulders stood high on end. I didn't know if he was considering me as food or judging my soul, but it didn't matter. The numbers came down against me. Hard.

"Jude, look out!" my sister yelled.

Cain attacked.

Chapter 41

WESLEY TACKLED me hard from the side, and together we tumbled away. Cain passed through the gate, and his momentum sent him spiraling directly past us toward a cluster of onlookers.

Then, finally, the spectators screamed.

The bouncer and I arced up and into the great empty void between the cage and the wall. We grappled in a cloud of sweat and blood. He snarled at me. I swung a haymaker, but the force spun me. He gripped a handful of my jacket and yanked me close.

"I'm trying to keep you alive," he hissed.

"You're still working for Retch?" I couldn't believe it.

"Make it look real." He hit me with a couple of solid rabbit punches. It didn't feel like he was pulling them one bit.

Cain hit an empty wall. The crowd scattered like low-gravity bowling pins.

I caught Wesley's next rockslide of a punch and twisted him around. We drifted toward the far wall. Without solid footing, I couldn't properly lock him out, but he made it look good. Good enough, anyway. The big dog launched himself straight at us.

Shit.

Cain understood how to move in low gravity. It arced slowly across the room, yellow eyes laser-focused on my jugular.

"Drop!" I told Wesley.

"You drop." He tried to twist, but my grip on his arm prevented any decent maneuvering.

I kicked off, sending myself laterally back toward the cage. Too low. The song wailed through the wildest chords. Time was running out.

Wesley's hand went to his gravity harness controller, and he immediately started to fall.

Not fast enough. Cain's jaws locked on his arm and shook, showering me with blood and saliva. The man screamed and pulled, but there was no way to get free. The dog weighed almost as much as he did. He wasn't escaping unless that dog let him escape. There was nothing I could do but watch.

Angel whistled. She hung from the open cage, with Runt at her hip. Cain spat out the injured bouncer and swung his attention to her. Wesley drifted downward toward me.

His arm bled from ruined chunks of flesh. His eyes were glassy and unfocused. I caught him by the uninjured arm as he drifted past and rode his momentum to the floor.

Black Betty finished, leaving the room with a resounding silence. My heart hammered. My mouth went dry. It was the moment of truth. Had Retch taken control of the Gravity Lounge?

My gravity harness lurched. Then the simulated zero-G of the Gravity Lounge transformed into a light upward tug. I gripped a railing on the floor to keep from floating away and hooked Wesley in place.

The crowds had thinned, but there were still gawkers, now falling gently upward. These assholes were the worst of the worst—here only for the bloody show.

"You going to make it?" I asked Wesley, the medic in me taking over. Ribbons of flesh dangled from his arm, and blood pooled in odd lumps by his side.

He scowled at me like he was regretting trying to help me, but finally landed on, "Yeah, I'll be fine. Medics are on the way."

My sister whistled again, seizing the giant dog's attention. Cain twisted, lips peeled back in a silent snarl. Angel dangled something in front of him, demanding his attention. Runt sat next to her on the ledge, meek and timid next to my sister's burning ferocity.

Cain didn't have a gravity harness, and neither did Runt. The big dog wasn't floating so much as reaching the top of a long, slow arc—an arc that would take him to the top of the cage where my sister sat waiting for him. Once his claws grabbed the cage, he'd be able to attack.

Above, through an opening in the ceiling, a flashing white strobe blinked a rapid report. That was Retch's signal. He had controls of the lights and he was telling me where to go to find the airlock gate. Petunia Alverez was almost there.

But she wasn't the only Alverez in the Gravity Lounge. My gaze fell on another familiar face moving against the panicked crowd: Reginald Alverez. He looked gaunt and hollowed out, his skin a pale gray compared to the hale glow I'd seen only a few days prior. When he saw me, his fists clenched at his sides.

"Purple Haze" by Jimi Hendrix blasted through the Gravity Lounge's speakers. The next countdown started.

Retch still controlled the system, and he was telling me exactly how much time I had left.

Reginald had a hard look in his eyes. He was there on a mission. Halfway up the long curve of the Gravity Lounge's wall, he launched himself upward toward the airlock entry.

There wasn't time to think about what Destiny's father was there for. Cain was on his way toward my sister, but as I prepared to jump at the dog, Angel waved me off.

"I got this, bro," she shouted over the wail of Hendrix's electric guitar. "Go get the scientist."

I jumped, my gravity harness pulling me toward the high dome of the ceiling. Using muscles trained in the punishing weight of the Heavies, I vaulted up the curved wall, grabbed the handholds on the upper stretch, and pulled myself over to the airlock entrance.

Cain slammed into the cage, his hooked claws grasped the bars, and he pulled himself toward my sister. My heart wrenched sideways. How could I *leave* her like this? What kind of big brother was I?

Jimi Hendrix wailed on his guitar. I only had seconds left before I needed to move. Hand over hand, I pulled myself toward the airlock passage and up into the hallway connecting to the smaller chamber. The hall sat at a sharp slope, leaning toward the open space below, but with the reversed gravity, I had no trouble scrambling up. Above, the white lights still flashed outside of the airlock. Reginald climbed and floated toward me as I pulled myself into the upper chamber. I tore my harness off and landed lightly at the top of the sloped passage.

"Demarco!" Reginald gasped.

I stood above him at the edge. Sweat beaded on his brow, even though it was his harness that did most of the work floating him up there. The man looked terrible. Grief had hollowed his features and sunken his eyes.

Below, Cain advanced into the cage. Angel sat between the big dog and Runt, with her arms outstretched to the big, snarling beast. I reached down to help Reginald up the slope.

But he didn't take my hand. Instead, he clawed his way up on his own. "I know enough not to trust you."

"Destiny didn't deserve what she got."

"She got you." He shuffled grasped a handhold, and I gave him more space. He swept back his coat to reveal a shining red pistol.

"Let's not get hasty, Alverez."

"I *trusted* you!" His hand closed on the pistol's grip.

"Careful," I said. "You wouldn't want to fall."

He let go of the handrail with his other hand and floated. "There's no falling in the Gravity Lounge." He drew the gun.

"I wouldn't be so sure of that."

"Purple Haze" ended with a Hendrix smash of drums and guitar rattling into the night. That was the signal for Retch's next change.

Nothing.

"Petunia's my *wife*, Demarco," said Reginald. "What she's doing out there got Destiny killed, and it'll do a lot worse if I don't talk to her."

"I thought you were going to apologize."

"I'll just talk."

"You don't need a gun for that." Shouts echoed from below, but I couldn't take my eyes off Reginald.

"She needs to listen."

"Step onto solid ground," I said.

His gun shook.

I silently swore at Retch and wondered if the kid had run

into trouble. Reginald was building himself up to violence, and there was nowhere for me to run. No way to stop him.

"Pull the trigger, then," I said, meeting Reginald's gaze. "Take God's judgment in your own sweaty hands and send me to the hell that I deserve."

Finally, all at once, every gravity harness in the lounge flipped, making people heavy instead of light. Reginald's feet hit the sloped floor hard. His knees wobbled. He grabbed for the handholds on the wall and missed. Panic washed across his face. The gun still gripped in his hands was forgotten.

The harness pulled harder. Below, the lounge was in chaos. The assertion of *down* beat bloody the most unrelenting patrons. Many of them couldn't even walk.

"Give me the gun," I said.

The whites of his eyes caught the flashes of the airlock behind me. His fingers finally closed on a handrail and he steadied himself. "She's almost here."

"The gun, Alverez," I said. "She left you a long time ago."

"Help me up!"

"Not while you have that gun."

He pointed the pistol at me.

The railing slipped in his fingers.

I stepped closer and offered a hand. "I'm sorry Destiny died. It was my fault."

The gears in his thick head seemed to turn as he considered his options. Give the gun to me or just the bullets?

"Make wise choices, Alverez," I said.

He handed me the gun.

I took his other hand in mine. Behind him, and far below, my sister backed slowly away as the monster Cain stepped forward.

Did she need my help? Probably not. Could she use a distraction? Maybe.

I shoved Reginald as hard as I could. He fell in a long arc with the powerful downward assist from his gravity harness. The arc wasn't exactly what I'd expected. The parabola was tighter and almost landed him short of the target—but he slammed into the cage with a resounding bang.

Cain, startled by the sound, spun. He was inside the cage by then, and Alverez was outside, but I could smell the fear rolling off the man, and so, apparently, could the dog.

Angel slipped past the dog and outside of the cage with Runt and slammed the loose gate back in place. The broken cage wouldn't lock. I had damaged it too much. Angel clung to the top of the cage, her useless legs dangling down over the edge. She had abandoned her harness, and her strong arms easily moved her from handhold to handhold.

"No!" shouted Angel.

The monstrous dog bashed the ruined gate. Reginald scrambled away and toppled off the cage to fall to the bottom of the lounge. He hit the floor with a resounding thud.

A dozen blue surrounded him. At the front of the police force stood Echo, who pointed up at me and shouted.

"No!" Angel commanded again. "Sit!"

Runt, next to her, sat down.

Cain left the cage through the ruined gate. His lips pulled back to reveal the broken smile of his teeth. His ears flattened, but his hackles were smooth.

"Sit," Angel rumbled in her most commanding voice. No creature alive could resist the insistence of that woman's words, but I didn't get the chance to find out what Cain did.

Above, the white strobes stopped flashing. The airlock door was finally opening. I pulled myself up into the receiving chamber. To either side of me, darkened hallways stretched out into the distance. I had done it. I'd made it there to meet Petunia at the gate. I could warn her of the danger. Send her back through to the colony, where she would be safe. If I accompanied her through the airlock, I could get her to tell me what Lorentz needed to know about the colonies.

A hiss of backlit fog burst from the enclosed airlock. I lowered Reginald's gun. The silhouette of a tall woman stepped forward into the doorway.

"Dr. Alverez," I said, "welcome to the Gravity Lounge."

"Funny," said a voice from the shadows to my left. "I thought that was my line."

Bishop Theodore Barton stepped from the shadows of an unlit corridor, pointing a gun at my head.

Chapter 42

PETUNIA ALVEREZ WAS A BIG WOMAN. She was soft in the middle and she carried tension in the muscles of her shoulders like nobody I'd ever seen, but her piercing gray eyes penetrated even the sourest of souls. Her hair was cropped short, and her square jaw clenched so hard I worried about her dental health. It wasn't hard to see why Reginald respected her so much—the word *powerful* fit her better than *beautiful*, but she was compelling nonetheless. Despite her overwhelming presence, she wore her Sunday best—a dark blue blouse and long black skirt—with the awkwardness one might expect from a career scientist.

"Drop the gun, Mr. Demarco," said the bishop.

There's a certain kind of truth that emerges only when a man points a gun at a fellow soul. Some men shake under the pressure. They know the decision they're about to make could destroy them. Others hold the gun steady, ready to do what needs to be done if they must. They made their decision long ago and thought through the consequences. Others, even more dangerous, haven't thought through anything at all and probably never will.

Then there's the fanatics. They're the most dangerous of all.

I tossed Reginald's weapon to the floor at Barton's feet. I'd never been much for guns, but the loss of this one seemed significant. At a gesture from Barton, I raised my hands and backed away.

"Out of the airlock," Barton said, aiming at the big woman. When she stepped forward, the lock closed.

"I'll remind you that you promised me sanctuary in your church, bishop." Petunia's voice was deep and commanding and laced with fury.

"This isn't a church," I said.

Barton's pale forehead glistened with a sheen of sweat. "I regret that it has come to this, Dr. Alverez. You have forced my hand with everything you have done."

"Trinity's Catholic sanctuary is the Bishop's loophole in the broken governance of this station," Petunia explained to me. Her voice tumbled from her like a bucket of gravel. "And he promised to extend his Church's protection to me for this visit."

Barton said, "Your colony project wouldn't *exist* without the protections offered here."

"How long have you been planning to kill me, Barton?" Petunia asked.

"You brought armed men. Trinity alerted me the moment they stepped into the airlocks."

Petunia stared at the bishop's gun. "I wonder why I felt they were necessary?"

"You've always wanted this church as your own," said Barton. "You've always wanted to control the launching point for your vile activities."

"Hold on," I said. "This is a church?"

They both looked at me like I was a half-baked idiot.

Petunia said to the bishop, "You're as guilty as I have ever been."

"I couldn't have known what you would *do*—"

"With what?" Petunia roared. "With the endless stream of helpless people you sent my way? With the animals you sent for my experiments? You're complicit, Bishop. The Church doesn't get to wash its hands when this all comes out."

Barton's eyes narrowed. "And that's why I'm here to make sure it doesn't." He put two fingers to his mouth and whistled.

A pair of big bouncers shuffled down the hall, preceded by the lights. If the Gravity Lounge was still officially designated as a church, then Trinity might not judge anything that happened in the lounge, but it still ran the lights, same as it did in any of the cathedrals. If I could escape into the dark, maybe I could disappear—but running wouldn't do Petunia any good, and now we were outnumbered. I didn't like our odds.

The goons didn't wear gravity harnesses, meaning Retch's manipulation of the system didn't affect them. It didn't matter. An increase in artificial weight wouldn't do much for this situation anyway. Wesley approached from another long hallway and picked up Alverez's gun. His left arm was bundled in a thick bandage.

"Back for more?" I asked.

He sneered at me.

"Here I thought we were starting to get along."

Barton gestured with his pistol at the far hall. "Dr. Alverez is here for the funeral. We had better not keep her waiting."

"You're still going forward with the funeral?" I asked.

Barton replied, "It's a sacred rite."

The goons nudged us forward, and, as a group, we moved down the curved hall at the top of the lounge. Petunia and I took point with Barton and his pistol bringing up the rear.

"Ideas are like a nasty virus, aren't they?" I watched the lights ahead of us as they lit the way down the hall. "They thrive in the medium of information, but ultimately, they're their own thing, and the worst of them spread like a disease."

The hall curved along the upper crown of the Gravity Lounge. We passed another balcony overlooking the cage below, but I could no longer see Angel and the dogs. Had she jumped like Reginald? The police flash of red and blue flooded the lounge below.

"For instance," I said to Barton, "Harold Mance was a festering pustule of bad ideas. You sent your three priests to follow him, but they weren't following him, were they? They were working with him and following *me*."

"Mr. Mance was a sick man," said Barton.

"That's not what made him dangerous."

"He was a killer."

"What I'm trying to work out," I said, "is how your priests knew how to find me. How did they track me down in the first place? For that matter, how did Leo Shaw keep catching up to me to collect on his debt? And how did the blue know I'd be at this morning's Mass? Seems like a lot of people knew where I'd be even before I figured it out."

Petunia said, "Maybe you're predictable."

"Maybe," I said, "or maybe I've been trusting the wrong people."

Ahead, a dull glow illuminated the hallway. Lorentz leaned against a big golden doorway with her arms crossed and a serene expression on her face.

The worst part was that some instinctual part in the back of my brain continued to trust her. Even as she gestured and the golden doors opened. Even as she greeted Barton with a nod like they were old allies. Even as she turned her serene expression my direction and didn't even flicker a smile.

"You were trying to keep me out of this," I said as I walked through the golden door.

"Things would have been so much better if you had been arrested." Lorentz fell in behind me. "There was no need to have you here for this."

"It sure got the blue's attention," I said.

Barton said, "They won't find their way to the chapel anytime soon."

"A man desperate enough to hope for rescue by the cops is a desperate man indeed," I said.

The hall curved upward, but the walls were no longer the dull gray of the minimalist corridors. This hallway made use of warm tones and faux wooden trim. Religious icons lined the walls like Stations of the Cross.

"Have you always been on Barton's side?" I asked Lorentz.

Lorentz had the decency to look ashamed. "I'm on the side of truth."

"Is that more important than 'Thou shalt not kill?'"

"It won't come to that," she said.

"It sure feels likely from this side of the pistol."

"The colonies claim to be the future of humanity. I need to know why."

"I bet."

Petunia said, "Our work will continue, even without me."

I glanced back at Barton, who walked behind us a fair distance away. The lights of the passage lit up when the rest of the group passed, but they dimmed around him. He walked in shadow.

Like me.

Pieces started to fall into place.

I said to Petunia, "You're experimenting on people. Human modification."

"An oversimplification." Petunia's expression was sour, like she'd bit into some bad fruit. Her accent was Hallow all the way—all crisp vowels and immaculate consonants. "Magdalene Moon is the most important project upon which humanity has ever embarked."

"Please," said Lorentz. "Tell us about it."

"Was this the deal?" I said to Lorentz. "You get to interrogate her before Barton kills us?"

Lorentz said, "There's something I need to know."

"This is my daughter's funeral," Petunia said.

Ahead, the hallway opened into a wild perversion of a cathedral. Backlit stained glass decorated the space, casting glittering color over rows upon rows of fiberstone pews. In the center of the space stood a massive altar covered in steel gray cloth and golden chalices. Above that hung a cross larger than any I had ever seen. Its length was decorated with gears.

This wasn't a typical Catholic space.

"What is this?" I asked.

Barton stepped forward and placed a hand on Lorentz's shoulder. "As I said, welcome to the true church."

Lorentz didn't shy away from him. She gazed up at the strange cross and around at the extravagant decorations, taking it all in. Barton had created a new church alongside the Catholic one below. How could something like this exist in a city run by Trinity? A Catholic AI trained on Catholic ideals would never leave an idol like this untouched.

Or would it?

"Sanctuary," Barton explained again, as if that somehow clarified things. "There are pockets of it throughout the city, centered in our predecessors' places of worship. Sanctuary means that people will not be prosecuted by mortal means so long as they stay within those borders."

Lorentz explained, "Each bead in Nicodemia used to have three major cathedrals. One top, one central, one bottom."

Only the central one had survived in all three beads. Here in the Hallows, Saint Lucy of the Light still stood strong as the beacon of Catholic belief. But even that cathedral was seeing waning numbers. Even that single church couldn't draw enough faithful parishioners to justify itself. Where, then, was everyone going, if they were going anywhere?

"You're a machinist," I said to Lorentz, eyeing the gear-laden cross.

"It's not like that," she said.

"It's exactly like that," I said.

All the chaos and madness in the world fell away and the only thing I could see were Lorentz's pleading eyes. She wanted me to believe. Desperately wanted me to be by her side.

And something in me wanted it too.

It wasn't her beauty, though she *was* beautiful. It wasn't her confidence, carried the way a police officer carries a baton. She *believed* something, and that tugged at the empty void in my heart. If I believed the way she believed, maybe I could fit somewhere in this broken world. I could finally find a place to hang my guilt.

But I couldn't. The only beliefs I had were in my own two fists, in the corruptible nature of man, and in the value of a good mushroom burger. Mine was an empty life into which God was too big to fit.

To Barton, I said, "You think that nothing you do here is wrong because Trinity doesn't punish you for it."

"We're not in the Sinless," said Barton. He gestured at the

shining walls with his pistol. "This isn't a temple in worship of nothing, Demarco. This place is a sacred sanctuary in worship of the holy laws of science."

"Ha!" Petunia's laugh was a belch of venom.

Barton spun on her. "You are the worst of them," he said. "You've read the books. You've learned the ethics of science and technology, but you reject them."

Petunia spat on Barton's feet.

His face went wine red with rage. "Tell them what you've done on your colony."

Everyone in the room looked at Petunia. She stepped back and searched each of our faces in turn.

"This is my daughter's funeral," she said.

"As good a time for the truth as any," said Barton. His gun was pointed at her heart, and it didn't waver.

Petunia watched him with dead eyes, her cold expression sending a shiver down my spine. She was a shark in the deep. A predator observing prey and trying to decide if she was hungry. It made me doubt my conviction to see her safely through. It made me wonder if there was a reason Barton wanted to kill her and if maybe that reason was a valid one.

But some final shred of my Catholic upbringing told me that killing wasn't right. It was never the way, even if the Church itself failed to obey that commandment. The Church was guilty of killing and kidnapping throughout its entire existence.

The missing people. The supply shipments. The kidnapped dogs. It was starting to make sense.

"Magdalene Moon isn't a *potential* colony," I said. "You've already started to populate it. Barton sends you his heathens."

"For reform. For punishment." Barton gestured at Petunia with his gun. "Not—whatever you have been doing with them."

What they have been doing was exactly what Lorentz was investigating. That was why they were allied.

Petunia's lips twisted up. "You live under a theocratic regime that thinks you're scum. This place has had you people under its thumb so long you think the crushing pressure is a warm embrace. Well, my colleagues and I are escaping religious oppression and building our own home on the moon. There isn't anything wrong with what we're doing." She nodded toward Barton. "The bishop here only has a problem because people like him aren't invited."

"You *change* people," said the bishop. "If I had known—"

"They *wanted* it!" Petunia snapped.

Barton looked like he might strike her to keep her from uttering any more blasphemies. He wrestled himself under control, but the tension twitched in the muscles of his neck. "God makes us in His image."

Petunia said, "God's image is flawed."

Lorentz watched, with her intelligent eyes sparkling and her hands folded in front of her. This was gold to her. An actual religious conflict played out as the two major sects prepared for a schism. "People should know about this."

"They will *not*!" snapped Barton. "It would be the end of Nicodemia."

I remembered Retch's expression as he read the journal. If the words dealt with changing people—if it told of a place outside the purview of the Church—then he had finally found the escape he was looking for. That's why he wanted to be here. That's why he hadn't wanted to speak his findings out loud.

A whiff of incense and aromatic oils on Barton triggered a memory that seemed like it came from a thousand years ago. I remembered the room where Destiny Alverez was killed. The room where Harold Mance had tortured and killed the girl who had started this whole business. It was that scent of incense that had confused me. Why would the hallmark heavy odor hang around a girl who had nothing to do with the Church? She probably hadn't stepped inside a sanctuary in years. Likewise, Mance wasn't the religious type. Monsters like him didn't see the point in ceremony unless it was part of their ritualistic murder.

But Theodore Barton reeked of incense. The smoke clung to him after the day's Mass, seeping into his clothes and his skin. Then I remembered the shape of a person in the blood spray. It had never made sense to me. How could that have happened if there weren't two people in that room? One slashed her throat while the other stood near the wall.

I said, "You read Destiny her Last Rites."

Barton aimed his pistol at me. The mirrored walls around us shone in the dull light. Petunia was a bundle of tension.

"But your presence wasn't recorded there," I said, "because you're excommunicated."

"I'm exalted."

"Same thing."

"It is not," he whispered.

"How long have you been invisible in the eyes of your god."

He broke away and stalked down the corridor. "Bring them," he ordered. Wesley moved to comply.

"Demarco, wait," Lorentz said.

But I didn't stop. I passed the altar into an ornate chamber decorated with angles of polished steel. White floors shone under brilliant lights above, and in the center of the room, on a raised section of floor, sat a coffin. This was the funeral chapel, and the far wall was open to the recycler.

Barton stood near the coffin. He still held the pistol, but his eyes were sunken and the overconfident thrust of his jaw had slackened to a quivering mess. "My sins will not be tallied."

"You value Trinity's judgment above all else," I said, stepping forward as the others entered the small chapel. "Above your friends. Above your flock. Are you guilty of Destiny's murder?"

"She was *Mance's* victim," Barton spat. "How could I have known what kind of monster he was?"

"He confessed to you. You thought you could control him—make him work for your cause."

Barton's jaw tightened in denial. "I didn't know what he would do."

"Why do I have trouble believing that?"

Barton said, "We've all had dark thoughts, and I had no way of knowing that he would act on his. He said that he could bring me the colony scientists."

"By killing their children."

Barton slumped. "I didn't know."

"You were following him that night in the garden. You knew that he was after Destiny, and you wanted to stop him."

His eyes darted to Petunia. "I was too late."

I said, "Another lie."

Petunia's expression was completely unreadable. Barton's only response was a choked sob in the back of his throat.

I stepped closer to him and spoke as quietly as my jangling nerves could manage. "You murdered a girl to protect the city."

"It was mercy—"

Petunia made an inarticulate noise in the back of her throat.

"You murdered her," I said.

"Mance—" Barton sputtered.

"*You* killed her!" I shouted. "As your reward, Trinity

excommunicated you." Barton had sacrificed his every belief to protect the city. It was the kind of thing that had resulted in my own excommunication.

"Exalted," he said.

"Sure."

"I released her from her pain," Barton whispered. "Mance had tortured her, and there was nothing else I could do. Mercy was the right choice, so Trinity rewarded me."

"You released her from pain that your own man had caused. You and he were quite a team, Bishop. You even went in for an encore with Lacie van Esters."

"God gave me license to do what needed to be done." His confidence returned, and the fear in his eyes turned to rage. "I'm doing His will."

"That's why you shot Saria van Esters in the greenhouse," I said. "After Mance murdered Lacie, you used your ability to rewrite Trinity to remove the record of the killing. You used your leverage in the Church to forbid the use of the cathedral's recycler. Then you sent Mance to locate Saria van Esters in the crowd. I threatened to disturb your plans there, so you recruited the priests to keep an eye on me."

"I knew you would slip up."

"That's a universal truth, isn't it?"

Petunia struggled, but the guards held her firm. "You son of a bitch," she spat. "You killed my daughter."

Barton flinched like the words stung. Maybe they did.

"Is what Demarco says true, Barton?" Lorentz said. "Did you kill Destiny?"

The two bouncers struggled to hold Petunia back. The woman looked soft, but she knew how to throw her weight around. "I'll have you disgraced for this, Barton. You think we're recruiting too many of your lost flock now, just wait till they hear about the monster leading their church!"

I said, "Give up now, Barton. We'll work something out."

He glanced down at his gun, then up at me.

"You regret killing Destiny," I said. "Believe me, I understand regret. My whole life is steeped in the stuff. Every night when you try to sleep, you see Mance and his blades. You're watching the beautiful Destiny Alverez bleed out in some shitty Sinless apartment. That guilt you feel is all the worse because Trinity doesn't acknowledge it and the police aren't bothering to look into it. You've gotten away with it. Nothing can stop your descent into the blackest night of the soul, but you'll never sleep in peace again."

"I don't need sleep. I only need the colonies to end. They are a threat to this city. To the Church." Barton flung open the coffin. "Do you understand what will happen if people can leave Nicodemia?"

"Then make Nicodemia somewhere people don't want to leave."

Inside the coffin, Destiny Alverez lay in state. Her skin was pale and waxy, her hair over-primped, and her clothes were Hallows formal like she'd probably never worn in life. The expression on her face was serene, with no evidence of the damage I'd seen that night in the Sinless.

Lorentz stared in horror. Petunia made a little gasp. Barton stepped aside as she touched her daughter's face. Tears streamed down her cheeks.

"I'm sorry, honey," Petunia sobbed. "I'm so sorry I left you."

"Let Alverez go, Barton," I said. "She's suffered enough."

Barton laughed a wicked, cruel laugh. "You think *she's* suffered? That's nothing compared to the suffering she's caused. Ask her where all those people went, Demarco. Ask her how much pain she's caused as she wrenched them away from God. How much pain she's caused to the families left behind."

"Was it their choice to leave?" I said.

"It was," said Lorentz, stepping forward. "You know he's right, Barton."

The air was heavy with tension. Barton aimed his gun at Petunia Alverez. "She's an abomination."

"That doesn't mean she has to die," I said.

Lorentz said, "Jude's right. You can't kill her."

Petunia wept, ignoring her imminent demise. Maybe she would have accepted her fate right then and there. Maybe she just didn't care what happened now that she saw that her daughter was really dead.

Lorentz snatched Reginald's pistol from Wesley and pointed it at Barton. The bouncer blinked rapidly and stepped back. Petunia struggled as the two other bouncers pulled her away from the coffin. She screamed and fought.

There wasn't an innocent soul in that chapel. The way Lorentz held the gun. The spite in Barton's eyes. The shamed bawling of the mother who had abandoned her daughter.

And me. There was always me and my guilt. If bullets flew in the Gravity Lounge, they weren't going to land on the innocent.

Barton's gun barked. Bullets slammed into Lorentz.

I tackled the bishop hard. Our momentum carried us into the recycler, triggering the recycling sequence. Lorentz staggered back and hit the far wall, leaving a bloody streak.

The recycler doors closed with a resounding boom.

Chapter 43

"RECONCILE?" Trinity asked in its deep, too-calm voice.

"Not today, Trinity," Barton and I said at the same time.

Clouds of corrosive chemical solvent emerged as the central pit opened. Barton stood across from the central processing platform, where he had fallen after I'd tackled him. I leaned against the far wall. My breaths came in short, acidic gasps.

Barton still had his gun. He could have shot me without a second thought.

But he didn't. He did something much worse.

He smiled.

"Trinity," he said.

"Reconcile?"

"Show Demarco the truth, Trinity. Show him the reason that the colonies must be stopped."

The walls went blank for a moment as the machine considered his words. What truth could sway me? What information could he use as a weapon against me now? He must have known the danger he was in. If not for his gun, I could overpower him, but there was something in his step that exuded righteous confidence. I was exactly where he wanted me to be.

"Open the doors, Trinity," I said.

"Leave them shut," Barton told the machine.

Corrosive mist rolled across the stark white floor. The air stank of its burning death. "Stop the pretreatment, Trinity," I said.

The mists stopped. The pit in the center of the room bubbled with corrosive sludge.

Barton raised an eyebrow. "You've done this before."

"Lorentz needs my help, Barton." There had been so much blood. I needed to get out and help her. "Open the doors."

"They will remain shut."

Trinity kept the doors closed.

"I'm a medic," I said.

"She is in God's hands."

"God doesn't give a damn about any of us." I said it with more venom than I intended, but less than it deserved.

The walls flared to life, projecting images of young Petunia Alverez and Saria van Esters sitting in the Cabrini Colony Lab down in the Heavies with two men in lab coats. One of them was a young, plump Reginald Alverez. The other, I didn't recognize. A single light illuminated the group, and the rest of the lab was shadowed in darkness.

"There's no way to move forward with this," said Reginald. "This sets us back a generation."

"*Another* generation," said the other man.

Petunia shook her head. "It's not the end. We can make this work."

Reginald said, "The full geological survey is complete. Both Magdalene Moon and Cabrini are loaded with chromium. Even if you scrub the atmosphere, there will always be trace amounts bubbling up through the regolith. Both locations are time bombs for colony collapse."

"Unless you change how the human body processes chromium," said Petunia. "There are ways forward if we can do that."

I circled the central recycling pit, but Barton mirrored my movements, keeping the pit between us. My fists clenched so hard they ached. "This doesn't make any difference."

"God made us in His image."

"Doesn't look to me like these people care."

On the screen, Reginald threw up his hands. "You're talking about the genetic modification of the human genome. There are rules we can't break."

"Those are Trinity's rules," said Petunia.

"It's blasphemy!"

"It's science." Petunia placed her hands flat on the table, as if forcing them not to close into fists. "This is bigger than God."

The man's face burned red. "You're going too far, Petunia."

"But there must be *something* we can do," the woman snapped back. "*Something*, Reggie. We have to make this work or we'll never—"

"Petunia," snapped Saria.

The group was silent for a long time.

"Trinity," I said, taking my eyes from the screen. "Open the recycler room doors."

"Keep them closed," said Barton. The doors stayed closed. Dammit.

"Lorentz is out there," I growled. "Bleeding. Dying. Come on, Barton. She's one of you. She believes in your God so hard she'd die for him, but that doesn't mean she should."

"She never understood what we faced."

"Bullshit."

His eyes narrowed. "She used me to get information, same as she used you."

"She's worth saving."

"Keep the doors closed, Trinity," Barton said.

In the center of the recycling chamber, the sludge belched an acidic odor. Barton watched me closely through hooded eyes. "What are they hiding, Demarco? You're the one with such keen investigative skills. What does Petunia Alverez want that she can't say in front of Trinity?"

"I think we're done here," snapped Reginald on the screen. He stood and briskly walked from the room. The other man followed, apologizing as he went.

Saria van Esters leaned back in her chair. She placed a hand on Petunia's, and the two shared a knowing look. "Almost," Van Esters said. "Almost."

"It's never going to work without this," Petunia said. "Not in a hundred more years. Not in a thousand. Someone needs to do something."

Saria reached across the table for a notebook and wrote something on an open page. Trinity's camera picked up enough that I could recognize the geometric design of their shared written language.

This was a language Trinity had never cracked because it was specifically designed not to be cracked by Trinity.

I said, "People don't make secret codes unless they're oppressed."

Barton glanced at the screen behind him, where the image of the notebook loomed large. Now, Petunia was writing in it in response to Saria. His attention snapped back to me before I could round the central platform and take his gun. Blue light played across his sad smile. "Every religion has its heathens."

I needed a chance to jump Barton, but he wasn't going to give it to me. It was a couple of paces to the slurry pit. Even if I crossed the pit, there were several more steps until I reached the bishop. Plenty of time for him to shoot me. If I jumped over the pit, he'd have the added bonus that my body would fall directly into the recycler.

Which would be pretty convenient for him, but not great for me.

As the two scientists sketched shapes in their notebook on the screen, I said, "Lorentz wanted the secrets in that notebook. She needed to know how the secrets in that notebook affected the truths being pushed by the Church."

"It's her obsession," said Barton. "It's the reason she hired you."

"You thought Destiny could read the journal. That's why you let her get her hands on it. Where did you get it?"

"Her father visited one of my Priests, seeking advice. His family has been torn apart by his wife's ambition. His daughter was in the process of ruining her own life, seeking a life of sin not becoming of a Christian." Barton glanced at the journal on the screen. "We told him to give the journal to Destiny, hoping that she would come to us when she learned what lay within."

"But it only made things worse because she then tried to get into the Gravity Lounge," I said. "She was trying to go to the colony to find her mother."

"She had the key to the code. When she died—"

"When you killed her."

"Mance did that!"

"You're the Spanish Inquisition, Barton. The power's gone to your head."

"Mance found her for me, but when she wouldn't tell him what she'd read in the journal, he took her away."

"Violently."

"It was the only way."

"After I spotted you in the garden, you went to track them down. Mance took her to her place at the college first to get her bandaged up. He must have thought she had the journal there, and he even knew where the good hiding place was. She'd already dropped the book in the garden. When he didn't find it, he took her to her place in the Sinless. You were there, weren't you? Mance attacked me—attacked Reginald—because you needed a distraction so you could escape."

"You were seconds too late to save her." Barton's jaw clenched. "God's plan—"

"God had nothing to do with it," I said. "Mance knew everything about Destiny because he'd been tracking her for as long as she'd been trying to get into the Gravity Lounge."

"He was a sick man."

"And you covered for him from the second he made his first twisted confession. As soon as you were excommunicated, you went back and erased all the records you could find of his murders. All those women, Barton."

"It had to be done."

"I don't know what's worse—his killing or your coverup."

His nostrils flared. "My sins are not yours to measure."

"You even fudged some records showing that Mance was in a prayer group at the time of the murder. The blue never even suspected you'd modified the timestamps. The tricky part must have been getting Mance to attend so that people would remember him."

"He was a regular attendee."

"Of course he was," I said. "When you found Destiny in the Sinless, she wasn't in such good shape."

"She wanted to tell everyone what the colony offered. Out of spite, maybe. Mance had tortured her, and she was broken. She aimed to get into the Gravity Lounge to meet her mother and leave for the colony, but now she was going to tell everyone before she left."

I said, "If she told everyone the truth—"

"Mance *forced* me to kill her."

"You murdered her. Sliced her throat while Mance stood aside." It was the only explanation I could figure for the blood spray pattern.

"I sacrificed everything to save the city, and Trinity exalted me for it." His voice dripped with anguish. He had killed her, choosing love of Trinity over anything his god had ever told him. That was why he was excommunicated.

I paced slowly. "I know the feeling."

"I spent a day in here communing with Trinity, learning how I could tell the machine to erase the events around Destiny's death." He took another step to the right to match my movement. "I learned about Saria van Esters' involvement."

"So you sent Mance to kill her daughter and covered it up using your access to Trinity."

"I didn't know he would kill the daughter."

"He's the flock following a shepherd."

"What do you know of flocks?"

"I know a little something about guilt."

"Guilt is how the Church controls us," he spat.

"Maybe the Church needs some more modern ideals."

The man went very still. Behind him was the closed exit. He could order Trinity to open the door and leave me if he wanted.

I said, "And now you've killed for your Church."

He pressed his lips together and regarded me for a long time. "I've done only what was necessary."

"That's what they always say."

"This is different!"

On the screen, Saria pushed away from the table. "This will work."

"I know," said Petunia.

"You'll have to leave Reginald," Saria said.

Petunia's voice dropped low. "It was going to happen anyway. He'll never understand."

"I'll send people," Saria said. "But Trinity will never let them return. You included."

Petunia said, "If that's the cost, then that's the cost."

I stared at the video as the two women clasped hands and wept. This was their pact, written in the odd code they had developed. Saria would send people to the colonies via the Gravity Lounge, and Petunia would change them so that they could survive on the colony. Here in the sanctuary of Barton's church, Petunia was safe from the machine—but not from him.

Barton became aware of their plan because people sent to the colony always left via the Gravity Lounge. It had been luck that finally delivered the notebook into his hands.

But he still didn't understand the full contents of that notebook. That's why he had gone to Lorentz, but she took the obsession as her own and tackled it in her own way: by hiring me.

"The Church has always been against human modification," Barton said, lowering his weapon. "It perverts God's will."

"There's one thing I don't get," I said.

His eyes glistened, but he waited for me to continue.

"Mance never took the journal. Destiny had it in her

purse. I found it in the garden. Mance never had any intention of making her decode the thing, did he?"

"He had to—"

"No, Barton. He never did. You didn't know what Mance was going to do because the bastard was going to do it whether or not you asked for his help. The only difference was that he directed his murderous tendencies wherever you pointed."

Barton rasped, "No."

"All right," I said. "Confession time's over."

"He wanted to help me."

"You're a piece of shit, Barton, but you've put it all on the table. You've killed. You've sinned. And now you've bared it all in the liminal space where Trinity can truly judge your sins. You've reconciled."

His lower lip quivered.

"Do you reconcile, bishop?" I asked. The screens around me went blank, having finished playing the memory that Barton wanted me to see. "Will you return to Trinity's fold if your sins are forgiven?"

"I haven't done my penance," Barton said.

"You've done nothing but penance. You've suffered in darkness. I *know* you have."

A tear ran down Barton's cheek. "I can't."

"You can. It's time. Imagine what it will be like to live in God's warm embrace again. You've suffered enough. Return like the prodigal son, Barton. You deserve it."

His whole body shook.

"Your penance is to live in the eyes of your God. You want the machine as your god? Fine. Have it. But it's time to return to the light. No more hiding."

Barton looked at the gun in his hand. He seemed to consider the depths of the shadows it cast, even in the whitewash of light inside the recycling chamber. It twisted in his hand so that he could examine it in profile—this finger of God which he used to reach into the darkest depths of humanity. He had used it to judge and kill Saria van Esters and Harold Mance. I could see in the sunken depths of his eyes that each judgment had cost him dearly. Each had left stains on his soul that he may never scrub clean.

"Yes," he finally said. "I reconcile. May God have mercy on my soul."

The screens flashed. Trinity said in its too-calm voice, "Theodore Barton, you have reconciled. Go forth in peace."

He dropped to his knees, weeping. The gun clattered to the floor.

"Open the doors, Trinity," I said.

Barton's eyes went wide. "No, not yet. Trinity, keep the doors closed."

But this time Trinity didn't listen to him—he was no longer excommunicated. Exalted. Whatever we called it, Barton didn't belong anymore. Trinity wouldn't listen to his commands. The doors to the chapel slid open.

Petunia Alverez stepped in, raised her husband's gun, and shot Theodore Barton in the head.

Chapter 44

PETUNIA LIFTED Barton's body with one hand and tossed him into the slurry in the center of the recycler. The sludge hissed as it returned him to the ecosystem. She threw his gun in after him.

Outside of the recycler, Lorentz lay still bleeding on the floor. There was so much blood. I moved to help her, but Petunia stopped me with a pointed gun and a hard look. I don't know which was more dangerous.

"You aren't going to be a problem, are you?" Petunia asked.

I said, "I've never *not* been a problem."

"You're smarter than you look." She kept her gun aimed at me.

Lorentz coughed. Blood glistened on her lips. I stepped out of the recycler as the coffin started to move. Petunia could have shot me. She didn't.

The monk was in bad shape. I touched her wound where Barton's bullets had torn through her gut just below the line of the ribs. A bad spot for a gunshot. She needed a full medical station and an army of surgeons. I found myself hoping that the cops would find us in time. A medic like me could only delay the inevitable.

But delay I did. I ignored Petunia. The scientist had her funeral. I didn't care anymore. She helped her daughter into the recycler, and it didn't matter to me one bit.

All I wanted was for Lorentz to be healthy again.

"I tried," I whispered to her as I bandaged her wound. I bound it tight so the trickle of blood oozing from her chest would slow. She'd need an infusion soon. Synthetic blood was easy to come by outside of the lounge. Surgeons were not. I needed help.

There was no help.

Lorentz's eyes opened a sliver, but I didn't know if there was comprehension in them. Behind me, the coffin thudded into place over the recycling pit and started to drop. Petunia stepped out of the recycling chamber, and the door closed.

"I was always on your side," rasped Lorentz.

I said, "I should have trusted you."

Her lips parted in a smile. "I wish I could live to see the day when Jude Demarco trusts someone."

"We can fix this, Lorentz," I lied, grasping her hands in mine. One more sin to add to the long list.

She squeezed my hand. "I love you, Jude Demarco," she said. "You're not easy to like, but you're sure as hell easy to love."

"I don't need your love," I said. "I need you to hang on. I'll have help for you soon."

But help wouldn't come. A gun cocked behind me.

I said, "It's the only way to keep your secret safe, Petunia."

"I wish he hadn't told you about the colony," Petunia said.

"You're changing people so they can live on the moon.

The Church thinks you're making abominations." I didn't turn to face her. "We both know that's a lie."

Her voice went flat. "What makes you say that?"

It was in the way Retch withheld information from the journals. It was the way Petunia and Saria held hands in Barton's video. It was the pattern of disappeared citizens. "You loved Saria," I said. "Did your husband know?"

"It wasn't any of his business."

I glanced back at her. There was a hardness in her eyes, and I had no doubt that she would pull the trigger if she needed to. I also took in the cut of her jaw and the gray in her close-cropped hair. She wore a woman's clothes—about as comfortably as a rottweiler in a tutu. "You dressed as a woman just for this visit, but that isn't what you are, is it?"

"This is a sanctuary temple, but the machine is always watching." Meaning that Petunia Alverez had transitioned to male, but saying it out loud was dangerous. Reginald had spoken of her starting to change back when she left him. She had dressed in women's clothes for the funeral, and that was enough to fool Trinity as long as we didn't talk directly about it. It was a subtle form of oppression, but there nonetheless.

They *changed* people on that moon in more ways than one. They gave them the ability to resist toxic levels of chromium. They made their bodies better suited for the low gravity. They let people *choose* their physical sex. *That's* what the Church was afraid of. Change. I dared not say any more for fear of Trinity's reaction. It might seal the airlocks if it wanted to punish Petunia. It would become even harder to smuggle people to the moon. The whole colony would be in danger.

"You could have told Destiny."

"That notebook was going to be my message to her, but it

went missing right before I left," Petunia said. "I thought it had been destroyed, but I gave her the key anyway."

"She had it tattooed on her chest."

"I always told her to keep it close to her heart."

"When she finally got her hands on the journal, she knew that the only way to get to you was through the Gravity Lounge. Barton killed her so she wouldn't tell everyone."

"That bastard."

When I spoke, I spoke toward Lorentz, so she could finally know the truth. "You turned your colonies into a secret refuge for people being persecuted by the Church. Why? Why not just tell everyone there was a way out?"

"The Church would never let us directly subvert their authority like that." Petunia lowered the weapon. "They hate us, but they tolerate us." She turned to leave.

"Wait," I said.

She stopped without turning around.

"Lorentz deserves to know," I said. "Tell her about the science. What truths about the universe have you unlocked?"

Petunia didn't move for a long time. Finally, she said, "It's not science. Or rather, it's not the kind of science you're thinking of." She glanced back at me. "It's also not new. Not even close. All we did was create an environment in which we allowed people to be who they wanted to be. Sure, gene therapies are new, and there have been revolutionary changes to our understanding of the human body, but at the core of it all is the idea that people understand themselves better than anyone else. We took the poor and the criminals and the rejected and we gave them back their idea of *self*. In almost every case, it led people to improve their own lives and the lives of those around them."

"Sounds like a real utopia," I said.

"Even utopias have conflict, Mr. Demarco. The only thing that's different in a utopia is how conflicts get solved."

I glanced at the gun still in her hand and finally lowered it.

"You should have this," I said, taking out the notebook containing the final words of Saria van Esters. "I have a feeling this was written with you in mind."

She took the book, and her expression softened. Her fingers touched the blood-darkened cover. "The better world that we fight for isn't for us, is it?"

"Not even if we deserve it."

"You're not a bad guy, Demarco," she said, "You know that, right?"

"There's someone you need to take with you," I said. "Can you wait for him?"

"I'll wait as long as I can," she promised, and she left in the direction of the airlock.

"She's gone," I whispered to Lorentz. "It's just us now."

Her voice grew unexpectedly strong. "Make sure she doesn't leave without the kid."

"I can't leave you here."

"I'm fine, Demarco," she said.

"You're not."

"I know my own body." She released my hands and pressed herself up on her elbows. Our faces were so close I could taste her breath. "I'm not dying from this, but if you let that woman leave without talking to Retch, you'll regret it." She choked on a wet cough.

I eased her back to the ground. "Be at peace, Ginnie." Her first name tasted like ash on my lips, but I owed it to her. Her pale skin glistened with cold sweat. "You always said knowledge is its own reward. God gives us truth, doesn't he? The colonies are all about science. People like Petunia will always lead the way, and now you know her secret. You know everything you wanted to know."

"Thank you," Lorentz whispered. Then, weaker, "Thank you."

She gripped the back of my head with her bloody hand and pulled me closer. Our lips touched, and the electric warmth poured from her. For a time, the whole world disappeared. There was only the warm, salty kiss, tasting of tears and blood. Lorentz wasn't a monk sworn off of mortal relations. She wasn't a woman driven by science and truth. She was only the woman I loved who loved me back. A pinpoint of warmth in the wide cold reaches of space.

And she was dying. Dying whether I helped her or not. Dying no matter how much she lied to me about it. Dying in my arms as I finally opened my soul to the touch of another human being.

This was why I had trouble trusting anyone.

"Go," she whispered in my ear. One last rattling breath forced its way out of her lungs, and then she breathed no more.

That soft part of me that loved Lorentz was cauterized by my rage.

A shadow passed over me. Retch stood with his arms crossed. He took in the whole scene with wide eyes. Behind him stood Wesley, a medical kit grasped in his one good hand.

Retch's jaw quivered. He stared at Lorentz's lifeless body. He was too late. Wesley was too late. Tears burned in my eyes.

Retch said, "Is she…"

"She's dead."

"Good," he said, but he didn't mean it. A wince of pain

danced across his face. "I'm sorry, Demarco. She was trouble."

"If anyone's trouble around here, it's you," I said. "And you know it."

That got a weak smile from him. "Yeah, I suppose that's true."

"You're going with Alverez." I rose from Lorentz's still form and stalked out of the room.

Retch followed. "You understand, right?"

"I brought you to the Sinless for your hormones. I've gotten you everything I possibly could, and supported every decision you've ever made, and this…" I gestured at the open door that led to the airlock chamber and we ran down the long hall. "I'm going to miss you, kid."

"Maybe I'll visit."

"That's not how this works," I said. "Once you're gone, you can't come back."

"I'd like to see them try to stop me."

Ahead, the whoosh indicated the opening airlock. Petunia Alverez had her way out. All she had to do was step in and close the lock. If I wanted to stop Retch, now would be the time to do it.

"I'll make sure they take care of Frida Ward," I said. "Your mother."

He stared at me for a stifling eternity. "Thanks."

"Petunia shot Barton," I said. "You better watch out for her."

The kid's nostrils flared. He didn't like having his beliefs confronted like this, but I needed to make sure he knew everything he needed to know. After a moment, he said, "The bastard got what was coming."

"It must be nice having such a straightforward sense of morality."

"I sleep well enough."

Retch was my only friend in a vast sea of angry faces. How could I say no to the kid now? He'd never forgive me, and he would be right not to.

"She's waiting for you," I said, realizing that enough time had passed that Petunia could have closed the airlock door.

"I know."

"I don't know if I can do this without you, kid."

Retch stuck out a hand for a shake. "Charm like yours? You'll have no trouble finding a new partner."

I ignored the shake and pulled him in for a hug, patting him hard on the back.

Then he was gone. He disappeared around the corner and I heard the whoosh of the airlock door closing.

The lights dimmed slowly, then fell to nothing, leaving me alone in the dark, the one last living soul in a whole empty world.

I was a failure to friends, family, and dead loved ones. I sat back against one wall and finally let myself wallow in the empty darkness. My palms pressed to my eyes and tried to contain the great wracking sobs that threatened to shake me apart.

When I opened my eyes, the lights were on again. Retch stood over me and extended a hand to help me up.

"Alverez needed someone to be the new recruiter in the Heavies," he said. "And who am I to turn down a steady, honest job?" He stared at me for a long time. "What? You didn't think I was leaving, did you?"

Chapter 45

"HE'S MEAN," I said.

"He's trainable." Angel sat in her wheelchair surrounded by statuary made of metal and glass. The hidden workshop in the back of the trolley repair station had been converted into a gallery for the one-time-only event. Great red cloths draped over the workbenches around the room, and refreshments were being served along the back wall, where Francesca Frank normally did her work. Both Cain and Runt sat attentively at Angel's feet.

The artist broke away from a group of patrons and crossed to us with a wide grin on her face.

"Hey, Frankie," I said as she approached. "Show looks like it's going well."

Frankie blushed. "Thanks for the chance," she said. "I can practically feel the Karma rolling in." Runt whined, and she turned her attention to the dogs, smooshing their big faces. "Oh, what good little boys." Cain outweighed her by at least double. The big dog nuzzled up to her until she gave him a treat.

"Mean, huh?" said Angel.

"He's spoiled."

"He needs love."

"I travel a lot," I said.

"Good," said Angel. "He's going to have trouble adjusting to the gravity down here, and you can bring him with."

"*We* weren't accustomed to the heavy gravity when we moved down here," I said.

"True," said Angel, "but Cain doesn't have a guilty conscience that makes him feel morally justified in his suffering."

"What are you implying?"

Angel whistled and the dogs both snapped to attention. "Training a dog will be good for you."

Frankie let out a long sigh. "This is more people than I've talked to in the last year, and it's exhausting, but…"

"Knock 'em dead," I said.

She hurried off to greet a new group coming through the wide entrance. They were Travelers, by the look of them. Frankie wasn't going to have any trouble finding a pocket deep enough to bail her out of her remaining debt.

Runt's stub of a tail wiggled at hypersonic speed. He cast around for someone approaching, and I had a pretty good idea who it was.

"Stay," Angel said in her calm voice.

Runt froze.

Retch emerged from the old trolley car in the center of the room, which now served as a giant display case for a whole flock of Frankie's twisted metal birds. Wesley, laughing about something extremely funny, trailed along. He cradled a golden-brown ball of floof in his bandaged arm. When Retch crossed to us, Wesley lingered behind.

"He's afraid of dogs," Retch said. "For some reason."

"Like that one?" I asked, nodding to the ball of fur in Wesley's arms. Its beady black eyes watched me.

"That's King," Retch said. "Turned out he was hiding in the Gravity Garden."

"You fulfilled your promise to find him," I said.

"It's important to keep our word." He cleared his throat. "When it's convenient."

"Even when it's not," I said.

"Speaking of which," said Retch, "word has it that your former client isn't too happy with you."

My mind flashed to Lorentz before I realized that he was talking about Reginald Alverez. "I thought he was arrested."

"He was. Turns out he shot the bouncer on his way into the lounge. That, plus the fact that they were coming after you was what let the police finally storm the place."

I said, "And once they were inside…"

"They found plenty that was interesting. That monk of yours knew what she was doing when she set the cops after you. Without that, they never would have had the political will to break up the dogfighting ring."

"Lorentz was a good person," I said.

"She was a celibate monk, Jude," said Angel. "You being with her was going to make her worse."

"True." I let out a long breath. The same arguments had been rolling around my head for days, and I'd almost had enough wallowing in self-pity. "He's still mean," I said, glancing down at Cain.

"So are you." My sister always spoke the truth. She clicked her tongue, and Runt launched at Wesley, planting his nose right in King's butt. Wesley cried out, and King wriggled and fought. Cain, seeing the excitement, bounded forward huffing giant hot breaths to take in all the scents. Wesley shot me a pleading look, but I shrugged. There wasn't much I could do to help.

"How did you get Cain under control, anyway?" I asked. "In the cage, I mean."

"You mean after you threw Reginald Alverez at me and disrupted everything?"

"It was the only way to keep him safe."

"You have a funny idea of what's safe, bro."

"He made it home," I said. "I checked in on him after everything. I'm pretty sure he won't be hiring me anytime soon, but he got the closure he wanted, even though he never made it up to the funeral."

"We can't place Cain with anyone who has kids because of his history," Angel said. "He plays too rough if nobody's there to keep him in line. I found a place that'll kennel him up in the Hallows on a regular basis, but only if there's clear ownership and someone to help train him."

"I can't afford—"

"I can." She gripped my elbow. "I'll pay, but you have to be the one to train him. Pay attention to him. Take him on walks."

"Just take the dog, Demarco," Retch said. He rescued Wesley by taking King, but that made him the center of canine attention. "You could use a friend."

"I thought I *had* a friend."

"Business partner," Retch said.

"Same thing."

Angel clicked her tongue and Runt backed away from Wesley. Cain flopped onto the ground. They both got treats. "Maybe someday you'll learn the difference."

"Not likely," said Retch.

"Speaking of friends," I said, "any word on Anders?"

Angel said, "Can't keep a good cop down."

"Not even if you try," said Retch.

"If only they weren't so rare," I said. He wouldn't have taken that bullet if I hadn't involved him in my business. "I'll stop by and visit before I head up the chain."

"Business?" Angel asked.

"Always," I said.

"Take the dog with you." Angel grasped Cain's jowls in her hands and gave him a shake. "He's a good boy."

The responsibility made my chest hurt. It gripped my heart in a vise and didn't let go. I was an investigator. A handyman. A medic. I wasn't anyone that any creature should rely on for support. Not after how I'd treated everyone who had ever cared for me. Not after how I'd let Lorentz die. Cain was better off without me, and Angel must have known it.

I looked into the dog's big brown eyes. I'd never been much of a dog person, but something about the monster's smooshed face and wobbly jowls was almost charming. The animal had enough muscle to work the docks of the heavies and big enough teeth to tear a hole in a bulletproof vest, but something in those eyes made him look as soft and cuddly as a white rabbit.

"He's mean," I said, reaching out to pet the big monster.

He growled as my hand approached, but I kept it still until he stopped. Then, slowly, I touched the bridge of his nose. When he allowed that, I scratched his ears.

"Even mean ones deserve to be loved, bro," Angel whispered.

I left Frankie's art exhibit and descended into the streets of Heavy Nicodemia. The city never slept, and every soul that wandered the streets was a mix of sinner and saint. Wherever I looked, in the dark or the light, there were problems wanting to be solved and not a single shred of hope that it would happen. I stepped into the shadows and a calm peace wrapped around me like a well-worn trench coat. I was the man who walked in the dark.

And if hope was lost somewhere in the black underside of the city, I'd find it.

I'd be that hope.

Bonus Content

Demarco's not done yet.

Interested in more? You'll get an extra author's note, huge discounts on more books, and access to piles of exclusive material.

You'll also get All Things Found, a short story about Demarco when he picks up a job investigating a murder that happened right there in the Saint Francis of Assisi cathedral. A priest is dead. A relic is missing.

There are some things that aren't so easy to fix.

https://anthonyeichenlaub.com/all-things-found-newsletter-signup/

Afterword

As I put the finishing touches on this novel, the bishop from the Diocese of Winona/Rochester—*my* home diocese—made national news for a statement condemning Minnesota's proposed Equal Rights Amendment.

This amendment, among other things, would enshrine gender identity as a protected class, ensuring that rights cannot be taken away from people simply because of who they are. It's a compassionate piece of legislation, putting into place basic human rights that many Minnesotans believe they already have.

And the Church opposes it.

There are a lot of things I like about the Catholic Church. It's one of my community's best supporters of the homeless. It opposes the death penalty and injustice in general. It teaches a mystical, mysterious brand of Christianity that speaks to my soul.

So, when I complain about the Church's stance on abortion or transgender rights or *any* gender equality, it doesn't come from a place of hate for the Church. It comes from a place of profound disappointment in an institution that I know has the power to do better.

I haven't been back to church since 2020, and I haven't given the Church money (except for some earmarked donations to the local homeless shelter) since long before that. No matter how much the ritual and mysticism speaks to my soul, I can't justify giving my time and money to an organization that continues to support and promote behaviors that I consider evil.

In the future of the All Things Found books, the Catholic Church has progressed a little. Women are allowed ot join the priesthood. Every time I write about Priest Cano, I wonder if I really believe that the Church might make that much gender equality progress in the next three hundred years.

Maybe?

We can hope, anyway, but when the most liberal Pope ever is heard making bigoted slurs and bishops openly campaign against equality and compassion, it dents the faith a little. It undercuts teachings that I once took to heart. It makes me think that change might not be on the horizon for my generation and likely not for a couple of generations after me.

But even when I write about the Church's miserable failings, I will always add a glimmer of hope. I will always hold onto the idea that maybe one day things will change for the better.

Also by Anthony W. Eichenlaub

Short Stories

Not Done Yet: Sci-fi Stories of Wisdom and Fury

All Things Found

The Man Who Walked in the Dark

Devil in the Gravity Lounge

Nicodemia Station Blues

Old Code Series

Grandfather Anonymous

Grandfather Ghost

Grandfather Guardian

Grandfather Zero

Grandfather Crypto

Cascade Crash

Colony of Edge

Of a Strange World Made

Upon Another Edge Broken

On a Forsaken Land Found

From a Barren Seed Grown

Above a Distant Sky Seen

Metal and Men

Justice in an Age of Metal and Men

Peace in an Age of Metal and Men

Honor in an Age of Metal and Men

Milton Keynes UK
Ingram Content Group UK Ltd.
UKHW030645240724
446081UK00004B/383